THE QUEEN OF ARCASIA

First Calliope Press paperback edition published 2021

Manufactured in the United States of America.

THE QUEEN OF ARCASIA
ISBN 978-0-578-33812-5

THE QUEEN OF ARCASIA

by

David R. Witanowski

CALLIOPE PRESS

THE REYNARD CYCLE

'Hope' is the thing with feathers -
That perches in the soul -
And sings the tune without the words -
And never stops - at all -

- Emily Dickinson

THE QUEEN OF ARCASIA

I

Danica was early that year.

Fewer than half the ewes had given birth and Crowning was still a month away, but as the sun boiled away the last shroud of dawn Lara caught sight of the old woman sitting atop her painted wagon, gently urging her mares up the trail from Perun.

Winter was not yet over, but Danica had come home. This was a rarity, and rarities were few and far between on the farm.

Farm, Lara thought, and snorted. The place did not even have a name. Even Perun was Perun, and what was Perun? Some two score cabins, a sawmill, and a tavern named after a brigand, nestled so deep in woods that all one could make of it from afar were greasy cookfires rising above the pines. Compared to the stories Danica had told Lara of Vassa (Vassa!) with its streets of silk, its grand bazaars, its tall tower of gold and jade . . . Well, dirt-tracked, greasy-smoked Perun was less than a pigsty.

And what did that make the farm?

Less than nowhere.

Lara was certain that she must once have lived in Vassa, or some other great city of the North. She could remember racing down long winding halls of white stone with high windows, laughing all the while, or creeping through rooms hung with colored fabrics and lamps of gold and silver, hiding beneath carpeted tables whenever footsteps sounded nearby. She remembered, ever so distantly, bathing in a metal tub steaming with hot water, and playing atop a bed far larger and softer than the prickly straw pallet she slept on now.

There were other memories too, less pleasant to recall: Long hands of papery skin gripping her shoulders tightly, tall men in suits of metal, their voices raised in anger, and shut doors of cold iron that would not open. Whenever she spoke of such things, however, Moder would merely look up from her work and say, "Those days are being in the past," and, "You must be putting them out of your head."

Of course, none of Moder's words could stop the dreams that came to Lara at night, the good with the bad.

Sometimes she dreamed of a red room. It had a door behind which some great beast was pressing, the wood warping and splintering as it forced its way through. "Don't look! Don't look!" a woman's voice would scream, as gloved hands wrapped over her eyes . . . And she would wake, her heart beating so hard that she felt certain that it would force its way out of her chest.

Often, when she woke thus, she would feel the warm, furry bulk of the farm's great white sheepdog, Pasha, pressing against her. All of the terrors of the night would lift from her then, and she would drift back to sleep.

Pasha stood beside her now as she watched the old woman atop the wagon coming slowly up the lane, his ears pricked. Any moment now he would race across the field- still brown despite the little yellow flowers struggling to blossom- and dance about both wagon and horse, his tail wagging mightily.

Lara longed to run to meet her too, longed for any scrap of news from the world beyond the farm . . . But that would mean putting down the buckets she was hauling up from the brook, the flock needing watering before being put out to pasture.

The sheep could wait, of course. But Moder would likely be cross with her for shirking her chores.

At last Pasha made the decision for her, bounding forward with a joyful bark. Lara knelt down, removed the yoke from her shoulders and followed, gripping at her skirt with one hand so that she would not trip on it.

When Danica saw Lara she did not wave, but rather pulled on the reins of the draft horses until her wagon rumbled to a halt. It was a grand-looking thing, dark wood polished and painted with animal scenes. Danica was far plainer by comparison, a woman of some sixty odd summers, her gray hair streaked white at the temples, and her robe and cloak so travel-stained that they were both as brown as the earth. But, for all the dirt she was still striking, looking far younger than her years . . . And dangerous somehow, especially when she stared, unblinking, with her flashing golden eyes.

"Shores rarely meet," Danica said to Lara, her face wrinkling as she smiled, "But people often do."

"You are early!" Lara shouted, leaping up and onto the seat of the wagon and embracing the old woman, who kissed her on the forehead in return.

"Spring is early too, I think," Danica said as she pulled away from Lara, and gave the reins a shake. "Were it a lioness it might jump down your throat!"

Danica often spoke this way: In proverbs and riddles. It made Lara laugh.

"Did you bring us anything?" Lara asked. Danica often returned from her travels with a little trinket, or child's doll, though it had been many years since Lara had played with such toys. Her oldest, named Brigitte, sat neglected on the shelf beside her pallet, her painted eyes faded, her violet dress worried and worn.

Danica nodded. "I learned a new story in Zelkova. Or, rather, I was reminded of an old one that I had quite forgotten. I've been polishing it all Winter, and it's become quite shiny. Would you like to hear it?"

"Yes," Lara said. "Yes, please!"

"Then you must be patient, for the others will wish to hear it as well. But what of you, little one? Do you have any new stories for Danica? Did you dream of the castle again?"

"Yes," Lara said, but suddenly feeling as though she had been tricked, she held her tongue. The two rode in silence for a while, Pasha panting as he trotted beside them, occasionally letting out a bark.

During the long nights of summer, Lara would often sit with the old woman on the porch of the farmhouse and speak to her of the place of white stones and high windows, Danica nodding now and then at her words as she blew smoke from her pipe. And when Lara ran out of words to speak, Danica would tell her of the cities of the North: Vassa, of course, where the Grand Prince Koschei held his court, but also bright Zelkova, and Lukomorie, and even Alkonost, which the Calvarians had seven times put to the torch, and seven times had been rebuilt. Seven was a cursed number, Danica said, for the demons had been seven, but it was apparently auspicious too: The Calvarians had never deigned to touch the city since the seventh foundations had been laid down. But, more often than not, when her stories were spent, the old woman would ask to hear about the castle, and of the other things that Lara dreamt.

Danica was always far more willing to listen to Lara's stories than Moder. Which was hardly surprising, for the old woman was a servant of the Watcher, and stories were a part of her trade. Every year, the day after the festival of Summer's End, Danica would hitch her mares to her wagon and travel from one place to another, singing sad songs of loves lost and hopes dashed as she plucked and strummed her guitar. And wherever the road took Danica, there was certain to be a warm fire and food and drink waiting for her at the end of the day, for to refuse hospitality to a follower of the Winter King, or to treat such a guest ill, was to invite the wrath of Wulf.

"Is that why you are our guest?" Lara had once asked the old woman at supper, when she was still too young to realize how rude the question was. "Because of the Watcher?"

Danica had merely laughed at that and had raised her cup to the girl and said, "No, my dear, but you make a guest feel most welcome."

Lara had nearly returned the gesture when she felt Moder's hand on her wrist.

"It is we who are the guests, Lara," she had said, gently but firmly. "This is Danica's home. We are . . . keeping it for her. When she is being away."

It had taken Lara several years to fully understand what Moder's words meant, but when she was thirteen summers old the blow finally landed: The farm was not her home, nor was Perun. Home was the place in her dreams, and even then she could not be certain if what she dreamed was true and what had sprung from the stories Danica wove, for when the Winter was over the old woman always returned to them with new songs to sing, and new tales to tell.

"You had best retrieve your burden, little cub," Danica said as the wagon rolled on, nodding to the place where Lara had left her buckets beside the track.

With a sigh Lara leapt from the wagon, took up her yoke and walked in the furrows that the wagon left behind it, beginning the slow climb towards the farm.

* * * * * * *

Despite Lara's distain, the farm was not a crude place. Unlike the logging houses in Perun, it had been built almost entirely out of worked stone, and its roof was tiled with copper shingles rather than thatch or wood. The green patina of the tiles closely matched the ivy that crept up the face of the stones, and red and white wildflowers grew in the grass beneath the farmhouse's eaves. Between the house and the barn there was a vegetable garden, its neatly organized beds divided by low hedges and lanes of gravel. A pair of fences ranged about the place, the first to keep the sheep out of the garden, and the second to keep the flock from wandering beyond their pasture. The fields stretched up towards the high fells of the mountain, where not even the hardy pine trees of the valley would grow. Even Lara had to admit that, had she not grown to be sick of the sight of it all, she would have found it pretty.

How such a place had come to be, so isolated and remote, was one of the first stories that Lara could remember Danica ever telling her. It had happened this way: Long before even the old woman had been born, the master of the mill had travelled north, along the course of the river Rusalka to the city of Irikosa, and there he had won the hand of a daughter of one of the Vargr, which is to say, he had taken the hand of one who was of the House of the Grand Prince. It is said that his bride laughed all the way to Perun, but upon seeing that place her laughter died, and from that day she refused even to smile, and lay in a state of profound melancholy. Wishing only to please her, the master sent for craftsman from as far as the capital, and with his wealth he built both farm and garden, acquiring a proper horse and carriage so that she might travel in the style she had once enjoyed. When that failed to cheer her, the master of the mill filled the house with many a rare and wondrous thing, but this merely served to remind her of the fine life that she had left behind, and of the mistake she had made in marrying a man of Perun, until, despairing, she weighed herself down with stones, and walked into the Rusalka.

Some expected the master of the mill to follow his wife down the long winding paths that lead to the halls of Domdaniel, but instead he shut up the house that he had built and set his mind towards his work, and after some time he married another. His second wife was the daughter of a charcoal burner, whose home had been a hut. To her, the wattle and daub home the master kept beside the mill was a delight, and so there the master and his second wife lived until they too came to know the number of their days.

As for the farm, the people of Perun quickly came to believe that it was a cursed place, where the shade of the master's first wife still lingered. Those who trod on the path that led to it were wont to rub a bit of earth on their foreheads, and whisper prayers to both Lioness and Firebird for protection. And so, it was shunned by the master's sons, and by his sons' sons, and their sons in turn.

But, as any of the wise might know, a place so shunned, and with such a history, was inevitably bound to draw the attention of one of the Watcher's servants. And so, one cold autumn night, a pair of loggers returned from their labors with stories of lights in the house's windows, and of smoke rising from its chimney. The men of Perun, grown prudent from years of listening to tales of wargs and spirits, waited until midday, with the full light of the Firebird to bolster their courage before they ventured up the path to the farm. And, when they came within sight of the farmhouse, they saw there a tall, bearded man dressed in gray leaning against one of the timbers of the porch, whittling at a stick with a bone-handled knife.

It was the great grandson of the mill master who had the courage to call out to the man, and to ask him who he was, and what his business was there. The stranger did not deign to respond at first, nor to look up from his work, but eventually he whistled, and from around the corner of the farmhouse loped a great black wolf. The hound stared at the mill master with pale blue eyes and, baring its fangs, it growled.

That was enough for the men of Perun and begging the stranger's pardon for their intrusion they quit that place, and seldom have they returned to it since. And so, the farm that had been built to delight a daughter of one of the Vargr became the home to one of the Watcher's servants.

The man in gray seldom spoke, but every evening, at dusk, he would walk to Perun and, finding a likely place near the fire of the tavern, he would play upon an old guitar and men would listen to him, and drink, and raise their glasses to Wulf and place coppers into the gray man's cup, for the taste of copper was the closest to a man's blood, and of old that was what the Watcher thirsted for most of all.

The man who kept the company of wolves made many changes to that place, as one might expect. The great canopy bed that the master of the mill had bought for his bride, now worm-eaten and moldering, its satin curtains having long since gone to dust, he chopped up for firewood, and many of the treasures of the house he sold. And with that coin he bought a small flock of sheep that had been brought to Perun to be slaughtered for the men who worked the sawmill, as well as tools for the felling and working of wood. He turned the carriage house into a barn for the animals, and the great lawn became their pasture, ringed by a long fence of pale white pinewood. And, in the garden that had grown wild with thorns and creepers, the man planted vegetables and herbs for his sustenance. But, perhaps fearing that the place might lose some of its dread, the man in gray set poles on the pathway to his house, and onto them he affixed the blackened skulls of the men and women who had died in Perun and been returned to the Firebird, so that all who came to that place would pass beneath the silent gaze of the dead.

And, at last, the man in gray and his wolf joined the skulls on their posts, affixed there by an apprentice he had trained from the village of Perun, and now the apprentice too grinned from atop a sharpened pole, a blackened thing that might have been man or woman. Danica had never told that tale, but she was now the Mistress of the farm, as the guitar that she plucked at had once been the man in gray's, and the farm built for the sad daughter of one of the Vargr was now her own.

Of course, the stories that Danica told often changed. Sometimes in the telling it was the master of the mill who had been driven to despair and walked to his death laden down by stones. Sometimes it was the maiden of Irikosa who had become one of the Watcher's servants, learning the secret language of the wolves and wargs of the forest. Sometimes the master of the mill and his wife lived happily, until the Red Death came, and sorrow fell on the farm. But whatever the case, the Farm belonged to Danica now, at least until the Watcher came for her.

"You were the girl from Irikosa," Lara had once said to the old woman, certain that she was right in her guess.

"No, little one," Danica had said, smiling her weird smile. "I was born in Perun, and of *that*, at least, you have my word."

* * * * * * *

By the time Lara had made the climb from the river, her shoulders aching from the strain of the yoke on her back, the wagon had come to a halt before the farmhouse. Danica had slipped from her seat and was speaking with Moder, their hands linked.

"The flock is wanting its water," Moder said, her deep blue eyes blinking momentarily as Lara took a moment to catch her breath. "And you are late."

As ever, Moder's pale blond hair was done up in a tight bun so as not to interfere with her work, and regardless of the dirt and filth of the barn, her patched attire was far cleaner than the stained cloak and robes Danica wore.

"I will help," Pinsard said, stepping out from the entrance to the barn. He was almost as tall as Moder now, lean as an arrow. His tousled hair was still matted to his head from sleep.

"The mares will want water too," Lara growled as he approached. "Get your own buckets."

Danica never raised her voice, but she had a way of sharpening it that almost made one jump. She did this now, saying, "I watered the mares in Perun. Now do as your *moder* says and see to the sheep, the both of you."

Lara made for the barn at once, Pinsard stepping aside to let her pass. Pasha whined softly and followed too.

The barn that had once been a carriage house was always warm in the morning, even in the dead of winter, for the mass of sheep huddled together during the night served almost as well as any hearth would have. The black-headed, black-legged flock was already lapping greedily at the trough as Lara and Pinsard emptied the buckets into it, the biggest of them shoving aside the weaker with their heads.

Pasha let out a reproving bark.

Still not enough water. Lara let out a sigh.

"They have all been milked," Pinsard said, shouldering the yoke himself. "One more walk down to the stream, I think. If we do it together."

Lara nodded in agreement and laid the buckets onto the yoke, and then took a third from a peg attached to the stall where Whisper was stabled, the old horse raising his head with ears pricked, nickering affectionately.

Lara let the great steed sniff and blow at her face and breathed softly back. When she had been younger, Moder had taught her how to ride on the great stallion, whose coat had been sleek and whose gallop had been steady, but now Whisper was nearly blind and his mane was streaked with gray. Still, Moder cared for him, grooming him with brush and pick and treating him with berries when they were in season, though he did no real work on the farm.

"He is a warrior," Moder had said once when Lara had asked why they kept him. "He is one of the gray. He is deserving his rest."

Pasha barked again, dancing about Pinsard as if to trip him as he walked out of the barn, looking back at Lara expectantly with his bright blue eyes.

"I'm coming," Lara said, and followed.

Danica and Moder were busying themselves with the task of unhitching the mares from the wagon, but Moder straightened as the two exited the barn, and watched as they went, her mouth a perfect line.

That usually meant trouble, and Lara quickened her step until she strode side by side with Pinsard.

"Did she tell you any stories?" Pinsard asked as they walked down to the stream, the buckets swaying in time with his stride. "Any new stories, I mean."

"You know she didn't."

"Did not," Pinsard corrected.

"Did not, did not," Lara mocked. "Did not you know how stupid you sound?"

Pinsard reddened a bit about his cheeks. "It is the proper way-"

"The proper wayyy," Lara drawled, and swapped at one of Pinsard's buckets with a bit more force than she perhaps intended, sending it clattering into the dirt.

"*Awirung!*" Pinsard swore.

"*Awirung!*" Lara repeated. "Psh. Do you even know what that word means?"

"No, I don't!" Pinsard barked as he picked the bucket back up. "Just- Just that Moder says it whenever she is angry."

For a moment Lara was silent. Pinsard rarely lost his temper.

"You said 'don't,'" Lara said, and giggled.

"I did not," Pinsard said, and then he laughed too.

The rest of the work was easy. Pinsard was lean, but very tall and strong for his age, and between the two of them they brought four full buckets up from the brook, which the sheep drank lazily. Eventually Pasha drove the flock out of the barn and into the high field beyond the house, where they could graze upon fresh grown leaf and clover. The farm's pair of rams nosed about within their own, smaller pasture, as Lara and Pinsard kept watch. To pass the time Lara kept an eye out for golden trefoil, which sickened the sheep, and for mint, which Moder used to scent her soap . . . Though she could not help but gaze back at the farm and wonder what Danica and Moder were saying to each other as they went about their business.

Some time before sundown Danica walked into the pasture and took a good look at the flock, paying particular attention to the lambs that had been birthed during the late Winter. She had a long sharp knife in her belt, and Lara knew what would come soon thereafter.

"Which one?" Danica asked of no one, rubbing one of the lamb's silky white heads. "This one?"

"Must you?" Lara asked.

"This is one of the uses of a lamb," Danica said, patting her blade and grinning crookedly. "We do not keep wolves here, or lions, do we?"

"It's just-" Lara started. "It's just . . . They don't know. It's-"

"It is cruel," Pinsard said, flatly.

"It is," Danica said. "And it is not. Would we live with sheep if they gave no wool? Gave no milk? Gave no meat?"

Lara chewed on her lip.

"This one, then," Danica said, and took one of the lambs by the crook of its neck.

A weird cry pierced the air then, loud enough that it startled even the old woman, who let go of the sheep in her grip and drew out her blade reflexively.

"Shrike," Pinsard whispered.

Lara nodded. Moder had shot one once, many years past, a scrawny thing that had been more bird than human. *"Always kill a shrike,"* she had said that day, though Lara did not know why.

She wondered if she should return to the house to fetch bow and arrow when Danica said, "No, not a shrike. Listen."

The cry went out again. Bird-like in a way, yes, but with enough of a canine bent that Pasha took to howling in response. The flock, troubled, huddled together as they began to make their way back towards the farm.

"This way," Danica said, sheathing her blade back in her belt.

At the far side of the ewes' pasture there was an old stone wall, older perhaps than even the farm, for there were weird black slabs mixed within the uneven blocks that made it up. The flock rarely came close to this place, perhaps because the mountain loomed so heavily above, or maybe it was because the wall was overgrown with nettles and creepers, and thick thorny branches grew between the rock. Even Pasha shied away as they approached and ran back to keep the flock together.

Lara jumped as the weird scream echoed across the pasture, far closer now. Pinsard squinted at the brush, his blue eyes darting.

"There," Danica said, pointing, her own yellow eyes grown quite wide. "An animal."

Lara drew closer to one of the thorn bushes, and saw that there was something within it, all twisted up in the branches and bloodied. It was hardly bigger than a hare, and its face was cat-like in a way, though its ears were high as a rabbit's. Its black hide was striped with silver and its tail was very long, whipping about as it stared at her with its honey-colored eyes. How it had come to be wound up in the thorns she could not say, but it hissed and chittered angrily at the sight of them.

"A fox-squirrel," Danica said. "A hawk or a hill cat must have been at it."

"Is it dying?" Pinsard asked, his face grown very still.

Danica nodded. "It will die. And die in pain if we do nothing. A touch of the Watcher's mercy, I think . . ."

Danica reached for her knife, but Lara took the old woman's hand by the wrist, surprising even herself for a moment.

"No," Lara said.

"So, you would leave it to die?"

Lara bit her lip again. "No. I will rescue it."

"Lara," Danica said, not unkindly, "This is not a lamb. You cannot milk it, you cannot shear it, and only a Prince would want it for the price of its fur. It has no purpose. You will shred your arm to tatters getting it out of there, and it will surely bite you for your trouble."

Lara breathed hotly through her nose, thinking, the old woman's yellow gaze, not unlike that of the squalling animal in the bush, directly upon her.

She released Danica's arm.

"There is a tree in your garden that grows no fruit," she said. "Should we chop it down because it's useless? And Whisper is nearly blind. Should we send him to the butcher in Perun, because he can't see? Every afternoon *that mountain* hides the Firebird. So, should we knock it down too, to better see the sky?"

Pinsard touched her arm, then. She did not realize how loudly she had been speaking.

"Very well," Danica said, stepping back. "Free the thing if you will."

Lara turned and looked at the fox-squirrel trapped in the brush, and leaned forward, extending her arm slowly through the thorns, wincing as they bit and tore at her, reaching her hand out towards the animal, who was cowering now, burring deep in its throat.

"Quiet now," Lara said, shushing, "It's alright. You're safe now, I promise."

Blood ran down her arm freely, from several cuts. Her hand was close to the fox-squirrel, whose sharp teeth were bared.

"Lara," Pinsard said, the worry in his voice clear.

"Shhh," she said, and piercing the palm of her hand upon the thorns, lifted free the branch that had trapped the animal.

And the fox-squirrel did not bite, but ran up the length of Lara's arm, its sharp claws digging into her skin until it came to rest beside her throat, and found comfort in the folds of her hair, shivering against the warmth of her neck.

Slowly, Lara withdrew her arm from the brush, not minding so much the pain as the thorns dragged at her, and stood up, the fox-squirrel still nestled against her neck, licking at its own wounds.

Danica's face had curled into an odd look, knowing, pleased even, but also sad.

"What a priestess you would make," Danica said. "If only-"

"If only what?" Lara said, straightening to her full height, trying to ignore the blood running down her arm.

"Those cuts need minding," Danica said by way of a reply. "And I am wanting supper. The sun is setting, and I have a new old story to tell. Bring your pup, and your scars. You will be siblings now, you know, for you both know the sting of the same nettle, and they say that always cuts true from the beginning."

Lara nodded, though she did not understand, and helped Pinsard as best she could to lead the flock back towards the farm, surprised perhaps to find that the little animal was slumbering upon her shoulder, so that she walked as lightly as she might so as not to disturb it.

* * * * * *

By dusk, Moder was fussing over Lara's arm, dressing it with gauze lightly soaked with the vinegar she would normally use for the spring's preserves. The animal's wounds she sewed up as well, though she wore thick black gloves over her hands, and dosed it with a tincture of poppy that she kept in a high locked cabinet within the kitchen of the farm, so that it would sleep as she worked.

"It is not being tame," Moder said when she was done, washing the thing's wounds as clean as she might. "It is *un-tydre*. A chimera. Dangerous."

"It didn't bite me," Lara said, thinking. "It was only afraid. And I won't make it stay if it doesn't want to."

Moder regarded her, the corners of her eyes crinkling slightly. Then she handed the animal over, setting it in Lara's lap.

"You'll feed it yourself," she said, removing her gloves.

"Yes," Lara said, gently stroking the dozing ball of fur. "Only . . . What does it eat?"

"That depends," Danica said, turning slightly from the hearth, where she was stirring a cast iron pot full of fresh cuts of lamb with the barley, carrots, turnips, and split peas that she had bought in Perun. "But it looks to be more squirrel than fox to me."

Moder's left eye blinked at that, her lip curling subtly before she picked up her knitting from the table. Lara stared at her for a moment, curious.

"See if it will eat seeds or nuts to start with," Danica said. "Though even a true squirrel will eat meat in the early Spring when food is scarce. Some of my broth will do it good when it wakes up, and in three days time you may find yourself a sister hard to shake off."

"Ssss," Moder hissed, undoing a bit of her knitting. "You are making me lose count."

"The broth is hot and ready," Danica said. "Where is that tall son of yours?"

"Chopping wood," Moder and Lara answered together, pausing to listen to the distant strikes of metal on wood as Pinsard grunted with exertion.

The phrase was a misdirection that they had grown so used to that even with Danica they could not help but use it. In truth, Pinsard was outside, beyond the garden and far enough from the barn so as not to disturb the animals, practicing sword cuts against a post wrapped in thick rope. Moder insisted that both Lara and Pinsard strengthen their arms in this way every day, while sharpening their use of the bow. After all, Moder said, there were wargs in the wilds, and shrikes large enough to carry off a young lamb, and there were wicked men in the world, brigands and raiders and the like.

"Is The Nightingale in Perun not named after such a one?" Moder had said time and again. And often, when the weather was good, Moder would spar with one of them for hours, using wooden swords at first, then blunted steel blades. Had she not torn up her arm in the brush, Lara too might have been out with her practice blade. It was thinner somewhat than the long sword that Pinsard favored, but still heavy.

Moder put a pair of fingers into her mouth and whistled sharply. *Come!* the whistle said. *And quickly!*

Lara and Pinsard both knew Moder's calls by heart. This one was meant only to summon, but there were others: *Stay put. Hide. Danger!* Moder used them all, every now and then, though Lara could not recall hearing the last two ever being used in earnest, so that Lara had begun to wonder at their worth.

Sure enough, within a few moments, Pinsard loped through the open door of the farmhouse, his practice sword sheathed and his face wet with sweat.

"Supper," Moder said, simply. Pinsard nodded and put his sword away before washing his face and hands in the basin put aside for such, rubbing at the back of his neck with the cool water from the well.

As he washed, Moder put aside her knitting and set out ceramic bowls and silver spoons. Then Danica ladled out her lamb stew. Lara let the fox-squirrel slumber atop her legs as she accepted her share, tearing a hunk of old bread from the loaf atop the table.

Pinsard waited for the others to be served and then spooned a portion of the meal into his own bowl.

"Let us eat," Pinsard said.

"And not bite our tongues," Danica replied, grinning. She had taught them this call and response many years ago.

They ate in silence for a time, for all were tired from the day and eager to fill their bellies but, as they became sated, they began to ask Danica of her travels: Where had she been? And what had she seen of the world beyond the farm?

Perhaps expecting this moment, Danica at last told the story she had kept for that evening's meal. It was, as she had told Lara, very, very old, but new all the same.

"A traveler once came to a village, far to the west of here, in Arcasia," Danica began, "Carrying nothing but an empty pot and a pale-white stone."

The fox-squirrel began to stir beneath Lara's hand, and she held a bit of meat beneath its nostrils. It sniffed at it and began to nibble at the offering.

"The villagers, seeing that the stranger had no coin to spend, turned him away from their homes and hearths. But some of the village saw that the traveler had gathered firewood from the forest, and water from the river nearby, and was cooking his white stone within his pot."

"Was he The Wanderer?" Pinsard asked, guessing that the traveler was one of the demons of old.

"No," Danica said, "Only a clever man. For the villagers began to gather about him and ask what he was about. He told them that he was cooking white stone soup, which he had lived on for some time, though it would taste better with herbs to improve the taste."

"So they gave him . . ." Lara began, not certain how to proceed.

"Flavor!" Danica replied. "Substance! Onions, carrots, lettuce, beef, salt! The white stone soup tasted better and better to the villagers with every seasoning added, until at last the traveler removed the miraculous stone from the pot and let all enjoy the broth."

"Himself included," Lara said, smirking.

"Of course."

"So he . . . *tricked* them," Pinsard said, picking out the word carefully as he put down his spoon. He had finished his meal rather quickly.

Danica nodded. "He did, but it did not end well for the traveler."

"But he," Lara said, "Surely they-"

"When the traveler fell asleep that night the villagers stove in his head, and took from him his miraculous white stone, and ever since then they have served the most delicious white stone soup west of the mountains and south of the sea."

Lara bit at her lip but nodded. Pinsard's cheeks flushed slightly.

"Must every story you are telling be ending with someone dead?" Moder asked, sighing, and not for the first time.

"I am a servant of the Watcher," Danica replied, "If you want cheer, go find the nearest fool. Speaking of which, there once was a servant of the Watcher who thought to give his stories happy endings-"

"I am guessing the end of the story," Moder said, pushing away her bowl. "And it is being bedtime, I am thinking."

"But Moder-" Pinsard began to complain. Lara too thought this unfair. The sun had hardly set.

"Bed!" Moder repeated, in a tone that brooked little argument.

Moder seemed to have forgotten about the little chimera, so Lara gathered it up in her arms and made her way up to her pallet in the loft that served as her bedroom. Pasha trailed after her, still a bit put off by the new addition to their family . . . But when she lay down the sheepdog curled up over her feet while the fox-squirrel settled upon her breast. Soon, both animals were sound asleep.

Pinsard rustled a bit as he slipped under the sheep-hide blanket he kept beneath the loft. He too was breathing evenly within moments.

Lara shut her eyes. Outside the wind was picking up. Rain began to spatter against the window in fits. Sleep would come easy enough. She was tired, after all, and the day had been a long one . . . But she could still hear the voices wafting up the stairs. Lara did not mean to listen, but eventually she could not help it. They might have been in the hall, it sounded so loud.

". . . to the question whenever they are found," Danica was saying.

"There are being more then? Since the rebels are taking Sirin? More . . . More, what is word, refugee?"

"Refugees, yes. And hundreds, yes, thanks to that general, the one with only one leg," she clucked her tongue. "Foalan?"

"Faelas. The judges must be regretting sending him to the South. He was learning too much of his enemy. War in Calvaria. *Between* Calvarians . . . It is unknown."

"They are cheering his name in Vassa," Danica said, "The Grand Prince has offered his daughter's hand to him, they say. And you should be glad. The more rebels there are of your people the easier it will be for you to hide."

"It is only the old ways," Moder said, so softly Lara could barely hear it. "It is being hard to change. Even now."

There was silence for a time, save for the rain. It was so long that Lara closed her eyes again and began to drift into the darkness.

"There has been a third," Danica's voice pierced the quiet. "A third false Larissa."

"*Awirung*," Moder swore. "Not another."

"I'm afraid so," Danica replied. Lara opened her eyes and would have sat up if it were not for the fox-squirrel sleeping atop her.

Larissa was her name. Her true name.

"And?" Moder asked, simply.

"What you would expect. A village girl, or a noble's bastard, propped up on a horse. They say her real name was Langwydere, but that didn't matter. A mob of idiots flocked to her banner before they all ended up dead on a bonfire. She would have joined them, but her head is on a spike above the gate of Carduel, like all the rest."

"Cruel, cruel, cruel," Moder said. "Has he no pity?"

"None, they say," Danica replied. "None."

There was silence again.

"So he is being busy," Moder said. "He is being in the West still?"

"Still, yes. But there are eyes and ears about everywhere, even in Irikosa. I have seen the placards. She is too-" Danica hesitated, and finished, "She must never be seen."

"She will not be being seen."

"But she cannot stay here forever."

"No," Moder said, softly, and Lara understood for certain then that they were talking about her, though she did not understand why. "No, she cannot."

"Then what?"

"A question being for another day, I am thinking," Moder answered. "It is being late."

"Bed is it? And so early."

"Goodnight, wolf-girl," Moder said, beginning to climb the stairs to her own room.

"Would that I were a wolf," Danica said. "Or a girl."

Lara heard the door to Moder's room creak open, then shut, listened to her settle into her bed, listened to the dull clatter of the tobacco jar, and then Danica's bare feet against the porch boards.

She hated to wake the animals, but it was too much. "Shhh," she whispered, cupping her hands about the curled-up fox-squirrel. It did not stir much, breathing easy as she laid it upon her pillow, and remaining still as she crept off her pallet and climbed down from the loft. Pasha whined and followed her down the steps before settling next to Pinsard. The boy stirred briefly as she passed him by, his right-hand twitching ever so slightly against the bare floor.

Danica was sitting on the porch of the farmhouse, smoking her long pipe, her face lost in a haze of smoke as rain pattered softly against the roof.

"You did hear then," Danica said.

"Hear what?" Lara said.

"I thought so." Danica drew on her pipe and blew out a long plume of blue smoke that curled away like a serpent.

"You were talking about-" Lara began, unsure. "You were talking about me, weren't you?"

"Amongst other things."

"I heard you say there was a third. A third . . . A girl, who died?"

"A girl who died."

"But- Who died? Who killed her?"

Danica breathed more life into her pipe.

"You should ask your mother," she said. "She knows more than I can tell you."

Lara did not answer. She stood on the porch, aware for a moment that she was cold, the skin of her arms gone to gooseflesh.

"Are you afraid to ask?"

Lara shook her head. "It's just- Just talking to her- Sometimes, it's like talking to a book. Like- Like she has no feelings."

Danica took the pipe from her mouth.

"Lara," she said, reaching out to take her hand. "Lara, your mother loves you."

"Then why?" Lara said, small tears springing to her eyes, "Why doesn't she show it?"

"Because people are not books, Lara," Danica said, squeezing her hand. "You cannot read them so easily."

Lara wept a little, though not long.

"You should be in bed," Danica said. "With your pup. There will be time for questions tomorrow, and I've already told you one story tonight. You can wait that long, yes?"

"Yes," Lara said, hugging the old woman before she retraced her steps to the pallet in the loft.

As she laid herself down the fox-squirrel nestled against her shoulder. She closed her eyes.

But still she could hear Danica's voice repeating: *She must never be seen, she must never be seen, she must never be seen.*

II

"Be getting dressed," Lara heard Moder say as she shook her from her sleep. "And come."

"What is it?" she muttered, squinting at the windowpane overhead. The sky was still dark, only the faintest hint of blue betraying the coming dawn. But Moder was already climbing down from the loft. She had never woken her this early before.

This too, was a rarity.

Danica told her, she cursed as she roused herself, throwing off her shift and pulling on her breeches, boots, and blouse, but she discounted the thought quickly. *No. She wouldn't do that. She likes to keep her secrets.*

The fox-squirrel let out an enormous yawn, its back arching as it stretched. It spun about a few times before resettling into the warmth of Lara's pillow.

"Lucky thing," Lara grumbled as she looped her belt and did up the lacing of her bodice.

"I am waiting," Moder said from below.

Lara tied fast the last knot, grabbed her gloves, stuffed them into her belt and hurried down the steps. Pinsard stirred, shifting atop his pallet, but he did not wake. Pasha's ears pricked and he opened his eyes, his tail wagging.

Moder put out a black-gloved hand and said, "Stay."

He obeyed.

Lara followed Moder out and into the yard. There was already some light cresting the horizon, painting the clouds a brilliant mixture of blue stained with rose.

Lara blinked at Moder. She was not wearing her dull breeches and sheepskin coat, but was clothed all in white, save for the black leather belt about her waist, her long black gloves, and tall black boots, polished to a lustrous sheen.

She wore a sword upon her belt. A real sword, with a gleaming steel pommel. And there was a long bundle of rolled up cloth in the crook of her left arm.

A chill gust of wind picked up, buffeting them. Lara shivered and rubbed at her arms.

"You are cold?" Moder asked without turning around.

"Yes," Lara said.

"That is good," Moder said. "Cold is keeping the mind sharp."

It puts me right to sleep, Lara wanted to say, but held her tongue.

They walked. Lara thought that they might come to a halt at the nicked-up practice post, but Moder strode right past it, making for the tree line north of the farm.

Where is she taking me?

"The water for the flock," Lara said, glancing backwards as she jogged to catch up.

"Pinsard will fetch it," Moder said, brusquely. "And Danica will milk the ewes."

Lara didn't argue. Moder's face was more expressionless than usual, almost as cold as the gusts that continued to tousle their hair.

They came to the edge of the woods. Moder stooped under the branch of a leafless oak and pressed on.

Lara followed, but she was beginning to wonder just how far they would go. She had been in the forest before, the place was not forbidden to her, but she rarely went very deep. Danica's stories about ravenous wargs and wicked faun had always scared her, and Moder had never been shy in reminding her that there truly were such things, and worse, lurking in the vastness of the world.

But I am safe, she thought. *Moder is with me. And she has a sword.*

"*There once was a girl who wore a cap the color of blood,*" she could hear Danica saying, "*Whose grandmother lived deep in the woods . . .*"

Lara stepped on a loose branch, snapping it in two. She started at the sound. Her heart pounded.

"Be watching where you step," Moder said. "It is being better to not make noise when walking in the forest."

Lara nodded.

You're being stupid. It was only a branch. Moder wouldn't take us someplace that wasn't safe. She wouldn't. Would she?

And so, it was something of a relief to Lara when Moder finally came to a stop. She had brought them to a small clearing, no bigger than the farmhouse itself. Oaks, spruces, and pines ringed it, the evergreens lending a hint of color amidst the gloom of bare branches and frost-coated leaves that stretched around them.

Moder walked to the center of the clearing and turned to face Lara, her deep blue eyes staring. Sunlight was beginning to creep through the wood, the long shadows of trees lengthening between bands of gold. The chill wind could not reach them there.

"You are having questions," Moder said.

"Danica told you?" Lara said, still not believing it.

"No," Moder answered, "But I am knowing all the same."

Lara blinked.

"How?" she asked.

"The day after Crowning," Moder said, with the faintest of smiles, "You will be knowing your sixteenth summer. I too was having questions when I was sixteen."

It was hard for Lara to imagine that Moder had ever been a girl. It was harder still to imagine that she had ever had any doubts.

"So," Moder said, her smile fading. "Be asking your questions."

All that she had heard the night before- the war, the dead girl's head on a spike, the talk of keeping her hidden away- none of it seemed to matter to her now. The real question, the one she had wanted to ask since before she could remember, had been nagging at her for so long that she had begun to take it for granted.

After all, it had only taken her first look in a mirror for her to realize that she was different from the woman who called her *dohtor* and the boy who called her *sweoster*.

"Who is my *moder*?" she asked.

"I am," Moder replied, but Lara shook her head.

"Who is my *real moder*? Who is my *faeder*?"

Lara saw a rare thing then. For a moment, brief though it was, Moder could not meet her gaze.

"Your *moder* and *faeder*," she said, quietly, "Both are dead. Dead. Like Pinsard's *faeder* is."

"Dead," Lara repeated, nodding to herself. Why else would she live with kindred who did not share the color of her skin?

"But who were they?" Lara pressed. "And how did they die?"

Moder straightened.

"This I will answer," she said. "But first, a gift for you."

Moder took the bundle from under her arm and balanced it between her hands. There was clearly something within it, for the cloth kept its shape.

"Open," she said, "And take."

Lara unfolded the bundle, slowly, feeling the palpable weight of what was within. It was a sword, long and narrow, safe within a leather sheath.

"Take," Moder said, again. "Is being yours now."

Lara took the thing, gingerly. This was no practice blade. The hilt was a lovely thing, wrapped in what looked to Lara like snakeskin and ringed with a ribbon of polished copper. Elegant loops of steel guarded the grip and the first knuckle-length of the blade itself.

She unsheathed it.

Its blade was far thinner than those of the practice swords she had trained with for as long as she could remember, and it gleamed in the light of the rising sun. She couldn't help but give it a swing, delighting at the noise it made as it sliced through the air.

"Where did it come from?" Lara asked, marveling at it still.

"Vassa," Moder answered, laying down the cloth, which she had folded into a tidy square. "Danica was bringing it two summers past."

Vassa! The city of the Grand Prince! Danica had been there before, Lara knew, but to have been there so recently, and to have bought such a fine sword . . . Lara did not know how much gold a blade such as this would cost, but surely it was more than what the villagers of Perun paid them for their milk and wool.

"But why?" Lara asked.

"Because I am telling her to," Moder said, crossing her arms.

Lara tested the edge of the blade with her thumb. It was quite sharp.

"Does it," Lara said, wetting her tongue, "Does it have a name? Like in the stories?"

Moder muttered something under her breath and shook her head.

"No," she said, smiling faintly, "It is not having a name. But you may be giving it one. If you must."

Lara's mind raced. All the great swords in the stories had names. Thunderclap, the soul-crushing blade of the Demon King . . . Or Wrath, the longsword of Kalin the Golden, and Cold-Night, which the traitorous Count Faisan wielded against his own countrymen.

"I can't think of anything," Lara finally said.

"Good," Moder said. "Sword must be a part of you, and you must be like sword. Strong, but able to bend, or you will break. So will sword. You are seeing?"

Lara nodded. This was not the first time she had heard these words from Moder.

"Stone is strong," Lara said, "But water is stronger."

"So," Moder said, unfolding her arms to take hold of her own blade. "You would still be knowing of your *moder* and *faeder*?"

Lara looked at Moder. She had changed her footing. Loose, but tense. A fighting stance. And there was danger in her deep blue eyes.

Lara hesitated only a moment.

"Yes," she said.

"Then I will be telling you of them both," Moder said, her words deliberate, "When you can touch me with the tip of that sword."

"Is that all?"

"You are thinking it will be easy?"

Lara opened her mouth, incredulous, then shut it. Moder might withhold the truth, might exaggerate, but she rarely, if ever, spoke in jest.

Lara shook her head 'no.'

"Good," Moder said.

The tops of the trees about them rustled in the wind. The sword was still cold in Lara's hands, but her palms were damp with sweat.

"May I put on my gloves?" Lara asked.

"Please," Moder said. "Is better for grip."

Lara slipped the naked blade into her belt and pulled on her gloves, flexing her fingers as she shook out her hands to loosen them.

"Your legs too are needing stretching," Moder said, though she remained still. "Muscles are being tight. Too tight and they tear, or are you forgetting?"

Lara frowned at her own carelessness. She always stretched before sparring. Moder had taught her that when she was ten summers old.

You're distracted, she thought as she stretched her calves and hamstrings, *Focus. The tip of the blade and she will tell me the truth.* She had done it before, against Pinsard, hundreds of times, more than she could count.

Pinsard is not Moder.

She knelt, placing the scabbard on a dry patch of leaves. She drew the sword from her belt as she straightened, saluting as she leveled the blade with Moder's eyes.

The white-clad woman nodded with approval. The wind whistled through the trees.

Lara lunged forward, blade extended, intending to land a quick blow to the top of Moder's shoulder, but as she neared both her sword and her arm were thrown aside by the sheer force of the older woman's draw. Before she could recover, Moder had danced past her and planted the flat of her own blade against the nape of her neck.

"Too slow," Moder said, leaping aside as Lara whirled to retaliate. The blade caught nothing but air.

Moder gained a little ground, gripping her sword with both hands as she kept it in a low guard. Lara huffed and came at her again, her hand held behind her to narrow her profile, but again Moder's parries were far quicker than her cuts, and after four exchanges the older woman had struck her twice: Once on the upper arm and once on the outside of her left thigh.

Lara hissed through her teeth. Moder was only using the flat of her blade, but there enough force behind her blow to make them sting.

You only need to touch her!

She launched herself forward. Moder would hit her, no doubt, but she would strike home. And Moder did hit her, but not with her sword. Instead, she dodged past the point of Lara's blade and bulled into her with all her strength, throwing Lara flat on her back.

Lara wheezed, the wind having been knocked from her. Before she had recovered fully, she felt the point of Moder's sword resting above her left breast.

"Body is weapon too," Moder said. She had not even broken a sweat. "Always be remembering."

Lara smashed Moder's blade aside with her own, leaping to her feet as the older woman gave ground. Lara came on again, slashing and thrusting, all technique cast aside.

"Anger is not helping you in a fight," Moder said, dodging one of Lara's blows almost lazily. "It will only be, what is word? *Distract*, yes, anger is only being a distraction."

Moder stepped into one of Lara's cuts then, their swords briefly crossing as the older woman caught hold of Lara's wrist and twisted her blade out of her grip.

The blade had hardly struck the ground before Moder had kicked it away.

"Again?" Moder said, stepping back and raising her sword into a high guard.

Lara stared, sullenly, and rubbed at her wrist.

"What is wrong?" Moder asked, relaxing her stance. "You are giving up so easily?"

"It's not fair," Lara said, "You are better than I am."

"How so?"

"You are faster than me," Lara answered, "Faster *and* stronger."

"That is being good," Moder said. "Would you be wanting a *laruwa* who was weak? One who is slow? One who could not be teaching you how to be quick? How to truly be strong?"

Lara felt a momentary flush of shame and shook her head.

"So," Moder said, sheathing her sword, "Be glad! For your *laruwa* is not being slow, is not being weak, and you are being quicker and stronger at sixteen summers than you are knowing."

"What is a *laruwa*?" Lara asked.

"I am your *laruwa*," Moder said. "As I am being Pinsard's. Teacher is word. One who is giving knowledge."

But not the knowledge that I want.

The thought must have been written on her face as plain as day, for Moder walked over to the place where her sword lay amongst the frost and picked up the blade.

"When you are learning this," she said, offering the weapon by its hilt, "I will be telling you what you wish to know. I swear it, Lara. By the name of my lufiend, I swear it. By him, I swear it."

Moder's voice had grown reedy and tight.

Speechless, Lara took the sword. Then Moder leaned forward and sealed her promise, gently kissing Lara on the cheek.

"That is being enough for today, I am thinking," Moder said, scooping up the folded bit of cloth and handing it to Lara. "Flock will be in pasture. But tomorrow we are coming here again. Yes?"

"Yes," Lara said.

"And why are we coming here? And not *chopping wood* in the yard?"

"Because," Lara chewed a bit on her lower lip. "Because no one can see or hear us here."

"Just so," Moder said. And as she walked from the clearing she added, "You are having leaves in your hair."

Lara tousled her head and followed, wrapping the cloth back about blade and sheath. And the wood felt far less ominous to her than it had that morning . . . if only because she knew that, one day, she would stand in the clearing and touch Moder with the tip of her sword, and she would know the truth.

Finally, they stepped from the trees and began to cross the old pasture. The sun was still rising, but it was already growing warm.

Moder had a long, easy stride. But, when they were halfway across the field, she slowed.

"It is being true, Lara," she said, softly, "That I am not your real Moder. But, every day, I am wishing that I am. Do you . . . Understand?"

Lara nodded.

"That is good," Moder said, and walked on.

Beyond the barn Lara could see Pinsard and Pasha, leading the flock out to graze. And there was Danica, leading Whisper down the lane, the old horse slowly clopping along with his head hanging low.

The stinging wind blustered against Lara's face, but she smiled.

* * * * * * *

And so, Lara passed every morning by practicing her sword work with Moder. Even when it was raining . . . Which was often, as the month that Danica called Blossoming was a wet one.

"Here are two, spared from the deluge," Danica would snicker whenever they returned, hair and clothing soaked through, but she always had cups of hot broth ready for them as they dried themselves by the hearth.

But rain or not, Moder insisted that Lara never miss the morning's work, though they did not spar again for many days. And at first Moder refined her cuts, thrusts, and parries, when to stand and when to advance, and how to properly grip her sword, which was far lighter than the dulled practice blades Lara was used to.

"Cutting wood at the post was making you strong," Moder explained, "But now we are making you fast."

They were not alone, either. Pinsard joined them every other day, rising even earlier to see that the flock was watered. He had been hiding a proper sword as well, more akin to Moder's steel-pommeled longsword than Lara's was and heavier to boot.

"When did she give you that?" Lara asked one blustery afternoon, when they had finished their exercises and were watching over the sheep.

"Last summer," Pinsard answered. "The day after Crowning."

"Does it have a name?"

"No," Pinsard had answered. "Does yours?"

"No," Lara had replied, "Not yet."

The fox-squirrel too began to follow Lara about, perching atop her shoulder or skittering through the dew grass before leaping from tree to tree. Whenever Lara would spar, the animal would chitter and scold from a high branch, occasionally letting out its weird bird-like cry. But always, when they were done with their mock battles, it would leap from the trees and race in circles about Lara's boots before bounding ahead of them, chattering merrily as its thick tail trailed behind it, occasionally shooting a look backwards as if to make certain that it was not too far ahead.

"It reminds me of something," Pinsard said of it eventually, grown pensive, "A flag I think. Or a banner."

"What does?" Lara replied, "Its tail?"

"No," Pinsard said, "Something else. Eh, I do not remember. But its tail *is* like a banner, I suppose."

"Bannertail," Lara repeated, and so the fox-squirrel, if not Lara's sword, was given a name.

But though a fortnight had passed, Lara still felt herself no closer to her goal. Moder was frightfully quick after all, and sharp-witted, and also very strong.

As for Pinsard . . . Well, he was another matter.

He certainly had more practice than she with a real sword, and more raw strength, but he was a novice compared to Moder, who regularly sent him tumbling onto the freshly grown grass of the clearing. *Moder* was, if anything, rougher with Pinsard than she was with Lara, and after their lessons he often had a fresh bruise or cut as a reminder of his mistakes.

After one such hard fall, Pinsard yelped out in pain and clutched at his right ankle. Moder gingerly helped him take off his boot and footwrap, asking him if he could move his toes. Pinsard grimaced as he did so, but Moder nodded.

"Is not broken," she said, "Merely twisted. Needs rest though, or it may becoming worse. No more for today. Go. Sit. Rest your leg. I will watch flock today. And Lara, Danica will have chores for you."

Lara knew there was no arguing, though she had done nothing that morning but practice what Moder called 'the cuts.' But she was also a bit relieved. By the end of the day she was often so tired that she had trouble climbing up the steps of her loft.

They found Danica in the old carriage house shearing one of the rams, the animal struggling futilely to free his head from the old woman's grip. She didn't even look up from her work as Lara entered the barn with Pinsard limping beside her. *Moder* grunted a 'morning' and went to join Pasha and the flock in the pasture. Lara sometimes wondered if the animals needed them for anything beyond the simple task of opening and closing the gate to their enclosure.

"Chickens need feeding," Danica said, clipping away. "And there will be some eggs. Come back when you are done and muck out the pens. We'll be needing compost soon."

She glanced at Pinsard and gestured to the stool standing next to the washbasin.

"Sit," she said. "And clean the fleece before I scour it."

Pinsard sat. Bannertail spotted something in the loft, a mouse no doubt, and scampered off in chase of it.

Lara walked to the shed that served as the farm's chicken coop. Danica only kept a half dozen of the birds, so they were fairly easy to care for, mostly feeding themselves when the weather was warm and there were worms and grubs about the farm's garden. Lara tossed a few handfuls of feed into the pen as she went to check the nests.

"Only two," she said, scooping up the eggs. "You lot had better watch it. Danica *loves* roast chicken."

The hens clucked as they pecked and scratched, a few cocking their heads at her with clear suspicion. Lara shrugged, and carried the eggs to the kitchen where a bowl was already waiting for them.

Sure enough, when Lara returned to the barn, Pinsard was picking dung and burrs out of the newly shorn fleece while Danica went to work on the second ram, the first one bleating nakedly in its pen. Bannertail was happily chewing on something up in the loft, perched atop a bale of straw.

Danica glanced up at Lara, wrinkling her nose.

"I know, I know," Lara said, and went to fetch the pitchfork, broom, and shovel along with the good wheelbarrow.

Lara led Whisper out of his stall first, hitching him to a section of the fence encircling the sheep pasture. The old stallion laid his head down on one of the posts and closed his eyes, seeming to bask in the brightness of the day.

"Good man," she said, and set her mind to mucking.

By the time she was laying down fresh straw for the stallion's bedding, Danica had finished washing the fleece. The old woman dried her hands on her apron and hung the wool from a peg.

"Girls need walking," Danica said, opening the stall that her mares shared. "Whisper too, perhaps?"

"I think he is too tired today," Lara answered.

Danica sighed. "Well, be done with the stalls before I am back. And rest that leg," she said, addressing Pinsard, who was scrubbing at his hands with a soapy brush.

Pinsard nodded, and then Danica led her mares from the barn and they were alone.

"I can help," Pinsard said as Lara began to muck out the larger stall.

"*Moder* and Danica told you to rest."

"It does not hurt so badly now."

"*Rest*," Lara said, raising a pitchfork laden with horse droppings, "Or you'll have more than your hands to clean."

"Alright!" Pinsard said, raising his hands in surrender. "But remember that I offered."

"I will," Lara said.

She worked in silence for awhile, save for the mournful bleating of the rams and the sound of Pinsard sharpening the edge of his sword against the whetstone he seemed to carry with him everywhere. Then

Bannertail leapt from the loft, skittering down one of the barn's support beams and laying the gory remains of a mouse at Lara's feet.

The fox-squirrel looked up at her expectantly.

"Thank you," Lara sighed, scooping the thing up with her shovel before tossing it into the wheelbarrow.

The fox-squirrel let out a tiny bark and proceeded to clean itself with its tongue.

Lara grinned, but she found herself drawn to the speckled bloodstain at her feet. She put her boot over it and scuffed, but when she lifted her foot the stain was still there.

"Pinsard," she said. "Do you remember your father?"

He passed his blade over his whetstone and grew still.

"Yes," he answered, not lifting his eyes from the sword in his lap.

"What was he like?"

"He was," Pinsard said. "A great warrior."

"And do you-" Lara hesitated, "Do you remember how he died?"

"A man killed him," Pinsard said.

The boy got up from the stool, sheathed his sword, and walked to the barn door, wincing every time he put pressure on his sprained foot. He stood there for a while, silent, and stared at the sunlit garden where the first green sprouts of cabbage, beets, and carrots were already breaking the soil.

Lara buried the head of her shovel into a bit of muck and joined him.

"Moder will not tell you who he is," she said, guessing at the truth.

"No," Pinsard said, gripping his sword tighter. "But she will, one day. And then I will find him. Find him and kill him."

"Don't say that-" Lara began, but stopped when she saw the look on Pinsard's face. His jaw was clenched and his eyes, normally so kind, had taken on a cold, predatory look, like that of a hill cat or mountain wolf that had been separated from its pack.

They are just like Moder's.

Pinsard grew aware of her silence and turned towards her, his features softening.

"I should lie down," he said. "It is too hard not to work, watching you."

"Yes," Lara said. "Go and rest. I am sorry if I-"

"No, it is I who am sorry," Pinsard said, switching his sword to his off hand and giving her arm a squeeze. "And you had best be quick to finish with the stalls. I see Danica coming back up the path."

Sure enough, the old servant of the Watcher was already making her way back from the west meadow, her two mares trotting alongside her.

"Shit," Lara swore. She was nowhere near done with her work.

"Good luck," Pinsard teased, and only half limped as he made way towards the house, his dark mood seemingly lifted . . . But for a long time afterwards Lara could not forget the hatred she had seen in his eyes and she wondered:

Is that how I will feel, when I have touched Moder with the tip of my blade?

* * * * * * *

The last of the Winter rains fell. The days grew longer, Pinsard's swollen ankle healed, Moder pushed Lara ever harder, and a growing sense of anticipation hung about the farm, for Crowning had finally come.

Even if Lara had not been counting the days, there were always signs. Having sheared the entirety of the flock, Danica now spent almost every evening in Perun, telling dreadfuls and playing upon her guitar, not returning to the farm until long after the house had gone to sleep. In the past Lara had tried to wait up for the old woman, hoping to hear a bit of news from the village, but she had never quite managed it. But every now and then she would wake in the darkness of deep night and hear the woman slipping into the house, her newly earned copper jingling as she dropped it into the jar above the hearth.

But the surer sign of the festival was the arrival of the silent man. Twice a year he visited the farm and, for as long as Lara could remember, he was the only man from Perun who was welcome there. Like Danica he always came by way of a horse-drawn wagon, though his was not the wondrous rolling home that hers was, it being made up of rough pine and iron going to rust. Into the wagon they would load sacks of fleece, blocks of cheese, jars of pickled cabbage, and the remainder of the male lambs . . . While Danica and he would sit on the porch, the old woman speaking and the silent man listening.

"Why does he never talk?" Lara had asked Moder some years ago.

"Because he does not have a tongue," Moder had answered,

shortly, and Lara had never pressed further.

Lara thought that the silent man would be strange even if he could speak. His face was somehow both old and young, depending on the light, and his smile charmed and unnerved her all at once. He rarely blinked, tending to stare, and year after year he wore the same clothes: A coal-black doublet with slashed sleeves and breeches over stiff white underclothes. His dress might have appeared lordly, were it not going to rot. Besides the numerous split seams and tears, his garments were always soiled, and white speckles of mold dotted his doublet, especially across his back.

He looked the same as ever as his wagon jostled its way up the path, the sunlight making his silvery hair glisten. A great patch of dry mud lay blossomed across his left breast, as though someone had thrown a clod of earth at him, and his boots were mismatched, the left so worn that his big toe was sticking out its front.

Lara was sweeping the porch when the wagon came to a halt in the yard, the silent man hopping down from his seat with more grace than his appearance might suggest. Both Moder and Danica were inside, airing out the rooms and dusting every shelf and cabinet, while Pinsard was with the flock. And so, for the first time she could recall, Lara and the silent man were alone.

He saw her and smiled.

Lara wondered if she should call out for Moder, but decided not to . . . At least, not right away. After all, for all his strangeness, Lara had never been afraid of the silent man. She did not know precisely why, though if pressed she would have said that he seemed *right* somehow, like an old friend.

"Good day," she said to him, miming a curtsy.

The silent man smiled at that. Then he bowed, very low, with his right hand extended so that it almost touched the ground.

As he straightened, he looked about questioningly.

"Moder and Danica are inside," she said. "Do you want me to fetch them?"

The silent man held up a single finger. It said, *'In a moment,'* as clearly as if he had been speaking. Then he pulled something bright and shiny out of his sleeve.

It was a small sheet of gold, thin as parchment. Thinner even, Lara realized, as the man began to fold it.

His fingers worked so quickly that they were hard to follow, and when he was done he went to one knee and held out what he had made on his palm, seemingly offering it to her.

"This is for me?" she asked.

He tilted his head and gave her a nod.

Lara took it carefully, for it was delicate, the silent man having folded the sheet of gold into a loop with upraised points. It was a crown, Lara realized, the kind that a doll might wear.

It would fit Brigitte perfectly, she thought. *But how could he know that? Unless . . . But no. How silly. It is Crowning tomorrow. He must know I'm not allowed to go. That must be it.*

But whether he was trying to comfort her, or was making mock of her, Lara could not say.

When she looked up from the miniature crown of foil, the silent man was staring at her expectantly.

"Thank you," she said. "It's very pretty."

The man made a noise in the back of his throat that might have been a chuckle.

She was not certain what else to say, but she did not have to, for just then Moder stepped from the house and onto the porch.

"I was wondering when you would be arriving," Moder said. "Lara, why were you not calling for me?"

Lara began to mumble an answer, hiding the little crown behind her back.

"You are hungry?" Moder asked the silent man, seeming to have already forgotten Lara, "There is being barley quick-bread and honey in the pantry."

The silent man shook his head.

Moder took hold of his doublet near the mud stain, rubbing at it slightly with her thumb.

"What mischief are you getting in?" she asked.

The silent man shrugged and grinned, revealing surprisingly white teeth.

"Be keeping secrets then," Moder sighed. "I can scrub it clean later if you are liking. And mend boot at least."

The silent man bowed, though nowhere near as low as before.

"May I die," Danica said as she joined them, sniffing at the air, "Is winter over already? Or has someone cut down a scarecrow and hung him here to frighten away the birds?"

The silent man lifted his right leg and placed his foot behind his left knee, his head and arms going limp.

"You couldn't scare a blackbird if you were Stormbringer himself," Danica sneered. "Fancy a bit of smoke, scarecrow?"

The man nodded, straightened himself, and followed Danica into the house.

"Lara, help me to be loading the wagon," Moder said.

Lara tucked the gold foil into her bodice and took trips to the barn with Moder stowing the spring fleece in the back of the silent man's wagon.

By the time they were ferrying the jars of pickled cabbage out of the root cellar, Lara could not contain herself any longer. The little crown the silent man had given her had been nagging at her thoughts with every trip they made, and so:

"Moder," she began, trying hard to sound indifferent, "It is Crowning tomorrow."

"Yes," Moder replied.

"Only . . . Well, I thought that I might go with Danica to the festival this year."

Moder was silent as she walked up the root cellar's steps and crossed the yard. She was silent too as she laid the crate of jars onto the rear of the wagon.

Then she said, "No."

Lara laid down her own crate. "I've been before."

"That was different," Moder said, stepping onto the back of the wagon and rearranging the crates so they were more secure. "You were much younger then."

"I could watch from Danica's wagon. I wouldn't go out, and you could come with me."

That was, in fact, the manner in which she had last seen the festival: Sitting atop Moder's lap as she gazed with wonder out of the rear door of the wagon, which Moder had allowed to be kept open so that she could see. She must have been eight summers old then, and the memory of it was vague. There had been bonfires and torches, noisemakers and masks, much dancing, and more song, and all of it enough to turn dreary Perun into a revel that the faun of the deep forest might have held in some secluded glade, lit by ghostfire.

"No," Moder repeated.

"Please, Moder," Lara pleaded. "I never leave the farm, and I only want to see the festival. I'll sit in the wagon and stay out of sight. No one will see me."

Moder raised an eyebrow at that, seemed almost to be considering it, but still she said, "No. It is too much risk."

"But why?"

This was the only argument Lara had left.

"I will be telling you," Moder said, "When you are touching me with the tip of your blade. Now, go and fetch Pinsard. And flock. And be getting the lambs onto the wagon."

Lara's head flushed up with anger, but she did as she was told and climbed up towards the pasture, letting out her breath in short sharp blasts. Behind her she could hear Danica playing upon her guitar for the silent man's amusement, the sound of the strings fading as she picked up her pace, putting the barn between herself and the house.

"Wulf!" she cursed, loudly, and stopped to catch her breath.

She saw a bit of golden trefoil beneath her feet and kicked at it until it and a patch of soil came loose under her assault, taking flight briefly before landing in a clump some distance away.

"Are you alright?" Pinsard asked when she finally came within speaking distance. Pasha sensed her obviously foul mood and whined, but the sheep paid her no mind and continued to graze.

"The silent man is here," she growled. "You and I must sort the boy lambs from the girls for him. Moder commands it."

Pinsard said nothing. He walked around the far edge of the flock and began to herd them towards the farmstead with his arms outstretched. Before long Pasha was guiding the sheep so well that both Lara and Pinsard needed only to follow.

When they had walked a good stretch, Pinsard cleared his throat.

"Moder will not let you go to the Crowning festival," he said. "Is that it?"

"Yes," Lara replied.

But I am going anyway.

III

That night, after the silent man had been sent away with exhortations to set a good price for fleece and fodder, Moder let Lara and Pinsard stay up late so that they might listen to the tales that Danica would tell at the festival on the morrow.

And so, as Moder knitted in the corner, Danica told them of the sadistic Vargr called Iskandar, who had sewn his adulterous wife into a bull before leaving her for the vultures to devour . . . And of The Lady of Diamonds, who drove her husband into penury and death for the sake of a necklace whose jewels were made of paste. She spoke in hushed tones of the man-eating ghouls that lived beneath the earth, made a poem of the infamous poison feast of the mad Queen Grisana, and wept as she sang the lay of Vasilisa the Beautiful, swallowed by the sea as she clutched at the Mirror of Truth, her fleet ablaze, the last of her servants joining her in death.

By then the fire in the hearth had turned to embers, and the candles were burning low. Moder had long since retired, and Lara and Pinsard were both stifling yawns themselves.

"Yes," Danica said, "Even for me it is time to sleep. I must rest if tomorrow I am to spin dreadfuls and play my guitar until dawn."

"Is any of it true?" Lara asked as she shooed Bannertail from her lap. "The old stories, I mean."

"Yes," Danica replied, smiling. "Now sleep well, my little ones. Sleep well."

But it was not Danica's tales that kept Lara up that night, wakeful in spite of her weariness. Rather, it was the question of how to slip away when Moder had finally gone to sleep . . . And how to return without waking her. She had done so before, of course, more than once, but that had been to gaze at the stars when she could not sleep or to pilfer a spoonful of jam from the root cellar.

She had never left the farm by night. Nor had she made the long walk to Perun alone.

Eventually, she fell asleep without realizing it, and woke the next morning to find Bannertail nipping at her toes through the sheets.

Lara sat up, sent the fox-squirrel scampering down the stairs with a half-hearted swipe, and rubbed at her eyes. Judging by the light streaming through her little window, she guessed that there would be no lessons with Moder that day.

Still, Crowning or not, there were chickens to tend, eggs to turn, rugs to be beaten, and floors to scrub with pail and brush. Moder spent the better half of the day in the garden, rooting out finger-grass and goosefoot, while Pasha and Pinsard shepherded the flock in the lower pasture. As for Danica, the old woman roused herself long past midday, fixed herself a quick meal, and made to ready her wagon for the ride down to Perun.

She would not return, Lara knew, until the Firebird had risen on the first day of Sowing: The first day of the new year.

"A cozy bed and a roof over one's head," the old woman muttered as Lara helped hitch the mares. "Far better than sleeping under a hedge or some cold ditch."

"You never slept in a ditch," Lara said, "Did you?"

"I have," Danica said. "And it's just as unpleasant as you would expect, especially when it rained. Of course, I was younger then. Quicker too. I used to be able to run down a deer if I wanted venison for my supper . . . But those days are long behind me. Now help me get these collars on the girls. The night is coming, and they are expecting me."

When the mares were finally harnessed, Danica climbed onto the wagon and set her weathered old warg mask on the seat beside her. The thing had probably been the color of blood at some point, but its paint was chipped, and a pair of cracks ran through it.

"You are a good friend, girl," Danica said, giving the reins a shake, "And that is worth more than a thousand poor ones. Remember that! If nothing else . . ."

"Wulf's Fancy!" Lara called after her, waving as she watched the wagon roll away . . . But she could not help but feel a twinge of guilt.

Would she still have said that if she knew what I plan to do when the lights are put out and Moder is asleep?

The thought lingered, worrying at her, but faded as she washed the windows, growing smaller and smaller with every swipe.

She was still at it when the Firebird sank below the pines, the tree line turning golden as twilight crept across the farm. The shadows in the yard stretched and lengthened, and then Moder whistled: *Come! Supper!*

Lara was rinsing the last of the vinegar from her rags when Pinsard walked into the yard with a book tucked under his arm. It was one of the older ones from the house, *The Downfall of The Demon King*, and it was in worse shape than Danica's mask.

"That thing will fall apart if you keep reading it year after year," Lara said.

"Me?" Pinsard sniffed. "I thought you liked it."

As a matter of fact, Lara did like it, having read it as much (if not more) than Pinsard, but the barb could not be ignored.

"It's alright, I guess," she said. "Even if it's a book for children."

"For children?" His cheeks reddened. "It is not a-"

"I'm joking!" she laughed. "You don't need to get so mad! I like it too, I do! Only-"

"Only what?"

"I just . . . Well, I wish that Zosia would do more."

"More?"

"More than be pretty, I mean."

"She kills the Demon King!" Pinsard sputtered.

"Does she?" Lara asked. "It's Aquilia that lands the fatal blow. And he has to rescue *her* from the ruins of Duskwalker's palace, not the other way around. Most of the time she's walking through glades or singing, or, I don't know, listening to the wind."

Pinsard chewed on that for a moment.

"What of when she scaled the side of the Iron Fortress?" he asked. "Or when she outwitted Graymask at the Stair of Grief? Or what-"

"I didn't say she was useless," Lara said before he could go on, "Just that I wish she-"

Moder's second, louder whistle interrupted her.

They hurried into the farmhouse, Pinsard laying the old book by the front door as they joined Moder for supper.

* * * * * * *

Long after sundown, dishes washed, barn and chicken coop locked shut, and Whisper's trough refilled, Lara lay in her loft, dressed in her sparring clothes, waiting for Moder to retire. She had settled by the hearth just as Lara and Pinsard had turned in for the evening, knitting a new mitten with her deft fingers, and she had hardly stirred since.

She knows, she thought as the needles clicked. *She knows! She must. She never stays awake this long . . .*

And then, just when Lara despaired that Moder would never cease her knitting, she heard it: Chair legs scraping against hardwood, a faint rattle from the kitchen, soft footfalls on the stairs and, finally, the creak of a door closing shut.

How long should I wait? Lara wondered, sitting up.

The house made sounds. Timbers settled. Pasha snored. Even the embers simmering in the hearth below seemed loud to her the longer she sat in the darkness, Bannertail nestled snugly on her lap.

Finally, she could stand it no longer. She scooped up the fox-squirrel, set it aside, and scooted forward as quietly as she could. Pasha stirred for a moment, yawned at her, and then went back to sleep.

She had set her boots next to the edge of the loft, but she did not put them on. She picked them up and stepped down the stairs, slowly, her feet bare.

Why am I so frightened? she thought, feeling foolish as her heart raced. *I've done this a hundred times before.*

The second to last stair creaked as she put her weight on it. She froze, waiting. She could hear Pinsard's breath, but it remained steady and regular.

She went on.

I need the privy, she rehearsed in her head as she padded down the hall, thankful for the rug beneath her feet as she passed Moder's bedroom.

I thought I heard something downstairs, she mulled over as she crept through the farmhouse's great room, the dull embers casting enough light for her to not bump into chair or table. *No, that won't do.* If she had really heard something downstairs she would have woken Moder.

At last, she was at the front door. She took hold of the metal latch.

I don't have to go. I could just use the privy and go back to bed. Danica will tell us all about it tomorrow. It's a long walk to Perun. In the night. In the dark.

She held her breath, opened the door, slid through, and closed it slowly behind her.

Yard and barn were bathed in pale light, for the skull-moon was half full and brilliant, and for a moment it seemed to Lara as if a ghastly apparition was peering around a doorway: A terrible moon-face, staring at her from the darkness, grinning its rictus-grin.

It's only the moon, she thought.

She tugged on her boots and began to walk.

Before long she was beyond the western pasturage and standing before the entrance to the wood. What had always been so normal by day- so *boring-* now looked like something out of one of Danica's stories. There was no wind, but the high branches were swaying. Beneath them there was a deeper darkness broken by the thinnest shafts of moonlight.

She looked back towards the farm and could only just make out its outline.

She went on.

The forest was silent, save for the occasional warble of some far away night bird. It was still too cold for the crickets and katydids to sing their song. She followed the path as quickly as she could, trying with varying success not to stumble into the tracks left behind by Danica's wagon.

Dry leaves crunched beneath her feet. Above her the branches creaked.

And then she came to the first of the skulls.

It perched atop a long pole upon which bones had been tied with twine. Most were ribs, but there were smaller ones too: Finger joints, perhaps, or the parts of a foot, as well as something that was either arm or leg.

Lara did not recoil, though she had never seen a human skeleton before, only those of the sheep and chickens on the farm.

All the bones were blackened, having been pulled from the ashes of a funeral pyre by either Danica or the servant of the Watcher who had preceded her. Or perhaps they were the bones of the man in gray. If there had ever truly been one.

"I don't suppose you'll tell me?" she whispered.

The skull did not answer.

She walked on.

Before long she came upon another skull, and then another, until both sides of the path were thick with them. They seemed to stare at her as she passed beneath them, judging with their empty eyes.

No wonder folk from Perun never come to the farm . . . Well, except for the silent man. But then, maybe he's not from Perun-

A twig snapped. It wasn't close, but it wasn't far either. She kept her wits and turned, peering into the dark of the wood, which had grown quite silent.

Snap! There it was again, closer now.

Something was on the path behind her.

She stepped into the woods, wincing as a carpet of pine needles crunched beneath her boot heels. She crept behind a tree and kept very still, shutting her eyes as she strained to listen.

For a long time, there was nothing. And then: *Crack! Snap!*

It's just a deer, she told herself, only half believing it. *Or a hill cat, maybe, chasing its supper.*

Whatever it was it was quickening its pace, panting as it crushed the dry leaves underfoot. It was as if a great warg was tracking her by scent alone, slathering as it came.

I should have brought my sword! Or even one of the carving knives-

She peered around the tree.

A tall dark shape came hurtling towards her, pale-faced with fierce blue eyes, great black wings streaming behind it.

Lara let out a wild cry and struck out with her fist the way Moder had taught her to.

"Owww!" Pinsard cried out, staggering backwards. His winter cloak wrapped around him as he fell, and then he was on the ground, clutching at his stomach.

His face was so wet with sweat that Lara guessed he had run all the way from the farm.

"Oh!" she gasped, stooping to help him up. "Pinsard, I'm sorry! I thought you were- Well, never mind, but are you alright?!"

"It's not your fault," Pinsard groaned as he picked himself up, shooing away her hand. "I suppose I should have known that you would be frightened."

When he was on his feet, she punched him again. In the arm this time, and not as hard, but not gently either.

"Enough!" he said, rubbing at his stomach. "I'm going to be sore enough tomorrow already."

"But how did you know I was gone?" Lara asked. "How did you know where I was going? And does . . . Does Moder know?"

Pinsard shook his head.

"Moder is still asleep," he said. "And I *knew* because Pasha came down to lie beside me. He only does that when you go to visit the privy for too long. And then you did not come back. I was worried."

"That's," she said, "Actually kind of sweet."

"I was worried that you had gone to the festival," he clarified.

"Well," she said, "I'm not there yet."

"I knew it!" he said, lowering his voice as his words echoed through the wood. "Moder told you 'no.' But you are going anyway?"

"I wasn't going to just walk into the middle of the festival and start dancing like an idiot," Lara huffed. "I just wanted to get close. Close enough to watch."

"But Moder said 'no.'"

"Why?"

"It is dangerous," he offered.

"Why?"

Pinsard struggled for a definitive answer, uncertainty lurking behind his cool, blue eyes.

"There are wicked men in the world," he said, using Moder's words.

"Well," Lara said, brushing herself down as she continued down the path. "I'll just have to steer clear of them, won't I?"

"Wait!" Pinsard called out and made to stand in her way. "Stop. You cannot go. I followed you so I could take you back to the farm, not so that you could get into trouble."

"Haven't you *ever* broken the rules?" Lara asked. "Do you *always* do what Moder tells you?"

"Yes," Pinsard answered.

Lara raised an eyebrow.

"I find that hard to believe."

"I suppose," he said. "That we both used to run off together . . . But we were a lot younger then. It was different. We never went very far, and besides, we always got caught by- Well, by some old woman. Do you remember her?"

Something strange happened to Lara then. Her chest felt tight. She could almost hear the click of heels against pale stone floors. She felt, as if in one of her dreams, hands gripping her, gripping her tight. A door splintering, breaking open. A red room.

"Lara!" Pinsard said. "Lara are you alright?"

She found herself leaning forward, steadying herself against an oak with one hand and she gasped for breath. She felt like vomiting.

"I'm fine," she forced herself to say, straightening. Pinsard was close, standing as if to catch her if she fell. "Something just came over me. I'm fine now, really."

"Now will you come back with me?" he asked.

"You'll have to drag me back," Lara said. "Is that what you're going to do, Pinsard? Drag me?"

Pinsard dropped his arms to his sides and sighed.

Lara stepped around Pinsard and went on.

His footfalls were slow at first, but they soon quickened to match hers. Before long he was walking beside her.

"What about what Moder said?" she smirked.

"She never told *me* not to go to the Crowning festival," he said, "And besides, I can protect you."

"*You* will protect *me*?"

"Yes."

"You *do* remember me knocking you onto your ass just now?"

"I was," Pinsard sniffed, "Surprised."

Lara let out a laugh. Whatever nightbird was warbling in the dark took flight, its wings flapping wildly.

Pinsard rubbed at his stomach, and they walked on.

* * * * * *

The walk was better with Pinsard beside her. They did not speak, but the forest felt less sinister somehow. The birds were just birds, the trees were creaking merely because they were old, and snapped twigs or rustling brush was more likely badger than warg.

And when the last of the mounted skulls were behind them, they could hear the unmistakable sounds of the Crowning festival: Laughter, voices raised in song, and the cry of pipe and drum wafting through the trees. Soon Lara could make out the gleam of the lanterns hung along the edge of the woods. Beyond them a pair of bonfires roared, ringed by a sea of torches being waved aloft. She could almost make out the figures dancing between the flames, and the bulky outline of the sawmill straddling the river Rusalka.

"We should get off of the path now," Lara said.

Pinsard nodded, and they made for a thick knot of trees, keeping brush and trunk between them and the revelers. They moved as Moder had taught them, crouching as they chose their steps, but it hardly seemed necessary. It would take ears sharper than those of a bat to hear their footfalls over the cheers and howls of the townsfolk, let alone the great rumbling hiss of the bonfires.

As they drew closer, an excess of smells overcame Lara. There was wood smoke, of course, and the slightly sweet aroma of freshly cut lumber . . . But there was also the strong scent of cooked meat and overripe fruit. Lara had eaten enough lamb and mutton over the years to recognize it easily, but she had never smelled anything like this. At least, not that she could recall.

She sniffed loudly.

"What is that?" she asked.

"Roast pig," Pinsard whispered. "And beer. A lot of it."

"How do you know that?"

"I used to eat a lot of pig, when-"

The ring of torches suddenly widened as the crowd let out a 'whoop!' It spun about crazily and then tightened up again.

"When I was young," Pinsard went on, "And everyone but *moder* and *faeder* drank beer all the time. Wine and beer."

Lara had tasted wine once or twice. Danica sometimes brought some home from the village in a bottle wrapped with twine, and Moder had allowed her a little bit in her cup. It had tasted awful to her, sour and oily at the same time. She wondered if she might find the taste of beer more enjoyable.

They had nearly settled upon a decent vantage point, a place between the trees shielded by a thick patch of tall brown grass, when they heard something rustling through the brush. It was coming their way.

Lara didn't have to tell Pinsard to sink deeper into the woods. He was already creeping back with as much speed as he dared, drawing the hood of his cloak over his head. She followed suit, hoping they would not have to flee just when they had gotten so close.

They settled behind a thicket and waited.

What came bursting from the grass was a man and a woman, the former leading the latter by the hand. He was stripped down to his breeches and a sweat-stained shirt, while she wore a gray gown and woolen cape. Both were wearing animal masks over their faces: An antlered stag for him, a button-nosed rabbit for her.

The man came to a halt near to the place where Lara and Pinsard had been standing just a few moments before, and then he pulled the woman close as he pressed his mouth to hers. His hand made its way from her hips to the lacing of her gown with half-fumbled efficiency. She leaned away from his embrace and helped to loosen her blouse.

As the man's hand began to quest beneath the woman's shift, Lara became acutely uncomfortable. It did not help that Pinsard was crouching beside her. She had, of course, read of such things in the farmhouse's books, and both Moder and Danica had explained the mechanics of love making to her (Moder with more mechanics, Danica with more color), but it is one thing to know of such things, and quite another to see it.

Her cheeks flushed, and she squirmed inwardly as the woman began to undo the lacing of the man's breeches, but she remained still. She wondered what was running through Pinsard's head.

"Take that thing off," the woman said, tugging at the man's mask. "No one can see us here."

Lara had to stifle a snicker.

"But I like my little kit," the man said, flinging her cape aside. "Don't you like your buck?"

"Take it off," she said, tracing her fingers along his thigh. "You won't be sorry."

The man let out a low sigh and tore off his mask with a sharp tug. She took her time.

The girl was snub-nosed and had round cheeks. As the boy slipped off his shirt Lara noticed that his chest was sunken and hairless.

They can't be much older than us. A summer or two, maybe . . . Or maybe not.

Lara felt herself transfixed. After all, how long had it been since she had seen a new face? Someone who wasn't Moder, or Pinsard, or Danica, or the silent man even? And yet there they were: The girl's nose crinkling as she smiled, the boy's desires so obvious that they might as well have been written across his forehead.

"Here," the boy said, reaching for the girl's mask. "I'll take that. These are expensive, after all."

"For a timber-man, maybe," the girl teased.

The boy ignored her, and made for a nearby tree, coming so close to their hiding spot that Lara was certain that he would see them skulking in the dark. But he was clearly distracted, searching the trees for a place to hang the masks. He settled on a dead branch before turning back to the girl, hopping as he kicked off one of his well-worn boots.

The masks twisted on the branch as the lovers continued to disrobe, stag and rabbit nearly as tangled with each other as their owners were.

Masks. Two of them.

To Lara's credit, some part of her did its best to stand in the way of the inevitable. Hadn't she only come to look at the festival from afar? it asked. How much more trouble would they both be in if they were caught? Was this really fair to Pinsard? What if someone recognized the masks? The boy had said that they were expensive, what if they stood out because of them? And what if Danica saw them? How long would it be before the boy and girl noticed that someone had stolen their masks?

Danica's repeated warning, 'she must never be seen,' was the last line of defense . . . But it shattered the instant that Lara rose from her crouch, padded quietly over to the dead branch, and lifted the masks from it.

"What are you-" Pinsard hissed before he remembered to keep his mouth shut. He hardly needed to worry. The amount of noise the lovers were beginning to make would have smothered a giant's footfalls.

Lara beckoned to Pinsard, and then pressed into the brush. When she had put some considerable distance between herself and the lovers, she stopped.

"Are you crazy?" Pinsard whispered once he had caught up. His normally pale face was very red, especially his cheeks.

"Maybe a little," she said, slipping the rabbit mask over her face. It smelled faintly of lavender flowers, and of beer, especially where the nose nearly met her lips.

"Here," she said, tossing the stag mask at his feet. "This one is yours."

"Absolutely not," he said, throwing up his hands. "I am not putting that on."

"Suit yourself," she said, making straight for the tree line.

"Lara!" he cried.

She ignored him.

And sure enough, by the time she'd stepped from the trees, he was beside her, still fiddling with the mask's strings.

"I hate you," he said.

"No, you don't."

* * * * * *

Had Lara had been more familiar with the festival of Crowning a few of her fears might have been considerably allayed.

First, nearly every man, woman, and child in Perun was drunk, with very few exceptions. Normally only the loggers and mill men began their days with a dark pint of barley beer, another during the midday meal, and another helping or two with supper . . . But on Crowning the drinking began with the rising of the Firebird and continued long into the night, and all were encouraged to take part.

Secondly, a degree of anonymity during the revel was encouraged, and the choice of animal masks was limited to those of rabbits, does, and stags. Crowning might be the festival of the Lioness, but enough of Perun's chickens and goats had been carried off by hill cats that the loggers and their wives had come to hate the creatures in a general sort of way.

And so, as Lara and Pinsard approached the mad revelry taking place between the bonfires, no one paid them much mind.

The heat from the fires was incredible, like nothing Lara had ever felt. To stand within fifteen paces of them was like putting one's arm inside an oven, and cinders were leaping from them high into the night. The smoke had a will of its own, or so it seemed, for wherever Lara stood it followed, making her eyes water and her throat tight.

Some of the people of Perun were making a game of how close they could withstand the heat, tossing logs or bits of furniture into the flames as they fled, but the bulk of them were milling about a tall wooden pole. After her long walk through the woods, Lara almost expected there to be a skull on top of it . . . But this was Crowning after all. The pole was crowned by three garlands, and hung with ribbons, yellow and green.

"We probably look a bit odd, ah, standing here," she said. "We should get closer. Shouldn't we?"

Pinsard shrugged, trying hard to look nonchalant as they stepped into the crowd.

She did not blame him. She was nervous too.

Once they'd begun to mingle, it struck Lara that she had never been around so many people, at least not that she could recall. There were also at least three men for every woman present, and she didn't care for the grins they gave her as she passed. It took her a moment or two to notice that she was the only female present who wasn't wearing a skirt.

The sight of her legs, even beneath her breeches, was clearly extraordinary.

"Your lover lose 'is drawers, miss doe?" a man with brown-teeth slurred, and took a clumsy swipe at her rear.

The man's palm was easy to dodge, and Lara was debating whether she should make an example out of him when a drum began to beat, and the entire crowd let out a collective 'WHOOP!'

"What is-" Pinsard managed before the crowd began to move as one, stamping rhythmically to the beat of the drum as they circled about the pole. Those closest to the pole took up its ribbons, wrapped them around their forearms, and began to dance counter to the direction of the crowd.

"The river!" A deep voice sang out. "The river flows into the sea!"

"WHAT CARE WE?" The crowd called back with one voice. "WHAT CARE WE?"

"Beneath the waves the fish are free!"

"WHAT CARE WE? WHAT CARE WE? WHOOO-AHWP!"

The crowd reversed their step. Flute, pipe, and horn joined the drum, as well the familiar thrum of Danica's guitar. Men and women lifted their arms into the air and shook them about. Those with torches painted the night with embers. Those with cups sent beer sailing. Those that were doused cheered and hollered.

"The seeds are floating on the breeze!"

"WHAT CARE WE? WHAT CARE WE?"

"And wargs are lurking beneath the trees . . ."

"WHAT CARE WE? WHAT CARE WE? WHOOOOOO-AHWP!"

They reversed again. Lara did her best to play along while keeping up the pace. It was harder than it looked. The call and response might have been simple, but the step and drumbeat were getting quicker with every verse.

In the middle of the fourth verse Lara caught a glimpse of the musicians. They were settled atop a platform just a short distance from the tumult, and behind them three immense barrels lay on their sides, cradled by wooden blocks. *The beer*, Lara assumed. She'd already grown used to the smell of it.

Danica was easy to pick out, her face hidden behind her mask as her fingers danced over the strings of her guitar. Beside her a barrel-chested man with a snow-white beard pounded on a wide drum as he led the call and response, a tattoo shaped like a sunburst spread across the better part of his bald head. It didn't take the sight of his shriven right leg, the foot of which twisted inwards, for Lara to guess this was Svarog, Perun's own resident smith-priest. Danica told her once that the men of Perun called him 'The Limper' behind his back . . . Though they would never dare to do so to his face. Lara could see why: His body looked like muscle stacked on muscle, and with each strike of the drum she wondered if the thing would break.

And while Lara could not name the three women stamping beside Svarog and his drum, she knew that even the smallest of villages were home to at least three priestesses of the Lioness. Such women treated ailments, groomed hair, and provided other comforts . . . For a price. 'Three' was the number holy to Sphinx, of course, but it was also practical: Three could do such work far easier than one and denying a priestess hospitality to save a bit of coin was practically begging for the Watcher's attention. And so, though Perun was no true town, an elderly matron with slate gray hair danced beside a plump little woman with rosy cheeks and a freckle-faced maiden whose long locks were nearly as fair as Pinsard's. All three wore dresses the color of chestnut, and as they spun their skirts blossomed, revealing muscular legs. They wore strings of beads about their left ankle, which clattered together as they whirled and stamped.

Can't stay here. But the dance isn't over yet . . . What if-

"WHOOOOOO-AHWP!"

Lara was nearly bowled over as the crowd reversed itself. She felt Pinsard's hand on her back, steadying her. At least she thought it was his hand.

Have to risk it, she decided. *Before Danica sees us.*

While they were still out of sight of the platform, Lara grabbed ahold of Pinsard and began to tug him out of the crowd. She had expected to have to shove through the throng, but men and women parted for them easily, knowing grins on their faces.

"WHEN A WOMAN WANTS A MAN!" they chanted, beating Svarog to the verse.

"WHAT CARE WE? WHAT CARE WE?"

"SHE WILL CATCH HIM IF SHE CAN!"

"WHAT CARE WE? WHAT CARE WE? WHOOOOOO-AHWP!!!"

Men whistled and women cried out what Lara took to be encouragement as they ran from the crowd. They ran from the pole and its ribbons, the brilliance of the twin bonfires, and the watchful eyes of Danica.

"Is that supposed to be enjoyable?" Pinsard asked once they'd put some distance between them and the festival.

"Perhaps it's more fun if you're drunk?" Lara answered.

She stopped for a moment to get her bearings. They were still on the eastern side of the Rusalka, near to one of the long cabins that the loggers shared. Lights shone across the river, illuminating a building that resembled the farm in its size and general shape. Firelight gleamed from its windows, and dark shapes moved about within.

The Nightingale! It must be.

Of all the things in Perun, Danica spoke the most often about its tavern, and how it got its name. Before its very doors had died the brigand Solovei, who had terrorized the road from Irikosa to Vassa. They had called him The Nightingale for he could whistle like a songbird, and it was said that if you heard his song and threw down your gold without a fight, he would let you live. Until, at last, the great warrior Ilya Vargr hunted him down with a score of royal lancers at the behest of the Grand Prince, chasing him and his band through forest, field, fetid marsh, and, finally, Perun. When Solovei refused to surrender, Ilya Vargr separated his head from his neck and rode off with the former tied to his saddle. And so the people of Perun could hardly hang Solovei's body from a tree . . . But it seemed wrong to send him to Domdaniel without a head to help guide him, so they burned his body on a pyre, only to discover that the great brigand had swallowed a belly full of jewels. And so, in honor of The Nightingale's generosity, the keeper of the old tavern renamed the place of his demise in his honor, and the men who drink there still raise their cups to him.

"We should start back," Pinsard said, scratching at an itch beneath his mask. "It must be past midnight by now."

"One last thing," Lara said, and made for the bridge that spanned the river. It was easy to see, for it was limestone and the skull-moon made it glimmer.

Pinsard caught her by the arm.

"Where are you *going*?" Pinsard asked.

"I want," she said, taking back her arm. "To see where Solovei died."

"It's-" He shook his head. "It is a patch of dirt, Lara. How interesting could it be?"

"I want to *see* it, Pinsard. And . . . I want to taste beer."

Noises came out of Pinsard's mouth, but none of them were real words. Lara tried not to snicker.

"*Awirung*," he cursed softly. "Fine. You are just going to do it anyway, aren't you? No matter what I say."

"Well," she said, "I could hardly go to a tavern without you there to *protect* me."

Pinsard shot her a particularly withering look, but he still followed.

As they walked, Lara tried to think of precisely how two strangers, one of them a Calvarian, might have come to Perun in the middle of the night. From what Danica had told her, the nearest village was a place called Kostroma, but that was at least three leagues away, and no doubt its people were celebrating Crowning much as Perun was.

In fact, the only outsiders Lara had ever heard tell of were tinkers, peddlers, and the occasional vagrant, and she and Pinsard were clearly none of those. And, by the time they crossed the bridge, she was beginning to wonder if the truth might be easier for the locals to swallow. After all, surely *some of them* knew that a Calvarian woman and her son lived in the farmhouse beyond the wood, caring for Danica's flock while she was away on the business of The Winter King . . . Though in all the time that she had lived on the farm, Lara had never seen Moder leave it.

At least, not without her.

The Nightingale stood between a thatch-roofed barn and a brick house with a tall chimney- a bakery perhaps, or maybe the smithy where Svarog spent his days hammering iron. But only the tavern was alight, the ash tree in its yard hung with lanterns shaped like birds in flight. Some of these dangled from The Nightingale's wide porch, casting shadowy feathers across the lawn.

It was easy to spot the place where Solovei had met his end. Not only was it the only patch of dirt before the tavern that appeared to have been stamped flat, but it was also devoid of even the smallest weed. A signpost loomed beside it, on which was painted the likeness of the brigand himself, lounging upon a tree branch. His clothes were a brilliant shade of green, and his right hand was half-cupped beside his mouth.

She was leaning closer to inspect the detail of Solovei's face when the front door of the tavern banged open, music and firelight spilling into the yard along with a wobbly-footed man who managed to step from the porch without falling. He made his way to the ash and promptly began to relieve himself, one hand pressing against the trunk for support.

"And she lifted, she lifted, she lifted her skirts," the man rasped, only half-singing, "And she lifted her skirts and she lay in the dirt, and she were the magpie's delight, yea sir, yea she were the magpie's delight . . ."

"Come on," Lara whispered, not wanting to draw the man's attention as she made for the door. The strumming of a lute muffled the tramp of their boots against the porch slats and then they were in.

The Nightingale's hearth was wide, and a cheery fire burned within it. There was a silver plate on the mantel, three pairs of lit candles, and the antlers of a stag upon a plaque. A handful of men sat beside it, all of them gray-beards or with hair that had thinned to a wisp. They were playing at cards on a tiny table set between them, but the lute player was sitting on a stool facing the flames . . . and though his back was turned, Lara felt a jolt of dismay run through her when she recognized his filthy black doublet.

It was the silent man.

Maybe he won't notice us, she thought. *And even if he does, well, who would he tell? He can't speak, remember?*

Opposite the fireplace a slab of varnished wood lay balanced across three brass-hooped barrels. Three men were leaning against it, sipping from red cups. Two of them had swords hanging from their belts, Lara noticed, though they hardly looked like soldiers. The third was a man who looked rather out of place: His green jacket had silver buttons, his boots were polished, and his dark beard was waxed and trimmed. As for the barkeep, she was a lean woman, her bodice stained, with sleeves knotted at the elbows. Her hair looked as though it had been shorn like one of Danica's sheep, no longer than the width of a finger. Three sturdy shelves ran the length of the room behind her, each one lined with bottles, jugs, and row upon row of red ceramic cups.

"Wulf's fancy," one of the card players said, looking up from the game. "Andrei's gone and turned into a girl. A pretty one too."

The comment prompted everyone in the tavern to turn and stare, save for the silent man, who kept strumming at his lute.

"Festival over already, is it?" one of the other card players said. "Can't be. It's not even close to sunup."

The man peered out a window, nodded, and went back to staring.

The Nightingale's barkeep sighed, set down a jug, and sidled around the slab, muttering as she did so.

"Master Laszlo send you?" she huffed, her nostrils flaring. "Well, you can tell him that if he wants another barrel I'm going to need to see some glimmer in my purse before I so much as pour him a-"

The barkeep squinted at Lara, and then shifted her gaze towards Pinsard, who was still lingering near the door.

"Here now," she said, "I know you?"

"No," Lara said. She didn't know what else to say and having so many strange men staring at her was distracting to say the least.

"Where'd you come from then?" She turned to the men at the bar. "This one yours, Polevoi?"

"Not mine, I'm afraid." The man with the rich clothes and the manicured hair said, stroking his mustache. "I think I would remember marrying a maid with legs like those."

The men wearing swords chuckled at that.

"You run away from home, girl?" the barkeep asked, a touch more gently. "You and this boy? Cause you're going the wrong way if you want to see the city. Nothing in Perun but trees that need cutting and men that need drink."

"No," Lara said, "I didn't- We didn't run away."

"Well!" The barkeep threw up her hands. "Then, by the Lioness, where *did* you come from and what are you doing here?"

Pinsard stepped between Lara and the tavern keeper.

"My *sweoster* wants a cup of beer," he said, standing very tall and straight. "So do I."

"This one's a Calvo!" one of the armed men spat, revealing a crooked set of broken teeth. "Wulf, but I never seen one this far south before . . ."

The men sitting beside the hearth began to murmur all at once. The men flanking the one named Polevoi both reached down to touch the hilts of their swords. Worse, the silent man had ceased his playing and was staring with the rest of them. Lara met his eyes. He looked surprised for a moment, or was it worry? Then he smiled, got up from his seat, and slipped through a door at the back of the room.

He's gone to fetch Danica.

Lara wondered if Moder would ever let her out of her sight again. She met Pinsard's gaze. He was clearly thinking the same thing.

"Here now!" one of the haler graybeards bellowed. "Peace, you lot! I've a guess as to who these two kits belong to."

The room grew quiet. The man reached into a pouch and began to slowly fill his pipe with tobacco.

"Some of you remember," he said, "There were a Calvo come here some nine years past. A woman. Were the summer that no good cheapjack ran off with Dimas' daughter- No offense, Master Polevoi."

"None taken," Polevoi said, taking a sip from his cup. "I happen to be a very good cheapjack."

"Well," the logger went on, "I saw it myself, and she come here riding with Mistress Danica on a big demon horse, black as coal. Not she, though. She were white as fresh snow. Some thought she were a ghost, come to live with the Mistress in the curse house."

"That's just too much wine talking," one of the card players growled. "No such thing as ghosts, nor pale ladies, nor demon horses either."

"Then where'd *he* come from?"

The man pointed at Pinsard. The men grew quiet again.

"He have the dark of it, boy?" the barkeep asked. "You come from the curse house, out in the woods?"

"Yes," Pinsard said. "And my name is not 'boy.'"

The woman smirked as the room once more filled with curious murmurs. The armed men relaxed somewhat, taking their hands off their swords, though they still stared.

"What about you?" the barkeep asked Lara. "You some faunling, lives in the deep forest, come to carry a babe away in the night?"

"No," Lara said, and laughed at the thought of such a thing. "I'm his *sweo*- His sister. We take care of Danica's sheep, when she is away."

"And your mother?"

"Moder does not leave the farm," Pinsard answered.

"Very well," the woman said with a cluck of her tongue, "You've come for beer, little doe and stag, and beer you shall have."

She bustled back behind the bar, set a pair of fresh cups upon it, and poured them both a long draught of amber from her jug.

Might as well drink it, Lara reasoned, stepping up to the bar. *I'll probably never have the chance again.*

"That'll be four drab," the barkeep grunted as Lara took her first sip. The beer was far more bitter than it smelled, and it tickled as it slid down her throat.

The barkeep was looking at her, expectant.

"I'll take a copper bit," the woman said, leaning forward. "If you don't have the drabs."

"Oh," Lara said, understanding what the woman was after. "I- We don't have any coins, if that's what you mean."

The woman's mouth turned, as if she had bitten into a rotten piece of fruit.

"You certain you're not Laszlo, dressed up as a girl?" the woman growled. "The Nightingale don't give out drinks to beggars."

"Ah, leave off the girl, Fanya," Polevoi said. "I'll pay for their drinks . . . Provided Mistress Doe here takes off her mask."

He grinned at Lara then and patted at the coin purse hanging from his belt.

Lara slipped off her stolen mask and set it onto the bar, giving her hair a shake for good measure.

"Why, you're not a girl at all," Polevoi said. "Don't you look a lady! Well now, why don't you come sit by me, lady . . ."

"Lara."

"Come sit by Polevoi, Lady Lara." He motioned for his sellswords to make room and patted the stool beside him. "And you, Master Stag. Share your drink with me."

"My name is not 'stag,' either," Pinsard grumbled, but took off his mask.

They sat. Polevoi dug a few coins from his purse and laid them on the bar.

"Here's a proper bit, Mistress Fanya," Polevoi said, "And two drab extra for your trouble."

Fanya scooped up the coins, mollified.

"These don't belong to you, do they?" she said, gesturing at the masks.

"No," Lara said. "We-"

"I can guess how you got them," Fanya said with a hint of humor in her voice. "I'll just go and hang them on the wall. We'll see just who's been tumbling with who sooner or later."

The men laughed with approval as Fanya tied the masks to a coat peg beside the front door. Then Polevoi raised his cup to Lara and tapped it against hers.

"Wulf's Fancy," he said, and took a swallow.

"Wulf's Fancy," she replied, and took one of her own. It tasted a little better now that she knew what to expect.

"Wulf's Fancy," the men in the room repeated, raising their cups.

Pinsard did not say anything but took a healthy swig himself.

"What is in this?" he asked, making a noise that was somewhere between a groan and a belch.

"Barley, hops, and a pinch of coriander," Fanya said with pride. "Good, isn't it?"

Pinsard nodded politely and put his cup down.

"Now then," Polevoi said, "Introductions. I am Polevoi, a wanderer with a full purse."

Fanya snorted. "He's a peddler with a head full of nonsense, more like."

"And these two gentlemen," Polevoi went on, seemingly unruffled, "Are my paid companions, Pyotr and Stellios. Can't be too careful on the road, what with goods worth the stealing."

The two men stared at Lara, hands on their cups.

"Now where has Silence got himself off to?" Fanya asked of the room. "Crowning's not over yet."

"Looking for a tree, most like, Fanya," one of the graybeards replied. "Saw him go out the back-"

Just then the front door slammed open.

Danica! Lara whirled about. *Or is it just the old drunk?*

It was neither, though the man standing in the doorway did look drunk. His nose was good and red, and his gray hair was so wet with sweat that he looked like he had dunked his head in the river. His leather jack hung open, his breeches were loosely tied, and his boots were speckled with muck. Even his thick brush of a mustache looked tousled.

"I'm surprised to see you up on-" Fanya began.

"Silence woke me," the man slurred, stomping towards Lara and Pinsard. "These two don't belong here, Fanya. They come from the house beyond the wood. *The curse house!* It'd be ill fortune to serve . . ."

He looked about the room then, confusion creeping across his face. He had clearly been expecting his words to carry more weight.

"How do you know all that?" Fanya asked. "Silence whisper it to you?"

"He, uh-" The man lowered his voice, though Lara was certain everyone could still hear everything he was saying. "So, you know they're from the, from the-"

"The curse house?" Fanya crossed her arms. "Yes, they said so themselves. Now, where *is* Silence?"

Yes, Lara wanted to say, *And who in the world are you?*

"He's- He went-" The man wiped at his damp forehead. "Look, Fanya, their mother- She's probably worried sick. Let me take 'em back to the curse house where they belong."

"Girl's too pretty to be your brat, Erlking," one of the graybeards snorted from across the room. "Boy's too pale. So, what are you going on about? You don't really know their ma. Do you?"

The man- Erlking- closed his eyes and rubbed at his brow.

"They're Danica's business," Erlking said finally. "That enough for you? Now you come with me, the both of you. I'll see you back home."

He took Pinsard by the arm. Lara winced. It would be easy for him to break the drunk man's hold, easier still to put him on the floor with a broken nose . . . But Pinsard did neither. Instead, he let himself be pulled from his stool, a sheepish look plastered across his face.

"Pinsard," Lara said. "What are you-"

"You too," Erlking said, turning to Lara. His breath smelt like vinegar and his lips were stained red.

"And what if the lady doesn't want to go?" Polevoi said, putting down his cup.

Erlking met the rich man's gaze.

"She has to," he said.

"Why don't we ask her?" Polevoi said. "How about it, Lady Lara? Do you want to go with this drunk old man, or do you want to stay and have another drink with me?"

Lara was still staring at Pinsard. Why had he let this stranger put a hand on him?

"Lara," Pinsard said with worry in his voice, "Maybe we should go."

He knows something, Lara realized, a hot streak of anger rushing through her. *He knows something! And he never told me.*

"I'd love another beer," Lara said to Polevoi, "Thank you."

She drained her cup.

"Lara-" Pinsard began to object.

"Stop calling her that!" Erlking hissed through his teeth and reached to take Lara by the arm.

One of the sellswords, Pyotr, grabbed him by the wrist.

"Lady said she wants another beer," the sellsword said.

For a moment Erlking looked as though he might throw a punch. Then he noticed the sword on the man's belt.

"So she did," he said. "My mistake."

The sellsword released his grip. Erlking backed off and took a seat at the very end of the bar, his face grown sullen.

"Is there any bread, Fanya?" Erlking asked. "Or milk? My head is pounding."

"I'll check the larder," the barkeep replied, refilling Lara's cup as Polevoi slid another pair of coins across the bar. The brass disappeared into her apron and then she slipped out the back.

"Wulf's Fancy," Lara said, glaring at Pinsard as she took a good long swallow. She was beginning to feel . . . Warm. And a bit light-headed.

"You may look a lady," Polevoi chuckled, "But you can drink like a lord."

"Why do you keep calling me lady?" Lara asked.

"Because you look like one," Polevoi replied.

"You probably say that to all the village girls," Lara said. She might have been young, but she'd heard enough stories from Danica to know what sort of a man this Polevoi was.

"Oh no, I don't," he said, sounding wounded as he began to dig around in his coin purse. "Well . . . Perhaps I do sometimes, but you *do* look a lady. See?"

He pulled a silver coin from his purse and set it on the bar, face up. A woman's profile had been stamped into it. She was beautiful and long-locked, with a diadem on her brow.

"I don't look like that."

"You must not own a mirror," Polevoi said, picking up the coin. "Here, turn your head."

She did so, feeling a bit silly, though also strangely flattered.

"What do you think, gentlemen?" Polevoi said, turning to his bodyguards. "Am I not right?"

"Huh," Pyotr grunted. "It does look like her. Almost."

"Yeah," Stellios agreed, "Almost . . ."

"Here," Erlking said, putting out his hand. "Let me see that."

Polevoi shot his companions an incredulous look, but then he shrugged and flipped the coin towards the drunk. Lara was more than a little surprised when he managed to catch it.

"Eh, you all must have grit in your eyes," Erlking said, squinting at the coin. "This one here's got a bigger nose, and a rounder chin. She's no Queen."

"And you're no gentleman," Polevoi said. "I'll have the lady back if you please. It's worth more than a Vassan talent, which is more than you earn in week, I'll wager."

Erlking shrugged and flipped the coin back. Lara wasn't certain what bothered her more: That the man had insulted her looks, or that she'd let the peddler defend her.

"Who was that?" she asked as Polevoi returned the coin to his purse. "On the coin, I mean."

"You don't know?" One of the man's eyebrows arched.

"That's the Queen of Arcasia," Stellios said. "Or she was. She's dead now."

"All the glitter in Arcasia has her face on it," Polevoi said. "Used to be crowns and nobles, but now they're all ladies. They even put her on the bit."

"How did she die?" Lara asked.

"Her cousin killed her," Pyotr said. "Her and her son. Poison they say."

"Naw," drawled the old logger smoking by the fire. "I heard it were a bolt through the heart. Some hired killer."

"You're both wrong," Erlking grunted.

"Either way, she's been dead for years," Polevoi said. "But everyone from Vassa to Therimere knows her face. Heh. She's prettier than the Grand Prince, at least."

"May The Firebird watch over him," Pyotr said, raising his cup.

"And Hydra drown his tax collectors," Polevoi added, finishing his beer. "Ah, that's good. Will you have another cup, Lady Lara?"

"She can have mine," Pinsard said, pushing his cup towards her. "And then we should be heading home."

"Without a dance?" Polevoi said. "Come, now, its Crowning! I've bought the lady a drink. The least she can do is give us a dance, eh gentlemen?"

"A dance! A dance!" the men of the Nightingale roared, stamping their feet. "A dance and a Crowning Queen!"

Polevoi got to his feet, and bowed as he held out his hand.

"I don't know how," Lara said.

"You'll never know how if you never try," Polevoi replied, smiling. "Besides it's easy. You just follow my lead."

"It is late, *sweoster*," Pinsard said.

Polevoi frowned. "And I say it's early yet. Just one dance, boy, and then we'll be done."

He took Lara by the hand and tugged. Surprised, she staggered forward and found herself in his arms, being twirled about.

"A dance and a Crowning Queen!" the men cheered. "A dance! A dance! And a Crowning Queen!"

"Ah, by Hydra's Teeth!" Lara heard the barkeep yammer as she came out from the back wielding a stale hunk of bread. "You lot see a Crowning pole in here? You want to dance with the girl, do it outside! Besides, Zlatomira was this year's Queen!"

"She's Queen of The Nightingale, then," Polevoi said. His grip was too tight. "And a Queen needs a King."

He leaned forward, his lips pursing. Lara reeled backwards, twisting her wrist.

"Let go," Lara said. "You're hurting me!"

When he did not loosen his grip she stamped on his foot, putting her weight behind her heel.

"You bitch!" he yowled. "What do you think you're-"

She drove her palm into his nose before he could finish. Not quite hard enough to break it, but enough to get him to loosen his grip on her.

"You drink my beer?" Polevoi blanched, trying to staunch the blood gushing from his nostrils. "Take my coin, and this is the thanks I get? Stellios, hold her!"

"Get back!" Pinsard snarled behind her.

"Keep out of this, boy," Pyotr shot back.

"My *name* is Pinsard."

"And I'm the Prince of Therimere," the man said, throwing a sloppy punch.

Pinsard dodged, caught hold of the man's wrist, and then sent him face first into the wall beside the bar. Chairs and stools began to scrape as the men of The Nightingle got to their feet.

"Stellios!" Polevoi shouted, looking about. "Wulf, where are you, you twist?"

"Not here," Lara said, throwing a punch of her own. The peddlar took the punch right across the jaw, and half-spun half-fell into the card table, toppling it.

"She attacked me!" the peddler cried out, clutching at his face as he tried to gain his feet. "You all saw! Just wanted a kiss . . ."

Lara heard a sword being drawn behind her. Pyotr had clearly regained his feet.

"No Calvo puts his hand on me and keeps it!" he barked. "Let's make this quick, boy."

She turned just as Erlking broke a stool over the sellsword's head. The man crumpled to the floor like a sack of potatoes. Pinsard looked just as surprised as she was.

Then someone took hold of the back of her hair and tugged, hard. Lara tried to keep her feet, but the floorboards proved as slippery as they were hard. She went down.

Later, she would blame the beer.

She shook her head, trying to clear it. When she saw Moder standing at the entry, sword on her belt and pale in her training whites, she shook it again.

"Get up, Lara," Moder said, staring at the peddler.

He still had a bit of Lara's hair in his fist.

"Who are-" Polevoi managed before Moder punched him so hard that a pair of his teeth came free before he hit the floor. When he wouldn't stay down, she kicked him square in the groin. He curled up then, rolling to one side before spitting up a stomachful of beer.

The Nightingale was silent.

Moder turned to the man named Erlking. "How bad?"

"Very," he replied.

She nodded, looking about.

"We are going," she said to Lara, and to Pinsard, who was still staring at the sellsword groaning on the floor.

"Are you angry?" Lara asked.

"I will be," Moder answered. "When I am having time."

IV

"We are needing more horses," Moder said, exiting while the locals were still staring.

Erlking followed, throwing the barkeep an apologetic shrug. Fanya's mouth moved, but no sound came out. Polevoi groaned.

"Thank you for the beer," Lara said, taking Pinsard by the arm. "It was very good."

The silent man was waiting for them in the yard, holding the reins of two saddled horses. They were not Danica's mares. One was a spotted gray, not much older than a filly, the other a bulkier gelding whose dark coat might have been shellbark or smoky coal. It was hard to tell in the light.

"Sellswords had a decent pair of steeds," Erlking said, hopping from the porch.

The silent man clicked his fingers at this, surrendered the reins to Moder, and 'spoke' with his hands. And, from the look on her face, Moder could clearly understand what he was saying.

So that's how he talks, Lara mused as Moder's frown deepened. *Another secret kept from me . . .*

"One of them must have been knowing," Moder said when the silent man had finished, peering down the road. "How far are you thinking?"

"Not too far," Erlking said. "I think I could catch him, if I-"

Moder shook her head, 'no.'

"Damage is done," she said. "Too many seeing. Too many talking. No. It is time."

Erlking nodded sourly and then hurried off, making for the stable.

"Go with him," Moder said to Pinsard, "And be quick. We must go, yes?"

"Yes, Moder," Pinsard said, breaking into a run.

"Find Danica," Moder said to the silent man. He padded off at once, leaping nimbly over the old drunk snoring on The Nightingale's lawn, his bottle still clutched to his breast.

Finally, Moder turned on Lara. There was anger in her eyes, yes, and disappointment, which Lara always found harder to bear . . . But there was something else. Something that made the hairs on the back of Lara's neck tingle.

Moder's afraid. Really afraid.

"Moder," Lara said, "Moder, I didn't-"

"Come," *Moder* said, handing Lara the spotted mare's reins. "You are remembering now how to ride horse proper?"

"I am," Lara said.

"Good," Moder said, and vaulted onto the gelding, who stamped and snorted in protest.

Lara hesitated. Even Danica's mares were touchy about being ridden, and she'd known them both as foals. This horse didn't know her at all. Perhaps, with more time and an apple for a bribe-

"Lara!" Moder barked.

Lara mounted, doing her best to be gentle and half-expecting the horse to bolt . . . But the spotted gray was seemingly unruffled, merely taking a moment to turn her head and prick up her ears at the sight of a girl sitting atop her. As though it was used to it. Like it was the most natural thing in the world.

"Yah!" Moder cried, digging in her heels. The gelding made for the limestone bridge at a trot that quickly became a canter. It didn't take much urging to get the mare to follow suit, delighting perhaps at the opportunity to stretch her legs.

They pounded over the bridge. The revelers of the Crowning festival stood between them and the pathway home, but Moder did not seem to care. She bore down on them, pale against the night, fearsome atop her coal-dark steed.

"It's the Vargr's daughter!" a woman shrieked. "Come on her demon horse!"

"Run!" a man cried out.

The crowd parted, men and women stumbling over each other as they made to flee. If Danica was among them, Lara could not see. The press was too thick.

They put the bonfires behind them and sped past Danica's wagon, which the old woman had parked beside the trailhead that led to the farm. Her mares strained at their tethers as they passed, shying away from Moder as much as the villagers had.

The woods. Moder slowed her gelding to a trot, wary perhaps of the ruts in the trail. Lara did the same. The ride felt longer to Lara than her walk had been, and she might have asked a dozen questions then. But something stopped her. Perhaps it was the silence, perhaps the Watcher grinning at them through the trees, or maybe it was the look she had seen in Moder's eyes . . . But Lara was afraid too. Afraid of what was waiting for them at the end of the trail.

They cleared the wood. Moder urged her gelding on, putting on speed until they were practically on top of the herb garden. She must have dragged on the reins then, for the gelding came skidding to a halt and reared, neighing so loudly that Lara wondered if the folk in Perun could hear it.

"Inside!" Moder huffed as she leapt from her saddle. She didn't wait for Lara, either, but marched straight through the farm's front door, leaving it hanging open behind her. Which was a rarity in and of itself.

Lara let her own mount come to a halt before she dismounted. Her feet had barely touched the ground when Pasha burst from the house, tail wagging, nearly knocking her over as he leapt to lick at her face. Then he took notice of the strange horses in the yard and let out a bark that might have been a 'hello.'

The gelding snorted back, pawing at the dirt. The mare lowered its head and nibbled experimentally at the garden's cabbage shoots.

Come! Moder whistled. *And quickly!*

Lara obeyed, and held her breath tight as she readied herself for a scolding . . . But Moder was not waiting for her. She was somewhere upstairs, tearing apart her room from the sound of it.

"Be lighting a fire!" Moder called down to her. "And candles! We are needing light!"

Lara took the tinder box from the mantle and struck steel to chert until she had a flame going in the hearth. She was still lighting the candles when Moder came bustling down the stairs, a packsack in each hand and another on her back.

"Your sword," Moder said. "Find it. And anything else you are wishing to keep. There is being room for one or two things."

"What do you mean?" Lara asked, "Where are we going?"

But Moder had already laid the packs on the dining table and was rummaging through the larder.

Lara looked at the packs. There were bedrolls strapped to each of them. She threw the nearest one open and blinked. Thick squares wrapped in wax cloth lay nestled within coils of rope. A tin canteen was tucked beside a wooden bowl. She shoved them aside. There were candles, fresh clothes, soap-

"Moder!" she called out, "Where are we going?!"

"Away from here!" Moder shouted back. "Find sword! And gloves! And good warm cloak!"

"Why? What's going on?!"

"You are being seen!" Moder answered. "That is what! Now go!"

Lara ran to her loft. Bannertail woke with a yawn and paced about her feet as she freed her scabbard from the wall. In her trunk she found her gloves and the mossy-green cloak that Danica had gifted to her when she was twelve summers old. It was trimmed with wolf fur (the old woman claimed she had skinned the animal herself) and too warm for spring, but Lara threw it over her shoulders anyway, hurriedly fastening its clasps.

She looked about, wondering when she would see her room again, wondering *if* she even would see it again. *What else to take?* There hadn't been much room in the packsack, and she didn't have many possessions. Mostly, they were things she had found in the pasture when there had been little to do but stand and watch the flock. There were a few interesting rocks, a pale blue robin's egg that had never hatched, a bleached mouse skull, and a collection of arrow heads made of chipped flint.

Nothing, in other words, that couldn't be replaced. Except maybe Brigitte, her old doll. She was a delicate thing, with glass eyes that made her seem just a little bit alive. She was laying beside the window, the silent man's tiny crown sitting atop her brow.

Lara tucked Brigitte her into her belt as gently as she could.

Surely, though, we'll come back. This is just Moder being, well, Moder. We'll spend the summer camped in the woods and then-

The fox-squirrel attacked the billowing rim of her cloak, shrieking its bird-like cry and lashing its tail like a whip. Lara might have laughed had her evening not taken such an unexpected turn.

"Stop that, silly," she said. "It's just my cloak!"

Bannertail glanced up at her, suspicious.

"Oh, come on then," she said. "Danica will skin you for sure if you don't."

Lara knelt and held out her palm. The fox-squirrel pounced, sped up her arm, and settled atop her shoulder.

She was halfway downstairs when Pasha began to bark wildly. Then she could hear it: Hooves pounding against the trail.

She flew down the rest of the steps, sword in hand . . . But it was only Pinsard who burst through the front door, muttering a quick excuse as he squeezed past her, mounting the stairs two at a time.

Erlking and the silent man came in next. They had packsacks of their own, and Erlking had a broad-headed axe strapped to his belt.

"There is being room in your packs?" Moder said as she returned from the larder. Her own pack was bulging.

"Some," Erlking said.

"Be getting as many-" She shook her head, irritated. "As *much* cheese, sausage, and per- Preserf- *Awirung*! Fruit. In. Jars. As much as you can! And being quick."

"We will," Erlking nodded. Then he and the silent man stepped into the kitchen.

Lara blinked. She had not seen Erlking until this very night, but *he* knew where their larder was.

Secrets! Secrets! she stewed, but she remained as quiet as the silent man as she slipped Bannertail into her pack.

She was tucking Brigitte beside the chimera when an old woman came panting through the front door, barefoot. Pasha followed on her heels, his tail practically spinning.

"Danica," Lara said.

The old woman smiled at her, the lines about her eyes crinkling like paper, and stretched out her arms. Lara rushed into the embrace, knowing only that she was terrified, though of what she did not know.

"I wish I could go with you," the old woman said, squeezing her tight. "But I'd only slow you down. My legs nearly gave out just running here."

"I-" Lara didn't know what to say. "I wish I could have seen it."

"So do I," Danica said, and released her.

"You will take care of Whisper?" Moder asked.

"I will," Danica replied, without any of her usual ambiguity. "And who knows? He may outlive this old wolf yet, have the run of the place. The sheep would like that, I suppose. Horses rarely eat sheep."

Moder embraced Danica. As they parted, Moder took the old woman by the shoulders and stared at her unblinkingly.

"Remember," she said, "Do not be lying. He will be knowing if you do, and he may be killing you for it."

"Would you leave words for him?" Danica asked.

Moder released Danica. From the look on her face, Lara guessed that she had not been expecting the question.

"No," Moder said at last.

"As you wish," Danica said. "Ah, Hirsent. I will miss the road. Though you've made this place so comfortable that I suppose I'll have to try and enjoy it. So, go then . . . And may you have the Watcher's own luck."

The old woman gave Moder a kiss on the cheek, and went to receive Pinsard, who had returned from above with his sword and a clean pair of shirts tucked beneath his arm.

"Don't grow too tall!" Danica said, patting him on the cheek, "It strains the neck to look you in the eyes enough already."

Pinsard bent to hug the old woman, said, "Thank you," and strode through the door, snatching *The Downfall of The Demon King* as he went.

Erlking and the silent man returned from the larder then, their packs full to bursting. Erlking bowed his head, but kept moving. As for the silent man, he put one his fingers to his right eye and pulled the lower lid down. Danica stuck her tongue out at him. He made a noise in the back of his throat that might have been a chuckle. Then he too was gone.

Pasha whined, and Lara reached down to stroke his ears, her throat tight.

"None of that now," Danica said, offering the dog a morsel she had been saving in her skirts. "Now, be off with you! Be off, or we'll never be parted. I could give you wisdom, and wish you warm days, cool evenings, and smooth roads ahead . . . But that is not the Watcher's way. So, remember me. When the moon is full and you long for a sad song or story, think of Danica. That will be enough, I think."

Lara wanted to wrap the woman up in her arms all over again, wanted to stay on the farm for the summer and the winter and the summer after that, but she could not, and so she followed Moder out the door and into the yard.

Now there were five strange horses in the yard. There was one for each of them, though none were as fine as the mare she had ridden there. Erlking had managed to calm the enraged gelding somehow, and he was walking it around the garden when he spied Lara.

"How was she?" he asked, nodding to the spotted mare. It was still nibbling at the cabbage. "Gentle, I hope?"

"Very," Lara said, glad of such a simple question. "She's a good horse."

"She can be," Erlking said. "When she's not being naughty. Mischief, I named her, but don't worry. I broke her for you myself."

"For me?"

"Of course," the man nodded. "And she's worth her weight in silver-"

"Talk is being for later," Moder said, giving the straps of her packsack a final tug. "Now, we are riding."

It wasn't a question.

"I'll see to your pack," Erlking said to Lara.

She was too distracted to object. She let him take it, and mounted Mischief, questions piling upon questions.

This man- a stranger- trained a horse for me. So that I'd have a horse to ride this night. Because I was seen. Because someone is coming . . . The one they keep talking about, the one who killed that girl and put her head on a spike.

And now he's coming for me.

By the time they all were ahorse, the skull-moon had sunk very low. But the night was still clear enough to see by.

"You lead," Moder said to Erlking. The man had taken the gelding for his mount. "You are knowing woods better than I."

The man nodded curtly and didn't even need to click his tongue to get the gelding moving. Moder and the silent man rode after him, having less luck with their hobbies. Lara had no doubts as to whether they had been stolen.

"You go ahead," Pinsard said to Lara as he came alongside her. His rouncey's coat looked as though someone had spilled whitewash over its neck. "I will take up the rear."

"As you wish, brave Aquilia," Lara said, and gave Mischief's flanks a gentle kick.

She only looked back once. Danica and Pasha were standing on the porch, the old woman filling her pipe with tobacco, the dog staring with ears upturned.

Then the lane turned, and they were gone.

* * * * * * *

Lara woke, half-expecting the familiar prick of her pallet beneath her. Then she saw canvas hanging where ceiling rafters should have been, and she remembered.

They had ridden all night, through wood and glen, fording the brooks that fed the Rusalka and at one point crossing an overgrown stretch of road far wilder than the rutted lane that led to Perun. Only twice did they slow, Erlking dismounting just long enough to search the ground, though searching for what exactly Lara could not say.

It was dawn when they finally came to a halt beside a rocky stream. There was some shelter amongst the budding willows that grew beside the waters, and Moder and the silent man had gone to work setting up tents (Tents! Was there nothing Moder had not packed?) while Erlking saw to the horses.

Lara would have helped, but she was so tired by that point that she had nearly fallen asleep atop a mossy stone. She just might have, too, but the squall of the fox-squirrel in her pack had jolted her awake. Moder had drawn her sword at that, looking as though she were ready to fight a warg, but when she saw Bannertail's head poking from Lara's pack she put her blade away and went back to work.

Lara did not remember having fallen asleep. She wondered if Moder had carried her to her tent. Or perhaps it was Pinsard, who was lying flat on his back beside her, using his cloak as a makeshift blanket.

She sat up and listened to the stream rushing over the rocks. Then the urge to make water drove her out of the tent and into the bushes. She could see Erlking sitting underneath one of the larger willows, dangling a line of catgut into the stream with the aid of a stripped branch.

She pushed further into the brush.

Lara guessed that it was well past noon, for The Firebird was already sinking. She could not remember ever having slept so late into the day, even when she had taken ill. Of course, neither had she stayed up all night, riding like someone hunted.

When she was done she hitched up her breeches and quietly made her way over to Mischief, where her sword had been stowed beside her saddlebag.

She pulled the blade from its sheath.

Truth-Teller, she thought. *That's not a bad name for a sword. Of course, it's not a sword that I want to tell me the truth.*

She pulled open the flap of Moder's tent, and hesitated. She had often seen Moder asleep, when the evening had grown long and she was sitting by the hearth with her head propped against the cushion of her favorite chair. She had always looked so serene. Not so now. Moder's jaw was clenched, and her right hand clawed at her bedroll, as though she were trying to catch hold of something. She did not rouse as Lara stooped forward, but turned over, mumbling something in her own tongue.

It felt unfair to do what Lara did next, but she did it anyway.

Moder woke with a start, reaching for her sword as her other gripped the blade whose tip was pricking her left shoulder.

"I have touched you with the tip of my sword," Lara said.

Moder stared at her with her piercing eyes.

"You have," Moder sighed.

Lara relaxed her grip. Moder brushed the blade aside, and got up, stretching.

"Food first," Moder groaned. She lurched from the tent, kneading her thumbs into the small of her back.

Lara followed her. Erlking had caught a fish from the stream, silver and glittering. He was gutting it, readying it for the glowing embers of a cookfire.

He must have been stoking it all morning.

Moder bent down to warm her hands.

"You are being drunk," she said to the man. "Drunk! The *one* day that this one is being . . ."

Moder chewed at her lip, clearly unsure of the right word.

"Rebellious?" Erlking offered.

"You are drinking too much," Moder said.

"It *was* Crowning," Erlking replied, spiking the fish on a sharpened stick. "And as I recall, M'lady, it was you who was watching her day and night."

"She is good at the quiet step," she said. "Better than I guessed. Is good thing, I suppose."

Erlking looked up from his work and flinched at the sight of Lara. He'd clearly not known she was there.

"Hrm," he grunted, and lowered his gaze. His hands shook a bit as he set the spitted fish over the coals.

Moder sat on an old stump near the fire and stared at the smoke wafting from it, the palm of her right hand rapping gently against her knee. Lara took a seat across from her, ignoring the damp of the ground. The simmering wood popped and crackled, and the smell of cooking meat roused Bannertail, who whined a few times before he gave up and disappeared into the brush.

"Pierrot?" Moder said, glancing at their makeshift camp.

"Sent him for nuts and berries," the man answered. "It's the best way to shut him up, I've found. But he should be back soon."

Moder nodded and went back to tapping at her leg.

"When-" Lara began to say.

"When Pinsard is awake," Moder said, and took the spitted fish from the heat of the cook fire. Its silver scales had turned golden brown, and it made a noise like a dry stalk of grass splitting as she pulled it open and examined the white flesh within. When she was satisfied, she broke the whole fish in two and held half of it out for Lara to take.

"I'm not hungry," Lara said.

"Eat," Moder said, laying the other half upon one of the stones near the heat of the coals.

Lara ate.

She had never had fresh fish before, had never even seen a fish alive, only the dry salty things that Danica sometimes brought back from Perun. This one still had its head, its black lifeless eyes almost accusatory as they stared back at her, but she ignored them. She had not eaten since supper the day before, and the hot flaky meat was delicious. She only wished that there were fewer bones to contend with.

"I can catch another if you wish," Erlking said as Lara picked the fish clean. "Your, ah-"

"Not enough time," Moder said. "Go, and ready horses. Pack tents. We cannot be staying here too long. Perun is still too close."

Erlking did not argue and went to work breaking down the tent he and the silent man must have shared. Lara tossed the remains of her morning meal onto the coals and watched them blacken.

Pinsard emerged then, his hair wild, his eyes bleary and his cloak wrinkled. Lara would have laughed, but not today. Today they were running. Today she had touched Moder with the tip of her sword.

Besides, she imagined that she looked little different.

"Sit," Moder said, gesturing for him to approach. "There is being food."

Pinsard walked over, slowly, his attention torn between Lara and Moder before he settled himself between them. He did not reach for the fish laid out for him. Somehow, he seemed to know what Lara had done.

Moder let out a deep breath and began.

"There is a man, Lara," she said, choosing her words. "He is looking for you. And he is promising much gold to anyone who will help him to find you."

"Looking for me?"

"Yes."

"But why?" Lara asked. "Who is he?"

"His name is Reynard," Moder answered. "And he is the Lord of Arcasia. He killed your mother, Lara, and now he is coming . . . Coming for you."

Moder's voice had grown quiet. Soft. It scared Lara more than her words did.

"Isengrim- Pinsard's *faeder*- he tried to stop him."

Moder shut her eyes.

"He died trying."

"Reynard," Pinsard repeated. His eyes had grown fixed and cold. "I remember him."

"And do you remember your *faeder*?" Moder said, her voice growing firm again. "Do you think you could kill the man who killed him? You? A boy who is not yet being twenty summers old? Can you do what he could not? Can you?"

"No," Pinsard said, dropping his shoulders.

"So," Moder said. "Now you are knowing why I am not telling you his name. So that you will not be running to him. So that you will not be fighting him! So . . . That I am keeping you safe. Both of you."

"I don't feel very safe," Lara said.

"Am I not telling you not to go to Crowning Festival?" Moder said, though there was no anger in her words. "Am I not warning you? And am I not teaching you sword? Am I not teaching you to be riding a horse, and how to be catching animals with snare? Am I not teaching what you must be knowing?"

Moder shook her head and sighed.

"I am only wishing that I could be teaching more. More summers you were needing, more teaching. But you could not wait."

Lara felt a flush of shame over what she had done, but she pushed it aside and rose to her feet.

"I have touched you with the tip of my sword Moder," she said. "Now tell me. This man, this Reynard, he killed my mother, but why? Who was she?"

"She was," Moder said. "You are-"

"Your mother, Majesty," Erlking's voice rang out, "Was Persephone the First, the Queen of Arcasia. Your father was King Nobel, who named her his bride before all of Calyx, on a Crowning some twenty summers past. And, when your father fell in battle, your older brother was crowned Lionel the First."

"The Queen," Lara said, "Of-"

"Then *Lord* Reynard poisoned your mother," Erlking went on, his rough voice growing hot. "And set his cutthroats to murder your brother, and all those loyal to him without a shred of pity. He calls himself The Lord Protector now, but know that as I am true, *he* is nothing. Nothing but a usurper, who sits on your rightful throne."

The man knelt then, his left knee sinking into the mud beneath it, and bowed his head low.

"For you are Larissa the First, the Queen of Arcasia, and I- I am Arlequin, who was your family groom as my father was before me. Please, Your Majesty, I beg you to accept again my service, for I will be loyal to you and your house for as long as I may live."

Lara stared at the man, not certain what to think, let alone say.

But the dreams . . . The dreams were real.

"Oh, get up," Moder growled, paying no mind to Bannertail as the fox-squirrel bounded on top of the now cold tail end of the fish and dragged it off to be devoured. "Tents need packing still."

"Yes, yes," Arlequin groused, suddenly ordinary again, just another rough man from Perun wearing clothes stained from working closely with animals. "And don't be cross with me. The Firebird would have set long before you found your tongue."

"Tents!"

Arlequin hustled off and began to break down the rest of the camp, working quickly. Moder got up and stamped out the coals.

"Then," Lara said, "It is true? I am . . . I am a Queen?"

"Yes," Moder answered. "And no. Queen is having servants. Queen is living in great hall. Queen has army. You are having these things?"

"No," Lara replied.

"And who are you thinking *is* having many servants, great halls, armies? Who is having everything? Everything that he wants?"

Everything but a Queen. Lara felt the sudden urge to leap onto Mischief's back and ride away from Perun as fast as possible.

Moder seemed satisfied by Lara's silence.

"Help Arlequin with tents," she said, continuing to scatter the campfire. "Pinsard, go and find Pierrot. It is being time to leave, I think."

Pinsard did as he was told.

Lara walked over to where the man who had called himself Erlking was rolling up Moder's tent, her head still reeling. The day before she had been herding sheep and shoveling filth out of stalls. Today she had a groom to tend a fine horse, a royal mother and father, a dead brother she did not remember, a title of her own . . . And a man who was hunting her.

The man who had killed her family.

"I- I accept your service," she said to Arlequin as she approached. It was all that she could think to say, but it felt right to her.

"You honor me, Majesty," the man said, keeping his eyes on his work as he bowed his head in deference.

"Pierrot," Lara said. "That is the silent man's name?"

"Yes, Majesty."

"And he was one of my mother's servants too?"

Arlequin snorted and began to roll up the bedrolls.

"He was your father's fool, Majesty, and after that he was your brother's. Now he is *just* a fool, and good for very little."

Something swooped past Lara's shoulder then, green and winged. A dragonfly she thought, or a katydid. It did a lazy loop in the air and then collided with the tip of Arlequin's nose. "Wulf!" the man swore, swatting at the thing as it drifted lazily to the ground, settling atop the bedroll.

It was a leaf, neatly folded into the shape of a miniature bird.

Lara turned around, and sure enough, there was the silent man, smiling ever so faintly. He placed his right hand over his heart and bowed.

"I sent you into the woods to forage, you colorless affliction," Arlequin spat, "Not to pick leaves!"

Pierrot let out a huff, and produced a small leather pouch, seemingly from thin air. This he presented to Lara, bowing as low as he had on the porch of the farmhouse.

"Thank you," Lara said to the silent man, graciously accepting the pouch and loosening its strings. Inside there were over a dozen or so violet frostberries, and half as many shellbark nuts that some animal must have buried beneath winter snow or secreted in the hollow of a tree. When she was younger, Danica had taught Lara how to crack open their shells with her fingers, and that they tasted much better when they had been roasted in a skillet.

She plucked two of the frostberries from the bag and popped them into her mouth. They were rather tart, but there was already some of the sweetness of Spring in them.

"Thank you," she said again, closing the pouch and tying it to her belt by the draw strings. "They're very good."

Pierrot bowed again, clearly pleased, though Arlequin crossed his arms, his mouth bending into a deep frown.

"All morning you've been in those woods," he said to the silent man, "And that's all you've found? A handful of nuts and berries?"

Pierrot put up both of his hands, urging for patience. Then he reached behind his back and rummaged about, clearly wrestling with something larger than the little pouch he'd given Lara.

Finally, he made a satisfied noise in the back of his throat and offered Arlequin another bird fashioned out of folded leaves. This one was easily three times as large as the one that had struck the groom in the nose.

Arlequin looked at the bird, and then at the silent man's toothy grin. Then he ripped the thing out of Pierrot's hand, crumpled it up, and tossed it as far as he could throw it, letting out a rather unintelligible curse as it unfurled itself in midair and sailed away.

"I'll fetch Her Majesty's horse," the groom growled, storming off. "In the meantime, let's see if Master Pierrot knows how to fold a tent and make *it* fly!"

The silent man seemed to consider the idea, and then went to work, shooing Lara away when she offered to help.

Lara threw on her cloak and shouldered her packsack, still thinking about her mother and father, and the man called Reynard, and how much had been kept from her, and of her dreams: The corridors of stone, the enormous bed, the thin hands holding her tight, and the red room, its door splintering as a chorus of voices screamed with terror.

She thought of all these things, and her throat felt very tight.

Then she stepped over the place where the silent man's second bird had fallen, its wings bent but still capable of flight.

He may be a fool, she thought. *But he does make me smile.*

* * * * * * *

Lara still had many questions of course, but as they made their way across pinewood and rocky hills shrouded with mist, driven on by Moder's urgency and stopping to rest only when necessary, she found that her chances to speak with anyone were few and far between.

When they were not riding they were either sleeping or eating, often not stopping long enough to bother with tents, let alone a fire. By the fifth morning the memory of hot, freshly caught fish and fresh frostberries seemed luxurious when compared to the hard biscuits, dried fruit, and salty lamb sausage that served as their regular meals. Were it not for the horses, Lara suspected, Moder would have driven them on until they all dropped, and she quickly found herself glad of bedroll and cloak when the Firebird set and the night grew chill about her.

Still, they had to slow from time to time, especially over rough terrain, and as they rode along a dry riverbed at the bottom of a steep-edged ravine, Lara slowed Mischief until she was side by side with Pinsard, who seemed to have taken to his rouncey well enough.

"Did you know?" Lara asked. "All this time, did you know who I was?"

"I knew you weren't my sister," he answered, keeping his eyes on the ground ahead of them. "And that you were a nobleman's daughter. I did not know you were a Queen."

"Moder never told you, or Danica?"

He shook his head. "Moder only told me that we needed to keep you safe and that I should be watchful of strangers asking about you, especially if they came to the farm without warning. And Danica-"

Pinsard paused as they both ducked under a skeletal-looking tree trunk that had fallen diagonally across the ravine.

"Danica told me that you were left on the doorstep in a basket, but I knew that was just another one of her stories. We used to play when we were little. When my *faeder* was still alive."

They rode in silence for a while. Lara was not surprised. Pinsard had spoken very little since he had learned the name of the man who had killed his father, and she guessed that it weighed on him.

"Do you remember what it was like?" Lara asked, softly, the way she might have to Whisper or one of Danica's fussy mares. "Before the farm?"

"Very little. I was very young."

"Tell me," Lara said, wishing that she could remember more than dreams and fragments.

"I remember that we never stayed in one place for very long," Pinsard said. "And there were always people with us. Men and women. The men were soldiers, I think. They all had weapons and wore armor. And they were all scared of *faeder*."

Pinsard quieted again. They passed around a slight bend in the riverbed before he continued.

"We used to live in a tent, *faeder* and *moder* and I, but it was *big*, almost as big as Danica's great room, not cramped like these ones." He patted his saddlebag for emphasis. "Other times we would stay in places with high walls and towers. Most of them were falling apart. Or they had no roofs. I suppose they must have been castles, or houses where nobles used to live."

"Used to live . . ." Lara repeated. "Were they abandoned?"

"Yes."

"Why?" she asked. "Was there plague?"

Pinsard shook his head, and said, "There was a war. *Moder* and *faeder* fought in it."

This was news, though it made perfect sense. After all, Moder was a Northerner, as was Pinsard in his own way, though he had never seen his homeland.

"Did they fight the Calvarians?"

"Yes," he answered.

"For my mother?"

Pinsard did not answer, and after a while he lightly whipped his rouncey's reins and overtook her. She held back from following and listened to the sound that Mischief's hooves made against the smooth stones of the dead river. Then the ravine leveled out, and Moder set them all to speed.

So, they went on, the forest growing wilder as they went, until finally Arlequin's steed stumbled over the roots of a large cedar, and even Moder's exhortations failed to move him when he stopped to tend to it. The woods here were stark and silent, the bark of the pines partially speckled with old sap and the uneven ground littered with branches. Some of the trees had been clawed at by something large, a bear perhaps, or a particularly large hill cat, though the marks looked very old.

"How long?" Moder asked Arlequin, sharply, her head craned as if she were looking for something above the trees. Lara looked upwards as well, but she only saw the treetops swaying gently, and above them the bright blue of the sky.

"We should rest 'til morning to be safe," Arlequin answered, lifting up the horse's left foreleg and squinting at the bottom of its hoof.

"No time," Moder repeated for what felt like the hundredth time. "How long?"

"Not too long, I think," he said. "But they'll all be lame if we keep up this pace, or worse. Ground here's too rough for them."

For a moment Moder looked as though she was going to argue, or bark another order, but then she nodded, once, and slumped forward in her saddle, clearly exhausted.

"Sit down and rest, Moder," Pinsard said, offering her his canteen.

Moder took her son's hand and dismounted, hissing with pain as she put weight on her legs. She took a few swallows of water and, finding the nearest tree, found a seat against its trunk, and closed her eyes.

"Eat," she commanded them. "Drink. Rest."

Then she fell fast asleep.

"You rest too," Lara said to Pinsard, who knelt to retrieve his canteen from Moder's loosening grip. "I can keep watch."

"I am not tired," he said, straightening himself.

"Then we can both watch."

Pinsard nodded and found a good spot amongst the pines to stand watch, but there wasn't much to see but trees. Pierrot tied up his shaggy-looking hobby and went off to forage while Arlequin walked his coal-colored gelding about a cluster of firs.

"What is his name?" Lara asked, gesturing to the horse.

"Surefoot, Majesty," Arlequin said, and chuckled. "An unlucky name for me to have given him it seems."

"He's yours then?" she asked, keeping pace as they began another circuit. "You didn't steal him?"

"No, Majesty, I didn't steal him!" Arlequin laughed. "Nor Mischief either. The Master of the Mill gifted them to me both, for helping his prize mare deliver a foal that would have killed her in the birthing. A lucky thing too, Majesty, or you might be the one riding one of that trader's sorry-looking animals."

"They don't look so bad to me," Lara said, glancing at the horses that the others had ridden out of Perun.

"The rouncey had a decent trainer, Majesty," Arlequin conceded, sparing a glance for Pinsard's steed. "But those two hobbies would see better use on a farm than this rough riding. So, thank The Firebird for Mischief, there. Your royal father would have had me whipped if I'd presented his daughter with anything less than a proper mount."

Lara tittered at that but quickly stopped, realizing from the look on the man's face that he was not speaking in jest.

"What was he like?" she asked. "My father."

Arlequin's face brightened. "Oh, he was a great rider, Majesty, with one of the best eyes I've ever seen for horses. You could show him an entire stable and he'd always pick out the best of the lot, quick as silver."

"Was he a good King?"

"There never was a better King, Majesty," Arlequin answered, without hesitation. "All Arcasia wept when he was taken from us."

"And my mother," she asked. "Did you know her well?"

"Not well, Your Majesty, no," he admitted, "A groom rarely sits at table with great lords and ladies. But Her Majesty was a more than fair rider herself, very kind and gentle. Ah, you should have seen her atop Gallant. Now, that was a proper horse for a Queen to ride . . ."

Lara wanted to ask the man more, but she quickly got the impression that he knew more about the horses he had raised for her family than he did about their riders. And she could not help but wonder how many of her father's servants had felt the lash of a whip or riding crop for displeasing him, or if her mother was truly kind or gentle. After all, Queen Grisana had bricked up her own children within the walls of Carduel, but the stories all agreed that she had been fond of her cats.

At last, Arlequin said, "Hoo there," and pulled lightly on Surefoot's reins, halting him with practiced ease. Then he took a second look at the gelding's hooves and nodded.

"No limp," he said. "No swelling. It will have to do."

He rummaged around in his belt pouch and brought out what was left of a carrot. Surefoot chewed it up and swallowed it down in three bites.

"That'll be the last of those for a while, boy. But the last one I saved for Mischief, Majesty. Would you like to feed it to her yourself?"

"Yes, thank you."

Arlequin was searching for the treat when the caw of a bird startled them both. It was answered by a second call, no louder than a throaty rattle.

"We should be going." Moder's voice was hushed but it carried. She had not only wakened at the sound of birdcall, but she had picked herself up and was making to remount her stubborn gelding.

"It's only a pair of blackbirds," Arlequin said, though he was scanning the trees too, his eyes worried.

"Perhaps yes," Moder said as she gained her saddle, "Perhaps no. We should be going either way."

A third cry, clearly some distance away, joined those of the others. Arlequin helped Lara mount Mischief and was about to go after Pierrot when the silent man came racing from the trees, carrying a bundle in his fist.

Arlequin mounted Surefoot, Pinsard his rouncey, Pierrot the shag-haired hobby, and they were off again, putting both pines and birdcall behind them.

They did not stop until long after dark, making their camp within a jumble of fallen tree trunks.

"These woods won't go on forever, Hirsent," Arlequin pointed out, after he had seen to the horses.

"Just a day longer," Moder said, leaning her head against a thick clump of moss. "Now let me sleep."

"What happened?" Lara asked once Moder had drifted off. "Back in the pinewood, I mean. What were you both so afraid of?"

"Shrikes, Majesty," Arlequin answered, darkly. "*His* shrikes."

Lara was tired. They'd ridden for over a fortnight with little food and less rest. Still, she found it hard to sleep that night.

His shrikes. Two simple words, but they were impossible to drive out of her head. *His shrikes.*

Just what sort of a man is this Reynard?

* * * * * * *

Lara spent the better part of the next morning wondering what might be waiting at the end of their journey. Perhaps a riverboat captain would take them to the coast, where a ship with tall sails could carry them far away, to Frisia perhaps, or Therimere. Or maybe they were bound for Vassa, to beg the aid of the Grand Prince, and she might see the city she had only heard about in stories.

Or, she thought to herself glumly as her rear began to chafe against Mischief's saddle, *More likely we're headed to a place smaller even than Perun, and we'll spend the next ten summers crouching in a cabin. One with only one room that smells worse than the sheep pen.*

Lara, they would call her. *The Queen of No-Place-In-Particular.*

But Arlequin had spoken true the night before. The woods *were* thinning, and by midday there was no longer any need to ride single file.

- 83 -

They covered great stretches at a full gallop, pausing only to water the horses from a stony brook.

They came to halt some hours before sundown. Through a break in the trees Lara could make out rolling hills dotted with solitary trees and patches of shrub. To Lara, it did not look in any way remarkable, but Moder stared at it for a long time before she motioned for them to dismount.

"Stay here," Moder said to Pierrot as she rubbed at her calves. "Be watching horses."

"Why are we stopping?" Pinsard asked. "Are you hurt?"

"Muscles are sore," Moder replied, waving the question away. "Is not serious. But go with Arlequin, both of you, and be seeing why we are stopping."

"What is it?" Lara asked as she made to follow.

"You will see," Moder said, frowning as Bannertail squeezed out of Lara's packsack and bounded after them.

"Step lightly, Majesty," Arlequin whispered as they approached the tree line. "We are not alone."

Lara felt a cold rush of fear at those words, but she saw nothing sinister beyond the trees. There were no riders or shrikes, only a house with a thatched roof built into the side of one of the hills. There was smoke rising from its chimney and a large gray cow grazing in a rude paddock. Half a dozen figures were working a strip of tilled soil, seeding it perhaps.

Do they all sleep in that little shack?

She leaned forward to get a better look, and then she saw why they had stopped.

A dirt lane led from the farm, joining a path that snaked west, curling about the hills. There were other farmsteads along the path, growing so close and thick that she supposed them to be a village far larger than Perun. But that was nothing. Beyond the farmland, towering over the hills and dwarfing the river that ran beside it, there was a city.

From a distance it looked as if hundreds of red-roofed houses had been piled atop one another in a great ring, from which a handful of dull-white towers loomed. Countless plumes of smoke rose from it, and high walls of stone encircled it. Ships of all shapes and sizes were moored in the river below it, and about its red gates were markets made of cloth, where merchants and buyers would haggle and argue and empty a cup for the Watcher when the deal was done.

It dwarfed everything that she had seen in her imagination, save for in splendor.

"Are all cities so large?" she managed.

"Far larger, Majesty," Arlequin answered, his hushed tone reminding her that their voices could carry far. "This is only Irikosa. Should Majesty ever come to see Calyx, or Arioch in the winter . . . Well, then this place would look quite small."

"Is that where we are going?" Lara asked, expectant. "Calyx? Or-"

"We are not going anywhere." Moder had joined them. She gripped one of the trees to help steady herself. "Not yet."

"You are certain, then?" Arlequin said, turning to Moder. "Those sellswords and that peddler you gave a beating both know my face. As does all of Perun."

"Is dangerous, yes," Moder said. "But we must be knowing."

"Knowing what?" Lara asked.

"How much danger we are being in."

Moder gestured towards the city by the river.

"You want him to spy?" Lara balked.

"I'll gladly play the spy for Her Majesty," Arlequin said, exhaling. "So. Who am I then?"

"Fur trader," Moder answered, the words already on her lips. "From Leshny."

"I have no furs," Arlequin pointed out.

Moder tossed Arlequin a black leather pouch. He caught it as neatly as he had the coin in The Nightengale. It jingled.

"You are looking for fur seller," Moder went on. "Road was bad. Horse nearly lamed by hole in road. Market closed, but you try in the morning. Find inn. Buy drinks and listen. And *do not* be drinking too much."

"I won't," Arlequin said, and began to make his way back to the horses. "I'll need both of the hobbies though, or it won't look right."

"Take them," Moder said, growing short. "But be back by dawn, or-"

"We won't be late."

Arlequin removed most of the gear from the hobbies and began to make his way towards the river, leading the animals by the reins and using the trees to stay well out of sight of the valley beyond.

Soon, Lara had lost sight of him herself. And once she had set Mischief to graze and had taken a bit of food, it became clear to Lara that there was little left for them to do but wait.

Moder, of course, refused to sleep for very long, and kept looking to the sky with her bow in hand and her quiver hanging from a nearby branch. Pinsard methodically practiced his sword cuts. Pierrot managed to amuse both himself and Bannertail with a colored string he'd woven between the fingers of both hands, the fox-squirrel occasionally batting at the figures he made until it grew bored with the game and scurried off, having spied one of the red-breasted thrushes that were nesting in the trees.

But as for Lara, she merely sat by the edge of the woods and looked towards Irikosa, watching its walls grow rosy with the sinking of the Firebird as dozens of lights bloomed within it.

Soon fires were being lit across the hills. The men she had seen in the field below quit their work, and a skirted figure with a pair of buckets emerged to milk the cow. She could almost hear them calling out greetings to each other, or complaining about the day's work, or arguing over a petty bit of housework that had gone undone . . . Then Pinsard joined her, still a bit red in the cheeks, and they watched together.

"Danica will be making supper," he said.

"She kept some of the lamb I bet." Lara's mouth watered at the thought of it. "Or finally chopped one of those lazy hens' heads off and made a stew."

"Pasha would like that," Pinsard said and, finding a place to sit, pulled the edges of his cloak tighter about his chest.

It grew darker. The waning skull-moon rose, and at last the door to the farmhouse shut, and the lights in the valley began to go out. Bannertail came slinking through the brush and climbed into Lara's lap to sleep. There was fresh blood around its mouth.

"He was my faeder's friend," Pinsard said, the Watcher's light making his face seem even paler than usual. "He was his friend, but he killed him anyway."

Lara did not have to ask who he was speaking of.

"I should have stopped you," Pinsard said. "On Crowning. I should have stopped you."

"It's not your fault. You didn't know."

"I knew enough. I knew, but I-"

Bannertail started as he rose.

"I failed Moder," he said. "And I failed you. I will *never* do it again."

"Pinsard-" she began to say, but he was already gone, his long legs carrying him as he went to relieve Moder of her vigil.

You didn't fail us, Pinsard, she thought as she stroked the top of the fox-squirrel's head until it curled up into a ball, its long bushy tail serving for a pillow. *You didn't fail us at all.*

I did.

* * * * * *

The sound of hooves woke her. She must have slept through the better part of the night, for the skull-moon was in the west and the lights of Irikosa had dwindled to a mere smattering. She set Bannertail aside and rose, hissing when it became clear that her right leg had fallen asleep.

She ignored the pain and half ran, half limped towards the others, coming up alongside Pinsard as Arlequin emerged from the darkness, riding one of the hobbies and leading the other by the reins. From the lather on the animal's thighs and necks, Lara knew that they must have been keeping a grueling pace.

"How bad?" Moder asked when he'd taken a swallow of water.

"That sellsword bastard couldn't keep his mouth shut," Arlequin answered. "By now, everyone with a thirst for gold from Perun to Lukomorie is hunting us for the bounty on Her Majesty's head. The smarter ones are already combing the countryside for our trail, and the Vargr's men are going from homestead to homestead, hoping to find us hiding in a barn or some such nonsense."

He took another gulp of water and went on.

"All that is bad enough! But one of the men rode here all the way from Vassa and he told me that the court of the Grand Prince had an unexpected visit from Reynard's personal emissary: That winged monster his Luxian spymaster calls 'daughter.' They say half the city saw her coming before she landed on one of the balconies of the tower of gold and jade."

"So soon," Moder said, and cursed. "What else?"

"No one but Koschei the Deathless and his lickspittles know for certain . . . But apparently, she demanded that the Grand Prince remove his soldiers from the Muraille and grant Reynard's army free passage within his borders."

Moder closed her eyes. "And?"

"The old fool refused, and said he'd have the next herald who spoke to him so boldly shot at once, human or chimera. That was four days ago."

"Then they are being in Solothurn soon. If they are not already . . ."

Moder chewed on her thumb, and then spat into the grass.

"We must cross river," she said. "By tomorrow night. No longer."

Arlequin scratched at the back of his head.

"There is a ford just north of Mira that should serve," he said. "But it is deep. Might need to lose some gear."

"Better we lose tents and packsacks than be caught on wrong side of river."

Arlequin nodded and began to walk the hobbies to let them cool as much as they could.

"What happens after we cross the Rusalka?" Lara asked.

"War is in the north," Moder answered. "War, too many eyes, and now *he* is coming as well."

"Then where do we go?"

"Mandross," Moder said, chewing at her thumb again. "High mountains between Mandross and Solothurn. Few passes. Easy to defend. It will be being hard to follow us there, even for Reynard."

All that Lara knew of Mandross was that mercenaries came from there. Mercenaries, and books written by dusty old men in dustier halls. At least, that is what Danica had told her of the place. Given the current circumstances, she liked Moder's description far better.

"Mandross then," Lara said, and went to unhitch Mischief without waiting for Moder's approval.

She was tired of being hunted, yes, and tired of secrets. But most of all, she was tired of not being asked what she thought they should do.

She was supposed to be a Queen, after all.

V

They had nearly forded the Rusalka, up to their necks and suffering in the crisp evening air, when a rider galloped down the far bank. He drew to a halt, the sun at his back and a long spear in his gloved fist. His helmet resembled an overturned pot.

Lara pulled up the hood of her winter cloak, ignoring the cold rivulets that ran down her back.

"You there!" the man called out. "You can't cross here! Don't you know there's a bridge up yonder?"

"Aye!" Arlequin called back. "And a toll too, we reckon!"

The man leaned forward and tipped his helmet to peer at them. "What's your business this far south?" he asked.

"Ours," Arlequin said. "Now, you going to let us pass? Or are we going to have to cross your stinking bridge?"

The man considered. His horse let out a low whinny.

"Two marks," he said.

"Two?" Arlequin balked. "You a toll collector or a brigand?"

"The bridge is upriver."

The man leveled his spear at them. Its leaf-shaped point looked very sharp.

"Alright, alright, by Wulf," Arlequin grumbled, and waded towards the rider with Surefoot in tow. Pierrot followed, then Moder and Pinsard. Lara brought up the rear and kept her head down.

When both he and Surefoot were free of the river, Arlequin rummaged through his saddlebag and pressed a pair of silver coins into the rider's outstretched palm.

The man relaxed his spear.

"There be a hostelry in Mira," he said. "If you're looking for a hot meal."

"We'll rough it," Arlequin replied bluntly.

The rider grunted and watched silently as the rest of them made the crossing. As she drew closer, Lara saw that he was an older man, his bristly moustache as white as his hair. He wore a dark tunic over a shirt of mail, its fabric embedded with metal bosses shaped like eight-pointed stars, and as Lara slogged her way up the riverbank he smiled at her, the lines around his eyes and cheeks wrinkling cheerily.

He was still watching her as they made their way up an overgrown lane, the sunlight glinting off both spear and helm.

"He knows," Lara said, glancing backwards.

"Yes," Moder said. "We must leave path soon."

Pierrot shot Moder a look, raising his eyebrows as he pantomimed drawing an arrow taut.

"Bowstring is wet," Moder replied. "And he is not worth the arrow."

Pierrot shrugged. *Ah well.*

"We could have taken his horse at least," Pinsard said, scowling as the man turned his steed back upstream.

"Ahorse or on foot," Arlequin said, "He'll make trouble for us soon enough. That was no toll guard or town watchman. That was one of the Vargr's men. You see his coat?"

"I did," Lara nodded. "But then why did he let us go?"

Arlequin blinked at her question. Then he let out a chuckle.

"What's so funny?" Lara asked.

"I beg your pardon, Majesty," Arlequin said. "But clearly you've never heard the tales of the great Lady Hirsent and her skill with a blade. Why risk certain death at the hands of the She-Wolf when you've already got two fat coins in your purse?"

"Do not be using those names," Moder said, her eyes narrowing.

"At any rate," Arlequin said, "We should steer well clear of Mira! Where there's one Vargr's man there's bound to be at least a half dozen more, as well as every brigand and jumped-up idiot within spitting distance looking to collect the usurper's bounty."

"This *bounty*," Lara said. "Just how large is it?"

Arlequin's voice grew hush, as if the brush itself might be listening.

"Six thousand *thousand* golden sovereigns, Your Majesty," he said. "Or millions as they're called. A truly frightful sum."

"Six millions," Lara repeated to herself, marveling at the sound of it. The number hardly seemed real.

* * * * * * *

When night fell, they made camp atop a knoll from which they could see for leagues, for the countryside west of the Rusalka was mostly scrubland, dotted by lonely pines that quivered in the wind.

They were not alone in the wilderness. As soon as it was truly dark Lara could see pinpricks of light swaying in the darkness like lightning-flies in summer. Torches, she guessed. They were far away, their bearers most likely following the false trail that Arlequin had laid, leading Surefoot alongside a stretch of bog they themselves had nearly ridden into before they changed their course . . . But they were still too close for her own peace of mind.

Eventually, she closed her eyes, and tried to imagine what six million coins could buy.

* * * * * * *

"Was Moder really a proper Lady?" Lara asked Pinsard the next morning, as they were making ready to ride. "Or was Arlequin just making a jest?"

"I'm not certain," Pinsard answered, testing the girth of his saddle. "But Moder told me once that the Queen of-"

Pinsard shot her a glance and cleared his throat.

"That your mother rewarded *faeder* and her for fighting so bravely in the war. So, perhaps she was?"

Lara looked at Moder struggling to resaddle the brown hobby that she was beginning to call Demon, her black boots and white breeches speckled with mud, and tried to picture her in a gown of damask, a fan in her hand rather than a blade.

"No," Lara said with a shake of her head. "It can't be true."

For three days they rode west by southwest, and every morning Lara woke to find the snow-peaked mountains of Mandross looming closer. But the signs that they were being hunted were growing as well. There were campfires too far from any proper road, many of them still smoldering. There were game trails marked by hoof and boot prints so fresh that a child could have picked them out. In other places the tracks crisscrossed or doubled back upon themselves, and Lara wondered how many of these bounty hunters were, in fact, tracking each other rather than themselves.

The thought cheered her, until they found the bodies.

There were five of them, all men, though one looked little older than Pinsard. Some wore well-worn leathers and roughspun, others fur-lined hide. One had a rusty set of greaves on his legs. Another still clutched the haft of the axe that lay by his side.

All of them were dead.

One almost looked as if he were resting against a tree until Lara noticed that he was holding his own guts in his hands, his eyes untroubled by the flies that were swarming over them.

Afterwards, when she had emptied her stomach and stopped gasping for air, Lara found the presence of mind to reason. It had only been a matter of time before two bands of armed men, driven by the promise of riches would chance upon each other during the hunt. Whatever words had been spoken, if there had been any, had not ended well.

"It is hard," Moder said as she laid her hand on Lara's back and began to stroke her the way she did when she was sick with a fever. "Always it is hard, to be seeing death for the first time."

But this isn't the first time, is it?

Don't look! Don't look!

She pushed the thought aside and forced herself to look at the men who had died because of her foolishness at the Nightingale. She suspected that these would be far from the last.

"Who were they?" Pinsard asked.

"They lost, whoever they were," Arlequin answered, studying the ground. "The winners took their mounts and rode west."

"They killed them for their horses," Lara said, quiet.

"Yes," Moder sighed. "Their horses and their boots."

"Come, Majesty," Arlequin said, "We must be away from this place. There's nothing that can be done for them now save burning, and a pyre may bring others."

She lingered a moment longer, listening to the creak of trees and the hum and whir of insects feasting. Then she gathered Mischief's reins and urged her onward.

* * * * * * *

The next day the first true thunderstorm of the year came roiling out of the west. Moder argued with Arlequin for the better part of a league as trees swayed wildly and sheets of rain pelted them, but when even Mischief bucked and whinnied at the lightning lancing overhead, they were forced to halt.

"Lazy girl who shirks her chores," Lara hummed drearily as they slogged their way out of the wood and took what little shelter they could within the confines of a long ditch. "When thunder roars, run indoors . . ."

She tried to remember the rest of the song that Danica would croon whenever the weather turned foul, but she soon gave up. After all, its sage advice rather depended on being underneath a sturdy roof rather than out in the open, huddling in a muddy pool of ankle-deep water.

The horses found some comfort in each other's company at least. The way they stood in a cluster reminded Lara of the farm's sheep.

Soon Lara's cloak was soaked through, and her teeth chattered as Bannertail shivered against her neck. Arlequin and Pierrot looked just as miserable, but Moder was sitting up straight, apparently untroubled by the wind whipping at her face. Pinsard was trying to do the same, but he kept flinching at the rain in his eyes. When he saw Lara smirking at him, he mouthed something foul and gave up.

Eventually the worst of it passed them by, the howling winds drifting eastward, and Arlequin led their horses up to higher ground. Lara followed, wringing out her hair with her hands. The fox-squirrel let out a yip as it leapt from her shoulder, landing in the wet grass before giving itself a shake.

As the Firebird broke through the clouds, Lara realized that the ditch they had been sheltering in ran alongside a proper road. No country lane she had ever seen was paved with stones or was wide enough to drive two carts side by side with room left to spare. She could see too that the wild thickets they had been traveling since crossing the Rusalka had given way to farmland. Not more than a league distant there was a village, its freshly tilled fields sharing the hillside with a ruined tower.

She felt dreadfully exposed.

"Border is close, yes?" Moder said.

Arlequin grunted in the affirmative.

"Shouldn't we get off the road?" Lara asked.

"No," Moder replied. "I think now we must be following it."

"But the men, the shrikes-"

"Eyes may be finding us on road or off," Moder said, "But *on* road we will not be being alone."

"I'm afraid she's right, Majesty," Arlequin said. "This is one of the high roads, old as Aquilia. If anyone or anything spies us riding over wheat fields or sleeping in an apple orchard with the high road so close . . . Well, they'll take us for brigands or bounty hunters at best. But, on the high road, Majesty, there are all sorts."

Lara did not like it, but she understood the logic. She mounted Mischief.

"Scout ahead," Moder said to Pierrot, who was testing the strings of his lute. "Stop before dusk and be waiting. But turn around if there is danger."

The silent man did not answer, but shouldered his instrument, mounted his shaggy horse, and set off at a steady canter. Lara felt a stab of worry as he went, but then she remembered that he was a servant of the Watcher. To do him harm in any way, to even lay hands on him . . .

No. No one who feared the gods, and the Watcher's wrath, would be so reckless.

"We too will ride separate," Moder said, gesturing to Pinsard as she fought to mount Demon. "Will look less . . . Odd, is word?"

"Odd," Pinsard said. "Yes."

Lara swallowed her objections. She had no doubts that Arlequin was trustworthy, or that he would do his best to protect her, but she also could not remember having been apart from either of them longer than an afternoon. And from the look on his face, she could tell that Pinsard was just as uncomfortable with the idea as she was.

"It won't be long," she said to him.

"Be careful," he said.

"Aren't I always?"

Pinsard took a deep breath and mounted his rouncey.

"Go now," Moder said to them. "We will not be far behind."

"What about Her Majesty's sword?" Arlequin asked, nodding at the blade Lara wore on her belt. "The horses I can explain, but that's no peasant's weapon."

Moder drummed her fingers against the horn of her saddle.

"Hide sword in bedroll," she said, unslinging her bow and quiver. "But take these. And if you see shrike-"

"Always kill a shrike," Lara said. "Don't worry, I remember."

* * * * * * *

They rode along the high road at a trot, Bannertail napping within Lara's saddlebag as Arlequin led the way. Every now and then she would glance backwards. Sometimes she caught a glimpse of the two pale figures following them, but more often than not there was nothing behind them but the long, gray road.

They rode like this for several leagues, passing meadows of golden scatterweed and thickets of pale white birch. Gradually the wind stilled, and the Firebird beamed down on them, driving a bit of the chill from the air, but still Lara shivered. Her clothes were damp, and the clear skies were no comfort. Her breath caught with each swallow taking flight and every hawk circling in the heights above looked like a shrike to her.

She was staring at one of them when she heard Arlequin call out, "Whoa now!" She reined in Mischief at once. There was a wagon on the road ahead of them, its bed laden with bales of fresh hay.

"Just a peasant, Majesty," Arlequin said. "Nothing to fear, I should think."

"Unless there are bounty hunters hiding in the hay," Lara replied, looking over her shoulder. Moder and Pinsard were nowhere to be seen.

"So," she said, arching her brows, "Who are we, then?"

"Hmmm." Arlequin stroked his moustache. "A stable hand and his daughter, running from the war . . . The horses were the innkeepers', but-"

"The inn burned down?"

Arlequin considered this and nodded.

"Where's mother?" she asked. "Dead?"

"Yes," he replied. "Of the fever-"

"But I was too young then to remember her."

Arlequin nodded again, but his expression grew somber, and they rode in silence for a stretch. Finally he seemed to remember himself and wiped his eyes with the back of his hand.

"I'll do the talking, Your Majesty," he whispered as they began to overtake the hay wagon, "With Majesty's permission, of course."

"Given," she breathed, doubting that she would ever grow used to being called 'Your Majesty,' or granting a man three times her age her *permission* to do anything.

As they neared, Lara saw that the wagon was being drawn by a bulky dray horse the color of an oak nut. A rheumy-eyed man wearing a wide-brimmed hat and a patched cape was leading it by a rope tied to its harness. A young girl, probably no older than six summers, peered at them from atop one of the bales, her mouth agape.

"Good even to you," Arlequin said, his voice growing coarser as he gave the man a nod.

"Good even," the man replied, and pinched the brim of his hat. "And where be you headed, this stark and stormy day?"

"South," Arlequin answered. "Be we near Gorynych?"

"Aye," the man said. "I be bound there meself, for 'twill be market on the morrow, and I've feed to sell."

"The road strikes me fair lonely then," Arlequin said. "I spied not a man all the morrow! Be there pox here, or poor harvest?"

The man paused and took a long look at the both of them before answering, his eyes lingering on their horses and the axe that hung from Arlequin's belt.

"No," he said at last, "There be no signs of the Sickener, Lioness be praised . . . But there be queer folk about. Saw such a one not an hour past, riding hard. And I 'erd there were trouble in Cvetko, as lies by the old mill. Thieves come out of the wood and killed the elderman and his sons."

"Brave you are, then," Arlequin said, "If there be bandits in the forest."

"Brave?" the man said, snorting. "Not I! But the Vargr's men hung half a dozen of the villains from the tree atop Tinker Hill yesterday morn, and my Lada will beat me royal if I don't 'turn from market with half a talent in me purse."

Arlequin chuckled. "Well, we be no villains, if you be afeard. Milos I am called, and Ziva here be my daughter."

"Dragos," the man said, patting his chest. "And this little one is Jalena."

Lara smiled at the girl, who hid her face behind her hands and peeked at her from between her fingers.

"Pardon my tongue, Master Milos," Dragos said, "But your daughter be even prettier than her mare. A fine horse, that."

"Aye, though it be not hers. Nor this one mine."

"Oh?"

"Both were the hostler's," Arlequin said, his face beginning to look appropriately haunted. "Won 'em in a game of Spoils some say, though more like it were from some wastrel what couldn't pay 'is bill. Either way they profited him not, for the Grand Prince's soldiers burned the crossroad inn afore letting the Calvos have it."

"Ah," Dragos sighed. "You come from the war then?"

"I had keep of the stables," Arlequin said, nodding, "Or I'd not be 'ere breathing. Took the horses and started riding soon as I caught sight of banners on the road. 'Twere not the first time they'd paid the crossroads a visit, and with my girl up and grown-"

"Ye need say no more," Dragos said, shaking his head. "And can't say as I'd 've done different, were it me own lass . . . But what brings ye 'ere? Must be many a league behind ye by now."

"I've a good-brother lives in Gorynych. Wed me sister ten summers past and took to prentice 'neath a cobbler. Might be he'll stake us a time, gods willing."

"Ye'll find your feet, have no doubt . . . But 'ere now, how be ye in the way of fare?"

"We've precious little," Arlequin said, and he was not lying, for their packsacks were considerably lighter than they had been a month earlier. "But 'twill be enough to last, if we spur harder."

"Save yer spurs," Dragos said, "And share the road with us a time. I've bread and cheese to spare for goodly folk."

"We couldn't-"

"Ye can," the man insisted. "Come, ride with us and I'll thank ye for it, for the day be waning, and I'd sleep easier the night with company about."

"Ziva," Arlequin said, turning about to face her. "Be ye hungry?"

"Yes, father," she replied, taking her cue.

"Then it seems we ride with you, Master Dragos," Arlequin said, tugging at his forelock in lieu of a hat.

* * * * * *

The skies were threatening rain again when they stopped just long enough for Dragos to relieve himself by the side of the road, whistling tunelessly as he did so. Lara felt a bit of the urge herself, but she could wait until there was at least a bush to hide behind.

"There be two riders behind us," Dragos said as he bent to pick up the rope tied to his dray. "Stopped like. 'Tis odd."

"You think they be brigands?" Arlequin asked.

"Can't rightly say," the peasant said, "But touch me if they don't have white locks, the pair of 'em."

Moder and Pinsard. She sighed with relief. *Must be.*

"Deserters could be," Arlequin said. "Or sellswords. I've heard Calvos can fetch a fair bit of glitter in Mandross, signing with one of the companies. But let's ride on. I'd be off the road afore it's dark."

Dragos didn't argue and, once he'd gotten his dray moving again, they went on. Lara began to count the byways they passed. Some were marked by fingerposts that pointed the way to Pilistak, or Lutyn, or a half dozen other places that Lara had never heard of. But then, she supposed that Dragos would merely scratch at his head if she told him she'd spent most of her life living near Perun. Even the name Irikosa might mean nothing to him, just as Gorynych had meant nothing to her the day before.

It was near one such post that they came upon a moly tree in full flower, its petals white as milk. In a hollow made by the tree's winding roots were three wooden statues, so worn and weathered that they only vaguely resembled women. A flat stone lay before them, strewn with melted candles.

Firebird, Lioness, and Maiden Green, or so the old rhyme went. *Daughter, Mother, and Heaven's Queen.*

Pierrot lay beside the shrine, his shabby boots propped atop a thick tuft as he strummed his lute. Closer to the road there crouched a pock-faced man in a filthy shirt. A sheathed knife dangled from his neck, and he had a leash wound about his wrist, at the end of which was a black she-goat. One of them had built a campfire.

"Good even to ye, Masters," Dragos said as his wagon rolled to a halt. "Tarry you here the night?"

"Aye," the man with the goat replied. "Though I speak not for him as sits yonder. He's not made sound all even, save on that humming-wood."

"Perhaps he's a half-wit," Arlequin muttered.

"Tsk!" Dragos clucked. "Don't either of ye know a servant of the Winter King by 'is sorrow song?"

"My pardons, Master," the man with the goat said, his face paling. "I meant no offense! I've no drams, but if ye've a cup I'll see it filled come morn."

Pierrot looked over the man's goat and nodded.

Dragos lifted a basket from his wagon and said, "I've nary a coin for ye either, Master, but I've bread 'ere for your song. Will that do?"

Again, Pierrot nodded. Dragos reached into the basket, tore a black loaf of bread in half, and offered it to him. The silent man took it with a nod, and then turned to Arlequin, expectant. Arlequin pursed his lips and pulled a copper from his belt.

"Here's a taste of what the Watcher fancies," Arlequin said, flipping the coin into Pierrot's outstretched palm. "Now sing us a song, if you can find your tongue."

Pierrot smiled crookedly and began to play, his lute seeming to weep as he coaxed the strains of Virago's Lament from it.

Dragos was true to his word and shared his supper with them. Lara felt nearly at ease as they ate around the little fire, though she started when Jalena let out a shriek at the sight of Bannertail slipping from her saddlebag to hunt. She also disliked the way that the man with the goat stared at her when he thought she wasn't looking.

Does he know? she wondered. *Has he seen my mother's face on a coin like that peddlar? Or does he just see a girl he'd like to lay with?*

The third time she caught him gawking she grew convinced that the latter was the case. She was, in fact, beginning to give very serious thought to flashing him the back of her fingers when the sound of a horse in full gallop drove the idea from her head.

The others heard it too, the men growing quite still. Pierrot ceased his finger work as Arlequin got to his feet and pulled his hand-axe from his belt. Its head was pitted with rust, but its edge looked keen enough.

"Get your bow," he said as the hoofbeats grew louder.

She sprinted to fetch her bow and was nocking one of Moder's arrows when a rider sped past their camp. He was bent so far forward that he almost seemed a part of the horse. She caught only a glimpse of him. There was blood on his face. Then he was gone.

"What was that-" Dragos began.

"Shush!" Arlequin said, cocking his head.

Another pair of riders tore past them, then a third. All three wore suits of blackened steel and had swords on their hips. Shields rode on their backs, marked with a golden emblem.

A skull, Lara thought. *A golden skull.*

The third rider slowed. Lara began to creep away from the firelight, her grip on Moder's bow tightening as she waited for him to turn about . . . But he rode on, the thunder of hooves fading until all she could hear was the fire crackling under the nickering of their own horses.

"You can come out, Ziva," Arlequin called out. "They're gone now."

Lara stepped into the firelight, her bow still nocked.

"Were those the Vargr's men?" she asked.

"Margrave's more like, girl," Dragos answered, "Hunting the rest of that lot from Cvetko. They'll snare him come morn, I wager."

"Cvetko?" the man with the goat said. "There be trouble there too?"

"How do you mean?" Dragos asked.

"A peddler came through my village two days past," the man with the goat said. "Said there'd been a family killed, lived a ways from Zosim. Wargs some thought, or a bear that 'ad the frenzy. But wargs and bears don't steal silver and plate, nor horses either."

"Men do," Lara said, glancing towards Dragos.

"Zosim is a long way from Cvetko," Dragos said. "Can't be the same ones as killed the elderman and his sons."

"The elderman of Cvetko?" the other man blanched. "Dead?"

"Thieves came out of the wood," Dragos said, putting his left arm about his daughter as he stared into the darkness beyond the firelight.

"We should put this out," Arlequin said, gesturing to the fire. "'Twill be no use to us if there be brigands near, and it marks us in the night."

"And how know I that you be not a brigand?" the man with the goat asked, staring at Arlequin's axe. "With your queer speech and fancy horses . . . Might be you stole those horses. Might be you'll slit our throats in the night with that knife when the fire's out-"

"My father's no brigand!" Lara snapped, her patience finally spent. "And if he was, he'd have put his axe through your skull and roasted up your goat for our supper by now. So, you can sleep elsewhere if you don't like our company. But call my father a brigand again and maybe I'll tell him the way you've been looking at me all night!"

Arlequin looked almost as astonished as the others by her outburst, but he recovered quickly.

"This true?" he said, fingering his axe. "You been sniffing after my daughter?"

"No!" The man threw up his hands. "No, Master, I-"

"She's a liar then, is she?"

"No! I mean, I gawped at her, tis true, but I meant no harm by it! I'll not do it again! The Watcher take me if I speak false!"

The man had hardly finished when he realized that he had made his oath before the feet of one of the Watcher's servants. Pierrot smiled at the man.

"Will that do, Ziva?" Arlequin asked.

"Yes," she said, "If he means what he says."

"I do!" the man pleaded. "By my oath, I'll not do it again!"

"See that you don't," Lara said. "Now help my father put out the fire!"

* * * * * * *

"Those riders," Lara said once the fire had turned to ash. "They were heading north. Do you think-"

"Fear not, Majesty," Arlequin whispered. "Lady Hirsent would not be foolish enough to camp within sight of the high road. I am certain she and her boy are as safe as can be."

"You shouldn't call him 'boy,'" she said, grinning. "He doesn't like it."

"As you wish, Majesty," Arlequin said, and took a swig from his canteen.

They were lying near the horses. Pierrot was keeping watch. Dragos and his daughter were sleeping beside their wagon. As for the pock-faced man, he was snoring under the moly, holding his goat close.

"I suppose," she said, rolling onto her side, "That was not very . . . Queenly. What I said to that man earlier, I mean."

"It is not for me to judge Her Majesty's manners," Arlequin said, "But, no. It wasn't."

"Moder taught me how to shoot a bird in flight," she said, cradling her hands behind her head. "What berries were safe to eat, what mushrooms to shun, how to start a fire without a flint and tinder . . . But she never taught me how to be a Queen."

"Perhaps not, Majesty," Arlequin said. "But you gave that rustic a fright *and* set him straight to work. That's half of it right there, fancy words or no."

"When we get to this town," she said, "Gorynych, how far will it be to the border then?"

"Majesty will be in Mandross the moment you ride through its gates," Arlequin answered. "Gorynych guards the pass through the mountains, you see. But we're hardly an invading army. There'll be a toll to pay, and questions no doubt, but we've more than enough silver to satisfy both."

"What about Moder, and Pinsard?"

"Lady Hirsent didn't give me *all* of the coin, Majesty," Arlequin chuckled. "Even if she had, the free companies have need of recruits from all corners. The Margrave's men won't turn two Calvarians away from the gates, mark me. But rest now, Majesty. It will be morning before long."

With that Arlequin let out a great yawn. Before long he was asleep.

Tomorrow we'll be in Mandross, she mused as she drifted off. *There are scholars in Mandross. Scholars reading dusty books. Books, mountains, and mercenaries. Mercenaries and scholars. Though Moder is already teaching me how to fight . . .*

Maybe a scholar could teach me how to speak like a Queen.

* * * * * * *

It was still dark when Pierrot roused her, a cup of goat's milk held out for her to take.

She thanked him hoarsely, drank it down and stretched. The others were already up and about. Arlequin was helping Dragos hitch his dray as Jalena was either chasing or being chased by Bannertail. The man with the goat was gone, walking the road to Gorynych, or so Lara hoped.

She returned Pierrot's cup and readied Mischief to ride. The mare's tail swished about as Lara undid the hobble round her legs.

I'm ready to be going too, she thought, hefting her saddle onto Mischief's back. By the time she was done securing it, the fox-squirrel was perched atop her packsack, licking at its paws.

"Nothing in there for you today," Lara said as she offered her hand. "Come on. Come up now."

The chimera sped up her arm and settled on her shoulder, its ears and tail erect.

Lara turned. Dragos' daughter was staring at her, her hands grasping at her woolen skirt.

"Do you like dolls?" Lara asked, kneeling to reach into her pack.

"Yes," Jalena said, rubbing the heel of her foot against her leg.

Lara found what she was looking for. The points of her foil crown were bent, and her dress was matted with Bannertail's fur.

"Her name's Brigitte," Lara said. "She's a princess. You can have her if you like."

Jalena looked at the doll, her lips parted, but did not move.

"It's alright," Lara said. "She'll like living with you. If she stays with me, she'll have to keep sleeping in this smelly sack and never meet a prince."

Jalena crept forward, took the doll, and pressed it to her chest. Then she ran back to her father.

"The wagon is hitched, Ziva!" Arlequin called as she regained her feet. "It's time we were off."

"Yes, father," she said, and took up Mischief's reins.

They walked the horses that morning, keeping pace with Dragos as the Firebird rose hazily in the east. Threads of mist hung over the countryside, shrouding village and wood alike. Thicker bands of fog clung to the mountains ahead. They were close enough that Lara could trace the outline of the pass as it zigzagged its way up to a jagged cleft. She guessed the greasy smudges rising from its base were the fires of Gorynych.

Dozens of footpaths met the high road, running through patchwork fields and farmer's cuts. There were folk on them. Most were on foot or leading carts like Dragos, but there were some riders. None were wearing armor, though.

Farmers. Just farmers like Dragos, going to market.

As the morning lengthened, a man cradling a wicker cage full of hens fell in behind them. Another with a brace of geese slung over his shoulders followed, a naked blade more rust than steel dangling from his belt. Then Dragos slowed, making way for half a dozen women carrying baskets laden with eggs and cheese coated with wax.

This last lot seemed to know each other. Lara listened as they gossiped about drunk husbands, foolish sons, and secret lovers (who were apparently not secretive enough.) And so, Lara came to know how briefly a local widow had worn her mourning gown, as well as how much she had paid for the brooch she wore over her heart.

"Ziva," Arlequin said to her, speaking softly in spite of the murmur. "Look up. But do it slowly."

Lara followed his gaze. There was a winged shape gliding high above them, far too large to be a hawk or a vulture. It was circling listlessly, buoyed by the wind.

She looked away, her hand fumbling for the clasp of her cloak.

"Keep your hood down!" Arlequin urged. "It might not be one of his, but even if it is, it will never spot us in this mob. Not if we don't stand out."

Lara let go of the clasp and tried to walk as casually as she could. Bannertail gave her cheek a lick and abandoned her shoulder for the packsack hanging from her saddle.

Over a hundred men and women were heading to market by now, the road widening as the high road gave way to a rutted stretch of mud and gravel. Gorynych was close, smaller than Irikosa but far more imposing. Timber houses seemed to cower beneath a citadel whose battlements ran across the mouth of the pass. Rush water cascaded from its culverts, draining into a silvery river that wound across the countryside. They would have to cross it soon, then make their way through the sea of canvas and canopy that lay before the gates.

Lara was trying to guess the height of the citadel when bells began to toll. There had been no bells on the farm, or in Perun, but still she knew their ringing.

Some memories, it seemed, died harder than others.

"Three bells," Dragos grumbled as the folk ahead of them slowed to a crawl. "And not yet to market."

"Some fool's axle's broke, I'll wager," one of the men behind them said, clearing his throat and spitting. "Or a horse's thrown its shoe."

"I think not," another said. "Look yonder, by The Jack and Spur."

Lara craned her neck, but all she could see was a thatch-roofed building standing by the side of the road. A boot hung over its red door, beneath which a woman sat, plucking the feathers from a duck.

Lara stole a glance upwards. The shrike was nowhere to be seen. Still, the road folk were beginning to murmur amongst themselves. There was worry in their words.

"What is it?" she asked. "What's wrong?"

"There be a bridge ahead," Dragos answered bitterly. "Just beyond that tavern. Margrave's men be stopping folk, maybe, afore letting them cross. There be no tolls on market day, but it will be my cursed luck if we come round that bend and find a warden waiting, 'is hand out for a drab."

"This the only bridge to Gorynych?" Arlequin asked.

"There be a ferry near Jagoda," Dragos said. "But that be leagues away. Best cross here and pay the Prince 'is due."

Arlequin grunted. Then he climbed onto Surefoot's back for a better look.

Lara was about to do the same when Pierrot coughed loudly into his fist. She turned to see Moder and Pinsard leading their horses not a hundred paces behind them. They were far taller than the Solothurnian peasants giving them a wide berth. If either of them noticed her peering back at them, they made no sign.

The shrike must have seen them. It must have! But where is it?

Lara searched the skies, but there was nothing to see. Not even a sparrow. They rounded the corner of the tavern.

Wulf, where is it?! We shouldn't have come this way. We should have swum the river on a moonless night, or worn a fetch's skin like Zosia at the Stair of Grief-

A horrid shriek pierced the air.

In the yard beside the tavern there were four men hanging from a gibbet of newly cut wood. The shrike was perched above them.

It was far larger than the one Moder had shot down and stood quite straight on its scaly legs. Its blue-black wings shone like a polished boot. Ivory teardrops spotted its neck and breast. It had a man's face, long and hollow-cheeked, but its lips were as dark as its pupilless eyes.

It glared at them, fresh blood dripping from its chin. Lara's heart began to race.

The shrike was not alone. A score of soldiers were standing before the gibbet, soldiers in blackened mail with brass filigree. Their shield-like besagues were embossed with jawless golden skulls. So was the barding of their hitched steeds, all six of which were proper warhorses like Whisper.

One of them tilted their helmet to scratch at an itch. Her face was scarred, hard-set, and her hair was going to gray. Another, leaning on a bow-like contraption that was nearly as tall as herself, yawned.

Women, Lara realized. *They're all women.*

A parchment had been nailed to a post by the side the road.

A REWARD, it proclaimed in bold red letters, *For the safe return of The Princess Larissa to the Royal City of Carduel, His Excellency the Marquis Reynard, Baron of Maleperduys and Lord Protector of Arcasia, offers the sum of six million gold sovereigns, and a promise of amnesty to any and all enemies of the realm. For intelligence regarding her whereabouts, or for aid in her capture, further rewards shall be honored according to their merit.*

Signed,

Tiecelin, Baron of Moulinsart, Warden of the Muraille
LONG LIVE ARCASIA

For the benefit of those who could not read, there was a woodcut of a young woman with long dark hair hovering above an impressive string of numerals. It was not a perfect resemblance, but it was close enough.

Arlequin leaned over and said, very quietly, "When I say ride, you ride. Don't look back."

Lara nodded, doing her best to keep between Mischief and Pierrot's shaggy hobby, dreading every step and painfully aware that Dragos was walking his dray directly behind her.

He's a good man, she told herself. *He thinks I'm a stable hand's daughter. He wouldn't say anything.*

She looked back. Dragos was studying the post, a curious expression on his face.

He might be a good man . . . But he's also a poor one with a family to feed. Don't fool yourself.

She took a deep breath and walked on.

Another dozen soldiers were keeping watch over the approach to the bridge. The locals were clearly too cowed to object. Lara watched as a girl carrying a basket of eggs was led from the throng and prodded towards a figure sitting atop a dark-maned bay.

"Too young," Lara heard the rider say, "Let her go."

The girl hurried back to the crowd, not slowing to retrieve the eggs that tumbled from her basket as she ran. As the rider turned to gaze down the line, Lara could see why. She was wearing a helmet of steel and brass whose visor was shaped like a skull. Were it not for the light of day, she might have taken her for the specter of some long dead chevalier, haunting a lonely road or crumbling ruin.

"What do they want of us?" a woman whispered. "Where be the Margrave's men?"

"Shut it," a man hissed back.

The shrike screeched again, the crowd gasping as it flew from its perch. It landed on the roof of the tavern, its claws digging into the thatch.

"Something's got Briser in a fit," one of the soldiers said, glancing at the chimera.

"Best take a closer look at this lot then," the scar-faced woman said, tugging her helmet back into place as she approached. "One of these lasses might just be a princess. You a princess, girl?"

For a moment Lara thought the woman had singled her out, but it was Jalena she was speaking to. The girl was shivering against one of the hay bales, holding Brigitte close.

"A shy little princess it seems," scar-face said.

"Princess," Jalena squeaked, raising her doll.

The soldier frowned.

"That's a fine-looking dolly for a peasant girl," she said. "Where'd you get it?"

"'Twas her Gran's," Dragos said.

"This your daughter?"

"My Jalena," Dragos answered. "Yes."

Mail clanked and shifted. Lara kept her eyes on her feet, but she could tell that the scarred woman was staring at her.

"And this one? She your daughter too?"

Dragos cleared his throat. "Ah-"

"She's mine," Arlequin said. "Why? You lot looking for recruits?"

"Could be," the woman chuckled darkly. "If she's any good with that bow. You there! Girl. Turn round now so I can see your face."

Lara began to turn, wondering how quickly she could mount Mischief without breaking her neck when the shrike leapt from the roof. It lit on the porch of the Jack and Spur, sending the woman with the duck scurrying, and cawed at a pair of pale-haired figures leading their horses off the road.

"Here now!" the scarred woman shouted, gripping the hilt of her sword. "You two! Get back in line!"

The other soldiers were reaching for weapons as well, the one with the enormous crossbow working its winch. But Moder and Pinsard did not slow.

"Halt I say!" the woman snarled, drawing steel. "Halt where you stand or die!"

"Majesty," Arlequin said, very hoarse.

"I know," Lara breathed, and then she barreled into the soldier with all her strength behind her.

To Lara it felt like running shoulder first into a stone wall, but the scarred woman had not been expecting it. She lurched forward, stumbling over an old wagon rut. Pierrot kicked her in the shoulder before she could regain her balance, sending her face first into the mud.

The shrike screamed. So did Mischief, threatening to rear as Lara swung into her saddle. The soldiers stared, dumbfounded, and that was all the time she needed.

"This way!" Arlequin cried as he brought Surefoot about, the horse springing over the tussock that grew beside the road. Mischief needed little urging to follow. The crowd wailed as it began to scatter.

Then they were tearing across a field, putting river and soldiers both at their back.

"It's *her*, you fools!" someone was barking over the din. "To horse! With me, with me!"

Arlequin cut left, swerving around a briar hedge. Mischief leapt right over it and kept galloping. There was an orchard ahead of them, its trees covered with pink blossoms.

From the corner of her eye Lara could see Pinsard's dark cape billowing as his rouncey picked up speed. Moder was right behind him. She was shouting something, pointing upwards, but Lara couldn't make out her words.

"SHRIKE!" she heard at last.

She ducked forward, yelping as the thing's talons caught hold of her cloak. The clasp bit into her neck, then snapped. The chimera screeched as it swooped about for another pass, its black eyes glittering.

"KILL IT!" Moder hollered, closer now. "KILL IT!!!"

Lara had bow hunted long before she'd been given a sword, and she'd brought down many a bird. But she'd never done it while riding on a horse.

She dropped her reins and caught hold of the bow just as the shrike began its descent. This time it was Mischief who dodged, veering sharply as the chimera swept past them. Feathers lashed Lara's face, the reek lingering in her nostrils despite the wind.

Lara freed the bow, her hands sweaty as she fumbled at her quiver. She could hear the thunder of hooves gaining on her. *Arlequin? Moder?* It didn't matter. She plucked an arrow, nocked the bow, and turned about to fire.

Pinsard was hot on her heels. Moder and the others were not far behind- But so were the soldiers. Half a dozen of them, urging on their chargers. Their captain was leading them, her skull-helm gleaming.

The shrike was banking. She drew, waited for the chimera to level out, and let fly.

Her shaft soared over the shrike's right shoulder, the arrowhead missing its neck by a hair's breadth. She cursed her aim, but then the thing beat its wings and began to climb. It listed off, giving up the chase.

No! It's flying back to its master!

She was reaching for another arrow when Pinsard shouted, "Look out!"

Something whipped across her back harder than any switch. She spun about, nearly taking another branch to the face as she realized that they were riding through the orchard.

She bent over the saddle, grabbing the reins. They weaved through a sea of pink, flying from the row as trees gave way to meadow. Wicker beehives stood amidst lavender and oxeye. Beyond there was a farmstead, its great house overlooking the river, and a country lane running through a dark wood.

We'll lose them in there. We have to.

"This way!" she hollered, praying that Pinsard could hear her as she urged Mischief on. Figures wearing long-sleeved gowns and woven masks were scattering before them. They kept the bees, she supposed.

She was closing on the wood when two riders in black armor erupted from the trees.

Impossible! she thought as both riders bore down on them. *No horse is that fast! Unless-*

Her heart sank. She had got turned round in the orchard and was riding back towards the river crossing!

"Bloody Wulf!" she swore, tugging hard on Mischief's reins.

The mare neighed wildly and began to turn about. She nearly collided with Pinsard's rouncey but quickly regained her stride.

As they turned Lara saw Moder making straight for the riders, her sword unsheathed. Then she and Pinsard were driving towards the river. A beekeeper dove out of their way, toppling one of the hives. Soon the air was thick with enraged bees, and the unmistakable sound of steel meeting steel.

Have to help! Have to do something, anything-

Suddenly, Mischief let out a high-pitched squeal and lost her footing.

The world turned upside down for a moment. Then Lara was flat on her back, gasping for breath. She didn't remember dropping Moder's bow, but it wasn't in her hands anymore. Mischief lay on her side nearby, her tail lashing wildly.

It had not been a bee that had stung her, but a crossbow bolt. Its head was buried in her left haunch.

"Lara!" Pinsard cried as he leapt from his rouncey.

Steel clashed over swarming insects and pounding hooves. Somewhere close a woman was screaming.

Then Arlequin was at her side, helping her to stand.

"Get-" Lara said, finding her voice, "Get back on your horse!"

"I'll hold them, Majesty!" he said, guiding her towards Surefoot. "You-"

Arlequin's hand went to his axe. Pinsard drew his sword.

"Don't move!" a voice rang out. It belonged to the soldier with the mechanical bow. She had dismounted to reload, and was circling about the fallen hive, her weapon trained.

Another three were approaching from the river, their captain riding at a trot behind them. One was prodding Pierrot along with the butt of her pike. The silent man shot Lara a sheepish look.

"My horse," Lara addressed the marksman, thinking of the sword wrapped up in her bedroll. "Please, she's hurt. Won't you let me see to her?"

"I said *don't move*." The woman squinted down the length of her bow. "Now stay put, or I'll put a bolt right through her eye!"

Lara froze. So did the others.

"Daulnoy!" the captain called out, bringing her steed to a halt. "Put down that bow!"

"Captain?" the marksman said, her bow wavering.

"That's the Princess you're aiming at!" The captain's helm made her voice sound hollow. "The *real* one! Baroness will have both our heads when she finds out you skewered Lord Reynard's prize! Now *lower* your weapon!"

Daulnoy lowered her bow.

His prize.

Lara shuddered. But a thought came to her then that she hadn't considered before.

They'll kill the others without a second thought . . . But they can't risk hurting me.

"Well, well," the captain clucked, "Aren't you as lovely as all the placards? Lovelier even. The She-Wolf did well to hide you under a rock. Now why don't you tell your watch dogs to drop their weapons and-"

"My horse," Lara said again, turning her back as she went to Mischief. "She's hurt."

Lara wished she could do something to ease the mare's suffering. She had crushed both quiver and arrows under her bulk, but not her packsack. Bannertail's head was poking from its flap, the chimera's long ears flat against the back of its head.

"Shhh," she hushed, and began to undo her bedroll. The fox-squirrel squeezed from her pack and danced around her feet, squalling.

"Captain, she'll bolt!"

"On that lame nag? Not likely."

Lara's palm brushed against the hilt of her blade. She tugged it free and whirled back about.

"Let Pierrot go," Lara said, leveling her blade. "Now!"

"Or what?" the captain asked, her head tilting. "You'll kill us?"

"If we have to," Lara replied.

The woman chuckled. A hollow sound.

"But we mean you no harm, Highness. Quite the opposite. Why, there's a throne in Carduel just waiting for you to sit on it. If you'd simply let us escort you-"

"Don't listen to this lickspittle, Majesty," Arlequin rumbled. "She's nothing more than one of the usurper's killers!"

"And who should she listen to?" the captain sneered. "You? Remind me who you were again- her father's boot warmer?"

"He's *my* groom," Lara said, stepping between Arlequin and the soldier with the bow. "And I'm certainly not going anywhere with you!"

"I see," the captain said, her tone hardening. "Tell me, Princess. Is it my helmet that frightens you?"

"No," Lara spat.

"You're a bad liar," the captain said, lifting the helm from her head.

Her face might have been beautiful once. Her lips were full, and her eyes were dark and lively. But she had no nose. In its place a red hole gaped, slit by a sliver of bone.

Lara could not help but take a step backwards.

"Better, yes?" the woman smirked as she slid from her saddle. On her feet, she wasn't much taller than Lara. "I only wear it to scare the troops."

Lara couldn't find her tongue.

"I thought as much. But then, they say you shouldn't judge a coin by its face. Even one pretty as mine. So, I tell you again: My mistress, the

Baroness of Thelema, has care only for your safety. As does the Lord Protector. As do I."

"Reynard is a liar, Hartnet," a voice called out, "And so are you."

Moder was striding across the meadow, her sword dark with blood. Lara saw several riderless horses wandering the far side of the meadow.

"She-Wolf," the captain said, turning to face her. "So. You remember me."

"I remember you," Moder said, coming to a halt. "I also am remembering that my *ceorl* killed the men who had dishonored you."

"Pity he wasn't quicker," the captain said, tapping the socket where her nose should have been. "But I suppose I'd consider repaying the favor. After all, Lord Reynard cares nothing for you or your pup. Give us the girl and we'll forget we ever saw you."

"You will have to kill me first," Pinsard growled.

"And me," Arlequin added.

The captain redonned her helm.

"The Pincher's grown, I see," she chuckled. "Not a man yet though, is he?"

"He is his *faeder's* son," Moder said. "And mine."

"You've grown too, She-Wolf." The helmet did her grinning for her. "Grown *old.*"

Moder sprang forward, her bloodied blade lashing like the tail of a scorpion. The solider with the bow had barely raised her weapon when Moder's sword sliced through her throat, severing the strap of her helm. The bow fell as her mailed hands went to her throat. Her legs buckled. She fell.

Lara knew how fast Moder was, knew she would do anything to protect them . . . But she had never seen her like this.

Moder flicked her sword arm, splattering the ground with blood. The captain growled deep in her throat and drove towards Moder, her sword flying from its sheath.

Moder sidestepped her lunge and landed a blow against her back, steel ringing as the blade glanced off mail.

"Take the Princess!" the captain bellowed, her sword whirling as she parried Moder's follow up. "Kill the others!"

One of the soldiers shoved Pierrot aside and leveled her pike. The other two advanced, swords poised to cut Arlequin and Pinsard down.

All for the sake of capturing me.

"Stay back, Majesty!" Arlequin urged.

"No!" Lara shouted, shrugging off his hand and making for the nearest soldier. Their swords met, the woman's eyes widening as she began to backpedal.

"If it's a fight you want," Lara said, gritting her teeth as her blade caromed off the woman's pauldron, "Then fight me!"

The woman gave ground, her alarm growing when Lara did not relent. At last, she swung back. The cut was half-hearted. Easy to deflect.

Lara's riposte slashed open the soldier's cheek. It was not a deep cut, but blood began to well from it.

Lara almost froze. She had never given Pinsard anything more serious than a decent bruising, and had never managed to so much as wind Moder . . . But this was not a training session. The soldier swung back, quicker and with more force behind her swing. Lara parried, riposted again, the edge of her blade screeching as it glanced across the woman's breastplate.

"You're lucky the Protector wants you alive, girl," the woman panted over the droning of the bees. "Now, come 'ere!"

The solider bulled forward, her mailed fist catching hold of Lara's sleeve. Linen ripped as Lara spun away. She caught a glimpse of Pinsard smashing aside a pike, Moder and the captain locking blades.

Have to focus.

"C'mere!" the soldier snarled, swinging her blade so hard that Lara felt the impact of it race up her sword arm.

She's angry. Distracted.

Lara riposted, stabbing, not caring that her sword couldn't cut through steel. The soldier gave ground, her guard raised. Her armor made her slow. Lara quickened her strikes, thrusting forward, driving the point of her sword towards the soldier's bleeding face. The woman thrust the blow aside with her gauntlet, stepped back-

The soldier's boots trampled the wicker hive before she lost her footing entirely, landing heavily as the bees erupted about her. The mail that kept her safe from Lara's blade could not save her from the swarm.

Soon she was covered with them. She began to scream.

Lara turned and ran.

The fight was nearly over. One soldier lay face down in the wildflowers, her helmet lost. Another was trading blows with Pinsard. Arlequin was on his knees. His axe was hanging loose by his side, the sleeve of his jack wet with blood.

"Surrender!" Lara cried, sprinting to join Pinsard.

"She will," Moder's voice rang out.

Lara turned. The captain was crawling towards them, steadying herself with one hand as the other pawed at her helm. Moder followed, her sword poised for a killing strike.

"Help me," the captain rasped.

She collapsed. Moder lowered her blade. The soldier threw down her sword.

"Your dagger," Lara said, trying to ignore the cries, the blood, the dead.

The woman undid her belt, letting it slide to the ground as she raised her hands.

"Are you hurt?" Pinsard asked, his eyes trained on the soldier.

"No," she replied, "Are you?"

Sweat was running down his brow. His hair was wild. But the blood on his sword was not his own.

"I'm alright," he said, catching his breath. "But Arlequin, his arm-"

"A scratch, Majesty," Arlequin said. "Pay it no mind."

He dropped his axe and clutched at his arm, hissing through his teeth.

"Stop that," Moder said as she strode towards them, wiping the blood from her blade with an oiled cloth. "Needs cleaning. Sewing. Not dirt."

Moder gave her blade a final wipe, sheathed it, and made a tourniquet from the man's belt.

"What should we do with this one?" Pinsard asked, nodding towards the soldier.

Moder stared at the woman, her face hard.

"Let her go to her *Heafodcarl*," she said. "She is dying, I think."

Moder stepped aside. Pinsard lowered his blade.

"Your praises," the soldier muttered, rushing to her captain's side. The words she spoke were too faint to catch.

"We must go," Moder said. "More soldiers will be coming."

"Where's Pierrot?" Lara asked.

The silent man stood up. He'd been crouching amidst a patch of lavender with Bannertail in his hands. The fox-squirrel let out a yip.

"Mischief!" Lara started. The mare was still lying on her side, suffering. "Will she be alright?"

"She may, Majesty," Arlequin said. "But-"

"But?"

"Majesty, I fear we must leave her."

"Leave her?" Lara balked. "But we can't! Not like this! Not alone!"

"She cannot run with that wound, Majesty," Arlequin said, softly. "But she's still a fine horse. Any fool could see that. She won't die here."

"You can't know that!"

"Lara," Moder said. "There is no time. We must run. Run, or face Reynard."

A ragged laugh cut Moder short. It belonged to the captain. She lay in the arms of her underling, her visor raised. Her teeth were red with blood.

"You'll never run far enough!" she wheezed. "Never! He'll find you, She-Wolf. He knew you were in Solothurn. He knew you'd try to cross the mountains. He knows . . . You think The Baroness' bloody girls were the only ones he set to watch the passes? They'll be be coming for you now. You, your whelp, the little Princess. They'll be coming. All of them."

The captain began to cough up blood, and yet she managed to choke out another laugh. She was still laughing as they rode away. Lara rode Surefoot, tears in her eyes. Arlequin took the captain's dark-maned bay. They rode hard, far from the high road, and did not stop until long after dark.

When Lara closed her eyes that night, she could still hear her laughing.

VI

There was smoke on the plain below. From the ridge crest it looked like drifting fog. Beneath it a patchwork of colors roiled, ebbing and flowing like paint spilled into a stream.

"What is that?" Lara asked, shielding her eyes from the sun.

"A battle," Pinsard said.

A crimson wedge rolled out of the fog and drove itself into a black mass. The mass bent, broke, began to scatter. There was a flash, and something like a thunderclap echoed off the rocks.

"Who is winning?" Lara asked.

"Reynard," Moder said.

Moder led Demon over the next rise. Pinsard lingered a while. Then he too followed.

They had kept to the foothills for two days, not daring to slow but wary of straying too far from the trees that grew on the heights. Lara had lost count of how many shrikes she had seen that morning, let alone the vast flock that now wheeled above the battle, waiting to feed.

"Reynard," Lara said, "The usurper. He is here?"

"Aye, Majesty," Arlequin answered. "Him, and all the traitors that serve him."

"How can you be certain?" Lara said, squinting. "It's so far away."

"Would that I might lend Your Majesty a spyglass," Arlequin said, stroking his moustache. "But I've served long enough to know the colors of many a lord, even from a distance. Can you see there, Majesty? The dark pennons?"

Lara nodded.

"Those belong to Koschei the Deathless and his Vargr." Arlequin scowled. "The Grand Prince will no doubt regret the insult he paid the usurper's emissary, before this day is through."

"A winged monster you called her," Lara said. "Is she a shrike?"

"So they say, Majesty. One that is almost human. And yet still a creature, like the one we saw at the crossing. They are all of them foul things, bred to serve as his eyes and ears."

He spat into the grass.

"But at least the chimera that do the usurper's bidding do not know right from wrong. For there, Majesty, on that far hill. Do you see?"

Lara followed his finger, but all she could see were dark red lines mixed with splashes of gold and ivory.

"What is it?"

"The ram of Tarsus and the owl of Osca," he growled. "Flying under the bloody fox of the usurper. Hydra's Teeth, have they no honor?"

He fumbled for his canteen, the dressing on his arm giving him some difficulty as he took a swig.

Lara shot him a look.

"Pardon, Majesty," he said. "'Tis bad enough that cutthroats and mercenaries flock to his banners, but to see such lords fighting for his cause . . . Well, Majesty, it saps my spirits."

A jest sprang to mind, but she held her tongue. It felt wrong to mock a man who would lay down his life for her. Even if he was overly fond of his drink.

Wind swept the hillside, the horses spooking as the tall grass rustled. With it came a whiff of something that made Lara's eyes water. She could almost taste it on her tongue: Bitter, yet rancid, like eggs that had spoiled, and a reek worse than the sheep pens in high summer.

Is this what war smells like? she wondered, stroking Surefoot's neck. She tried to imagine what it was like on the plain, pressed together amidst smoke and blood, and found she could not look at it any longer.

"We should go," she said. "Before we fall too far behind."

"Yes, Majesty," Arlequin said.

By the time they caught up with Pinsard there was a hillside behind them. The rumble of foul engines spitting death grew so faint that Lara could hardly hear them above the jingling of the horses' bridles.

But something still nagged at her.

"Arlequin," she said, "Are there no *loyal* lords left in Arcasia? He can't have killed them all. Can he?"

"No, Majesty," Arlequin replied, his eyes on the footing ahead of them. "There are many in Arcasia loyal to your cause. And you have allies across the sea, powerful ones, who'd see you restored to your rightful throne."

"Well, where are they then, these *allies*?" she asked. "Why haven't they overthrown the usurper and come to find me, if they're so powerful?"

Arlequin didn't answer at first, his silence as deep as Pierrot's as he led the bay around a moss-covered rock.

"They are afraid, Majesty," he said at last.

"Tsch," Pinsard clucked. "They are cowards then."

"I would agree with you were it so simple," Arlequin replied. "I would spend my own life gladly if it meant putting a blade through the usurper's heart. But I am a man without. I have no children, and my Columbine . . . Well, she dances midst the stars, if there's any justice left in the world."

"She was your wife?" Pinsard asked.

"Something like that," Arlequin replied.

"I am sorry. I did not know."

Arlequin closed his eyes and sighed heavily.

"In that matter at least the great lords of Arcasia cannot match my luxury, for the usurper holds their children hostage at Carduel. All who would defy him face a heavy risk."

Lara used to shudder at the tales of Carduel, where Elissa and Tantilis dined on sweetmeats as they watched men burn, and the shades of Calidor and his brothers scratched and shuffled behind the walls . . . But those were just stories, old long before Danica had been a girl. She had never thought of it as being a real place, a place she would surely be taken if she fell into Reynard's hands.

"I heard Moder and Danica talking," Lara said, trying to remember their words. "Danica said there'd been a rebellion. Something about a 'false Larissa,' and a girl who was beheaded. Lyndemere, I think her name was."

"When was this?" Pinsard asked. "You never told me this."

"I have my secrets too," Lara snipped. "Was she the daughter of a great lord, Arlequin?"

"No, Majesty," Arlequin said. "She was naught but a peasant girl, and the third pretender now to wear your name. The first was your own royal cousin, Lettice of Lorn. Poor girls, the lot of them."

"Why would she pretend to be me?" Lara asked. "Did she wish to be Queen so badly?"

"I doubt she wanted anything of the sort, Majesty," Arlequin said, shaking his head. "But her father, the Count Firapel, believed you to be dead, and sought to put her on the throne in your stead, reasoning that the usurper would not dare harm his daughter. Especially if the common folk believed her to be their Queen, kept a prisoner in her own palace."

"He was wrong," Pinsard said.

Arlequin nodded, grimly.

"When the Count called for his vassals to march on Calyx, the usurper had Lettice beheaded, and put her head on a spike for all to see. So, when the time for battle came, all but the Baron of Landuc deserted. So died Firapel, Lord Simeon his heir, Esclados the Red, and many more besides. Few have doubted the usurper's cruelty since."

"Awirung," Pinsard swore, and quickened his step.

Lara could not tell if he was angry, scared, or simply tired. He'd been quiet since their fight with the soldiers, and moodier than ever.

Whatever the case, he'd clearly heard enough.

"And yet," Lara said, when Pinsard had gained some distance, "She- My cousin, Lettice- She *wasn't* the last?"

"No, Majesty" Arlequin sighed. "As long as the throne sits empty there will always be pretenders. Pretenders and the ones who'd rise alongside them. After all, who was the usurper before happenstance lifted him from the gutter? A common thief! A no one. A wretch, stealing from his betters."

"He hardly seems common," Lara said.

"Perhaps, Majesty," Arlequin said. "But the songs, even those that would praise him, all tell the same tale: 'Reynard the Fox, sprung from nothing, the Anthill rat who bested a lion.' Feh."

"They sing songs about him?" Lara asked, incredulous. "Like the ones about Clever Jacques or Wandering Tomas?"

"The Wanderer more like, Majesty," Arlequin said, shaking his head. "But yes. Reynard's a monster, dyed in the wool. A killer of men, women, and children. But the common folk . . . Well, they all love a rogue, the fools."

* * * * * * *

It was Pierrot who found a place to rest that night: A rocky shelf overlooking a piney gulch. They didn't bother to make camp. They'd ditched all but one of the tents, fire would attract attention, and besides, there wasn't anything to cook. The soldiers had stocked their saddlebags with salted venison, hardtack, and little bricks of tobacco. There were a few bits of cheese, bread that was as tough on the teeth as the tack, a grease-stained deck of playing cards, and little else. Moder had her bow, but she only had a handful of arrows, and those she was saving for the shrikes.

"We'll starve in these hills," Lara said after they'd eaten, Bannertail snoozing in the cradle of her lap. "Won't we?"

"We'll manage, Majesty," Arlequin said. "You'll see."

"No," Moder said. "Lara is right. Is death for all if we stay here. Death, or worse."

"But where can we go?" Pinsard asked. "Not South."

"Border is being watched," Moder agreed, shaking her head. "Guarded everywhere. Was stupid to try."

"Don't say that," Lara said. "We couldn't have known-"

"Reynard knew," she said. "Now, he knows he was right. Was stupid."

"Still have some decent coin," Arlequin said, shuffling his feet. "Might be enough to buy us passage, if we can make it to the coast."

"Between us and sea," Moder said, "Is Reynard, Grand Prince, and Calvarian army."

She did not need to elaborate.

"Why don't we go west?" Lara asked.

"West?" Pinsard balked, "Are you serious?"

"I am," Lara said, ignoring his stare. "Arlequin, these allies across the sea, who are they? Do you really think they'd help us?"

"Well, yes, Majesty," Arlequin said. "The Princes of Frisia certainly have no love for the usurper. They openly defy him by sheltering the heirs of Lorn and Engadlin on their shores, but-"

"And the Calvarians, they aren't blocking the ports in Arcasia?"

"No, Majesty, but-"

"Then why don't we go there?" she asked. "Reynard is here, in Solothurn, you said so yourself. Isn't Arcasia the last place he'd think we'd run to? If we could slip around his army and cross the border, we could make straight for the sea!"

"They do say that the Muraille has more holes in it than a sieve, Majesty," Arlequin mused, "And I'll follow wherever you are bound . . . But the usurper's spies and soldiers would be everywhere. If they caught us-"

"We'll fight them," Pinsard said, straightening somewhat. "And this time we will be ready for them."

Arlequin snorted at that, but quieted when he saw the look in the younger man's eyes.

"That's three," Lara said, looking to Pierrot, her brows raised.

The silent man shrugged nonchalantly and went on folding playing cards into fanciful shapes.

That left only one of them.

Moder had been listening, silent, her left thumb worrying the back of her closed right fist.

"You think it's too dangerous, don't you?" Lara asked. "Or stupid. Or both."

"What is not being dangerous now?" Moder said, shrugging herself. "But plan . . . Plan is not stupid, Lara. Is clever. Is being dangerous- very dangerous, yes- but clever. And that is real problem."

"Why?"

"Because it means Reynard has also been thinking of it. Long before we are sitting here. If we go west, we may be sneaking past soldiers and shrikes and spies and be thinking we are clever. Until it is too late, and snare is round our throats. Reynard is called Fox for reason, and we are hare."

Whatever shred of hope Lara had mustered fled from them then. She could see it in their faces. Arlequin reached for his canteen. Pinsard scooped up a loose stone and sent it clattering across the shelf. The fox-squirrel stirred at the noise and cracked open its honey brown eyes.

"So," Lara said. "It's pointless then."

"Is it?" Moder said, her lips thinning.

"We can't go south," Lara said, spreading out her hands. "We can't go north, and we can't go west. The only way we can go is east, all the way back to Perun where we started from."

"And what is east of Perun?" Moder asked.

"The farm," Lara answered.

"And beyond farm?"

Lara blinked. There wasn't anything east of the farm. Nothing but woods, and the little glade where she and Pinsard sparred with Moder.

"Forest?" she offered.

"Nothing *but* forest for leagues," Arlequin nodded. "There might be some trapper camps south of Leshny, but beyond that . . ."

His eyes widened.

"No," he said. "You can't mean-"

"Reynard is clever," Moder said as she met his gaze. "And without relent. Men, mountains, tricks- These things will not stop him. But there *is* a place that even he may be fearing to follow us into. And there we must go."

Lara had only ever seen one map, and that was in the book that Pinsard carried in his packsack. On it, Solothurn and the islands of Frisia were still marked as provinces of old Aquilia. Calvaria was called Skollmania, Glycon was Helia, and the city of Kerys had yet to be swallowed by the waves . . . But east of Solothurn and the mountains of Mandross, no landmarks or rivers were charted. Just a drawing of a cockrel-headed dragon and a simple warning: 'HERE BE CHIMERA.'

"Vulp Vora," Lara gasped. "You want us to go to Vulp Vora."

"I am not wanting to," Moder said, "But if we are ever escaping from Reynard, then I am seeing no other way."

"And then what?" Arlequin sputtered. "March Her Majesty across the Plain of Glass? Assuming of course that we aren't all eaten, or- or gods know what else!"

"Let her talk!" Lara said.

Arlequin shut his mouth at once, though Lara could see the corners of his jaw working.

"When I and-" Moder wet her lips. "When *we* were in Calyx, many years ago, there was being a Glyconese. A messenger from the high priestess who is calling herself 'Dragon.'"

"Remember him," Arlequin muttered. "Had a blue-coated Nisian, and those glass-eyed bodyguards."

"That one, yes," Moder said. "High priestess of Glycon was angry. Wanted to frighten Queen. Wanted her to stop pirates off of coast. Pirates from Frisia."

She locked eyes with Arlequin.

"And Frisia is where allies of Lara are, yes?"

"Hirsent," Arlequin pleaded. "This is madness. There'll be no food, and the water there is poison!"

"There must be some," Moder said. "Or chimera would not live there."

"The horses will be useless in the jungle."

"We will free horses. Go on foot."

"We'll be torn apart by chimera, mutants, monsters-"

"Not if we kill them first," Pinsard said.

"If we must," Moder added.

"If we must," Pinsard repeated.

"Good," Moder said, and gave his leg a pat.

Arlequin turned to Pierrot and barked, "Say something, curse you!"

Pierrot pursed his lips and spread out his palm. On it was a playing card. He had folded it into a ship with two triangular sails.

"Majesty," Arlequin said, getting to his knees. "I beg you, please! The stories they tell of that place- They are horrible, horrible! At least with the usurper's soldiers, we stand a chance. But, to go to Vulp Vora! Well, we'd have to be-"

"Mad," Lara said. "Reckless. Desperate."

"Oh, thank the gods," Arlequin breathed, kissing his thumb and pressing it to his brow. "I knew Your Majesty would see reason."

Lara nodded, absently. Even Danica, a servant of the Watcher and a warg of sorts herself, never spoke too freely of the place. Her tales were dreadful things, certainly, but they were still about people, and the world of men. Tales seldom came out of Vulp Vora. Monsters did. Everyone knew that.

"It's not a very clever plan," Lara said to Moder.

"No," Moder said, itching the nape of her neck. "It is a terrible plan. Very terrible."

"And that's why we must do it," Lara said.

* * * * * * *

The village was bigger than Perun, but only just. Thatch-roofed cottages with sheltered gardens were bunched about a crossroad. A smithy shared its yard with what was either a brewery or a cooperage judging by the number of barrels piled beside it. There was a two-story inn beside the bridge that forded the river.

It all looked rather ordinary. Dull even. The meadow where they crouched behind a fallen tree was rocky and patched- Hardly good farmland. Were it not for the bridge, Lara doubted there would be anything here but weeds.

But something was wrong.

"The women aren't moving," Lara whispered, squinting to make certain, "Only the men."

Three men were working the forge, hammers ringing. A dozen others sat before the inn, laughing over their drinks. Two more were fishing off of the bridge . . . But all the women were still. One sat with the drinkers, a girl in periwinkle, her cup untouched. Another leaned against a chicken coop, a dead hen in her lap. She wasn't plucking it.

Moder shifted, her eyes narrowing. She had brought her bow and three of their remaining arrows- But there weren't any shrikes about.

At least, none they could see.

"Women are dead," Moder whispered. "Is ambush. Those are Tybalt's men."

One of the men lifted the girl from her seat and (*Don't look! Don't look!*) began to twirl her about. The others kept time.

"Tybalt?" Lara managed.

"He was," Moder said, "Being most cruel of Reynard's servants. Always. Even before . . ."

"Before what?" Lara asked.

"He killed your brother," Moder said. "And *lufiend* of Arlequin. And many others Reynard wanted dead. Tybalt was cutting out tongue of Pierrot. Killing is game to him. His men- *those men*- are the same."

"Tybalt," Pinsard said, blinking against the sun. "But, if his men are here, then-"

"Yes. He must be here also."

Lara turned her head, glancing at the hedgerow behind them. Arlequin and Pierrot were there, keeping watch over the horses. She wondered what they'd do when they learned who was waiting in the village beyond.

"I do not see any horses," Pinsard said. "Not even a mule. But they must have them."

"Where?" Moder asked.

Pinsard considered.

"That warehouse," he offered. "Horses inside instead of barrels."

"Warehouse," Moder nodded. "Or old barn, there, on other side of river. More men too, hidden. Many more."

"Then what do we do?" Lara asked. "We have to cross."

"We wait," Moder said.

Lara swallowed. That very morning over two dozen soldiers with scarlet sashes across their breasts had ridden past them at a clip. One had been carrying a gray banner with a fox on it, its head turned as if searching for threat or prey. Had they not been in such a hurry, they might have seen them hiding in the brush.

"Tybalt is *not* being patient," Moder said. "Always was easy to distract. And we are not only ones wanting to cross bridge."

"You mean," Lara said, "Wait for someone else to- To-"

"If we are lucky, there will be a fight," Moder said. "Then we cross."

"But they'll kill them!" Lara exclaimed.

Moder cupped Lara's mouth shut, her eyes growing wide. Lara did not fight it, but kept still, wishing all the while that she could turn invisible.

They waited.

Someone at the inn began to pluck out a tune. A fisherman on the bridge shouted something she could not make out. The drinkers all let out a laugh. The man with the corpse slowed to a sway.

Moder withdrew her hand.

"They'll kill them," Lara repeated, quieter this time.

"I know, *dohtor*," Moder said. "I know. But we must cross."

Lara knew Moder was right. They had seen so much smoke from the hills that she'd wondered if the whole country was on fire. There were soldiers guarding the crossings to the north and soldiers in the woods behind them. There were flocks of shrikes in the skies now, *flocks*, swarming like migrating birds.

They had to cross. Here and now, or not at all.

But knowing that didn't make it any easier.

"Alright," Lara said. "We wait."

"Tell the others," Moder said. "Both of you. I will watch while you ready horses. And when I whistle- *if I whistle*- we all will go, yes?"

"Yes," they answered, and began to creep back towards the hedgerow.

They had not gotten far when a loud crash sent them to their bellies. Behind them, the laughter was dying. The player had ceased his plucking. Had they been spotted? Were they coming for them?

Don't look. Don't look.

But she had to see.

The door of the inn hung open. A peppery-haired man in thigh high boots was leaning against it, brilliant in crimson. Behind him loomed two figures: One lean and long-locked, the other black-cloaked and pale as a Calvarian. They all had swords. The one in crimson wore a breastplate over his finery. There was no mistaking them for village folk.

That must be him.

Tybalt stepped from the threshold. The men parted for him the way sheep would have for Pasha.

"How are we boys?" he called out. His voice was sour, almost casual, but it carried. "Having fun, are we? I do hope I'm not interrupting."

"We was just having a lark, sir," the man with the dead girl replied. Lara could hear the panic in his voice. "Dancing with the lady, like."

"Ohhh!" Tybalt crooned, turning on his heels to address the others. "Now that does sound like a laugh! Not as entertaining as, say, doing as we're told. Certainly not as much fun as waiting in ambush for the Queen of bloody Arcasia . . . But that does get dull. Does it not, Jacquet?"

"It does, Captain," the long-locked man said. "Terribly dull."

"Indeed," Tybalt said, turning back to the man. "So, go on then. Dance."

The man didn't move. Tybalt slapped his brow.

"Oh, dear me!" he cried. "How silly! I nearly forgot: You must have music! Corsablis, be a good man and play, will you?"

Someone began to play a lively tune.

"Now *dance*," Tybalt said.

The man took a few halting steps, struggling to keep the dead girl aloft as he turned her about.

Tybalt slowly drew his hand across his breast. Metal flashed in the sun.

A knife.

He tossed the blade into the air, caught it, and sent it spinning. It sank home in the dead girl's back. He drew another.

The man spun awkwardly, trying to keep the girl between himself and the blade. Tybalt flicked his wrist. A knife drove through the dead girl's forearm.

The man yelped, let go. The dead girl fell in the dirt.

"Well, that won't do," Tybalt said. "Don't you know how to treat a lady?"

Tybalt drew again. Two knives now.

"Go on," he said. "Pick her up! And do it properly, or the boys will be dancing with you next."

The man scrambled to get the girl back in the air, grunting as he got her spinning.

Tybalt threw. The first knife sank into the girl's neck. The other drove through the hem of her skirt, pinning it to the ground.

The man stumbled, nearly fell. Then the skirt gave. The men laughed as he slammed into a table, but he kept on dancing.

"Come on!" Pinsard hissed. He was already a few paces ahead of her. "Now, while they're distracted!"

She crawled after him.

They were slipping through the hedge when Lara heard an anguished cry. It was followed by a raucous cheer.

She began to gasp for air.

"Lara!" Pinsard reached out to steady her. "What's wrong?"

"A moment," she panted, brushing his hand aside. "I'm fine. Just give me- Give me a moment."

Pinsard stared, worry in his eyes, but kept his distance. And, shortly, she was breathing easier.

"It was *him*," she said. "Tybalt. He killed her."

"Killed who?"

"The old woman," Lara said. "The one who used to chase us. I was there. I saw it."

* * * * * * *

"Tybalt, eh?" Arlequin said and spat into the brush. "So, Pierrot, the prince of shit himself has come to collect the rest from us! What've you to say to that?"

The silent man pressed his fingers to his lips, kissed them, and then flashed the village the first pair.

"Agreed," Arlequin said, and threw Lara a sheepish glance. "Forgive me, Majesty, for our crude speech. The man, he-"

"I understand," Lara said. "Moder told me."

Pierrot stirred, his lips pursing. She wondered what he would say if he had a tongue.

"Then," Arlequin said, lowering his gaze, "Majesty has not, ah, changed her mind? About our course?"

"She has not," Lara replied. "And she wishes her groom would stop asking."

"Majesty, I did not mean to-"

"I'm sorry," she said. "I didn't mean to say that. Well, *I did*, but I'm- I'm very tired."

"We all are," Pinsard said.

"Well," Arlequin said, "We'll rest easier when we've put a few leagues between us and the usurper's filth. What's a Vulp Voran tiger or two compared to the likes of them?"

Arlequin made an effort to grin. It wasn't very convincing.

"Best be ready then," he muttered, and started to unhitch the horses.

The jangling tack brought Bannertail out from the brush. It looked up at her expectantly, a freshly caught songbird locked between its jaws.

"At least you'll never go hungry," Lara smirked.

She did her best to ignore the fox-squirrel as it chewed the bird's head off.

They mounted. Lara peered through the hedge, keeping a tight grip on Demon's lead. She knew Arlequin disapproved, but Demon and the dark-maned bay did not get along. And so, rather than risk being kicked or thrown, he'd kept his peace and handed her the rope.

And they waited.

At first, she kept her eyes on the road west of the village. What wagon or group of riders would come creeping out of the hills, she wondered, blissfully ignorant of what lay in wait?

When that grew tiresome, she tried to guess what was happening on the bridge. The 'fishermen' slowly crossed to the far side of the river, only to be replaced by a trio carrying their own poles- Or were they spears? It was too far to tell.

Moder was closer, but she was much harder to see, even with her blond hair and grass-stained whites. If Lara hadn't known where she was crouching, she would have taken her for a large, pale rock.

"White stone soup," she murmured to herself.

"What did you say?" Pinsard asked.

"Nevermind," she said, rubbing the bridge of her nose. "Gods, we've been here for hours. I'm not even scared anymore."

"That is good," Pinsard said. "I was worried."

"I'm sure it won't last long," she said. "But, what about you? Are *you* alright?"

"How do you mean?" he said, turning to face her.

"I mean, we haven't talked, *really* talked, since-"

Since you killed that soldier.

"Well, since that day at the orchard."

"I suppose not," he said.

"Do you," she offered, "Want to talk about it?"

"What is there to talk about?"

"It's alright," she said, "If you don't want to-"

"She was one of *his* soldiers," he said, bluntly. "They all were. They would have killed us. Killed us, and taken you."

"I know," she said. "I'm sorry."

"Don't be," he said, and might have said more, but Pierrot had begun to snap his fingers.

"Majesty!" Arlequin said, pointing. "Something's coming down the road."

'Something' was an understatement. A line of men (or women, perhaps) was advancing down the road, with a huge horse-drawn wagon and more on foot coming up behind. There were riders as well: Thirteen she counted as another pair came streaking over a hillcrest. The entire column quickened its pace, several of the riders doubling back as others raced ahead, making straight for the bridge.

"Soldiers," Arlequin said. "A whole company, Majesty, or what's left of it."

"They're not the usurper's?" she asked, guessing the answer from the way Tybalt's men were hustling into position, finding cover amongst carts and barrels, or behind walls that didn't face the road. The soldiers would see frightened peasants, fleeing for shelter. If they saw them at all.

"They're not wearing his colors, Majesty," Arlequin said, scratching at the back of his neck. "Or any others I know of. This could be it."

The riders slowed at the crossroads but did not stop. If they saw the corpses posed about the village, they were clearly in no mood to tarry.

Lara heard a distant whistle.

"Right then," Arlequin grunted, but Lara put out her hand to hold him back.

The call had not been one of Moder's.

"The barn," Pinsard said.

Lara followed his gaze. There was an old cowshed there, half swallowed by ivy. Its doors were opening.

The men on foot had reached the edge of the village and were moving aside to let the wagon pass. The riders were starting to cross the bridge. She could hear men shouting, horses neighing. Surefoot whinnied. Demon pawed at the soil, snorting with impatience.

"Easy," she soothed, suddenly aware of her own heart pounding. "Easy now."

One of the riders made the crossing and galloped onto the far bank. The rear of the column caught up with the wagon and pounded towards the center of the village, the slowest amongst them beginning to trail behind.

Tybalt's men remained as still as Moder, if not the dead women they skulked amongst.

A second rider reached the far bank. Then a third.

If there was call or signal, Lara didn't hear it, but suddenly doors and shutters were swinging open as men emerged from behind garden wall, woodpile, and the underside of the bridge itself. Men on horseback burst from the barn, swords gleaming as they swarmed towards the bridge. More poured from the cooperage. The cries of men began to fill the air.

"Gods," she breathed as the soldiers began to fall and scatter. Some surged back down the road, clambering desperately over roof and fence, but most had nowhere to run. Whoever was driving the wagon whipped its team forward, desperate to escape but unable to turn around.

Someone shot him before he could reach the inn. His body fell under the wheels as he tumbled off, but the wagon kept rumbling on.

The riders were faring little better. Of the three that had crossed, two had already fallen. The third drove his horse headlong into the river before being carried away by the rush. A handful of others bolted for the woods, Tybalt's riders in hot pursuit.

The fight spilled into the meadow as Tybalt's men abandoned their positions to press the attack. Many were racing to cut off the soldiers' retreat, leaving both inn and bridge undefended.

Lara leaned forward, tilting her head as she listened for Moder's whistle.

But no whistle came.

Lara shot Pinsard a look. He shook his head, 'No.'

The wagon and its team roared over the bridge, Tybalt's riders on the far bank making way for it as it bore down on them. There were only a handful of them left: A half dozen maybe. They were wheeling so close to one another that it was difficult to keep count.

Now! Lara wanted to shout. *NOW!*

Still, Moder was silent.

"By the bloody blue beard of Wulf!" Arlequin swore. "What in the world is she waiting for?!"

"Maybe she sees something we do not!" Pinsard said through gritted teeth. "Be patient!"

Demon neighed loudly and began to toss his head. It was only a matter of time before he would bolt. And the battle, if one could call it that, was nearly over. There were soldiers fleeing in every direction.

Some were heading their way.

"Majesty, please," Arlequin urged. "We cannot stay here! If we-"

"We wait for the signal!" she managed. One of the men running towards them fell forward, an arrow in his back. "Moder knows what she's doing."

Arlequin knit his brow. "As you wish, Majesty."

Another arrow sailed into the dirt, just shy of the hedgerow. It quivered. A soldier ran right past Moder. Either he did not see her or, if he did, he did not care.

Demon reared. She let go of his lead, and he took off at a gallop. He nearly ran one of the soldiers down and made for the rolling hills they'd spent the last day and a half skirting around.

But as Demon shot past the men fighting and dying in the meadow, a second host of riders came thundering out of the hills. The banner riding at their head bore the emblem of a mailed fist, and behind it a jawless golden skull.

The Baroness' bloody girls, the noseless captain had called them. Arlequin had a more colorful title at hand.

"It's the slattern's whores again!" he spat.

The Baroness' riders charged, their number fanning out as they sped towards the fray. How they could distinguish the Grand Prince's soldiers from Tybalt's men, Lara could only guess. As they began to cut men down left and right, it hardly seemed to make a difference.

Moder whistled. Lara drew her sword.

The soldier that Demon had nearly trampled threw himself into the dirt as they broke from the trees. Another made straight for her, his gloved hands outstretched. Perhaps he hoped to pull her from Surefoot, but when he saw her blade he turned the other way.

Across the meadow, one of the archers lowered his bow and began to wave. He was shouting something. Then he keeled over, an arrow protruding from the front of his leather jack. *One of Moder's,* she realized.

She brought Surefoot skidding to a halt beside the fallen trunk. Moder was already nocking another arrow.

"Demon bolted!" Lara shouted at her. "Ride with me!"

"Better I take her!" Arlequin cried out, bringing the dark-maned bay about.

Moder aimed at a man running towards the bridge and loosed. She didn't wait to see if the shaft struck home, but shouldered her bow, took hold of Arlequin's hand, and vaulted onto the back of the bay, her long legs dangling well past his own.

"Ride!" Moder cried, gripping Arlequin as the warhorse took off at a gallop. Surefoot sprang around the tree trunk after them, and then they were speeding towards the inn.

There were more dead men than dead women in the village now. There were bodies in the yard and bodies in the street. There were bodies everywhere. Pinsard's rouncey ran right over one as they tore past the cooperage. Lara caught a glimpse of ruined wagons within, a pile of boots heaped before them.

Then they were in the village. There were men on the lane ahead of them, straining to push a cart between them and the bridge.

They know, Lara thought, but then she saw the shock on their faces as she and the others came barreling towards them. Now she could see the armor beneath their roughspun tunics, and the blades hanging from their belts.

"By the Teeth!" one of them shouted, leaping backwards just as Arlequin and Moder shot past him on the bay. "It's her!"

She felt something heavy brush against her leg. She lashed out with her blade and heard a shriek. Something whizzed past her head.

"Keep going!" Pinsard cried out.

She focused on the inn. 'The Drowned Man' the sign hanging above its gateposts read. A pair of painted skeletons were on the posts, bottles cradled in their arms.

Come in, come in, they seemed to grin as Surefoot shot past them. *Come in and end your cares.*

"The Princess!" men were calling out. She rode past the dead girl in the periwinkle skirt. "The Princess on the bridge!"

They clattered onto the span. A horn, or something like it, was blowing wildly behind them. Men were crying out in alarm as horses screamed.

Don't look! Don't look!

She looked anyway.

The Baroness' soldiers were trying to cut their way to the bridge. Tybalt's men weren't making way. A group of them were dragging one of the women from her horse, striking her with cudgels as she fell.

They're fighting each other!

She didn't have long to relish the thought. There were riders on the far side of the river, making for the bridge at a steady clip. Some were ponying horses beside their own.

Tybalt's riders had caught their quarry and were returning with their spoils. The men they had left behind had dismounted and were ransacking the wagon beside the barn, tossing sacks and jars from its bed as though they were searching for something.

Me. They're looking for me.

"The wagon!" Moder shouted as they cleared the bridge. "Make for the wagon!"

"The wagon?" Arlequin shot back. "Are you mad?"

"Supplies are in wagon!"

Arlequin let out a string of oaths but turned his charger. Lara turned Surefoot.

Food! The thought raced through Lara's head as they picked up speed. On the run or not, soldiers needed to eat. The sacks might have flour in them, or fruit, or wheels of cheese, or perhaps there were jars brimming with butter and honey . . . But after two days of nothing but scatterweed roots and pine needle broth Lara didn't care if the wagon was full of hardtack and salted fish.

She would kill a man for something to eat.

"ARCASIA!" Arlequin roared as they thundered forward. "LONG LIVE LARISSA!"

"FYRR ME SEALTIAN!" Moder howled in her own tongue.

"GRIEF!" Pinsard cried out, his sword whirling. "GRIEF, TERROR, AND BLOOD!"

Lara let out a long wailing scream.

She didn't know any battle cries.

All but two of Tybalt's men ran at the sight of them. Whether it was the bounty or the fear of their captain that made them bold, no one would ever know. Pinsard cut the first one down as he was loading his crossbow. The other managed to duck under Arlequin's axe. Then the dark-maned bay kicked him so hard in the chest his breastplate split open.

Surefoot carried Lara well past all of this. By the time she brought him back around, Moder had leapt from the bay and was climbing into the seat of the wagon.

"The whole thing?!" Lara panted.

"Whole thing!" Moder replied, casting about for something just beneath the footboard: The reins.

Pinsard brought his horse alongside Surefoot. His cheeks were flushed. His eyes met hers, but there was no time for words.

"They are coming," he said.

"I am seeing!" Moder snapped, the team whickering as she snatched up the reins. She gave them a flick.

The horses did not move.

"Awirung!" Moder swore, and slammed the reins onto the seat. *"Salnes-an-Stan!* Pierrot! *Hit-eall beon corst,* you are driving cart to market, YOU drive this thing!"

The silent man slipped from his shaggy hobby, gave its rump a slap to set it to running, and leapt onto the wagon with far more grace than Lara might have expected. Then he took up the reins and whipped them, hard.

The team took off, turf flying as they made for an overgrown track running straight through the pines.

"Jackleg fool," Arlequin growled.

"Come on!" Lara cried, spurring Surefoot on.

She looked back only once. The Baroness' soldiers were fighting for the bridge, only a score of men holding them back. Tybalt's riders were racing to join the battle, deaf to the cries of 'Princess!' echoing throughout the village. If they saw the wagon hurtling into the pinewood, they were clearly ignorant of who rode with it.

It was not until much later, the wagon abandoned, the team cut free, her pack stuffed with dried beef, fruit, and cheese in black wax, and her belly full of buttered bread (the butter had begun to turn and the bread was coarse, but it was still *bread*, not hardtack) that it finally sank in.

They had done it. They crossed the river. Reynard, The Baroness, and the killer named Tybalt- they had slipped past them all.

There was nothing between them now and Vulp Vora.

VII

At first, the forest east of the river did not seem all that different to Lara than the one that the lumbermen of Perun had been dulling their axes on for generations. Its pines were taller perhaps, or thicker, and the ground was rockier- in places nothing but great shelves of stone that looked as though they had been shoved from the earth by some tremendous force- but otherwise there was nothing particularly sinister about the place.

Nor did the sounds of the wood bother her. She knew that the screams and groans at night were those of owls and badgers, and the frantic thumping at dawn and dusk was only the beating of grouses' wings, not the drumming of some chimera war party.

They were familiar sounds. They helped her feel safe. It was when the woods were quiet that she felt afraid.

They would be leading the horses through a clearing or around a jumbled pile of stone, and the birds would grow silent, and for a long time the only sounds she could hear were their own.

"There's something in the woods," Lara said, after they had finished their soldier's supper of cheese and barley cakes. The Watcher had waned to a sliver, and she longed for a fire, a lantern even, anything to drive back the darkness.

"It is us who spooks the animals, Majesty," Arlequin reassured her. "Men do not come here often, I think."

Lara nodded, but she was not convinced. She took first watch with Pierrot that night and, though she heard nothing but the rustling of Bannertail hunting in the brush, sleep eluded her long after Pinsard had taken her place.

The next morning, not far from their camp, they came upon a dead tree, its trunk and exposed roots coated with moss. Dozens of trinkets dangled from its branches, hanging from rotting cords and strips of vine. There were rusty coins and wooden talismans marked by slashes, circles, and spirals . . . But most were nothing more than splintered bits of bone, hide, and teeth woven with what looked like human hair.

There were hoofprints in the soil around the tree, but they were unlike those of any sheep or deer Lara had ever seen. For one thing, they were not staggered: Something on two legs, not four, had made them.

She pressed her boot into the mud. When she lifted it back up, the prints looked nearly as fresh as her own.

"Faun," Pinsard said, casting a glance over his shoulder. "Chimera."

"Yes," Moder said. "Many *un-tydre* were here."

"But why did they not attack us?"

"Perhaps this is a sacred place," Lara suggested.

"Nothing is *sacred* in Vulp Vora, Majesty," Arlequin said.

Pierrot plucked one of the coins from the tree and squinted at it. Just then, the woods grew quiet.

Lara held her breath, half expecting something to come creeping out of the mist, bestial, with goat-like faces and curling horns: Duskwalker, the mother of monsters, favored children.

Pierrot gave the coin a flip. Then he tossed it to Arlequin, who caught it with a scowl.

"Ass," he muttered, slipping it into his jack.

Somewhere in the woods, a pair of crows began to caw at each other. At least, Lara thought they were crows.

"Let's not linger here," Lara said, and they walked away from that place in silence, not stopping until the Firebird was well past her zenith.

* * * * * * *

Gradually, the forest thinned. Tree and brush gave way to rush grass, some of which was so sharp-edged that it could draw blood. The soil beneath their feet grew soggy, until they were slogging through the mud with every step. Instead of clearings there were stagnant pools, and the air swarmed with midges. Other insects were far too large to be normal. Bannertail caught one of them, a bright green thing that was either a fat dragonfly or a multi-winged beetle and gulped it down before Lara could stop it. But whether the bug was poisonous, or merely tasted foul, the fox-squirrel vomited it back up, and was content from then on to dine on Lara's scraps.

Bannertail was one thing. The horses were another.

In Solothurn, even in the hills, they had been able to graze. Now there was almost nothing for them to eat. No one trusted the lurid marsh plants, but even the ones that looked innocuous were anything but. What Lara had taken for lacecrown was actually snakeroot, and Arlequin cautioned her to steer Surefoot clear of the fiddleheads that sprouted amongst the ferns. When eaten they would bring the staggers, blindness, and eventually death.

And yet, to turn the horses loose seemed cruel. Where would they go and what would become of them in this place where chimera walked, and the memory of the demons still lingered?

To abandon them here, Lara thought, *would be as good as killing them.*

"Tomorrow," Moder said when the day was done and they had found what shelter they could amongst the reeds, "Tomorrow we will be freeing them."

But when the dawn came, they did not drive them off. Instead, they saddled them, fed them what was left of the shriveled apples from the wagon, and pressed on.

No one questioned why.

There was *some* beauty in the mire. At night delicate flowers bloomed. Some had violet petals with blue-green stamens. Others were white and pale as the Watcher and gave off a sickly sort of light of their own. The birds of the marsh were dark as jet, and red of eye and throat. Their cries were like the wailing of spirits lost in Domdaniel, eerie and lingering, and they made Pinsard shudder. That made Lara laugh, and the sound of laughter in that place was a welcome thing.

Then, after three nights of sleeping in the damp, her gloved hands clamped over her ears for fear that some insect might creep into them, the wetland finally broke. They had reached the edge of a great forest . . . If forest was the right word for the thing that stretched beyond the edge of the marsh. Its trees were bulbous, stalk-like things, their limbs dense with blue ivy. Furry white fronds clung to their roots, and the pooled resin that bled from their trunks looked to her like glassy eyes of amber.

"The ground," Pinsard said. "It looks . . . Alive."

He was not wrong. Clumps of moss and lichen were shifting as the soil swelled and collapsed. It was almost as if the forest floor itself were breathing.

"Is only *gost-aeir*," Moder said, dismissively. "Vapor, trapped below. Nothing more."

To prove her words, she climbed the nearest embankment and gave the soil a solid kick. There was a deep, throaty sigh as air escaped from the rent.

Moder sniffed, her nostrils flaring.

"No fires here," she warned as they climbed out of the marsh. "Not even a spark, or vapor will catch."

Lara nodded silently but, as they walked, she wondered if anything besides the air would burn here. The ground was nearly as damp and spongy as the marsh, and the ivy glistened wetly.

The stench of the place, rotting and yet sickly sweet, was bad. The heat was worse. Before long Lara's clothes were soaked through with sweat and reeking, and she longed for a breeze or (better still) a cold pool to bathe in. Even Moder, she noticed, was toying with the uppermost button of her coat, fastening and unfastening it again and again.

When they finally stopped to rest beside a rocky streambed, Lara sat upstream from the horses, removed her boots, and plunged her feet into the brook. The fox-squirrel lapped up a few mouthfuls of water before flattening itself belly first against a rounded stone. When Arlequin saw that the horses were content to drink here, he did too, followed shortly by Pierrot, who practically dunked his whole head into the rush.

"We should boil-" Moder began to say, then knelt down and drank. Pinsard removed his cloak, stripped off his gloves and splashed his face with water before doing so as well.

Lara cupped her hands and dipped them into the stream. She drank. If the water was deadly, it at least tasted fresh.

When all had slaked their thirst, they took out their rations and ate.

"The Baroness and Tybalt," Lara said, as she nibbled on a slice of cured beef. "Back at the crossing, their soldiers were fighting each other .. . But why? They both serve the usurper."

"Soldiers do as their captains do," Moder answered. "And there is being no love between Tybalt and Rukenaw. She was never forgiving him for Maleperduys."

"Rukenaw," Lara said. "That is her name?"

"Yes."

"And . . . Maleperduys?"

"It was long ago," Moder said, and tore a dry hunk of bread in half. "Are you remembering Rukenaw, Pinsard?"

"The Fairlimb," he said, nodding.

"A pretty name for the usurper's harlot," Arlequin said, clearing his throat. "If Majesty will forgive my speech."

"Is that so?" Lara asked. "She is his lover?"

"Rukenaw?" Moder pondered. "I am thinking not. She was more like *dohtor* to him. Or *sweoster.* But who is knowing? Many summers have gone since then. It could be."

Moder bit into her bread and chewed for a while.

"Was long ago," Moder repeated, and stood. "Is not important."

With that she walked off, making for one of the larger trees.

"Were they friends?" Lara whispered to Pinsard. "Moder and The Baroness?"

"I do not think so," Pinsard answered. "Moder was very angry with me once when she found me in her camp. And she- Rukenaw- she hated Faeder, I think."

"Why?"

"I do not know. It was-"

"Long ago," Lara sighed.

Lara caught Pierrot looking at her, smiling, the fingers of his left-hand drumming against his cheek.

"Shut up," she said, and fed the rest of her meal to the fox-squirrel.

* * * * * * *

Night fell, and the forest around them came alive.

Insects rattled and sang to each other. Strange animals scurried amongst the ivy. A shaggy, shell-backed creature with stumpy legs and a long beaked mouth lumbered directly across their path, grunting as it snuffled at the forest floor. Overhead, gossamer-winged reptiles swooped, feeding on insects, and being fed on themselves by loathsome, leathery predators that were not quite bird and not quite rat. Some of these hung from trees on serpentine tails. Others crawled about on segmented legs. No two were truly alike.

They were chimera, all of them, of that Lara had no doubt. And by comparison, Bannertail looked practically ordinary: It was easy to see where the fox began and the squirrel ended, easy to spot the dash of wild cat that lent it both face and temper.

Not so with the things that peered at them from the shadows. That some of them, even the ones that slithered on their bellies and had stalks for eyes, might have sprung from human stock was not lost on her. She kept her hand on the hilt of her sword as they walked and listened to their cries.

When it was too dark to see properly, they stopped, though Lara would have gone on walking until she collapsed. She was exhausted, of course, and woozy from the heat. But falling asleep out in the open, knowing that they were being watched by a hundred hungry eyes? That was difficult to imagine.

"Perhaps there's a better place to camp nearby," Lara said.

"Better?" she heard Moder ask.

"Safer," she clarified.

"There is no 'safer,'" Moder said, her white face looming out of the darkness. "Or we would not be being here, yes?"

Lara nodded and found herself wishing that she had listened to Arlequin, back in the hills west of the Vodyanoy.

"I will be watching first," Moder said.

"We could light a fire," she heard Pinsard say, hopefully. It was not a bad idea: The ground had stopped 'breathing' hours ago, and some of the dead tree limbs might be dry enough to catch.

"No," Moder replied, and that was that.

Lara did her best to hitch Surefoot, and put down her packsack gently. Bannertail scampered out of it, but not too far, and eventually the fox-squirrel crept beside her and sat with its ears pricked and tail aquiver.

"Rest, Majesty," Arlequin said, startling her somewhat as he knelt beside her. He was looking rather pale himself, and his skin was beaded with sweat. "I will keep watch for you."

"You should rest," she replied. "I am not tired yet."

She yawned.

"Rest your eyes then," he chuckled. "They're hardly any use in this gloom."

Lara shut her eyes. It did no good.

"Do you know any stories?" she asked. "Happy ones, I mean."

"I know horses, Majesty," Arlequin said and coughed into his fist. "And game, and as much herb craft as I could from old Madam Syrinx, who helped to bring the both of us into this world . . . But stories?"

He cleared his throat.

"I don't know any stories, Majesty. At least, not proper ones."

"Then tell me an improper one," Lara said.

"How my Columbine would have taken to you," he laughed. "*She* would have had a tale that would shrivel your ears."

"You must know *one*," Lara insisted. "Shrivel away."

"Well," he hemmed. "I do know one, Majesty, about King Leodegrance and his prize stallion. My uncle used to tell it when he was in his cups . . . But, well, it's hardly fit for- for-"

"Tell it to me," she said. "Your Queen commands it."

"Very well," he said. "So. Hm. He, Leodegrance that is, was one of the sons of King Leander, in the days of Old Aquilia. But he was the youngest of them and no one ever thought that he would be King . . . Only, well, old Leander had married two wives, you see: One a proper Aquilian lady and the other a Telchine princess with golden skin. Leodegrance's brothers were from the first wife, and he was from the other."

"And?"

"Well," Arlequin went on. "Leander loved his second wife more than the first for, well, she was, hrrm, sweeter than the other. Honey sweet, he called her."

He coughed.

"So, late one night, while they- the King and she- were abed, she told him about an old Telchine custom: Whenever a Queen died, those who wished to wear her crown would choose the best of their horses-"

"Stags," Pinsard said in the dark.

"What's that?" Arlequin said.

"The Telchines rode stags, not horses."

"Stags, then," Arlequin muttered. "So, they would sit astride their *stags* at dawn, facing east, and the first of them to-"

The insects quieted. Arlequin's words died in his throat. Lara opened her eyes.

"What is it?" Pinsard whispered.

"Hssst," Moder shushed.

A tree branch snapped. Something let out a shrill cry, once, twice, and then it too was silent.

Lara leaned forward, cocking her head to one side. Arlequin put his hand on the hilt of his dagger. She could see his hand shaking.

Another limb snapped, closer now, and then:

"Is someone out there?" a voice called out of the dark. It was distant, but very clear.

It sounded like a child's voice. A girl's maybe.

"I'm stuck," the voice whimpered. "Don't leave me here. I'm stuck."

For a moment, despite where they were and against all her instincts, Lara was tempted to call back. After all, what if it *was* a child? Who knew what people might live here, far from the Calvarians and the Grand Prince's tax collectors? It was not impossible.

"Come find me," the voice begged. "I'm stuck."

That's no child, Lara told herself, and kept still.

Another pair of limbs cracked. Something nearby let out a bone-shaking growl and moved off, pressing deeper into the woods. Whatever it was, it sounded very large.

"Mother," the voice cried out pitifully. "Is that you? Where are you? I can't find you, mother. I can't find you . . ."

Whatever was out there picked up its pace. Limbs split and rustled . . . But the sounds were growing fainter. It wasn't coming their way.

"Don't leave me," the voice said, almost a whisper. "I'm stuck. Don't leave me."

One of the horses let out a whinny. Lara bit her lower lip as she stifled back a scream.

"Mother?" the voice called out, uncertain. "Is that you?"

Lara held her breath, as she imagined they all were, and prayed to the Lioness for the horses to keep quiet as well. She could hear someone, Moder or Pinsard, slowly freeing a blade from its sheath.

"Come find me," the voice called out, clearer than ever. "I'm stuck."

Go away, Lara begged, beginning to tug on the hilt of her own sword. *Go away, go away, go away.*

"Don't leave me, mother," it sobbed. "I'm scared. Don't leave me."

Lara squeezed her eyes shut and *listened.*

She could hear Arlequin shivering in spite of the heat. She could hear the horses shifting, and the low rumble of their snorts. But she could hear something else. Something very soft: A low, knowing *giggle.*

"Don't leave me," the voice sighed.

Then it was silent.

Somehow, when the insects were singing again and the chimera were croaking and burbling in the dark, Lara managed to fall asleep . . . But she did not sleep well. Again and again, she would wake with a start, half expecting to feel the blast of hot, rancid breath against her cheek, and to hear a child's voice whisper "don't leave me" in her ear before it sunk its teeth into her throat.

Then, sometime before dawn, she felt a gloved hand come to rest against her right temple.

"I am here," she heard Moder whisper to her as she began to stroke her head. "I am here."

And- for an hour or two, at least- she slept.

* * * * * * *

No one spoke of what they had heard the night before and, as soon as it was light enough to see, they left that place, making as due south as they could with only the Firebird for their guide.

By mid-morning they had put a league behind them. There were many tracks in the mud: Hooves, paws, and mysterious furrows. But if they were being hunted, Lara could not tell.

By midday they came across another freshwater stream. They followed it, winding their way through a wide gully, glad of the breeze that blew through it, putrid as it was to the nose. The only chimera here were little lizards with tufts of fur on the ridges of their backs.

By midafternoon they began to breathe easier. And it was then that Lara realized that something was wrong with Arlequin.

At first Lara had thought that he was merely exhausted. After all, he had insisted on keeping watch all night, and she suspected he had been letting her sleep far longer than he should whenever it was her turn to relieve him. His eyes were a bit sunken, true, and he was sweating profusely, but then they were all tired and sweating.

Then she remembered how pale he had seemed the night before, how long he seemed to have been stifling a cough, how his hands had trembled that morning, as he'd unhitched the horses.

It was when he began to shiver that she truly knew something was wrong. The day had started hot and only gotten hotter, but as he led the bay along the streambed, she noticed that he was using his free hand to clutch his leather jack close to his chest. His teeth were rattling.

"We need to stop," Lara said. "Arlequin is sick."

"It's just the stink, Majesty," the groom said, shaking his head. "'Twill pass. Fresh air's all I need, fresh air and a drop of-"

He shivered again and stumbled, his left foot slipping as he set it on a loose slab of shale. He let go of the bay's reins and began to tumble over . . . But before he could, Pierrot caught him by the arm, his lips parting as he let out a wordless yelp.

"Ah, leave off!" Arlequin growled as he steadied himself and wrestled his arm from Pierrot's grip. "I'll build my own pyre before I let *you* lead me about."

Pierrot let his arm drop to his side, but he continued to stare as Arlequin pressed on. As did Lara. As did they all.

He had forgotten that he had been leading the dark-maned bay. The horse's reins lay where he had dropped them: In the dirt.

"Arlequin," Lara said, her mouth suddenly dry.

"Majesty," he said, stopping in his tracks. He did not turn to face her.

Moder came up beside him and peered into his eyes.

"Not red," she said. "That is good."

"It's the air is all," he said. "'Minds me of Old Quarter, when the wind come over Render's Row-"

"Keep mouth shut," *Moder* said, stripping off her glove and pressing her hand to his forehead. He shuddered and held his arms tight against his chest.

"Chills?" Moder asked. "Chills, and sweat?"

He nodded.

"Rest now." She frowned. "We will all rest, yes?"

Arlequin shook his head 'no,' but he walked over to a nearby stone and sat down heavily all the same.

Pierrot joined him.

"Pinsard," Moder said. "Go and see if there is better place to camp."

"Moder?" Pinsard looked as stunned as Lara was. Moder used to wring her hands when he was late for supper. And that was on the farm.

"*Go*," she repeated. "And be quick."

He got on his horse and went.

Surefoot and the bay wandered as Moder rinsed her hand in the stream.

"It's not the air," Lara said. "Is it?"

Moder scooped up a stone from the streambed and began to roll it in the palm of her hand.

"No," she said.

"What is it then?"

"Fever," Moder answered.

Lara swallowed.

"Will he-" Lara lowered her voice. "Will he die?"

"Without rest," Moder said, "Yes."

"And *with* rest?"

Moder let go of the stone. It fell into the stream with a 'plop.'

"You don't know?" Lara asked.

"I was *Fisicien* in Calvaria," Moder said. "*Fisicien*, second-class. Broken bones, wounds, saw and stitching. These things, Lara, I am *knowing*."

Moder wiped her hand against her hip and slipped it back into her glove. Then she went to round up the horses before they strayed too far.

Lara looked at Arlequin, bent over double with his hands resting against his knees. Life had felt so small to her before he had bent his knee and told her who she truly was. How long ago that seemed, and how great and terrible the world had grown since then . . . But it was not so terrible as it would have been if she had been forced to face it alone.

Then Arlequin caught her staring. He straightened.

"Don't go worrying on Arlequin's account," he said, puffing out his chest. "Just a breath or two off my feet, Majesty, and I'll be right straight again. Straight as a nail, you'll see."

Lara nodded and forced a smile as she turned away.

She kept her back to him so he could rest in peace.

He can't die, she told herself. *Not here. I won't let him.*

And who are you? The Queen of Heaven? You're not even really a Queen . . . At least, not in any way that matters.

Bannertail rubbed up against her legs then, the fox-squirrel's tail wrapping about her ankle as it scurried up her side. It sniffed at her face and gave her cheek a lick. It was easy to see the scars it had taken from the thorn bush. Her own were hidden beneath glove and sleeve, but they were there.

He won't die, Lara decided. *Not if I can help it.*

Pinsard returned much sooner than she would have expected, his rouncey kicking up clods of soil as they came skidding down an embankment. His cheeks were very red.

"We can't stay here," he panted.

"What is it?" Lara asked. "Chimera?"

"Worse," Pinsard said, trying to keep steady as his horse wheeled about. "Come on!"

"Not without-" Lara began to say, but Moder was already ahead of her. She dragged Pierrot up by his collar and pointed at Arlequin.

"Get him on horse!" Moder ordered. "You lead. Yes?"

Pierrot nodded.

Arlequin was too tired to object as the silent man got him to his feet and helped him to mount the bay. He sagged in the saddle as the horse scaled the embankment and broke into a trot, but he kept his seat. Sick or not, he was a better rider than Lara could ever hope to be. She felt like a loose sack of turnips as they took after Pinsard, Surefoot struggling over the lip of the gully and up the steeper slope beyond.

Moder loped after them on foot.

Showers of rock cascaded downwards as they climbed, the sharper ones biting the skin as they leapt into the air, but Pinsard kept on, making for the wooded top of a saddle-backed rise. There was a switchback trail snaking up its western side, and Lara wondered why they were not taking it until Surefoot crested the ridge, and she turned about. She knew then why Pinsard had come rushing back for them.

There were men in the gully. Scores of men, and just as many horses. They were less than half a league away. Then a flight of birds burst from the forest, and she knew there were more of them moving beneath the trees.

"Who is it?" Lara asked, half-guessing the answer.

"Tybalt," Moder said, trying to catch her breath. "Or mercenaries Reynard is hiring. Is too far for being certain."

"It can't be," Lara heard Arlequin wheeze. "It can't!"

"You are not knowing how stubborn he is," Moder said, and edged away from the lip of the hill.

"There's a way down here!" Pinsard called out. He was on the far rise by now. "We'd have to lead the horses, but there's a valley- We could cut through it, maybe lose them in the woods again?"

"Better than staying here!" Lara wondered if the men could see her as well as she could see them.

"Hirsent," Arlequin croaked. His voice was as raspy as a crow's caw.

"What is it?" Moder said.

"Hirsent!" The croak was harsher now.

They turned. Arlequin was bent over the horn of the charger's saddle. Pierrot, white with dust, had tilted his head back and was blinking with alarm.

Lara followed his gaze.

There were shrikes perched in the branches of one of the larger trees. They had looked like part of its boughs as they'd come up the hillside, but now she could see them clearly. The largest was a male with a brilliant red-breast, shocks of white streaking its glossy black feathers. The others were smaller, brown-winged and speckled, but their faces were far more human.

"Hirsent!" the largest shrike cried, spreading its wings as it glared at her. "Hirsent, Father! Hirsent!"

"Rohart," Moder gasped, her hand reaching for one of the arrows that had gone galloping off with Demon.

"Doom!" the shrike cawed at her, and took off, shrieking her name.

"Hirsent!" the others echoed, their wings beating wildly as they made to follow. "Hirsent, Father! Hirsent! Hirsent-Hirsent-Hirsent!"

"It knew you," Lara said as the shrikes sailed away, wheeling as they began to descend. "The shrike. It knew you."

"Yes," Moder said, and snatched the charger's reins away from Pierrot. "It knew me."

* * * * * *

It *was* Tybalt.

By nightfall they could hear him. He was laughing as he and his men crashed through the woods below.

"Can you hear me up there, long-legs?" he called out. "You can, can't you? Must be slow going, eh?"

Lara could make out his words perfectly. They cut through the foul night air and bounced off the rocks.

"How are those legs of yours, by the by?" he sniggered. "Still fit? Still lovely? They ought to be, from all of the running you've been doing."

Branches snapped and popped. Hooves clipped against bare rock. They were getting closer.

"Did you miss me, lovely-legs? I should hope so. I've certainly missed you. Why, we all have, haven't we boys?"

"Faster," Moder whispered.

That was easier said than done.

They had already crossed the valley, scattering a flock of feathery-winged lizards as they scaled the opposite rise. Then they had backtracked over sheer rock, turned due east and backtracked again. At dusk they had crossed a chasm, leading the horses over a bridge of frayed rope and rotting slats before cutting it loose behind them. Now they were hiking up a narrow game trail that cut straight up the side of a jagged cliff.

But Tybalt kept gaining on them.

Lara was not surprised. After all, he and his men had the shrikes to guide them. None of *his* men were sick either, so sick they could hardly walk. And, even if they were, Lara doubted that Tybalt was the sort to care.

At least it's dark, she thought, peering at the night sky. *The shrikes can't see us in the dark. Can they?*

She squinted. If there was anything gliding overhead, she couldn't see it.

"Of course," Tybalt kept rambling, "Some of the boys are more than a little cross with you. I can't say that I blame them. I'm a bit cross with you myself. You killed five of my men, after all! You, and your little white-haired whelp!"

The dark-maned bay whinnied as a bit of rock came loose beneath its hoof. Lara winced as it skittered down the cliff face, but whether Tybalt and his men could hear it made little difference. They already knew they were close. If they didn't, Tybalt wouldn't be taunting them.

Or would he? He certainly seems to love the sound of his own voice.

The bay shook its head and refused to go a step further. Moder snarled something low and ugly, and clicked her tongue, but still the horse would not budge.

"Get," Arlequin coughed. He sat up a bit as the bay plodded forward.

Lara allowed herself a smile. Arlequin had been delirious when they'd started their climb. Moder had wanted to tie him to the bay's saddle, but Lara had objected, fearing that if the horse stumbled over the cliff's edge he would be helpless.

He didn't seem so helpless now.

Then Tybalt's laugh wafted up from below, and her smile died.

"Five of my men, Hirsent!" Tybalt sounded a bit winded himself, the rhythm of his speech broken by pauses, and Lara could picture him and his men panting as hard as she had at the trail head. "*Five!* Is that how you treat old friends? And worse, before I can even get a good look at you, you ride off on *my* supply wagon . . ."

Tybalt quieted. Lara thought she could hear the thin warble of one of the shrikes. Or was it one of Tybalt's men? Whatever it was, it sounded very far away.

"Granted," Tybalt went on, "I'd not had it for very long, that wagon. But my boys and I, well, we'd grown rather fond of it! Isn't that right?"

"Don't listen to him," Moder hissed.

They were coming around a bend now, and Lara could see the summit of the cliff.

"But the worst of it, dear Hirsent - the *worst* of it, my darling love - is that we're all *here* now because of you. Here! In Vulp Vora! I swore I'd never set foot here again don't you know? Swore it by my mother's name! And yet, here I am! Did you know there are chimera here, Hirsent? Oh, yes! Chimera and worse! Something killed Jurfaleu just this morning, my sweet, something that looked like a boar and a bull had a tumble . . ."

Moder rounded the bend, leading the bay. Pierrot padded behind the horse, ready to catch Arlequin if he should fall. Lara went next with Bannertail perched on her right shoulder, then Surefoot, and then Pinsard and his rouncey.

"And so, my dear, darling Hirsent," Tybalt went on, "I am less than pleased with you! Those two idiots with you, those bootlickers, *them* I could almost forgive. They were never one of us. Wulf! They didn't even have the good sense to stay dead after I'd gone and made it so easy for 'em! But *you*, Hirsent . . . You! You *saved* him! Could have left him to die at the Samara, run off, had your whelp in peace! You ever think about that?!"

"Don't listen to him," Moder said.

"But, no! You saved his *life*, Hirsent! And you could have had it *easy*. You could have had it all! Right now, you could be sitting your pretty ass on a bed of cushions in Kloss, and the worst I'd have had to do would be to watch my *manners*! But you couldn't do it, could you? You and that high and mighty idiot, the both of you couldn't leave well enough alone! And now he's dead, and you're as good as dead, and I'm in bloody VULP VORA!!!"

Tybalt's last words echoed as they reached the top of the trail, where the woods were just as thick as they were below. Then it was quiet again, save for the song of insects.

Lara put her hands on her knees and panted. Bannertail scurried across her back. A wind blew. She took a deep whiff. The air was not as foul up here.

"They climb now," she heard Moder say to her. "No time to be stopping."

"It's true, isn't it?" Lara asked, straightening. "He isn't lying."

"No," Moder said. "He is not."

"You saved his life. Reynard's."

"I did."

"Was it-" Lara's voice quavered. "Was it before he-"

"Yes, Lara," Moder said, her head drooping somewhat. "It was long before. Now come. Please."

Lara nodded. Her face was hot with shame.

They went on.

Not far from the edge of the cliff, the trail split. It was hard to see in the darkness, but one path veered left before driving straight into the trees. The other snaked around a large rock before it too disappeared. Something horrid was shrieking in the woods.

They halted.

Ride to the left, lose your horse, Lara could hear Danica reciting over a pair of spoiled eggs. *Ride to the right, lose your head*.

"Which way?" Lara asked.

"Left, Majesty," Arlequin answered. His voice was ragged, but there was still some strength behind it. "Yes. I will go left, leave a clear trail."

He cleared his throat.

"And you, Majesty, will go right."

"No," she said.

"Majesty, please." His eyes crinkled as he smiled at her. "I've slowed you long enough already."

"No," she said again. "You can't. You'll- You'll-"

She could not say it.

"You never finished your story," she said instead. "About Leodegrance's stallion."

Arlequin managed a chuckle, and then grimaced as he slipped from the bay's saddle and bent his knee. His face was slick with sweat.

"You know very well that the Watcher comes for me, Majesty," he said. "And with him I must go . . . But not yet, my Queen. Not yet. And there is time enough, I think, to do you one last service. If you will but give me your leave."

"I- I forbid it," she stammered.

"Would," he wheezed, "Majesty make of me a rebel?"

Lara shook her head.

"Then I will go," he said, and rose shakily. "Keep Surefoot. He is yours now. But I will need the charger. And the rouncey too, or they'll know at once."

"Chance," Pinsard said quietly. "His name is Chance."

"A good name." Arlequin cleared his throat. "Say your goodbyes to him, Master Pinsard, and fetch your pack. Then I will be off."

Pinsard nodded and spoke something low to the horse as he gave it a pat, already slipping free the canteen that hung from the rouncey's saddle.

"The rest of the food," Arlequin said to Moder, steadying himself as he fiddled with the bay's saddlebags. "And the coin. There's not much, but I won't need it. Heh. And here I thought I'd end up in some chimera's belly."

"Let me," Moder said, and gently pushed him aside.

She freed the bags with a single tug. They looked practically empty. Then Pinsard helped tether Chance to the bay.

"Let Majesty ride," Arlequin said. "And stay off the path if you can. They may-"

"Arlequin," Moder said, taking his hand and pressing something shiny into his palm. "For the pain."

"I don't need-" he began to object, but Moder worked his hand closed. She leaned forward then and touched her lips to his brow. He murmured something back to her and slipped a blue stoppered bottle under his jack.

"Now," Arlequin said, "Give me the reins."

Pierrot was holding them. Arlequin glared at him.

"The reins, lack-wit," he said, struggling not to cough. "Or have you gone deaf as well?"

Pierrot tilted his head quizzically. Then, with the fingers his free hand, he began to make a tally: One, two, three, four, and five.

"And?" Arlequin snorted.

Pierrot held up one finger. Then he made it four. He tilted his head again.

Lara understood. So did Arlequin. His eyes narrowed.

"You're *not* coming with, jackanape," he said, reaching for the reins.

Pierrot would not surrender them. He held up two fingers, then three, and gestured to the horses.

"I *know*, curse you!" Arlequin spat. The effort of it winded him. "But you! You will stay! You . . . sponge-backed, Anthill rat! Stay and serve, or by Wulf-"

Pierrot hisked and wagged a slender finger. *Tsk-tsk.*

Arlequin might have lunged at the silent man then, weak though he was, but Moder stepped between them.

"They *climb*," she said.

It was all she needed to say.

Arlequin mounted, quaking as he shrank into his saddle. Pierrot turned to Lara and bowed, very low, the way he had when he had given her the crown of foil. He bowed so low that his battered lute nearly came loose from his back.

"Fool," Arlequin sighed and clicked his tongue. The dark-maned bay stirred and broke into a walk. Pierrot kept pace.

Bannertail chirruped, and leapt after the pair, dancing a while between Pierrot's legs. Then the fox-squirrel saw that Lara and the others were not following.

It squalled at the two men, its tail lashing. But they did not stop.

They were nearly out of sight when Lara called out: "Arlequin!"

Arlequin turned round. He bowed his head. She could not make out his expression.

"Goodbye!" she cried, hating the word. "And may Fenix guide your path!"

"And you, my Queen!" he rasped back. "Long . . . May you reign!"

They veered to the left. The woods swallowed them.

She wanted to curse. It wasn't right. It wasn't enough. She should have said more. She should have held them both when she had the chance. But it was too late.

They were gone.

* * * * * *

They abandoned the trail as soon as the clouds cleared. The Watcher was not full, but he was as bright as a pearl. Out in the open, the shrikes would spot them easily.

Lara led Surefoot into the brush as Moder covered their tracks. Pinsard went as far as to break several branches farther down the trail before backtracking to join them.

"Might not even see it in the dark," he muttered.

"Maybe," Lara said. She knew a false trail wouldn't fool Reynard's trackers for long. But every moment seemed to count.

They pressed into the undergrowth, Lara doing her best to ignore the slick fronds and sticky-headed buds that brushed against her legs.

The footing here was rocky and uneven. The moist-barked trees leaned drunkenly, and the rocky shelves were thick with roots. After her third stumble, Lara wished that Surefoot could lead them. He was certainly handling the ground better.

The wind picked up a bit and drove off some of the heat. Chimera chirped and hooted.

They had to retrace their steps more than once. First they came to a rent in the earth that was far too wide for any of them to jump. Then they came upon a stretch of forest where nothing grew, though clear pools of water dotted the ground. The trees were leafless, the soil was white as chalk, and the air itself stung to breathe. They turned away from that place without a second thought.

Often, though, the woods alone were obstacle enough.

"Too thick," Moder said, slipping from a tangle of fallen branches. Her head and shoulders were coated with something like dust. It glowed in the dark.

"Moder," Lara said, pointing.

Moder stared at the glimmering flakes, her deep blue eyes glazed with exhaustion.

"Awirung," she muttered, and brushed herself down.

"We could stop, Moder," Pinsard offered. "Wait until it is lighter."

"They will be catching us before then," she said, and began to walk back the way they'd come.

"They need to sleep too," Lara said, as she turned Surefoot about. "Don't they?"

"If they sleep," Moder said, "Tybalt will kill them."

"And when he sleeps?"

"He won't," Moder said, and kept walking.

Sometime later, an hour perhaps, Moder nearly tumbled into a wide crevice. It had been practically invisible until they were right on top of it. She would have fallen were it not for Lara, who caught her by the arm, dug a heel against a rock, and tugged backwards.

"Thank you," Moder huffed, shaking her head as if to clear it.

"Are you alright?" Lara asked, a terrible feeling beginning to settle in her gut. "Dizzy?"

"Just tired," Moder said, her voice firm. "No fever. I promise."

Lara nodded, putting the thought away. Moder might have kept the truth from her all these years, but she had never lied to her.

"Sit," Lara begged. "Just for a bit."

"A bit," Moder said, and flopped heavily to the ground.

"We've been here before," Pinsard said grimly. He was peering over the side of the crevice. "Look. That tree."

Lara looked. The tree he meant was an old husk, its trunk split in half by a lightning strike. They'd seen one just like it not far from the trail.

"Can't be," Lara said. "We've been going downhill for hours."

"I suppose," Pinsard said. "Only-"

"Wait," Lara said, holding her hand up.

She could hear something in the wind. It was a man's voice.

He was singing.

"A dress I must have as dark as the night . . ." The man's voice had a husky twang that reminded Lara of the lower strings of Danica's guitar. "With the stars of heavens bedew-ooo-ooooed . . . A dress I must wear if we are to wed . . . And a dress I must have before I am bed . . ."

"Corsablis," Moder whispered.

She stood up, slowly. Pinsard put his hand on the hilt of his sword. Lara stroked Surefoot's withers and prayed he would not neigh.

"Rose red, the slippers she bore . . ." He was louder now. Closer perhaps. It was hard to know for certain. "White the shroud that her mother wore . . ."

There was quiet again. Leaves rustled. Branches creaked in the wind. Something let out a caw and took flight.

Lara's eyes met Moder's: *What do we do?*

Moder held up her palm and scanned the trees. Finally, she pointed: There were pinpricks of light bobbing in the woods above them. There were only two at first, but soon they were a dozen. Then two dozen. Then more.

Surefoot pricked his ears and let out a snort. Bannertail poked its head from the saddlebag, sniffed the air, and yipped.

"Shush now," Lara said.

"Tch," she heard Pinsard hiss. She turned. He had climbed a spur of rock overlooking the crevice and was leaning as far over the gap as he could. Then he turned back and shook his head.

They were boxed in. If they stayed here, there would be nowhere to run. But, if they backtracked, they might only find themselves hemmed in someplace else. Worse, they might run right into Tybalt's men.

And, of course, there might be *no* way forward. For all they knew, they were already trapped.

Moder knew it as well as she did. "Choose," she whispered, her eyes weary but still alert.

Lara hesitated. She'd made so many poor decisions. This could be her last.

"A dress I must have as bright as the sun . . ." the singer crooned sweetly. "All her golden feathers ah-blayyyze . . . A dress I must wear, if with me you wouldst lie . . . And a dress I must have, 'afore I must die . . ."

The pinpricks on the heights bobbled as whoever was leading their pursuers came to a halt. Their light dipped low, vanishing for a moment amidst the undergrowth.

"Let's go," Lara breathed. As long as they kept moving, she reasoned, there was hope.

They traced the edge of the shelf backwards, and then kept on. The wind picked up, blew fierce, the boughs overhead showering them with droplets that clung to their skin.

"This way, I think," Pinsard said, pointing towards a fern-covered slope. He slipped a bit as he skidded down it, his black cape dragging through the muddy tracks his boots made, but it looked sound enough.

Lara began to lead Surefoot down as well, but just shy of the slope the gelding came to a halt, his ears flicking as he nickered softly.

"Come on, now," Lara soothed, trying not to sound panicked. "Just a little further."

Surefoot took a tentative step, snorted, and withdrew his hoof.

"Fair the maid . . ." the man's voice floated through the trees. "With the slippers of rose . . ."

"Fool," Moder muttered under her breath. "He gives them away, thinking to be scaring us."

He scares **me**, Lara thought as she took another step down the slope, her own boots sinking into the soft soil as she gave Surefoot's reins a firm tug.

"*Come!*" she hissed, as loud as she dared.

Surefoot huffed and threw his head. But he obeyed.

"Red her lips . . . Red the moon . . ."

The footing was bad. The ground was too wet, the topsoil too loose. If Surefoot slipped and fell, he'd roll right over her.

"Almost," Lara said, taking another step. "Nearly there."

"She runs to her love, but ever too soon . . ."

Near the bottom she began to slip, the soil giving way beneath her. She resisted the urge to lift her feet and leaned forward, drifting backwards until she felt Pinsard's hands bracing her from behind.

"Red her steps . . . Red her doom . . ."

"Watch out," Lara grunted, stepping aside as Surefoot lunged down the last stretch of the slope, driving straight into a patch of pitcher-shaped stalks.

The plants quivered and shriveled at the horse's touch. Surefoot neighed and broke from the things at a quick trot, snorting sharp blasts as he came to a halt. Bannertail sprung from the saddlebag and pounced into a nearby brush, squalling.

At last, both horse and fox-squirrel were quiet.

"Did they hear?" Pinsard whispered.

"I don't know," Lara whispered back.

Lara held her breath for a moment and listened. The wind blew. The trees swayed. Things rustled in the brush.

"Cold, the kiss he stole from her lips . . ."

The lights above them were shifting.

"Cold, the blade he wore at his hip . . ."

"Go!" Moder hissed and made to skid down after them.

Then she froze.

Lara stared at her, confused.

Then she heard it too.

It was far off, so faint that, were it not for the others, Lara would have thought she was imagining it. But there was no mistaking it: Someone was strumming the strings of a lute.

Pierrot.

A thrill ran through her.

They haven't caught them yet.

Moder did not waste any time, and slid down the embankment, mud coating her backside. Lara crept towards Surefoot, giving the shuddering stalks a wide berth.

The men on the heights were arguing. It was impossible to follow all of it, but she could make out snippets as they crept away.

"Snare, I say," one was griping. "Waiting behind some rock . . . a trap! White demons-"

"Bloody priest!" another snarled. "Lost 'is tongue-"

"Tracks," another added. It was the singer, she thought. "Clear as day . . . off the path, right?"

"Light soon," the griper said, hopeful. "Better by day?"

"Orders, right?" the snarler answered. "Orders is orders! Or did you forget?"

"So, you follow then," the singer said. "And we'll cut the bastard's strings."

Too many men began speaking at once.

"Chimera-"

"Bloody chimera, what about-"

"She-Wolf-"

"Chimera, waiting-"

"Tell that to him! Not my-"

"Bloody priest!"

"Never should have-"

"We all go- when it's light-"

"Light?!" That was the snarler again. "And if the Princess slips us? What then?"

"Not my fault-"

"Not mine either! He won't care . . . kill us both! Right?!"

"I'm not the one who-"

"You keep your mouth shut!" the snarler bellowed. "'Less you want steel in your belly! Now get on with it!"

That put an end to the discussion. They were passing beneath a felled tree dripping with creepers by then. It had fallen over a deep cut filled with luminous moss.

Lara turned back. The men were splitting up. The better part of them had changed course, drawn off by the strains of Pierrot's lute. But the rest were still following *their* trail.

A dozen at least, counting by the lanterns alone.

They trudged on, but not very swiftly. The growths hanging from the trees exhaled clouds of glimmering dust if they came too close, and the forest floor was riddled with knots and burrows. Moder was slowing again, sucking air with every tenth step.

She must have twisted her ankle.

Every time Moder winced, Lara looked back. Every time she looked the lights were closer. They were faster without the others it seemed. If the singer was still with them, he had lost his taste for song.

They came to the edge of a meadow whose pale, thick-stemmed grasses grew well over even Surefoot's head.

Lara said, "Stop."

Pinsard, who was a good ten paces ahead of her, turned about and pointed back towards the lights, his arm all but vanishing against the silhouette of his body. She doubted she'd be able to see him at all if it weren't for the moonlight.

"We'll hide here," she whispered. "In the grass."

"What if they find us?" Pinsard asked.

She gave the hilt of her sword a pat.

She couldn't see his face well enough to make out his expression, but she could see him nod. He had been listening to Moder's groans for just as long as she had.

They parted the grasses together, clearing a path for Surefoot, and dropped his reins in a clearing. Then they helped Moder hobble to a nearby patch. She was too exhausted to complain.

They settled in to wait, sipping a bit of water from their canteens. Moder's head drooped as she began to doze. They let her sleep, rubbing at their own eyes as they tried to stay alert.

Eventually, Lara realized that she could no longer hear Pierrot. There was only the wind whispering through the grass.

Bannertail was missing too. The fox-squirrel had been following her heels back in the woods. Had it crept back into her packsack?

She was about to get up and check when she heard someone cough. Rays of lamplight were streaming through the trees.

"Quiet," a rough voice hissed. "She's close. I can smell it."

Lara put her hand on Moder's shoulder and gave her a gentle shake. Her eyes opened. She blinked. Lara put her finger on her lips.

"In the grass?" another man queried. He spoke with a flat accent that Lara could not place.

Shafts of light spun as the man holding the lamp took a few steps forward. Pinsard shifted into a crouch.

"Fan out," the rough one whispered.

The lamps hovered at the edge of the trees. A gloved hand was gripping the lead lantern.

Lara gripped the hilt of her sword and loosened it from its scabbard. She wondered how many there were. Would she hesitate to lash out if one of them came pressing through the grass?

Pinsard wouldn't. She knew that by now.

Someone was pressing the grass aside on her left. She steeled herself.

Then, somewhere in the dark, something let out a throaty bark. There was a flash of steel in the lamplight as one of the men drew a sword.

Grass rustled as something shot through the brush.

"Wulf!" someone cursed. "What was that?! Ran right past my leg-"

Bannertail broke from the grass, panting. It took shelter under Lara's legs, curling its tail over the length of its body.

"Just a chimera, Aelroth," another man chuckled. "A little one, I swear. I'll skewer it for you!"

Bannertail shook with fright and screamed its bird-like howl. Lara bit back a curse.

Then a voice called out from the trees.

"Did they hear?" it whispered. It sounded like Pinsard's voice . . . But Pinsard was crouching right beside her, his sword half-drawn.

"I don't know," she heard another voice answer the first. It took her a moment to realize that it was remarkably like her own.

Bannertail whimpered and went still.

"Watch out," she heard her voice grunt.

Something like a horse neighed in the brush.

She could hear the men shifting, their mail jingling as they moved away from them.

"Almost," a voice- her voice- coaxed. The brush rustled. Something snorted like a horse. "Nearly there . . ."

"We can hear you just fine, Princess," the flat-accented man drawled. "Come out. We won't hurt you."

"I'm hurt," the voice whined. A girl's voice.

"Rugis can carry you," the one she took to be their leader grunted, taking another few paces into the forest with lantern held high. "Now come out! All of you!"

There was no answer. The reeds swayed in the wind.

"I've got her!" the flat voice cried out, triumphant. "She's hiding behind this . . . Wuh-"

He didn't get any further. Something giggled. There was a heavy *smack* followed by a yowling shriek, like a hill cat in heat. The man gave out a single, horrible cry.

Then he was quiet.

"Chimera!" someone shouted.

"Close ranks!" the leader ordered, and then a shape leapt out of the dark, its eyes flashing green as it bowled him over. His lantern flew from his hand and went spinning into the brush.

"Close ranks," he burbled, thickly. "Oh, gods- Oh, gods, no. My leg-"

He let out a low groan. Another terrible yowl split the air. It sounded like a woman screaming.

Bannertail bolted into the deeper grass.

One of the lamps spun about wildly. For a moment Lara could see the bearded face of the man who carried it, his eyes wide with terror. Then something the size of a stag dashed past him on four legs, its fanged mouth and mottled quill-backed hide at odds with its cloven hooves and long tufted tail.

"They're everywhere!" he cried out. Then he fell forward, his hand still gripping his lamp as he was dragged screaming into the brush.

"Run!" another man howled.

Tybalt's men began to scatter. Their lamps made them easy to pick out in the darkness. Screams filled the air as they ran. It was hard to tell which of them were human.

Lara scrabbled backwards on her hands and feet, shoving the grass aside with her shoulders. Someone gripped her by the arm. It was Pinsard. He hoisted her up.

"Slow," she heard Moder whisper. She had her knife drawn. "Go slow."

Lara tried not to hurry as they pressed backwards, trying not to stumble but unwilling to turn her back on the curtain of grass that stood between them and the noises she could hear: The screams, and the wet sound of flesh tearing.

She bumped into Surefoot. Bannertail was half curled around the horn of his saddle.

"Oh gods," a voice cried out behind them. It sounded like the leader, but it wasn't him. It was far too high-pitched. "My leg."

Lara and Pinsard parted the grasses. Moder led Surefoot.

"My leg," the voice cried again, a bit deeper. "Oh gods . . . Oh gods- Ran right past my leg. I'm hurt."

Ahead of them, somewhere beyond the tall grass, Lara could make out the distant outline of a solitary tree. It looked black against the twilight.

Somewhere behind them a scream split the air. Lara didn't look back. She kept her eyes on the tree and tried not to listen.

"Close ranks," the voice moaned. Then again, deeper still: "Close ranks . . . My leg. Right past . . . my leg . . ."

The voice sighed. Groaned. The resemblance was close enough.

"My leg . . . Oh gods, I'm hurt . . . Come out! Just a chimera . . . A little one. Won't hurt you . . . My leg . . . Close ranks. Close. I can smell it . . . A little one . . . I'll skewer it for you . . . My leg . . ."

VIII

There was a dry plain beyond the grasses, flat and treeless. The only plants that flourished there were swollen, fleshy things covered with spines. Their fruit was temptingly lush but, like everything that grew in Vulp Vora, they dared not touch them.

The plain dwindled to a stony wild broken by dark tabled hills, tall as towers. They slept in the shadow of one, waiting for the cover of night as they watched for signs of pursuit.

They saw none. No men. No shrikes. No wild chimera. The only living things amongst the rocks were lizards, beetles, and long bushy-tailed mice.

At night they walked, Lara leading Surefoot as they traced the edge of a high sandstone bluff. She could not see what lay below. The dark beneath the precipice looked bottomless.

Then the Firebird rose, and Lara saw that they stood above a vast sea of dust. It stretched east, as far as she could see: Clouds of grit driven by the wind, and leagues of sand as white as salt.

Ships lay in the sand. At least, the ancient, rusting hulks that sprawled amidst the dunes were shaped like ships. They made the ones Lara had seen moored in the Rusalka look like toys. The largest could have kept a hundred Peruns or more hidden within its belly.

"Ships of metal," Lara said. "But they have no sails."

"No water to sail on, either," Pinsard said. "The sea here must have dried up."

"Who built them?" Lara asked. "Giants?"

"Giants," Moder said, squinting as the wind threw fistfuls of dust into the air. "Or dead men, long ago. Come. This is not the sea we are seeking."

They turned west, towards the jagged mountains that shielded Mandross from the land of demons and walked until the heat and stinging wind became too much to bear.

There was no real shelter to be found. The best they could do was to nestle between two spurs of exposed rock and wrap their cloaks about them. Surefoot stood by miserably, head low, his neck muscles quivering.

"Water," Moder said, her lips puckering as she dug out her canteen. "Be drinking. But not too much."

Lara took a long swallow from her own canteen and, when she was certain that Moder was dozing, poured a bit more into her palm and let Bannertail lap it up. The fox-squirrel kept licking her palm long after there was no water left to drink.

"I know," she whispered. "I want more too."

The fox-squirrel pressed its nose to her fingers one last time and then scurried beneath her cloak.

She looked up. Pinsard was staring at her, his bright blue eyes peeking from the folds of his hood.

Lara stared back.

Don't tell.

His shoulders rose and fell. Then he reached into his packsack, pulled out the bowl he'd been using as a plate since they'd fled the farm, and filled it with the contents of his own canteen. He laid it on the ground near Surefoot and watched as the horse drank.

Were it not for the heat she would have hugged him.

The day lengthened. Lara's stomach rumbled, but she did not eat. She knew that the dried beef in her packsack would only make her thirstier. Instead, she leaned back and stroked Bannertail's soft fur as the wind sang against the rocks.

She thought about the others. Arlequin wouldn't have gone down without a fight, that much she knew for certain. Would they even bother to take him alive? Pierrot couldn't speak, but he was still a servant of the Watcher. He could read and write. Might they spare his life only to torture him? And what of Danica and Pasha back on the farm? Or Fanya, Svarog, and all the others who lived in Perun. Even old Dragos and his shy little Jalena. Were they safe? Or had Reynard's men taken them all away?

Taken them . . . Or killed them for trying to protect her.

The wind howled. The dust bit at her eyes. She told herself that was why she was crying.

* * * * * * *

"Lara," she heard Pinsard say. "Get up."

She yawned, and got to her feet, her muscles protesting. It was still light out. "What time is it?" she asked. She didn't remember having fallen asleep.

"Time to go," Moder replied, Surefoot's reins already in hand. She'd clearly been up for some time: She had neatened her hair, and her boots were newly brushed.

Lara touched her own tangled locks and pulled free something that looked like a cocklebur. She shook it loose from her glove as she fell into step behind the others.

That day was very hard. The wasteland went on and on. In places it was rocky, and in others the rock had been ground to a fine powder. They came upon patches of bone-dry scrub brush, and long tracts of cracked soil that might once have been rivers, but the only water they could see was in the clouds high above them.

Then, well before dusk, they came to a halt.

There was something on the horizon: A structure perhaps. Through the dusty haze it resembled an enormous black dragonfly, listing on its side. Its 'wings' glittered as they spun, windmill-like in the breeze.

"What is it?" Pinsard asked.

Moder shook her head: She didn't know.

"It's not moving," Lara pointed out. "Why don't we get closer and take a look?"

Moder's hand worried at Surefoot's reins, but she nodded.

As they crept towards the thing lying in the sand, Lara could see the thick lengths of ruddy tarp draped over its carapace and heard the tinkling of the glass chimes hanging along the length of its tail. Closer still she caught a whiff of woodsmoke and something else: Meat, she thought, roasting in garlic and onion. It smelled remarkably like Danica's lamb stew.

Just beneath the dome that served as the dragonfly's head, a pair of vaguely horse-like creatures stood, tethered to a low beam. Beside them a wide stone cylinder jutted from the sand. A rope and pulley hung above it.

It was a well.

"It's a camp," Pinsard said.

"Or a tavern," Lara said, pointing towards a green patch amidst the red. "I think that's a sign."

"What is it doing all the way out here?" Pinsard asked.

"There is water," Moder said. "Even chimera must be drinking water."

"And eating," Lara said, taking in a whiff of whatever was cooking beneath the tarps.

"Eating what, though?" Pinsard asked. "That place is not The Nightingale."

"It smells like mutton to me."

Bannertail smelled it too, and slipped from Lara's packsack, chittering.

"You can't seriously want to go in there?" Pinsard balked. "We could all be killed!"

"We'll die anyway if we don't get water," Lara said.

"I know, Lara, but," Pinsard sputtered. "We could wait for dark- I could creep up and-"

"No," Moder said, cutting him off. "We all will go. And not to be stealing."

Pinsard turned, his brow furrowing.

"Others are riding here," Moder said, gesturing to the creatures tethered near the well. "Riding . . . And riding away. South, could be. Could be taking us with them, I am thinking."

"And what if they," Pinsard said, swallowing, "Will not?"

"Then it is good," Moder said, "That we all are knowing how to be chopping wood."

The tethered animals raised their heads as they approached, black eyes blinking. One resembled a cross between a deer and a horse, the white stripes running up its hind legs contrasting with its ruddy hide. The other was more bizarre: A scaly bipedal thing with a long narrow neck and an even narrower head crested with iridescent feathers. The tongue that darted from its mouth was startlingly turquoise and as long as Lara's arm.

Lara didn't know if these were chimera or merely animals native to the desert, but she couldn't imagine riding either of them.

Bannertail leapt to Lara's shoulder. Surefoot let out a nervous whinny.

"Stay," Moder said, dropping the horse's lead in the sand rather than tying him to the hitching post.

He stayed. For the moment at least.

He might run off, Lara thought, *but at least he won't break his neck trying*.

Now that they were standing beside it, Lara could make out the great stone lid sealing the well shut. It didn't look as though a human would even be able to move it.

Perhaps there's a trick to it.

"An old mill, maybe," Pinsard said absently, staring up at the trio of blades spinning overhead.

Lara shrugged, shifting her gaze to the green sheet of metal propped against the thick folds of the tent. The pale symbols stamped on it were nonsense to her. If they *were* letters, or numbers, they were none that she had ever seen.

"Let's hope they say, 'Welcome to The Dragonfly,'" Lara said.

Pinsard shot her a curious glance. She shrugged. Perhaps the place looked like something else to him.

Moder coughed into her fist, straightening as she shifted the weight of her sword belt. Pinsard did the same, and tilted his head slightly, puffing out his chest.

Not long ago, Lara would have snickered. But she had seen blood on Pinsard's sword, seen how easily he had leaned from his saddle to strike Tybalt's man down. She had to admit that, standing side by side, both he and Moder looked very tall and very serious. Dangerous, even.

She shooed Bannertail from her shoulder, ignoring its squalls, pulled another fistful of cockleburs from her hair and did her best to follow suit.

She was still shaking them free when the crimson folds of the tent parted, thrust aside by a pair of clawed hands laden with ornate rings. A demonic-feline face peered out at them, tusked and whiskered, its fierce amber eyes gleaming beneath the horned headdress that topped its wide head.

"*Oraya kim gider?*" it rumbled at them in a rich basso voice. "*Dost yada düsman?*"

"*Wes hal,*" Moder replied crisply, bowing her head ever so slightly. "*Sprece thu Calvar?*"

The cat-faced thing sniffed the air, its lips curling back slightly as it looked them over. It was impossible to tell if it was smiling or simply baring its teeth.

"Are you . . ." Moder tried again, slower this time, "Knowing Aquilian?"

The thing did not answer. Instead, it craned its neck to get a better look at Surefoot. Then it extended one of its clawed fingers towards the horse, the bracelets hanging from its wrists jangling musically.

"O ati getirdin mi, soluk iblisler?" it queried, its words seeming to roll from the bottom of its throat. *"Igdis edilmis midir?"*

It kept its finger extended and stared at them expectantly. Lara winced as the fox-squirrel scrambled back to the safety of her shoulder, its tiny claws digging into her skin.

"What does it want?" Pinsard whispered.

"Something about Surefoot," Lara whispered back. "I think."

"Ic paet ne undergiete," Moder said, shaking her head. "We . . . are not understanding you."

"Huurrrf," it snuffled, its mouth yawning wider, but it appeared to be pleased with Moder's response, and stepped to one side as it beckoned for them to enter.

"Biz ticaret yapiyoruz!" it said. *"Evet? Evet."*

The scent of savory meat wafted from the opening. Lara could faintly make out what lay beyond: Woven carpets and over-stuffed cushions, a low brass brazier simmering with coals, hanging lanterns that sent stars and spirals drifting across the walls.

She could make out other shapes as well, all of them vaguely human. She couldn't see their eyes, but she had no doubt that they were all turned towards them.

"Iceri gel, soluk iblisler!" the chimera urged, waving them forward. *"Iceri gel! Seni isirmayacagim!"*

Moder nodded ever so slightly, and breathed, "Remember the cuts," as she slipped through the open fold.

Lara followed, noting that their 'host' was wearing nothing but metal bands and a woven knee-length skirt over its tawny hide. The skirt was held in place by a dagger-like brooch, and a tail dangled from its folds. She caught a whiff of its fur as she brushed past: A musky animal-tang mixed with something that reminded her of freshly cut pinewood.

She had smelled worse things.

Her eyes adjusted quickly to the dimness. The belly of the dragonfly was hollow, it seemed. Hollow, and ribbed like the insides of some great animal. In the places where its dark carapace was not masked by hanging cloth, Lara saw tangles of veiny tubes and ovals of clouded glass. There were symbols behind the glass, white, like the ones on the sign outside, but other things quickly drew her eye.

Of all the tent's inhabitants, Lara would be hard pressed to say which she found the oddest. The five figures huddled near the brazier looked human enough, but they were encased in sandy, skin-tight leathers that covered their bodies from to neck to foot. Shawls veiled their heads, cloth ends pooling atop the yellow knives they wore on their hips. They were staring back at her, their hazel eyes unblinking, wiry beards the only measure of their sex.

Nor were they alone. Leaning against one of the dragonfly's curving ribs, her arms crossed, was a woman whose teal robes looked drab compared to her golden skin. Lara took it for paint at first, until she saw the metallic shimmer of the woman's blue-black hair and the winged beetle tattooed across her left cheek. She was a Telchine, like Stheno the Wily or the wicked Queen Elissa. As the woman uncrossed her arms and took a sip from the ceramic bowl cradled in her right hand, Lara noticed the spear resting at her side. It was taller than the woman by a head, its steel tip a wavy leaf.

An immense suit of dented armor lay beside the Telchine, sagging against the wall like some drunken giant. It looked empty to Lara at first, but then it stirred, metal fingers splaying against the carpet as whatever was within began to rouse itself. But even as it sat up, it somehow seemed less alive to Lara. Its long arms and legs were completely out of proportion to its thick torso, and its helm had no visor: Just a collection of mismatched sockets.

Finally, there was the shrike. It was lounging on a bed of cushions, a single clawed leg casually splayed across a low table. It had vaguely human proportions, but there the similarities ended. An orange crest hung over its gray and noseless face like a beak, and its ashy wings lay on the carpet like an unshouldered cloak. In its elongated talons it clutched a pipe stem attached to a silver vase by a cord. The tendrils of smoke that hung about its head had a sweeter bite than the leaf tobacco Danica kept, but they made Lara's eyes water all the same.

For a moment Lara could not help but gawk. Then she heard the tent folds rustle as they closed, shutting out what was left of the day.

The cat-faced chimera gestured broadly towards an empty recess and huffed.

Sit. That much was clear. Moder bowed her head and led the way. Even inside the tent, she and Pinsard still had to stoop. The roof of the dragonfly had clearly not been built with Calvarians in mind.

They sat, setting their packsacks down beside them. Bannertail sought the relative safety of Lara's lap. The Telchine sipped her drink. The shrike placed the pipe stem between its orange lips and took a pull.

"Istedigin yere otur," the cat chimera muttered as it padded towards the brazier, the seated men making way as it reached for something in their midst. *"Ve sonra ilk ticaretimizi . . ."*

The chimera's bands clanged and rattled as it lifted a steaming bronze pot from the floor. It held it up, fixing them with its gaze.

"Simdi," it purred, *"Gidi, ve icecek ticareti de."*

With its free hand it pointed to an alcove, where a large clay pot stood. A ladle and a stack of bowls were laid out on the chest that stood beside it.

"Simdi ihtiyacin var, evet?" it grinned.

"Food," Pinsard said. "Water."

"But not for free," Lara guessed.

Moder reached into her packsack and produced a pair of silver marks.

"Is this being enough?" she asked.

"Bozuk para yok," it said, its nose wrinkling.

Moder's hand disappeared back into the sack. This time she held out a golden talent.

"Gold," she said. "Enough?"

"Bozuk para yok!" the chimera repeated, shaking its head with irritation. *"Ben bir tuccarim, mezar degil!"*

"Maybe it doesn't want coins," Lara said.

"What else would it want?" Pinsard asked.

"There is already being food here," Moder reasoned. "And water."

The shrike pursed its lips and exhaled a thin plume of smoke.

"Huh," Lara murmured, and reached into her own coin purse. There weren't any coins inside, just a few spare strips of dried jerky, the rest of the soldier's playing cards, and one of the little bricks of tobacco that the Baroness's soldiers had carried. She'd completely forgotten about them, until now.

She pulled out the brick and held it out for the chimera to see.

"Bu nedir?" the cat-faced chimera said, peering at the brick in her hand. *"Şeker?"*

Lara brought the brick up to her nose and took a theatrical whiff before exhaling as the shrike had done.

"Hah," the chimera chortled. *"Tutun! Tutun! İyi bir ticcaret!"*

The chimera turned to Moder.

"Tutun, soluk iblisler?" it queried.

Moder reached into her sack and pulled out the rest of the tobacco: Four little bricks in all. The chimera's eyes widened as she laid them on the carpet.

"Is enough now?" Moder asked.

The Telchine let out a quiet snort. The veiled men began to make gestures to each other.

"Uc tugla icin uc ogun," the chimera said, and set down the pot. Then it reached forward and plucked up all but one of the bricks- the one still in Lara's hand.

She leaned forward, offering it as well.

"Ceyiz icin," the chimera said, waving away the brick and loping towards the clay jug, its bracelets and bands jingling as it went.

One by one, the cat-faced chimera brought them bowls of water, and empty bowls to scoop into the iron pot. The stew within was mostly chunks of meat and onion in a thick and fiery sauce.

"Thank you," Lara said.

The chimera nodded, and hauled the pot away, slipping through a beaded curtain at the far side of the tent.

They dug out their spoons and ate.

"It is like mutton," Pinsard admitted, swallowing. "Almost."

"Yes," Moder said, frowning at her bowl. "Almost."

"They're not eating us, at least," Lara said.

"Not yet," Pinsard replied.

Lara sipped her water and tried not to think too much.

They were still eating when two of the veiled men broke away from their companions and shuffled towards them across the carpeted floor, walking on their knees while keeping their backs quite upright. They came to a halt just short of arm's-length and resettled themselves.

They were Southerners like herself, tawny beneath their paler second skin. One was older than the other, his beard gray as slate. The other had a white scar running directly across his left cheek. Neither of them spoke.

Moder set down her bowl. Lara and Pinsard did the same.

The older man bowed his head ever so slightly. Moder returned the bow. Then the younger man grunted and began to make signs and gestures with his hands and fingers. It was far more complicated than Pierrot's miming. Lara could understand none of it. It did not help that the scarred man's expression remained fixed and mysterious . . . But she did notice that his gestures kept drifting towards *her* before returning to focus on Moder.

When he was finished, he placed his hands over his knees and waited.

Moder stared back at them, clearly uncertain. Bannertail sat up and yipped at the men softly. They ignored its cry.

"They want to trade," a woman's husky voice broke the silence. It belonged to the Telchine. She'd finished her drink and was toying with the fingertips of her gloves.

"You are understanding them?" Moder said.

The Telchine smirked. "You should be more surprised that I can understand *you*."

"What do they want?" Lara asked.

"You," the Telchine answered. "They would haggle for the boy too, but he is clearly of your elder's blood, and that might give offense."

"I am not-" Pinsard began to say, but Lara grabbed him by the thigh and squeezed.

"Tell them," she said, "That I am not for sale."

"I could," the Telchine said, pushing away from the arch and sauntering towards them. "But what will you give me in return? More *tutun* from some distant land?"

"Is that what you want?"

"No," she said. "But I will tell them."

The Telchine kicked a cushion towards them and sat atop it neatly. The older man eyed her with an unfriendly glare, but he bowed his head as she grunted and began to move her hands. She was not as quick as the younger man had been, but her movements were far more elegant.

When she was done, the younger man grunted, and touched the hilt of his dagger before making a few curt gestures.

The Telchine turned to Moder.

"You are certain you will not sell?" she asked, arching one of her brows. "They are willing to pay half her weight in water."

"She is my *dohtor*," Moder said, bluntly.

"Ah, well," the Telchine said, and delivered their response, her gloved fingers dancing. There was clearly more to it than a simple 'no.'

The younger man took in a deep breath, his chest puffing. Then he covered his nose and exhaled as he backed away. The older man followed, but continued to gesture as he did so, his arms rising and falling as he bowed once, twice, and then a third time before he finally shifted back towards the brazier.

"What was that all about?" Pinsard asked.

"They accept your refusal," the Telchine answered.

"And that is being all?" Moder said, skeptically.

The Telchine sighed heavily.

"He *also* says that the sons of Mirgas and the sons of Olc split ways long ago . . . And there cannot be two suns."

She yawned, unfolded her legs, and stretched out her right arm until her elbow popped.

"I think he was trying to be clever."

"Can they not speak?" Lara asked.

"They *can*," the Telchine said, "But they are tribesmen from Eresh. The deep desert. There is no water there. To speak would mean opening their mouths, and that is a luxury they can seldom afford."

"What did they want with me?"

"What do you think?" the Telchine said, fixing her gaze on Lara. Her eyes shone violet, but perhaps that was just a trick of the light.

"Will they try to be stealing her?" Moder asked.

"Not before the new moon," the woman said, and brushed a bit of sand from her skirt.

"Why not?" Pinsard asked.

"It would be *rude*," the Telchine replied, in a tone that suggested she thought it a very stupid question.

Lara tried to remember whether the Watcher was waxing or waning.

"So," the Telchine said, "I take it you mean to cross the mountains."

"How did you know?" Lara asked.

"No one comes here for the stew," the woman answered, her smirk widening.

Moder shot Lara a familiar look: *Keep quiet.*

"We might be going that way," Moder said, attempting to sound disinterested. "Is faster, maybe, than going across the desert?"

"That way lies The Plain. I wouldn't go there. Unless you've grown tired of drawing breath."

"You have been to The Plain of Glass?" Pinsard asked.

"I have seen it," the Telchine replied.

"And you," Moder said, "Where are you going?"

"With you," the woman answered. "Maybe. It depends on whether or not you can afford me."

"And why," Moder asked, "Would we be traveling with you?"

"Why?" The Telchine snorted. "To guide you, of course. But you knew that."

"We don't even know your name," Lara said, ignoring Moder's glare.

"It's Arsinoe," the woman said. "So! Do you want a guide, or not?"

Moder shut her eyes and took a deep breath. When she opened them, she said, "We do."

"Go on then," the Telchine said, opening both her palms. "Charm me."

"We are having coins," Moder said, catching hold of her packsack. "Will *you* take them?"

"I might. Show them to me."

"How many?" Moder asked, cagily.

The Telchine rolled her eyes. "A few of the ones you tried to buy your supper with will do."

Moder retrieved a coin purse from her sack and spilled its contents onto the carpet between them. There were a handful of copper bits and brass drabs, half a dozen silver marks, and two gold coins. One was a talent, with Koschei the Deathless' grim bearded face stamped onto it. An eagle-headed chimera with the body of a great cat was on the other. Under it was a name: 'Lionel.'

"Hmmm," the Telchine hummed. "Clean coins. I have traveled where they can spend, but they are useless to me here."

"Useless?" Lara said. "Because they are . . . clean?"

"I will show you," the Telchine said, and plucked the golden talent from the pile. "Just to be certain."

Then, before Moder had the time to object, the Telchine twisted about and flicked the coin towards the armored figure slouching behind her. It bounced off its massive chest with a 'ping!' and landed on the carpet beside it.

"Dramsind," the Telchine called out. *"Fesis bujeti?"*

Whatever was inside the armor slowly swiveled its head towards the coin. Then it reached forward, its oddly flat gauntlet hovering over the coin as something inside its chest whirred and clicked.

"Buse," a thin voice murmured. *"Jekute."*

The clicking ceased. The metal glove retracted. The thing's visorless helm swiveled, drooped, was still.

"You see?" the Telchine said, shifting back around. "Your coins are too clean. Do you think the hollow men trade in metal? It is the colorless fire they seek, not glim and glitter . . ."

Lara was only half-listening. She was still staring at the suit of armor.

"So," the Telchine said. "No fire. No water either I take it?"

"No," Moder replied, tersely. "And I am wanting coin back."

"Yes, yes," the Telchine said, "I am no thief, *soluk iblisler.*"

"I am meaning no offense," Moder said.

"I take none," the Telchine replied. "But tell me, how about the horse?"

"The horse?" Moder said.

"Your horse," the Telchine said, her smug smile returning. "Now *he* is worth something. Is he stallion or gelding?"

"*Geldingr*, he is," Moder said, her Aquilian faltering. "But how-"

"Prahasta smelled him coming," the Telchine said. Lara assumed that she was speaking of the cat-faced chimera. "It's why he let you in. But, the horse, he *is* a gelding?"

"He is," Moder nodded.

"A pity," the Telchine sighed. "He'd have made some chimera a happy bride, no doubt."

Pinsard turned his head and coughed into his fist.

"Still," the Telchine went on, "Prahasta doesn't know that yet. Is he healthy, at least?"

"He needs feed and water," Lara replied.

"But no shakes? No sleeping sickness?"

"No," *Moder* said. "It is as Lara says."

"Good," the Telchine said with a clap. "Then I am willing to take the gelding as payment. Provided that *Lara* is willing to sell."

Across from them, the shrike let out a muted caw, its claws clacking against the table as its crest bristled.

"Me?" Lara said.

"He's your horse, isn't he?"

"He was Arle-" Lara chewed on her lip a moment. "Yes. He's my horse."

"And?"

"What will happen to him?" Lara asked.

"I will sell him to Prahasta. Prahasta will sell him to someone else when he realizes he is not a stallion. That is where my knowledge ends."

"He . . . Won't be eaten?"

"Eaten?!" the Telchine balked. "Is the North so barbaric? Or are horses there so cheap?"

"No!" Lara said. "It's just that- Well, chimera, they- They'll eat anything, won't they?"

"You have a chimera in your lap," the Telchine pointed out, squinting at Bannertail. "Yet here you sit."

"That's different," Lara said.

"Tss," the Telchine hissed, and bared her teeth. The fox-squirrel nestled closer to Lara's belly, hiding its face behind its tail.

The shrike cawed again, louder this time.

"We all have fangs, girl," the Telchine said. "Don't let Prahasta's fool you. He would sooner eat the three of you than that horse. Speaking of which . . ."

The beaded curtain rustled as the cat-faced chimera returned, his bands jingling. A growl rumbled from his throat as he spied the woman sitting by their side.

"*Arsinoe!*" he yowled. "*Orada ne yapiyorsun?*"

"*Ticaret yapmak,*" the Telchine answered.

"*Ticaret?*" The Chimera padded forward, the tribesmen shifting aside as he strode straight through them, wringing his clawed hands. "*Ne ticareti, Arsinoe?*"

"Don't mind him," the Telchine said, "He thinks I'm trying to steal his trade."

"Is that *not* what you are doing?" Pinsard asked.

"He's a quick one, isn't he?" the Telchine quipped as the chimera loomed up behind her.

"*Ne ticareti, Ahr-sin-oh-ay?*" he growled again, his teeth grinding against each syllable of her name.

"*Bir an, Prahasta!*" the Telchine snapped. "Now, do we have a deal? Yes or no?"

"You'll guide us?" Lara asked. "Over the mountains?"

"Yes," Arsinoe panted.

"And, after the mountains?"

"*After?* What else? I go my way, you go yours."

"No deal then," Lara said, and shifted her gaze to the chimera. "This woman is bothering us, Prahasta."

"*Ismimi biliyor?*" the chimera growled, his amber eyes narrowing as he took hold of the Telchine's right arm. "*Beni kandirmaya mi calisiyorsun, ici bos kizligin kizi?*"

"Fine!" the Telchine said, her calm beginning to dissolve as the chimera leaned forward and snuffled at her hair. "I'll guide you to the Eridanos. Now, say we have a deal!"

"The Eridanos?" Pinsard said, shooting Lara a subtle look.

The woman clapped her hand over the chimera's wrist and tugged. "It's a river!"

"Does it run to the sea?" Lara asked.

"Yes!"

"Guide us to the sea then," Lara said. "And we have a deal."

"*Yapmalisin!*" the chimera snarled, tugging Arsinoe from the cushion.

"The sea!" she yelped. "The sea, by The Ruiner! Now say it! *Bir pazarligimiz var!*"

"*Bir,*" Lara repeated, "*Pah-zar. Ligimeez var.*"

"Close enough," Arsinoe gasped as the chimera released her.

"*Bir anlasman var?*" the thing grumbled, his tail lashing against the carpet.

"*Yapariz,*" Arsinoe huffed, rubbing her arm as she got to her feet. Green bruises were already blossoming on her shimmering skin.

"*Kahretsin!*" the chimera spat. "*Cakallar! Cadirimdaki cakallar!*"

With that he went to see to the shrike's needs, his bands rattling as he waved a path through the smoke.

"He didn't take that well," Lara said. "Did he?"

Arsinoe snickered, the beetle on her cheek seeming to stretch its wings. "Imagine how mad he'll be when he finds out I own your horse."

"When are we leaving?" Moder asked, scooping up the loose coins and returning them to the purse.

"As soon as I settle things with Prahasta," the Telchine answered, brushing down the front of her robe. "Unless the idea of sleeping here appeals to you?"

"It does not," Moder replied. "And I am still wanting my coin."

"Is she always this testy?" Arsinoe asked, turning to Lara.

Lara did her best to keep a straight face.

"We still need water," Pinsard said. Lara could tell from the tone of his voice that the woman irritated him. "And food."

"And here I thought we'd go without either," the Telchine said, giving her forehead a slap. "How fortunate these two are to have someone like *you* looking out for them."

"Now listen," Pinsard said, and began to stand up.

"No," the woman said. "You listen, boy. I swore by The Ruiner that I would guide you to the sea, and that I will do. But I will do it *my* way. Not yours. Understand?"

Pinsard's nostrils flared as he glowered back at the woman and took a step towards her. She was shorter than him by at least a foot, but she did not flinch.

"Pinsard is always being full of care," Moder interjected. "What is word? Cautious?"

"Cautious," Lara nodded.

"Cautious," Moder went on. "With strangers. Like I am being. He, too, means no offense."

The Telchine crossed her arms.

"We have an understanding, then?" she asked, not breaking her stare.

"We do," Moder said.

She nudged Pinsard.

"We do," Pinsard repeated, sullen.

"I'll make my own arrangements then," the Telchine said, and gave the bruises on her right arm a brush as she went to collect her leaf-headed spear.

"Who does she think she is?" Lara heard Pinsard mutter.

"Our guide," Lara whispered. "Now keep quiet."

"You have other supplies?" the Telchine called to them, bending down to rifle through something resembling a packsack. "Carry-rolls, or the like?"

"They are being on the horse," Moder said.

"Go and get them," she said, retrieving something from her gear. "The two of us will join you presently."

"Two of us?" Pinsard said, his eyes narrowing.

"Dramsind," the Telchine said. *"Bufo fesis mona."*

Again, the suit of armor shifted, the fat fingers of its metal gauntlet plucking the gold talent from the carpet. Its long right arm served to steady it as it rose to its feet, tilting its head forward so as not to strike the dragonfly's shell.

*It **is** a giant*, Lara thought. *Or at least, it's as tall as one.*

Whatever it was, it clearly wasn't human.

The tribesmen turned to watch as the thing crept forward, metal plates shifting as its left arm stretched- no, lengthened- to offer Moder the coin.

She took it.

"You should probably make your farewells to your horse," Arsinoe said, and made her way towards the cat-faced chimera and the shrike on its cushions.

"Prahasta," she exclaimed, batting at the smoke. *"Simdi ticaret yapacagiz, degil mi?"*

* * * * * * *

- 181 -

The skull-moon was waxing, Lara noted, remembering the tribesmen's eyes. Waxing, and not yet full. It almost made up for the dark.

The dark, the stinging wind, and her aching legs.

It was a struggle to keep up with Arsinoe as she sprinted over sand and rock, occasionally using the butt of her spear as a fulcrum. The Firebird had set fully while they had been inside the dragonfly, and they had only the light of the Watcher and the stars to guide them, but the woman was not slowed by the darkness. She could see as well by night as a cat or owl, it seemed, and she never stumbled.

The same could not be said for the rest of them. Pinsard in particular seemed determined not to be outpaced, but his boots kept catching on loose stones and cracks in the soil.

"Slow down, *soluk iblisler,*" the Telchine said to him after one of his stumbles nearly sent him into a patch of thorny scrub. "You might scrape a knee."

"Awirung," he swore under his breath as he picked himself up, but he went more carefully after that.

The Telchine was fast, but the giant was faster. Partly it was the length of his legs, though occasionally he would tilt forward and run on all fours before righting himself again. Lara thought of the giant as being a 'he,' rather than an 'it,' though she couldn't entirely say why. There was nothing masculine or feminine about the giant, except for the tinny voice that occasionally answered Arsinoe's brisk commands, and even that seemed to spring from somewhere far below what Lara thought of as its head.

He moves like an insect, she thought, watching his legs pump back and forth. *Is that what's inside of that armor? Some enormous beetle, like the one on that woman's cheek?*

The thought was too bizarre. She put it out of her mind and focused on keeping her footing.

They stopped to rest only twice before dawn, just long enough to take some water and relieve themselves amongst the rocks. Even then they did not stop entirely, for Arsinoe did not halt until she had found a shelf of stone large enough to shelter them from the sun.

"Here," she said, unshouldering the bundle she called a 'carry-roll,' and set it beside her spear. "We'll eat here, and sleep until she's in our eyes again."

They set down their own packs and sat in a huddle. The giant's head swiveled back and forth, his arms going limp as he sank to his knees.

"How far?" Moder asked, eyeing the mountains.

"Two days," the Telchine replied, rooting through her pack. "And two more to make the passage if we're lucky. Now eat. We'll need all the strength we can get."

They had to carry all their supplies, now that they were without Surefoot. It had been hard for Lara to watch the cat-faced chimera lead him away, and she doubted any other horse than one that Arlequin had reared would have done so willingly. Demon would have bitten off the chimera's fingers, she thought, before letting a chimera stroke his withers.

At least the Telchine had sold Surefoot to Prahasta for quite a sum. Not only had the chimera refilled their waterskins from his well (the lid was not as heavy as it looked), but he'd opened his larder. Arsinoe's carry-roll he had filled with smoked meat, loaves of flatbread, and a large jar of red paste.

Arsinoe doled out the former sparingly, breaking up one of the loaves and passing out several ribbons of whatever had been in the stew. Then she stripped off her right glove and dipped a finger into the paste before placing it between her lips, savoring the taste of it before swallowing.

"Ah," she sighed, and dipped her finger into the jar again.

There was something odd about the Telchine's hand. The back of it looked as green and bruised as her arm, though those marks were already starting to fade.

When she saw Lara staring at her, Arsinoe let out a sigh.

"Try some," she said, "If you're so curious."

"May I?" Lara said as the woman slipped her hand back into her glove.

"'May I,'" the woman repeated as she handed her the jar. "Well, aren't we proper?"

"I don't think Moder would agree," Lara said.

"Hmmmph," Moder murmured, chewing her bread.

"Don't eat too much," the Telchine warned as she dipped the corner of her flatbread into the paste. "It will make you thirsty."

"What is it?" Lara asked.

"Scald," the Telchine said. "Minced lizard, garlic, and nightshade for kick."

Lara lifted the bread to her mouth and took a nibble. It made her lips a bit numb, but it wasn't bad.

"Doesn't *he* eat?" Lara asked, glancing at the giant. He was half sitting, half leaning against the shelf, his head resting directly against his chest.

"He had his fill at the *Carsi*," Arsinoe answered, and reached for the jar.

"*Carsi*," Lara said. "Does that mean dragonfly?"

"No," Arsinoe said.

Lara surrendered the jar. The Telchine sealed it shut, pulled the hood of her robe down over her eyes, and settled down to sleep.

"Should I take first watch?" Pinsard said.

"Dramsind will keep watch," Arsinoe said, scooting closer to the stone at her back.

"He is sleeping," Pinsard said.

"Is he?" she yawned and gave her hood another tug before falling silent.

Pinsard took a long look at the giant. He looked as though he had been squatting in the dust for over a thousand years.

"I will take first watch," he said, planting his scabbard beside him.

Lara nodded and finished the rest of her bread before drifting off, the shifting wind cool against her face.

* * * * * * *

It was Bannertail that woke her, slipping out from under her cloak.

She cracked her eyes. The Firebird was in the west, and the Telchine was eating more of the paste, this time with a little wooden spoon. Pinsard had fallen asleep leaning against his sword, but Moder was on her feet and practicing her cuts.

"Sleep well?" Arsinoe asked, licking the spoon clean. Bannertail watched it and the jar disappear into the Telchine's pack, and let out a low whine.

"I guess," Lara said. Her mouth was dry as the sand. "Bannertail, come."

The fox-squirrel's nose quested in the sand beneath the Telchine's feet for a moment.

"Come," she said again, patting her leg. Bannertail bounded back to her and menaced her right hand for a while.

"Your chimera," Arsinoe said. "Is it boy or girl? Or a bit of both?"

"I don't know," Lara answered.

"A boy then," the Telchine said. "You'd know by now if he were a she."

"How's that?" Lara asked, but the Telchine was already on her feet.

"Wake up," she said, kicking a bit of soil in Pinsard's direction. "We've a long way to go before the next sunrise."

Pinsard woke with a start and caught his sword by its hilt. It was half-drawn before he saw the Telchine smirking at him.

"You're quicker than you look," she said. "Keep it up, boy, and you might end up impressing me."

"Don't call him 'boy,'" Lara said.

"I can speak for myself," Pinsard huffed, and tromped off to practice his own cuts, grunting with more enthusiasm than usual as he swung his blade.

"There I die a dozen deaths," the Telchine said, taking hold of her spear and leaning on it. "He's an angry one, isn't he? But his form's not bad."

"He's called Pinsard," Lara said, but quietly.

"'Boy' is easier on the tongue," Arsinoe replied. "Besides, I don't need to know his name. I don't need to know his mother's name, either. The less I know the better, trust me."

"Better?"

"I'm your guide *now*, but who knows? I could be someone else's guide someday. Someone interested in an Aquilian girl with two *soluk iblisler* for a family. Wouldn't you rather I didn't know who you are, if and when that day comes?"

"Aren't you the least bit curious?"

The Telchine rolled her right shoulder and winced.

"Let me guess: You're running from something. Something serious enough that it makes a place like Vulp Vora seem warm and inviting. So, you're running, and you're going to keep running until whatever it is that you're running from is far, far behind you. That sound about right?"

"Yes," Lara said, "But-"

"The 'buts' of the world will drag you under, girl," the woman said, and gave the giant a tap with her spear. *"Dramsind, fiki."*

"Wopa," the giant replied, lurching upwards.

Bannertail lost all interest in Lara's hand and slipped into her pack.

"We should be moving," Arsinoe said, retrieving her carry-roll. "Or do you feel the need to fight the wind as well?"

"I could fight you," Lara replied, and touched the hilt of her sword. "If you like."

The Telchine chuckled.

"What I'd *like*, girl," she said, giving her spear a lazy twirl, "Is to be free of the lot of you. But not that way."

Then she gave her spear another spin, this one much swifter. When she was done, Lara found herself staring at its sharp, gleaming point.

"Not yet," she finished, and put up her spear.

Lara took a step backwards and took a deep breath. *She could have killed me.*

She still could.

"Go on, girl," the Telchine said, pursing her lips. "Stretch your arms. Dramsind and I can keep ourselves amused while we wait."

Lara nodded and went to join Moder. She could feel the Telchine's eyes watching her as she went.

"Do you really trust her?" she asked Moder, who was still practicing her diagonals.

"Do you?" Moder asked.

"No," Lara said. "But-"

The word died on Lara's tongue. Then she drew her sword and slashed at the air until her head cleared.

IX

It was well past midnight when Dramsind came skidding to a halt, all four limbs plunging into the sand as he cocked his head like a dog questing for scent.

Arsinoe immediately stopped in her tracks. Lara didn't need to see the back of her upraised palm to know that they should stop as well.

Lara caught her breath as she scanned the stretch of desert ahead of them. She couldn't see very far, but it looked as unremarkable to her as the last two leagues had been.

"Dramsind," she heard Arsinoe whisper. *"Biwu? Mototo?"*

The giant didn't answer immediately, at least not with words. With a tug it freed its right hand, chittering and clicking as sand sifted between his flat fingers.

Arsinoe took a step backwards. Then another.

"There is colorless fire here," she said. There was no humor in her voice, Lara noted. "We must go another way."

No one argued. Of all the evils left behind by the demons, the fire was the most terrible. It was invisible to the eye, and those that it did not kill it warped and twisted. Or so the stories said.

They retraced their own steps quickly, Arsinoe repeating her whispered question until the giant finally spoke.

"Buse," it said, the word sizzling in the air like fat in a skillet.

This seemed to satisfy the Telchine, and she took a moment to study the stars before making a new course, tentative at first but, as they went, she began to put on speed. Lara noticed that she always kept the giant between herself and the place where the colorless fire burned.

After a long while, Arsinoe slowed, and took a swallow from her waterskin.

"We're lucky," she said. "I've only seen him do that once before, and that was . . ."

She trailed off, rubbing the bridge of her nose as she wrestled with some old and unpleasant memory.

"No matter," she said at last. "Dramsind's steered us right. Anyone else would have walked right into it."

"Why did we come this way, then?" Pinsard asked.

"It wasn't here before," Arsinoe answered, flatly. "Now take some water, and let's be on."

Lara found that she wasn't thirsty. Neither was Pinsard, apparently. He was looking back over the moonlit desert, his lips parted ever so slightly.

"Drink," Moder said, holding out her own canteen. "Both of you."

They drank.

The ground grew rockier as they went on. The larger stones were cracked and pitted, and they grew larger as they went. Some stood alone, taller even than the giant. Others lay together like felled trees. Just past daybreak they scaled one such pile, climbed along a ramp of fallen rock and left the shifting sands for firmer soil.

Green things grew amongst the rocks here, a welcome change from the luminous blooms and repulsive growths of Vulp Vora. There were prickly shoots, wild mint, and golden-headed shrubs that smelled faintly like burnt pine. Arsinoe chose a place near to some of these for their camp and gathered a handful of them as they settled down to eat.

"I am not knowing these herbs," Moder said as the Telchine laid her bundle on a nearby stone.

"The Glyconcese call it iron-point," Arsinoe said. "Tea's supposed to be good for curing wounds, but they use it for just about anything else you can think of. Me, I just like the taste."

"Hmmm," Moder murmured, and found a place to lie down.

"The Glyconese," Lara said, "They come to this place?"

"No," Arsinoe replied. "The peaks are too high. But seeds drift on the wind more easily than people."

Lara looked to the mountains. If anything, they looked taller than the ones that guarded the Mandrossian border. It was high summer, and there was snow on every summit.

"I don't see any passes," Lara said.

"That's because there aren't any," Arsinoe said, and began to poke around in her pack.

Lara and Pinsard shared a look. Moder sat up.

"Then," Lara said, "How are we going to get over them?"

"We aren't," the Telchine said, still rustling through her things. "We're going under them."

"Under?" Pinsard said.

"It's the opposite of over," Arsinoe said, shoving her arm all the way into the bag. "Volk! I swear if that chimera's run off with my scald-"

"We know what 'under' means," Pinsard said. "But what I mean is, how?"

"Aha!" the Telchine exclaimed, producing the jar. "The knot unravels."

"*How?*" Pinsard repeated, his nostrils flaring.

"There are tunnels under the mountains," the Telchine answered, unscrewing the jar's lid. "Old ones. I didn't think you'd object, boy. After all, I'd always heard that your kind lived in caves."

"He is not a Calvarian," Moder said, some color beginning to show in her cheeks.

"Strange," Arsinoe said. "He looks an awful lot like one. So do you. Must be all the sand in my eyes."

Moder's lips quivered a bit, but she kept her peace.

"How about you, girl?" the Telchine asked with a tilt of her head. "Are you scared of the dark?"

"Not really," Lara said, "It's what's *in* the dark that worries me."

"Smart," Arsinoe said, and ate her paste.

* * * * * * *

It was still light when they caught their first glimpse of the door- if 'door' was even the right word for the massive slab set into the face of the mountain.

The archway it guarded had looked like a cave to Lara at first, the largest of the clefts dotting the approach to the higher bluffs. But though wind and water had smoothed its edges, it was far too perfect to be natural. Someone had carved it, just as the door had been built to fit it. If any path or roadway had led to it long ago, it was gone now. The only approach was the gravely remains of a rockslide.

The door itself, lichen-encrusted and large as a city gate, looked like a solid piece of stone. Or perhaps it was metal: The green and yellow lichens that carpeted it made it difficult to tell. It had no seams or hinges that Lara could see.

"How are we going to get through *that*?" Pinsard asked.

"With sorcery," Arsinoe said. "But we'll need to get closer first."

With that she began to climb, testing the ground with her spear as she stepped from rock to rock. The giant followed her with less caution, going to all fours and scuttling up the hillside like a massive crab.

"She's joking," Lara said. "Isn't she?"

Pinsard shrugged. Once the rocks dislodged by the giant had settled, he mounted the nearest boulder with an easy leap.

"Show off," Lara grumbled.

Lara was scooping Bannertail up by the belly when she noticed that Moder was standing very still, her deep blue eyes locked on the doorway. Her breaths were very shallow.

"Moder?" Lara said, "What is it?"

"Nothing," Moder said, and licked her lips. "I am coming."

The Firebird was behind the mountain by the time they had scratched and scrabbled their way to the foot of the door. It was even larger than it had looked from below, almost black in the early twilight.

Crickets chirped in the brush. Something began to howl in the badlands below.

"Now what?" Lara asked when she had caught her breath.

"Watch," Arsinoe said. "Though you might want to take a few steps backwards."

They took her advice and watched as she put some distance between herself and the giant.

"Dramsind!" Arsinoe shouted. *"Mifuf Nasali!"*

Stones rustled as the giant shifted his weight. Then his head swiveled to face Arsinoe, peering over his left shoulder like some great metal owl. Lara couldn't help but gasp.

"Motaju," the giant said, his voice crackling.

"Motaju kutuju!" Arsinoe called out, taking another step backwards as she shielded her mouth with her glove.

At first, nothing happened. The giant did not move, and the door did not open.

Then, with a loud click, the giant's head swiveled back into place and he began to stride forward, his right arm lengthening as he swept a boulder from his path. He straightened as he went, until he stood before the door at his full height.

And then he froze. But Lara could hear something now, faint at first but growing louder. She wasn't certain if it came from the giant, the door, or from the air itself, but it was high and thin, like the echo of a distant bell.

It grew louder. Bannertail let out a raspy hiss and slipped into Lara's packsack.

Lara hardly noticed. A pinprick of light had blossomed in the center of the door, blue as the noonday sky. It swayed and flickered, and then something lanced between it and the giant, bright and delicate, like a spider's thread laden with dew. It was gone in a flash, but when Lara blinked she could still see it behind her eyes.

The ground shuddered. Stones shook and jumped. The blue blossom faded, and the door with no seams began to slide apart.

Sparks flew as the door ground against rock. A pair of cracks ran through the face of the mountain as sheets of stone broke free, tumbling about the entrance. One fragment struck the giant's shoulder and burst apart, showering the ground around him with chips and slivers. Dust clouds billowed from the rock strikes, and soon the air was so thick that Lara could hardly see the giant at all.

Lara covered her mouth and held her breath as dust washed over them. The grit got into her eyes instead. Lara blinked until there were tears running down her cheeks. Moder swore. Then the air cleared.

"You could have warned us!" Lara growled at the chalk-white figure striding towards them.

"I said 'stand back,'" Arsinoe said, and gave her head a shake. "The door's open, isn't it?"

"Yes," Moder said. She and Pinsard looked like a pair of statues guarding the approach.

"How did you-" Pinsard began to say. "How did *he* do that?"

"I told you," Arsinoe said. "Sorcery."

It was hard to argue with her logic. What else would explain what they had seen?

"What is he?" Lara asked, glancing at the giant with renewed interest.

"Dramsind?" Arsinoe said, her eyebrow arching. "He's one of the hollow men. I thought you knew."

"The hollow men?"

"The old servants of The Dreamer," the Telchine said, speaking the name of the eldest of the demons aloud. "There are many like him near the waste, empty shells with spirits living inside them. But don't worry. Dramsind's my friend. Trust me, you'll be glad of his company when we're down there in the dark."

Lara opened her mouth, but no words came.

"Come on!" Arsinoe said, slapping her thigh as she made for the archway. "We can dust off later! But the door won't stay open forever."

Lara tousled her hair, hitched up her packsack, and followed. The crunch of stones told her that Pinsard and Moder were right behind her.

As they passed the giant the Telchine uttered something low, and he fell into step beside her.

Arsinoe paused at the threshold and sniffed at the air. The door had carved a shallow groove in the rock, but the stone beneath their feet was otherwise quite smooth. Lara could sense the enormity of space that lay beyond the archway, but all she could see was darkness.

"Hurry now," Arsinoe said, and trotted over the groove.

"It's pitch black in there," Lara said, hovering at the lip of the threshold. "How will we see?"

"Sorcery!" Arsinoe snapped. "Now come on!"

Just as Lara stepped forward the doors began to close, much faster than they had opened. She was nearly thrown off her feet as the earth lurched beneath her, but then she was through the gap.

She turned, the screech of metal filling her ears as Pinsard and Moder raced towards her, their arms windmilling as they struggled to keep their feet. Stones were showering from the heights behind them.

The giant was the last to enter. He crossed the gap with three easy strides.

Then the doors met, and all was dark.

Lara caught her breath. The air was very stale. It smelled somehow like the taste of metal against her tongue.

"We all here?" Arsinoe's voice floated from the darkness.

"Here," Pinsard said.

"Here," Moder said, and coughed.

"I'm here," Lara breathed. "I think."

"Give it a moment," Arsinoe said.

Lara brushed away some of the dust as they waited. Bannertail wriggled within her packsack, but she dared not free him.

As she was patting down her right arm, she realized that she could see the outline of her hand. Then her arm. Then the palm-shaped patches on her blouse free of dust. Gradually, the pale forms of the others grew clearer as well, even the dark bulk of the giant.

She looked up and saw, high above them, a thin stream of pale blue light. It was not flickering.

"Where are we?" Lara asked, looking about. The chamber was so immense that she could not see the walls.

Arsinoe brushed a bit of dust from her shoulder. "The mouth of one of the tunnels."

"Does-" Pinsard said, stopping to spit out a bit of grit. "Does anything live down here?"

"Bats, mostly," the Telchine replied. "Bats and insects, and the things that feed on them."

"Things?"

"Slimes for one," Arsinoe said. "The fishers are the worst of them, but I know the signs."

Arsinoe squinted at the head of her spear and retrieved an oily rag from her carry-roll.

"There are also some of my kin," she said as she polished, "Lost in the depths while searching for The Maiden. Pale, silver warriors of old turned cannibal. Ghouls, men call them."

"Sackmen, you mean?" Lara scoffed. "But they're just stories-"

"No, Lara," Moder said, her voice low but firm. "They are real, the deep men. Even my *ceorl* was afraid of them."

"*Faeder*?" Pinsard said, his fingers brushing against the hilt of his sword. "Afraid?"

Moder nodded.

"We'll be safe enough," Arsinoe said. "As long as we do not stray. They can't stand the glare of the ghostfire, weak though it is."

Lara glanced upwards.

"And who hung the . . . Ghostfire?" she asked. "Who built this place?"

"Oh, the demons I expect," Arsinoe said. "Or their slaves did. I doubt the likes of Skindancer or Duskwalker spent much time hauling rocks."

"But how can you be certain?"

Arsinoe looked up from her spear, her lids heavy.

"Do you have many such places as this," she asked, "Where you are from?"

Lara shook her head.

"You could have told us all of this days ago," Pinsard said. "Why did you wait?"

"Would it have made a difference, boy?" Arsinoe said, turning her attention back to her spear. "You needed to cross the mountains, so we are crossing them. This way is far better than The Plain, believe me."

"I'm not certain that I do," Pinsard replied sourly.

"Well, you're more than welcome to go back the way you came," Arsinoe smirked, "If that's how you feel about it."

"This way is being good," Moder said, catching Pinsard's gaze as she stepped between them. "Hard for others to be following, yes?"

"Yes," Pinsard admitted, his lips curling into something that resembled a smile.

Lara glanced at the black slab standing behind them.

She grinned too.

Let's see Tybalt get through that.

Arsinoe gave the head of her spear a final polish and tucked away the rag.

"This way," she said, taking a moment to orient herself before heading into the gloom. *"Dramsind! Kelali."*

The giant sprung to life and began to walk. He soon overtook the Telchine and forged the way ahead, not needing the light to find his way. In his wake more lights began to glimmer, leaking from cracks in the tiles that made up the floor, or running like roots across the expanse of the chamber's far wall, outlining a wide arch.

"Don't dawdle," Arsinoe called back to them, though it was hardly necessary. The lights directly overhead were already dimming, and Lara didn't imagine any of them fancied being left behind. In the darkness. With the ghouls.

* * * * * * *

The first of the tunnels was just beyond the arch, but it was far from the last. Off the central corridor there were branches and intersections, and recessed slabs gone green with rust: Doors, Lara assumed, like the ones that guarded the entrance. Every so often there were stairs that led to sagging balconies, and circular holes in both ceiling and floor, as if some great worm had bored up through the rock before driving towards the surface.

Nor were the tunnels empty. There were huge, wheeled things, like great wagons or carts, strangely curved slabs, raised pedestals, and stretches of drooping coils coated with mold, the chalky droppings of bats, and what looked to be centuries upon centuries of dust.

At one branch they were confronted by a grim sight. The mouth of the corridor was choked with skeletons wrapped up in robes of mottled cloth. The bulk of them had perished while pressing against some invisible barrier. Black handprints and smudges seemed to hang in the air before them.

"Glass," Pinsard said, taking a step back as he wondered at the sheer thickness of it. "It's glass. A door all of glass."

"They were trying to get out," Lara murmured, staring at one of the skeletons. The metal rings hung round its neck and wrists were black, as though scorched by some terrible heat.

"Maybe it's best they didn't," Arsinoe said, and kept moving.

The way forward was far from straight. The earth, it seemed, had shifted since the age of demons. There were rifts in the earth, and collapses. In one place the tunnel itself looked as though a pair of titanic hands had twisted it into a crazy spiral, forcing them to scale the walls until they walked on what had once been the ceiling.

The lights had failed here entirely, and for a time they hovered at the edge of the dark as the giant lumbered onward.

"Shouldn't you stop him?" Pinsard asked.

"Just wait," Arsinoe said, glancing over her shoulder. The lights behind them were dying one by one.

Sure enough, the sound of the giant's heavy footfalls were beginning to fade when a new line of lamps- or ghostfire, or whatever it was that lit their way- sprang to life along the length of a distant corridor. They scrambled to reach it, stumbling and sliding until the floor beneath their feet was level again.

"Is it all like this?" Lara asked.

"No," Arsinoe wheezed. "Some of it is *difficult*."

On and on they went. And the further they went, the more convinced Lara became that it was actually the giant who led them, and that if Arsinoe did not call out for him to stop, saying *"Dramsind, babalu!"* he would simply keep on stomping through the underworld until he reached the other side of the mountains.

Eventually, the temptation to try it herself grew too great to ignore. She waited until Arsinoe's steps were slowing and called out, *"Dramsind! Babalu!"*

The giant kept on plodding, but Arsinoe shot her a withering look before she repeated the command herself.

"Tch," the Telchine clucked as the giant lurched to a halt. "If it were that easy, girl, I'd have died long before meeting you."

"I was only curious," Lara said.

"Said the cat to the Watcher," the Telchine drawled. "But by all means, stop. This is as good a place as any for a piss."

They never stopped very long, just enough to take some water and rest their legs while they took turns finding some privacy. This was not difficult, for the lights that hovered about the giant did not carry very far, but Lara never felt at ease as she skulked out of sight. The thought of some clammy hand reaching out and taking hold of her by the hair had her squatting with her back to the walls.

She noticed that Bannertail did not wander either, even after she let him out of her pack. He kept as close to Lara as he could or, failing that, he would press up against one of Pinsard's legs, his ears flat against his head.

He was doing just that as Lara returned from the shadows. At the sight of her his tail wagged halfheartedly.

"What time is it do you think?" Pinsard asked, giving the chimera's head a scratch.

"The sun will be up soon," Moder said.

"You sound so certain," Arsinoe said.

"I am a Calvarian," Moder replied dryly. "Yes?"

"Hm," the Telchine murmured, and set down her jar of scald. She had scooped it quite clean.

"Should we rest here?" Lara asked, adding: "*Can* we rest here?"

"I'd rather we pushed on," Arsinoe replied. "It's a touch too quiet for my taste. And the next stretch can be . . . Tricky."

Lara looked to Moder. She was already finding her footing. Pinsard was rising too.

"Alright," Lara said. "Let's go then."

Arsinoe caught up her spear and stepped towards the giant. She was about to give him a tap when she froze and shot Lara a glance.

"Should I, girl?" she asked. "Or would you like to do the honors?"

Lara couldn't see the smile on the woman's lips, but she could hear it.

"Dramsind," Lara said, *"Kelali."*

The giant's head swiveled to face her. Something clicked inside his chest, but he did not move.

"Oh, very good," Arsinoe said, and for once her admiration sounded sincere. "You've been paying attention. Only, that word doesn't mean what you think it means."

She tapped the giant with the tip of her spear.

"Fiki," she said, and when she walked Dramsind followed.

The tunnel grew more ruinous as they went on. Or perhaps the stretches of bare rock that jutted into the corridor were deliberate. Whatever the case, the metallic tang in the air gave way to an earthier smell, musty though not entirely foul. After a while Lara noticed that the stones were damp. Water was trickling through cracks in the rock, water and-

"There's a breeze," she said. "I can feel it."

"I feel it too," Moder said.

"Is it the way out?" Pinsard asked.

"No," Arsinoe said, skirting around a fallen chunk of masonry. "But there are cracks and vents running all through this place. We wouldn't be able to breathe otherwise."

With her next step, Arsinoe plunged into a shallow pool. The splash startled all of them.

"Slow down a bit," Arsinoe said, giving her boot a shake. "We're not at the vault yet, but where there's water there's danger. Watch your step and be sure to keep an eye on what's above you."

"What for?" Lara asked, giving the pool a wide berth.

"Some of the slimes like to cling to the ceiling," Arsinoe replied. "They drop down on you while you're walking underneath. Others sit at the bottom of pools and latch onto whatever steps on them. Either kind can burn through cloth just as easily as skin, so be careful . . . And I'd tuck away that mongrel of yours, girl, unless you want him to end up as something's meal."

Lara coaxed the chimera into her packsack and made sure that the straps were secure. Bannertail poked his nose through one of the creases and sniffed at her fingers, but that's as far as he could get.

"She gets under *my* skin," Pinsard whispered as he fell in beside her.

"Mine too," she replied.

"This place," he said. "It's . . ."

"Like something out of a dream?" she offered.

"I suppose," Pinsard said. "I'm not sure what to make of it. I am scared. Very scared. But I can't help but feel drawn to it, somehow."

"I know what you mean," Lara said, reaching out and tracing one of the lines of light running through the wall. "Still, what I'd give to sleep in a bed again. Any bed."

"And take a bath."

"And spend all day watching over the flock," Lara sighed. "I never thought I'd miss that."

"Me either," Pinsard said.

They reached the end of the tunnel. A sheet of water formed a thin curtain between them and whatever lay beyond.

Arsinoe motioned for them to stop. The giant recognized the gesture as well, and let his arms go limp as he ground to a halt.

"Just in case," Arsinoe said, and poked her head through the curtain, the water running down the back of her robe.

Then she lurched backwards, cursing.

Pinsard loosened his sword from its sheath.

"What is it?" he hissed.

"The water!" the Telchine shivered. "It's freezing!"

"But it's safe?" Lara asked.

"Oh, I wouldn't say that," Arsinoe said. "Have a look for yourself."

With that the Telchine plunged back into the water. The giant raised one of its arms as if to shield her from the spray, but he was too slow.

Lara held her breath and raced through the wet. The water *was* cold, though to her it felt no worse than a dip in a summer stream. She might have bathed in it, had their circumstances been different.

She'd hate our winters, Lara mused. She swept her hair from her face and found herself standing at the head of a wide stairway.

She wiped the water from her eyes, and for a moment she thought the Telchine had lied, or was playing some trick on them, for it seemed as though she were standing beneath the night sky, cloudless and moonless, its vastness swept with glimmering stars . . . But these were no stars that she had ever seen. Where was the swan and eagle? Where the dolphin, or Parisa chained to her stone?

Then she noticed that the glimmering lights overhead were moving. A handful winked out as others swayed to and fro, like willows in a breeze.

They're not stars, she realized. *They're alive, like lightning flies, or those flowers in the marshes. But there's dozens and dozens of them . . .*

"It's beautiful," Lara said in a hush. She could hear Moder and Pinsard coming up behind her, their boots squelching.

"It looks that way, doesn't it?" Arsinoe said. "Tell me, Calvarian, what do *you* see?"

"*Lim-angel,*" Moder said warily. "*Creopan* with snares."

"Yes," Arsinoe said. "Though I call them 'fishers.'"

"They're slimes?" Lara said, drawing back from the steps.

Arsinoe leaned on her spear. "The lights attract bugs. The bugs attract bats. But what you can't see are the sticky threads dangling underneath them. When they get a hold of something, they coil up and yank. Harder than you'd think."

"But they're not strong enough to, uh . . . I mean, they catch bats, right?"

"One of them caught hold of my arm, the first time I came through here." The Telchine gave it a shake for emphasis. "Tugged like a jackal, and my struggling attracted the others. My gloves ended up saving me, but they had both my feet off the ground before I could get free."

"So how do we . . ." Pinsard began to say as he looked about the chamber.

"Keep close," Arsinoe said, hugging the wall as she crept down the stairs, testing the air with her spear as she went. "And don't get hooked."

"What about Dramsind?" Lara asked. The giant was still standing in the spray, his arm extended. His head was swiveling back and forth, as though he was looking for something.

"It's better if we go first," Arsinoe answered. "They can't hurt him, but he'll stir them up when I call."

Lara nodded and tried not to trip as she followed in the Telchine's footsteps.

There was no ghostfire here, but the gleam of the slimes was strong enough to suggest the outlines of the chamber. It was vaguely circular, rock-walled, and three corridors branched from it. The floor looked uneven and was strewn with lumpy-looking swells of pale, reeking filth.

At the bottom of the stairs Arsinoe came to a halt and pointed at a glistening tendril that hung in the air an arm's length from her face. It didn't look very thick to Lara, but neither did a frog's tongue, and she'd seen one of those snatch up a field mouse easily enough.

She kept her distance as they slipped past it.

They soon came to another stalk, then another, and another. They gave each a wide berth, but the further on they went the thicker they dangled.

"Fire," Moder grumbled. "Fire is best for *creopan*."

"Have some tucked away, do you?" Arsinoe asked, holding her spear close to her chest as she slipped between a pair of tendrils. One of them curled upwards as she passed, its tip probing the air.

"They can feel us!" Lara hissed as she stepped through the gap, keeping her eye on the questing stalk, extremely aware of the one that was dangling behind her.

"They feel the air moving," Arsinoe said. "No more. Just go slow. And don't panic."

Lara took another pair of steps. Something soft and wet crunched under her foot. She ignored it.

Then she was clear.

"See?" Arsinoe said. "Not so bad."

"Heh," Lara puffed, and watched as Pinsard sidestepped past the tendrils, his chin tucked against his neck. Moder went next. She glided through easily, her gloved hand pressing her scabbard against the length of her thigh.

"Which way now?" Pinsard asked.

"That way," Arsinoe said, indicating the mouth of the midmost corridor. It was by far the largest of the three, but she could see dozens of the fisher's lures hanging between them and it. "The one on the left is a dead end."

"And that one?" Lara asked, looking to the corridor on their right. It was smaller, but the way to it looked clear.

"That is leading further down," Moder said. "See water draining?"

She was right, of course. The spill from above had formed pools and eddies across the chamber's floor, but it all streamed towards the mouth of the right-most corridor.

"There's no fishers either," Arsinoe said, giving the entryway a quick glance.

"Isn't that good?" Lara asked.

Arsinoe shook her head. "If there's no fishers, that means there's nothing alive down there for them to snare. No bats anyway. It could just be empty, but it could also be miles of tunnels filled with chokedamp. Could be colorless fire. Could be anything. It's not worth the risk."

The Telchine turned her back on the corridor and made for the larger passage, treading carefully about one of the stinking piles before settling into a low crouch.

"Besides," she said. "This is the right way."

Arsinoe crept onward, her head ducking low as the lures swung and writhed overhead.

Lara steeled herself and followed.

They could only stoop for so long. The floor rose as they went, and the fishers grew thicker with every step. By the time they reached the mouth of the passage Lara was practically crawling through the filth, sticky droplets of slime dripping and trickling through her hair and down the back of her neck. It tingled against her skin the way the scald had on her lips.

"Let's not do that again," Lara said as she found her feet, doing her best to shake some of the filmy stink from her gloves.

"We may have to," Arsinoe muttered, taking a few steps into the gloom.

"What do you-" Pinsard began to say, when he let out a startled cry.

Lara spun around and saw that, in his rush to stand up, he had not entirely cleared the last of the fishers. One of the dewy filaments was already curled around the back of his cloak, and tugging upwards, digging the clasp into the base of his throat.

"Take it off!" Arsinoe shouted.

Lara reached out to Pinsard as his hands flew to the clasp, but then a second tug tore him off his feet. He let out a muffled cry as the cloak wrapped around his head, then another as a second tendril latched onto the first and dragged him backwards.

Moder's sword flashed through the air before he could go any further, severing the first tendril at its midpoint. As the other stalk whipped about, its grip went slack. Pinsard tore open the clasp, and then he was panting flat on his back, his fur-lined cape being born away like an enormous filth-smeared bat.

When he had crawled back to the safety of the corridor, Moder offered him her hand. He waved it away.

"You were saying," he gasped once he'd gotten back to his feet.

"Look," Arsinoe said, shrugging her head at the way ahead.

It was blocked. The ceiling had collapsed entirely, filling the passage from head to foot with huge chunks of rock.

"A cave-in," Lara said. Danica had taught her the word when part of the root cellar had crumbled. She never thought she'd see a real one.

"I wonder," Arsinoe said, taking a few steps towards the debris.

"Wonder what?"

"I wonder if this was really a cave-in," the Telchine said. "What do you think, *soluk iblisler*?"

"I was not one of the tan," Moder said, taking a closer look. "Am not being stone worker. But I have seen a, ah, *cave-in* before."

"And?"

Moder craned her neck and squinted into the dark.

"Maybe if there was being more light?" she suggested.

"Let's not be *too* hasty," Arsinoe said, walking to the foot of the collapse. "Not yet, at least."

Lara moved up to join her, but she felt rather foolish. To her eyes it looked no more sinister than any other heap of rocks they had seen.

"What is this?" Pinsard queried. He was standing on the right-hand side of the corridor, next to a cylindrical opening in the wall.

"A side chamber," Arsinoe said. "I had thought that we might sleep in it. Now I'm not sure that we should."

"Does it lead anywhere?" Pinsard asked, taking a step towards it.

"No," Arsinoe answered. "Why?"

"There is a draft," Pinsard said, removing one of his gloves and holding out his palm.

"Can't be," Arsinoe said, stepping away from the piled rocks to stand by his side.

"Do you feel it?" Pinsard asked.

Arsinoe readied her spear and took a cautious step forward.

"The boy's right," she said.

Pinsard glared at her.

"Is it a way around?" Lara asked.

"I don't know," Arsinoe replied. "I can't see."

"More light," Moder said.

"Nothing else for it, I suppose," Arsinoe sighed. *"Dramsind! Pito-fiki!"*

Lara didn't catch the words of the giant's rattling answer to the Telchine's call, but the clatter and splash he made as he stomped down the stairs and crossed the chamber echoed off the walls so loudly that anything listening in the dark would be sure to hear it.

Far from being troubled by the slimes overhead, Dramsind wrenched several of them from their perches as he advanced, their glowing frames squelching against the chamber floor as their lures failed them. Others let him pass after a few exploratory tugs. Whether this was because he was too heavy, or if the mindless slimes could sense that whatever dwelt within the suit of metal was not for eating, Lara could not say.

Then Dramsind was standing at the mouth of the corridor, the tendrils wrapped round his head, arms, and torso writhing and quivering in their death throes.

A stream of ghostly light pulsed across one of the walls and bled into the ceiling. Another ran through the cracks running about the circular doorway, flickered, and died. Something popped and crackled like a dry log on a fire as a burst of white-hot sparks briefly illuminated the side chamber. Lara saw dusty slabs standing in rows, and ropey growths hanging from holes in the ceiling. Then it was dark again.

"Volk," Arsinoe spat.

"I saw another doorway," Pinsard said. "Or an opening at least."

"I saw it too," Arsinoe sighed. "Convenient."

"Isn't it?" Lara asked. "It could be a way forward."

"It probably is, but it wasn't there the last time I was here. Neither was this cave-in."

"What are you saying?" Lara asked. "That someone collapsed the whole tunnel just so we'd go this other way?"

Arsinoe rolled her tongue against the inside of her cheek. "You left out the part where they figured how to snuff out the lights."

"Deep men," Moder said.

"Or something worse," Arsinoe sniffed, "Waiting for us to wander in there blind."

"So, what then?" Pinsard huffed. "Do we just turn back?"

"No!" Arsinoe snorted. "I just want to make sure you know exactly what we're getting ourselves into. And if I'm going to die down here, eaten alive by ghouls, I'd prefer it if you'd have the common decency to take down a few of them with us."

"In the dark?" Lara said, staring into the gloom.

Arsinoe scratched at her jaw.

"Do you have any spare bowls?" the Telchine asked. "Or cups? Anything metal will do."

"You can have mine," Lara said, loosening one of the straps of her pack. Bannertail attempted an escape, kicking at her arm as she grasped for her nesting tins.

"No-no," she said to the chimera. "You stay."

Bannertail stilled, but stared at her with accusatory eyes as she sealed him back in.

"Oh shush," she muttered. "I wish *I* could sleep in a bag while someone carried me through all this."

She held up the bowls for Arsinoe to see.

"Will these do?"

"Perfect," the Telchine said. "Now use them to scoop up some of the slime. And don't touch any of it with your bare skin."

Lara looked at the luminous muck splattered against the cavern floor. Some of it had painted the joint of Dramsind's left hip. It was still glowing, bright as any flame.

"How long-" Lara began to ask.

"Not as long as we'd like," Arsinoe replied, and snapped her fingers. "So, hurry up."

"I'll help," Pinsard said.

Lara handed him the other bowl.

They used loose rocks to shovel as much of the slime as possible into the bowls. The glowing sludge smelled like sheep piss and old cheese and made Lara's eyes water like fresh cut onions.

Whoever wrote The Downfall of the Demon King, Lara thought as she tried not to breathe through her nose, recalling the passages concerning Skindancer's fastness beneath the sea, *Clearly never smelled a slime up close.*

When they were done their bowls were both nearly full.

"That's good," Arsinoe said. *"Dramsind, foteli. Jiwos tuji."*

The giant swiveled towards the bowls and stretched out his hands, his palms facing upwards.

"Bufo," he said.

As they placed the bowls in his hands, his fingers dug against them. He squeezed. The tin buckled and crinkled like a piece of parchment beneath his grip, and then it was as though they were a part of his hands. He held them both aloft steadier than any human hand would have.

"Alright," Arsinoe said, and led them to the doorway. Dramsind followed dutifully, the light illuminating the pale mold spread across the damp of the walls.

"Will he be fitting through there?" Moder asked, indicating the doorway.

"He's very flexible," Arsinoe said.

"And strong," Moder said, her mouth twisting askew.

"Too strong," Arsinoe said with a wave. "He could accidentally kill all of you while trying to protect me. If I let him."

Lara believed it. He'd smashed the falling boulder at the doorway as easily as swatting away a fly.

"Can't he protect *all* of us?" Lara asked.

The beetle on Arsinoe's cheek flexed its wings. "Now where'd the fun in that be?"

"I'm being serious."

Arsinoe made a noise deep in the back of her throat. "I wish that he could, girl, but he seems to have the idea locked in his head that I need safe keeping. I'm afraid it doesn't apply to anyone else."

"Why?" Lara asked.

"Well!" Arsinoe said, considering. "I am the one who woke him. Perhaps he thinks I'm The Maiden reborn? He wouldn't be the first . . ."

The corner of her mouth twitched at that, and the beetle seemed to scuttle.

"So," Lara said. "Should we draw our swords then?"

"Depends," Arsinoe replied, glancing at the thin blade Lara wore. "Have you ever used it?"

"Yes," Lara said.

"Then, yes, girl," the Telchine said. "You should."

Lara drew her sword. Moder and Pinsard did the same.

"Careful there, boy," Arsinoe said to Pinsard. "That's no child's toy."

"I've killed before," Pinsard replied. The coldness in his voice made Lara wonder how much of it was an act.

"I'll bet," Arsinoe said, and stepped through the doorway.

****

They did not stray far from Dramsind. His every sway drove the shadows back, but to Lara it seemed that the darkness itself had a shape and weight of its own, greater even than the mountain hanging over them.

The giant followed Arsinoe, his legs and arms shortening as he squeezed through the doorway on the far wall. The tunnel beyond was low, and thick with black sinews that ran along the walls. Behind them water dripped against stone, but the way ahead was filled with a terrible stillness.

"Someone walk beside me," Arsinoe whispered after they had gone a ways. Her voice had lost its easy swagger.

Lara squeezed past the giant, ignoring the way his head followed her.

"You have slime on your bodice," Arsinoe said, pointing at a glimmering smear just below her ribs. She turned back and saw the patch of Dramsind's leg she had swabbed clean.

The fabric was beginning to smoke.

"Will it burn through?" Lara asked.

"Shouldn't," Arsinoe said. "But don't touch it."

Arsinoe shifted her grip on her spear and went on.

They padded through the dark. There were no echoes here. Even the clanking of the giant's metal boots sounded dull to Lara's ears.

Then the passage came to a T. Arsinoe waited for Dramsind to catch up to them and took a glance down the left-hand path.

"Main passage is this way," Arsinoe muttered.

"Shouldn't we take it?" Lara asked.

"We have to," Arsinoe said. "But I don't like it. It's too simple. Too easy to get hemmed in."

"But we have to?"

"We do," the Telchine said, and poked her head around Dramsind's bulk. "Watch your backs, *soluk iblisler.*"

Leather creaked and fabric rustled in the dark, but Lara could only see the white shock of hair as Moder traded places with Pinsard at the end of their file.

"Quiet now," Arsinoe said, creeping down the left-hand passage. "We might as well try to slip past unnoticed."

"What about him?" Lara nodded at the giant lumbering behind her.

"He's not the only one of his kind down here," Arsinoe replied. "And not all of them sleeping like The Dreamer. If we're lucky, whatever is listening will think he's on some long-forgotten errand, alone and unappetizing."

"Shhh," Moder hushed.

"Yes, yes, I know," Arsinoe said, and was quiet.

The passage branched to the right once, twice, and then a third time, but Arsinoe kept going straight. As they passed the turns she would slow, readying her spear to skewer whatever might leap out at them . . . But there was nothing to menace them but darkness, and the unsettling feeling that something watched them, just out of sight.

At the end of the passage there was an archway. Beyond it, the dim outline of a grooved causeway stretched across a dark gulf. A twisted guardrail ran along its length, flaking with rust. Lara grabbed hold of it instinctively as she took a step onto the causeway and peered over the edge.

Nothing. She couldn't see anything beneath them and, when she looked up, she couldn't make out the ceiling. All she could see was the causeway, the railing, and Arsinoe peering over the other side, testing the bridge's strength with her foot. *Nothing. Not even an arch or a column for support. But then . . . What's holding us up?*

Dramsind stepped from the passageway and put his full weight onto the span. The bridge groaned.

Lara squeezed her eyes shut, expecting to feel the bridge give way beneath her, but her footing remained sound. The causeway remained as firm as solid rock.

The sound, however, carried. Lara couldn't see them, but she could hear the groan echoing against walls and shafts above and below.

"Buse foteli," Arsinoe said. The giant handed the Telchine one of the glowing bowls and released the thing from his powerful grip. *"Babalu."*

Dramsind straightened back up. Something clicked inside of him, and he was still. Lara could see Moder and Pinsard holding the passage behind him, ready to cut down anything that came loping after them.

"Hold this," Arsinoe said under her breath, and handed the bowl to Lara.

She took it and cradled it in her palm, all too aware of how badly her hand was shaking.

"Follow me," Arsinoe said, pressing forward. "And if something grabs my leg, stab it."

Lara nodded and tried to keep her footfalls as light as the Telchine's were.

Fifty paces later, the causeway ended. The break was very neat. Deliberate. It didn't look the like the result of a collapse at all.

"Hmmm," Arsinoe chewed, and leaned over the edge.

Lara joined her, standing as close to the precipice as she dared, and stretched her left arm out, the bowl cupped in her palm. Sure enough, there was another stretch of causeway directly opposite the one they stood on. But the gap was too far for any human to jump.

"I've seen something like this before," Arsinoe said, her voice hushed. "I'll bet this bridge can stretch the way Dramsind does."

"How?" Lara asked.

"There might be something on the other side. If we could . . ." She tilted her head back. "Volk, I can't see a bloody thing. But maybe if we tied a rope-"

"We don't have any rope."

"We could fashion one out of cloth, tie it round someone's waist. Hmmm. How far can you jump?"

"Not that far."

"How about your blond brother? He's got long legs."

Lara knew that if Arsinoe asked Pinsard whether he could safely jump off of a cliff, he would do it, rope or no rope. And so:

"I don't think so," Lara said. "But, what about-"

"Dramsind?" Arsinoe gasped, feigning shock. "No! Not him! Why, he could fall and hurt himself!"

"I don't think that's very funny," Lara said.

"Neither do I," Arsinoe said, turning to face the gap. "So, alright then. *I'll* do it."

"You will?" Lara balked. The Telchine was taller than she was, but not by much.

"Do you want to get out of here?" Arsinoe asked.

"Of course, but-"

"Then I'll do it," Arsinoe said. "Now, let's see about making that rope."

As they turned from the gap, Lara saw Pinsard creeping across the darkest part of the causeway, his hands extended for balance. She assumed it was Pinsard and not Moder, for all she could really see of him were the pale contours of his face, but Moder would never do something so-

Stupid! Lara fumed, some choice words beginning to form on her tongue. *Not even using the rail. He'll get himself killed, and for-*

Then she saw the glint of the figure's eyes. Its filthy claws. Its naked chest, white as bone.

It wasn't Pinsard.

"Sackmen!" Lara cried out.

"Hrh!" Arsinoe grunted, readying her spear as she broke into a sprint.

The ghoul lunged backwards, caught hold of the causeway, and swung onto the underside of the bridge. Arsinoe whirled about, her spear lashing through the air where the ghoul had been, when another shape came loping out of the darkness.

"Behind you!" Lara cried out.

Then something wrapped around her ankle and wrenched her leg towards the edge of the causeway.

The rail saved her. She couldn't grab hold of it without losing her sword but, as it slammed into her ribs, she wrapped her arm around its length and held on.

There was a flare of light as the contents of the bowl sloshed. The slime ran down her glove and splashed against her bodice, but she managed to cling to it, dimly aware of Bannertail struggling to escape from her packsack.

The rail dug into her armpit as whatever had her by the leg gave it another yank, ragged nails digging into her thigh as it sought better purchase.

"Get off!" she cried, kicking as she fought to pull herself back up. A silvery-white face snarled back at her, squinting against the light as it clawed at her thigh.

Behind her, Arsinoe let out a whooping shout. Something landed on the causeway with a 'whump.' Throats hissed and hooted in the dark.

A ribbon of slime slid across Lara's wrist, burning as hot as an open flame. She screamed and hurled the bowl at the ghoul's head.

The slime spattered it from the top of its hairless head to the nape of its neck. It let out a shrill cry, its skin popping and sizzling as it released her. She kicked it in the chest and hefted herself upwards, wiping her wrist against her bodice and wincing from the pain of it.

A ghoul lay on the causeway, its dark blood pooling into the grooves beneath it. Arsinoe's spear lay nearby. Faintly, she could see the woman struggling with another of the creatures, her bone-handled knife in her hands. For a moment she was on top of it, driving her knife towards its throat. Then it rolled over and pinned the Telchine's arm under one of its flat, hoary feet as its hands grasped for her neck.

Lara ran her blade directly through its ribs. It let out a raspy hiss and tumbled off the edge of the causeway.

Lara stared at the blood running down the length of her sword, wondering how she could even see it without the bowl.

It's me. The smell of burning fabric filled her nostrils. *I'm glowing.*

"Look out!" Arsinoe shouted, her spear back in her hands. Lara turned, impaling a ghoul as it leapt at them from above. The impact nearly took her down with it.

"They're on the ceiling!" Lara shouted.

"I know!" Arsinoe shouted back and caught hold of Lara by the crook of her left arm. "Now come on!"

"What about the bridge?!"

"Forget the bridge! Run, girl, run!"

They ran. Lara could hear naked feet padding on the causeway behind them. An arm shot over the side of the bridge. Lara slashed at it, felt her blade meet bone. She kept running.

There was more trouble ahead. The headless body of a ghoul lay at the feet of the giant, who was wavering back and forth as he kept the other lantern steady. Moder was tangling with a live one, her back to another, who was crawling down the wall as easily as a spider might. Pinsard was in the tunnel, his hair wild and drenched with sweat.

"They're coming!" Pinsard yelled as the ghoul on the wall leapt towards Moder. She spun before it could land, and slashed open its bone-white chest, but its momentum bowled her over. The other ghoul pounced, hissing, its emaciated frame belying its strength as it stomped on Moder's sword.

"Moder!" Lara shouted, her legs pumping faster.

Bannertail finally tore his way from the packsack, squalling and hissing. The chimera landed neatly and kept pace with her as she whipped through Dramsind's legs.

The ghoul turned, its filthy hand lashing out as she thrust at it. It screeched as steel tore through the inside of its palm, and again when Bannertail dove directly at its eyes. It staggered backwards, its clawed hands swiping at the ball of fur and teeth ripping at its face, and then Lara drove her sword through its breast.

"Fiki!" Arsinoe hollered, helping Moder to roll away the quivering ghoul. Whatever was inside of Dramsind rattled and chimed sourly, but he turned about, his free arm swinging wide as he sent one of the ghouls scampering behind them over the causeway's edge.

"Hurry!" Pinsard cried.

Lara could hear the hoots and clicks wafting out of the passage now. They were getting louder every moment.

"You know the way?" Arsinoe growled as Moder gained her feet, still too winded to speak.

"Keep right!" Lara replied, snatching Bannertail from the ghoul's lolling head. The chimera whined in protest as the burn on her wrist sent waves of pain lancing up her arm.

"Good girl!" Arsinoe said, driving her spearhead into the gut of a ghoul slipping around Dramsind. "Now, run!"

"Moder-"

"Go!" Moder shouted. "We are behind you!"

Lara ran into the passage.

Pinsard loomed out of the darkness. A ghoul lay sprawled before him. The front of his shirt had been torn wide open.

"Go!" Lara shouted above the wails filling the tunnel.

He didn't need any encouragement.

It grew dark as they ran. Their only light was that of the slime burning through Lara's clothes, and that was dimming rapidly.

They raced by one of the side corridors, but no ghoul leapt out at them. A hundred paces more and they passed another. Still, there was nothing but the rising cries of the ghouls to trouble them.

"Oh-aaah!" Lara shrieked as the slime seeped through her bodice.

There was nothing for it. She let go of Bannertail and tore at the lacing. The slime was doing some of the work for her. As she tugged, the left strap of her bodice split.

"Help!" she shrieked as slime sizzled against her skin, dropping her sword as she tore off the rest of her bodice, the fingers of her gloves smoking as they wiped at the glowing muck. "Help me!"

"Keep still!" Moder barked, her belt knife in her hands. She cut, her hands as nimble as they were with her needlework, and hurled the glowing heap away.

They both tore off their gloves.

"My sword-"

"Here!" Moder breathed, grabbing it by the hilt.

Something in the darkness exhaled. Then a white shape came hurtling from the passage ahead of them. It drove itself down the length of Pinsard's sword, spitting and hissing. But Pinsard was not thrown. He let out a growl and kicked the thing to the ground as he slid his sword free.

Arsinoe raced up the passage behind them, Dramsind hot on her heels. He had lost his lantern.

"Run!" Arsinoe cried. "Run! Run! Run!"

The passage behind her was so full of ghouls that they were practically climbing on top of each other as they advanced. Half of them were scurrying along the walls, gripping at the hanging sinews.

Moder tossed Lara her sword. She caught it. Bannertail leapt onto her back.

They ran.

Lara traced the wall with her right hand, nearly recoiling from its icy touch, but too afraid to miss the right-hand turn.

They passed another branch on their left. A pair of ghouls skidded out of it, snarling like hill cats. Moder bowled the first of them over, the hilt of her knife jutting from its neck as it fell. The other raked at Arsinoe as Dramsind trampled it underfoot.

Three passages. One more, and then right! Or were there only three?

Lara couldn't remember.

The frigid stone beneath her fingers fell away.

"Here!" she shouted, nearly tripping over her own feet as she turned. "This way!"

She could hear boots sliding against stone as the others followed. She couldn't see a thing. She wouldn't know if there were ghouls waiting in the dark ahead of them until they took hold of her, hissing and shrieking as they tore at her. Or, worse, what if she had got turned around, and led them down the wrong way?

But then she saw it: A patch of gray, a hundred paces ahead of them. Light. Light from the main passage.

"There!" she cried.

"We are seeing!" Moder's words were almost lost in the cacophony rising behind them. It was as though all of Domdaniel were shrieking at their heels.

Fifty paces . . . Twenty . . .

"Hwaah!" Arsinoe roared somewhere behind her. Something struck the side of the tunnel with a 'crack.' A frigid gust rushed through the tunnel.

Ten paces . . . Five . . .

Metal squealed. Rock shattered. Dramsind's voice sputtered something in his weird tongue, and a ghoul let out an ear-piercing screech.

One!

Lara swerved through the doorway. Bannertail climbed onto her shoulder and dug his claws into her blouse. She hardly noticed.

She slipped on a wet tile as they spilled into the main passage. Moder's hand gripped her before she could fall. The cavernous chamber ahead was dazzling to her light-starved eyes.

"Fishers!" Lara shouted, daring a glance back as they raced towards the curtain of tendrils blocking their escape.

If she thought that Arsinoe was fast before, leaping amongst the dunes, it was nothing compared to the blur of teal that came racing from the side chamber. The archway behind her flew apart as Dramsind broke right through the wall. An angry red glare was burning behind the sockets of his helm.

"Don't stop!" Pinsard cried, and dove into the muck beneath the fisher's reach, sliding easily through the filth. Moder did the same.

"Hold on!" Lara shouted at Bannertail, slipping her sword into her belt. Arsinoe shot past her, her spear sailing into the gap before her.

Something deep and horrible was grating inside the giant. Stones skipped and clattered as dozens of naked feet and callused palms slid across stone. A howl rose up. Of dismay? Triumph?

Lara dove.

She hit the ground harder than she expected, but she ignored the pain in her side, ignored the agony lancing up her arm, ignored the shrieks and burbles echoing at her back, and scrambled forward, dragging her sword as she shimmied through the muck.

There was solid stone beneath her when she finally collapsed. She was gasping for air, so weak that she could barely lift her head. As she rolled over, she saw that Bannertail was circling about beside her, his shoulders quivering as he shook himself off.

She heard one of the ghouls let out a shriek. The others fell silent.

Boom. Boom. Boom. Boom.

Something large was coming towards her, and with it a sound like a thousand angry wasps, skipping and stuttering as it drew closer.

Then Dramsind was looming over her, the fire in his head blazing, the seams of his armor hissing. The fisher lures wrapped about him were misting, like water in a hot pan.

The ghouls were hovering just beyond the archway, breathless themselves. One of them was dangling in the air halfway to the ceiling, a trio of tendrils wrapped round its thrashing head.

Dramsind took another step, the chorus within it squealing angrily. It turned its head to regard her.

"*Kutuju,*" Arsinoe croaked. The word was barely audible.

Lara turned. The Telchine was hunched over her spear, spent, blood running freely down her leg.

Dramsind's arm shot out, his metal fingers splayed. It took all of Lara's strength to twist aside. The giant's hand smashed into the rock where her head had been.

"*Kutuju!*" Arsinoe managed to bellow. "Dramsind! *Motaju kutuju!*"

Dramsind paused. His head turned to face the Telchine as the hive within him roiled.

"*Motaju?*" his voice called out, almost lost in the swarm.

"*Kutuju,*" Arsinoe said, slumping forward. "*Kutuju,* Dramsind. *Kutuju. Kutuju . . .*"

Arsinoe's head met the floor.

The hive quieted, was still. The blaze within him faded. Something blue flickered above his right breast, flashed, and was gone. His arm slid back to his side. He straightened, his head looking about the chamber in a way that made Lara think he had no memory of how he had come to be there.

A dark, filthy shape rose out of the sludge on the opposite end of the chamber. It was Pinsard. Moder followed, the muck dripping from her as she pushed herself from the chamber floor. A dozen or so tendrils were already dangling between them as the slimes re-cast their lures.

"Stay there," Moder said as she gave her arm a shake. "We are coming."

"Can someone help me up?" Arsinoe wheezed. "Please?"

Lara got up slowly, making certain there were no lures dangling overhead, crept over to the Telchine and helped her rise. The woman was as shaky on her feet as a new-born lamb.

"You're hurt," Lara said.

"Just hungry," Arsinoe groaned, and tried to open her carry-roll, but she couldn't keep her fingers still.

Lara reached for her packsack but found that it was gone. Either the slime had burned through the straps, or one of the ghouls had snatched it from her back.

"Here," Lara said, undoing the Telchine's roll for her. The woman shoved her filthy glove into the bag and pulled out an entire loaf of flatbread before stuffing the corner of it into her mouth.

"You fought well back there," Arsinoe managed between bites, "Who taught you how to thrust?"

"Moder," Lara said, turning about. The ghouls had retreated from the archway, but they were still there, a score of them at least, shielding their eyes from the fishers' light as they clicked and hooted.

"Oh, shut up!" she shouted at them.

Arsinoe snickered as she chewed.

"He would have killed me," Lara said, staring at Dramsind. One of the fishers had snagged his arm and was coiling about it pointlessly.

"I told you," Arsinoe said, tearing the rest of the loaf in two, and stowing the larger half. "He won't know friend from foe when his blood is up. Do you remember what I said to him? To calm him down?"

"Koo-tuh-jhu," Lara said. Dramsind's head swiveled towards her, and something shifted beneath his breast.

"Good ear," Arsinoe said, tapping her forehead. "You tuck that away, girl. Don't know if it'll save you, especially if he thinks you're a threat . . . But it can't hurt, can it?"

"I wish I could say the same for my wrist," Lara said, looking to her wound. Her skin was dark and swollen where the slime had touched it. She patted her chest. It felt tender, but nowhere near as bad.

"Lara," Pinsard coughed as he and Moder slipped past the last of the fishers. "Are you alright?"

"Are you?!" she asked, staring at the blood running down his bare chest.

"It is just a couple scratches," Pinsard said, trying to sound casual.

"Oh, please," Arsinoe said.

"We all must be cleaning wounds," Moder said, "But not here."

"No," Lara said, staring at the reflective eyes gazing back at them from the dark.

Lara turned towards the stream of water that ran into the right-hand passage. The others followed her gaze.

"Well," Arsinoe exhaled. "This is it then, isn't it? I'm going to die down here, surrounded by idiots."

The Telchine bent to retrieve her spear. Something popped in her back.

"Volk," she grimaced. "And I'm not even comfortable."

X

The passage was low, but very wide. A dozen horses could have galloped down it, racing side by side, and never come close to touching. It was also eerily clean: The irregular blocks that made up the walls, the sloped ceiling, and the floor beneath their feet were free of mold and grime. Even the stream that ran along its length had failed to tarnish the stone beneath.

"The demons must like it tidy," she said.

"The demons are dead, Lara," Pinsard replied wearily. "Or sleeping so deeply they'll never awaken. The Demon King was the last of them."

"Let's hope so."

For a while they let the water guide them, ignoring any turns or branches in favor of the larger tunnel. Dramsind served as their torch, the luminous slime having coated him from head to foot during their escape from the ghouls.

Lara marveled at his resilience. His armor- or rather his body, she supposed she should think of it as such- had suffered a few scrapes and dents, but he was otherwise unharmed. Whatever he was made of was far stronger than stone.

Strong or weak, it was not the giant's body that lit their way, but the slime. And, as they trod onwards, its radiance grew dimmer until, finally, it died.

The passage became very dark indeed. And yet, somehow, Lara found that she could still see. Faintly, and not very far, but she *could* see.

"Ghost-light?" Pinsard whispered.

"I think it's in the walls," Lara said, peering at one of the irregular blocks jutting from the ceiling. Threads of metal ran maze-like along its surface, as twisted as the boughs of an old oak.

"We stop here then," Moder said, and lay down her pack. "Wounds need cleaning. Then we sleep, Arsinoe, yes?"

The Telchine nodded absently. The woman had not spoken a word since they'd entered the passage, merely sniffing at the air and casting the occasional glance towards Dramsind, a grim expectancy written across her face.

"Is safe to sleep?" Moder asked, raising her voice ever so slightly.

"Safe enough," Arsinoe said. She put her back to the wall and slid heavily to the floor. "We're not dead yet, at least."

"Should we wash?" Lara asked, dipping her boot into the stream. Bannertail mimicked her with his paw.

"Is filthy," Moder frowned.

"We're filthy ourselves," Lara pointed out.

"Quickly then," Moder said. "Wounds will fester if I do not clean."

It would have taken hours to scour all the filth, blood, and caked dirt from their skin, let alone their clothing, but Lara did her best. When she was done, she could see the angry white marks the slime had left on her wrist. The pain was not as intense, but it itched terribly.

"Do not be scratching," Moder chided. "Is like burn. If I had vinegar, or honey-"

"I won't scratch," Lara said.

"Are you having cuts? Bites?"

Lara shook her head. "One of them was clawing my leg, but it couldn't get through my breeches."

"And . . . un-tydre?"

"Bannertail," Lara said, crossing her arms.

"Bannertail," Moder corrected herself. "Is hurt?"

Lara shook her head, having given him a once-over as she'd tried (less than successfully) to bathe him.

"That is good," Moder said, and turned to Pinsard. "Now, open shirt."

"One of the deep men has done it for me," Pinsard said, exposing his chest. Moder clucked at the claw marks running across his left breast and pulled a flask from her pack.

"What is that?" Pinsard asked.

"Distilled wine," she answered.

"Where did you get it?" Lara asked.

"Farm," Moder said, soaking a strip of linen. "I was hiding it from Arlequin."

She dabbed at Pinsard's wounds. His lip twitched a bit, but he kept quiet.

"Shirt is ruined," Moder said as she wrapped his chest with the rest of the linen. "I have spare in my pack but save this one. We will be needing the cloth."

Pinsard nodded soberly and stripped to the waist. His ivory white skin was mottled with bruises old and new.

"You next," Moder said, giving Dramsind a wide berth as she made her way towards Arsinoe.

"How's that?" Arsinoe murmured.

"Your hip," Moder said. "I will clean."

"It's just a scratch," Arsinoe said. "I'll do it myself when I've slept."

"Hip," Moder said. "Show me. Now."

"Well!" Arsinoe sniffed. "I don't usually open my skirts for strangers I met in a *Carsi, soluk iblisler.* But if you insist . . ."

Arsinoe shifted as she cinched up her robes, revealing more than her shimmering legs. Pinsard averted his eyes. Lara tried not to stare.

"Leg is very bruised," Moder said, kneeling for a closer look. "But where is cut?"

"Here," Arsinoe said, tapping her hip.

"Wound looks old."

"It is," Arsinoe replied. "So, you can keep your needle and thread to yourself. I'll take a swig of your rakija, though, if you can spare it."

Moder was so distracted that she handed over the flask. Arsinoe took a quick swig and handed it back.

"Can I sleep now?" Arsinoe asked, tugging her skirts back into place.

"Yes," Moder replied, and got to her feet.

Arsinoe was snoring before Moder could find her own seat alongside one of the glowing blocks.

"What is it?" Lara asked, seeing the curious look on Moder's face. She was nearly asleep herself, with Bannertail curled atop her belly.

"I have seen Telchines before," Moder answered softly. "When I am in war. I have set their bones, sewn up wounds. . . I am seeing many. But I am *never* seeing one heal so fast."

"She *is* from Glycon," Pinsard said, pausing to examine the nicks along the length of his sword. "Could she be a naga? They say some of them shed their skins twice a year, and so keep their youth."

"Who says this?" Moder asked, her brow knitting.

"I read it somewhere," Pinsard muttered.

"I thought of Stheno too," Lara admitted, "When I first saw her."

"Hmph," Moder snorted. "That book again. It is just stories for children."

"Some of them seem real enough to me," Lara said, turning her gaze towards Dramsind. The giant appeared to have taken an interest in the wall beside him, clicking and chittering as he pressed his palm against it.

"Perhaps," Moder said. "But I am not thinking she is chimera. I am thinking that the place where she is from must be very, ah, hard to be reaching. More so than farm, even."

"Why do you say that?" Pinsard asked.

"She is a Telchine," Moder said. "One of full blood, not mixed. Like pack of dogs on a small island."

"I'm not certain she'd care for *that* comparison," Lara said.

"It is not being a good thing," Moder said. "Can be very bad. Too many *ieldran-* parents of the same blood- and there will be mutants."

"Is that what you think she is?" Lara said. "A mutant?"

Moder considered this for a moment.

"Not how you are thinking," she said finally. "But, yes. Wound is only hours old. Is not normal."

"It hardly seems like a bad thing," Pinsard said, "To have wounds that heal so quickly."

Moder did not answer, and eventually her head drooped as she tucked her legs to her chest . . . But Lara could tell that she was still awake, long after Pinsard was breathing soundly.

"Moder," she whispered.

"Yes, Lara?"

"Am I one?" she asked. "A mutant?"

Moder lifted her head. "You?"

"Because my parents-" Lara started to say. "I mean, in all the stories, princesses marry princes. Except for Lady Virago, and she went blind-"

"Your father and mother were Southerners," Moder said, her voice gentle yet firm. "And Southerners have much mixed blood. Any Calvarian would tell you that. If anyone here is being a mutant it is your *moder* and *broder*. Not you."

"So," Lara said. "I am like a pack of dogs, running free?"

"You are like something," Moder huffed. "Something that needs rest."

* * * * * * *

Lara rolled over, groaning. She could not remember dreaming, and her body ached all over. The burn on her wrist throbbed, tiny needles dancing up her arm with every heartbeat.

A hand was shaking her by the shoulder.

"Lara." It was Pinsard. "Lara, wake up. Something is happening."

"Alright," she growled and opened her eyes.

She found herself squinting. The passage had grown light. Well, *lighter*. The silvery threads running through the walls were gleaming.

Bannertail was peering down the passageway, his back arched and hackles raised. Arsinoe was up as well, one hand on her spear as she munched flatbread with the other.

Dramsind was missing.

"Where is giant?" Moder asked, shifting her belt as she regained her feet.

"Search me," Arsinoe said, chewing. Sleep seemed to have restored some of her cheek. "But if it's all the same to you, I'd rather we didn't wait for him here."

Moder nodded as they followed the fox-squirrel's gaze. Something dark and distant was coming, so large that it was dousing the lights as it came.

"The deep men?" Pinsard asked.

Arsinoe licked her lips. "Something else."

Bannertail let out a nervous yip.

"Which way?" Lara whispered. They'd passed a junction before stopping to rest, but she couldn't remember how far back it was.

Arsinoe examined the veins running along the walls, sniffed, and broke into a jog.

"Come on!" she barked. "There's a side passage just ahead!"

"How do you know?" Lara hollered, but the Telchine didn't answer.

She scooped up Bannertail and did her best to keep up.

The dark tide swept towards them, and with it a sound like hard rain drumming against a roof. It coated the corridor from floor to ceiling, its surface swelling and undulating as it came.

"Here!" Arsinoe cried and dove into what looked like a dimmer section of the wall. Lara half expected her to collide with it. When she didn't, Lara dashed after her.

It was a turn. Her eyes had been fooled by the shape of the blocks.

Then Arsinoe came skidding to a halt. Lara did as well, Bannertail squirming in her hands. The corridor was far narrower than the main passage. It was also a dead end.

"*Awirung!*" Moder growled behind her. Arsinoe began jabbing the wall ahead of them with the butt of her spear.

"Get behind me!" Pinsard shouted, his words almost lost in the approaching din.

Lara looked back just as the tide swept over the passage behind them. It wasn't a deluge, or some vast slime, but a galloping carpet of brassy insects, each one as big as a dog. They looked a bit like the pill bugs that hid beneath logs and rocks, with scurrying legs and groping feelers. They whined as they boiled past, legs ringing against each other like-

Metal! They're not alive, they're made of metal.

Several of the things spilled from the passage, either dislodged from the ceiling or jostled by their brethren as they passed, but they took no notice of them, not even Pinsard standing with his sword ready to strike, and they quickly scuttled to rejoin the stampede.

And then they were gone. The stream running down the middle of the passage was gone. They had drunk it dry.

"That was close," Lara said, letting Bannertail go.

Pinsard sheathed his sword.

"What were those things?" he asked.

"The reason there's nothing living down here," Arsinoe said, still fiddling with the wall. "That's my guess."

"What are you doing?" Lara asked.

"What does it look like I'm doing?" Arsinoe gave one of the blocks a push. "No one builds a blind alley underground. Not even the demons."

"The Wanderer might have," Pinsard said.

"Does 'The Wanderer' strike you as the sort to settle down, boy?"

Arsinoe set her spear against the wall and pressed both her hands against another block.

"Dramsind was doing that," Lara said.

"When?" Arsinoe asked.

"Last night," Lara said. "Or this morning- When you were sleeping."

Arsinoe stopped pressing. "Can you show me where?"

"It was back in passage," Moder said.

"Let's go then," Arsinoe said, hefting her spear.

"Those things-" Pinsard said, guarded. "Those beetles. What if they come back?"

"We'd best be quick then."

They hurried back down the passage, emboldened by the way the threads running through the wall were dimming.

"It was this one I think," Lara said, pointing to one of the higher blocks. "Or one of these. He was pressing his palm to it."

Arsinoe tried her spear against the block. It didn't budge.

"Did it move?" Arsinoe asked, trying the block next to it. "Or get brighter?"

"He was just standing still," Pinsard said. "I thought he was resting."

"Hrm," Arsinoe grunted. "Who knows? Maybe he was."

Arsinoe moved down the hallway, testing each block. Still there was nothing.

"What is Banner-squirrel doing?" Moder asked, pointing at the chimera. He was slinking beside the wall, his ears perked and his tail low.

"He hears something," Lara said.

"Wicja?" Moder asked, glancing down the passage. Lara presumed that she was referring to the insects.

"I don't think so," Lara said.

"Then this has to be it," Arsinoe said, retracing her steps and giving each of the blocks another prod. When that failed to elicit a response, she used the flat of her hands. "Maybe there's a catch between the seams . . . Can someone hand me a knife?"

"Mine is still with the deep men," Moder said.

"So is mine," Lara said, brushing her hand against the lip of one of the seams. "But maybe my sword-"

The block lit up beneath her fingers, the threads pulsing before growing dark. Then the entire wall began to open, the individual blocks drawing back to form a new passage.

Arsinoe raised an eyebrow. "That's a neat trick."

"I just touched it," Lara said, staring at her hand.

"Maybe," Arsinoe drawled. "Or maybe you're a great-great-granddaughter of one of the demons. Duskwalker, perhaps. You've got the legs for it."

"Or maybe she is not wearing gloves," Moder pointed out. "And you are."

"That's also a possibility," Arsinoe muttered and stepped through the opening.

Lara followed, Bannertail trotting at her heels. The corridor was dark, but she could see a pinprick of light at the end of it. Moder and Pinsard fell in behind her.

Stone scraped against stone as the passage closed behind them.

The corridor led to a cylindrical chamber whose ceiling was lost to the dark. Four identical passages ringed it besides their own, each one flanking a hollowed recess.

In one of the recesses there was an armored giant. Bands of light pulsed through the cracked seams all about it.

"There," Lara said, but then she saw the sloping shape of the figure's tall helm, its rusting breastplate, its missing right arm.

It wasn't Dramsind.

"Is it," Pinsard said, "Asleep?"

"I'm not sure," Arsinoe said as they stepped into the chamber. "But I've also never seen Dramsind *rust*."

"Here's another," Lara said, pointing at the inhabitant of the alcove closest to them. This one looked much like the other, but its feet had failed it. Its torso lay in the jumble of its limbs.

"It looks dead," Lara said.

Arsinoe nodded, only half listening as she looked about.

"Come on," she said at last, gesturing to one of the tunnels with her spear. "There's light down this way."

The passage was shorter than the first, and when they reached its end, they came to halt. Even Arsinoe was struck dumb.

A silent chamber stretched before them, whose far wall was a massive sheet of gold. Beneath it, a block of green marble stood, as dark as it was unknowable. Galleries ran along the curvature of the room, all of them empty, but kneeling upon the floor were rows of metal figures.

Some were giants. Others were smaller than Lara. A few lay in the dust, prostrate.

"What is this place?" Lara asked.

"It's a temple," Pinsard said, kicking up dust as he took a few tentative steps forward.

Lara followed him slowly. "A temple to who?"

"The demons," Pinsard answered. "Look. Up there on the wall."

He gestured towards the wall of gold. Five tall figures stood carved upon its face, shimmering despite the gloom. They had powerful frames and graceful limbs. Flowing robes hung from their rigid shoulders, simple yet elegant. One wore a fulsome beard, and beside him a shapely woman stood, her arm extended . . . But the sex of the others was harder to determine. For though they were shaped like men, there was something about their faces that made them seem less than human. It was their expressions, she decided. They were cold, forbidding, and without pity.

"There are seven demons," Arsinoe said. "Not five."

"No," Lara said, taking a few steps forward. "No, I think he's right. That one there on the left is The Ruiner. Look, he even has his lance."

The golden figure had a crested helm perched atop its brow, but the spear it grasped was even taller.

"'The Wanderer wore a cloak for rain,'" Pinsard recited, directing their gaze towards the next figure. "'And a wide-brimmed hat to shield eyes from sun. But his wand, like serpents coiled, he kept within his sleeve, and with it many evils he did weave.'"

"Hrm," Arsinoe sniffed, either unconvinced or unimpressed. "So, who's this then?"

She waved at the central figure, whose head was ringed by a disc. It held a curved sickle in one hand, while in the other it clutched the severed horn of a ram. Fruit was spilling from the horn alongside stalks of grain. Heaps of plenty lay at the figure's feet.

"The Hollow Maiden, her hunger never sated?" Lara guessed, though there was nothing womanly about the figure. "Or is it meant to be Duskwalker?"

"That one is Duskwalker," Pinsard said, indicating the queenly woman with arm outstretched. Lara nodded, but still she wondered. The figure on the wall was cradling a babe to her breast, not a monster.

"The hairy bastard must be Stormbringer, then," Arsinoe shrugged. And, sure enough, the bearded figure was clutching a fistful of lightning bolts. "But then where is Skindancer? Why isn't The Dreamer dozing up there if these are meant to be his servants?"

Arsinoe gestured to the metal men.

"Maybe The Dreamer built this place," Lara offered.

Arsinoe clucked her tongue. "If you thought you were a god, girl, and you built a temple, would you leave yourself out of it?"

"I guess I wouldn't," Lara said.

"'The Dreamer fell in the land called Hiva,'" Pinsard said, unshouldering his satchel. "'And built about him a dome of . . . of . . .'"

He paused to fish out his book and began to thumb through its pages.

"'And built about him a dome of *lead*,'" he exclaimed at last. "'Where not even Stormbringer could do him harm.'"

He flipped a few pages and continued.

"'. . . And so it was that Skindancer, still seething with envy, did lay claim to the sum of the seas, raising even Domdaniel from its depths-'"

"So, what are you saying?" Arsinoe said. "While Dreamer napped and 'Dancer cried 'sour grapes', the other five held hands and made nice with each other?"

"As nice as demons can be, I suppose," Lara said. "Until The Wanderer grew bored. Heh. You've clearly never read my *broder's* favorite book."

Pinsard ignored that last remark and kept moving forward, his focus shifting between his tome and the golden mural.

"Maybe the ghouls have it right, then," Arsinoe said, tapping her spear against one of the kneelers.

"How's that?" Lara said.

"Right about the Maiden, I mean," Arsinoe said. "If that really is her up there. After all, *she's* the one standing in the middle, not the so-called Demon King . . . Who knows? Maybe she *is* here somewhere, right beneath our feet, just waiting for the right person to find her."

"Maybe," Lara said, doing her best to sound nonchalant. Still, she felt uneasy. In all the tales she'd ever heard, The Hollow Maiden had been the queen of the underworld . . . And where were they now, if not there?

Lara walked down the central row, peering at the blank faces of the men of metal as she went.

"They seem so sad," she said. "All alone, down here in the dark . . ."

Lara reached out and touched one of them, pressing her palm to its arm. Would it come to life? she wondered.

"Don't do that," Arsinoe said.

"You did," Lara replied, but she let go. Her palm was black with dust.

"Is there anything in book about how to be getting out of here?" Moder's voice echoed through the room.

Neither she nor Bannertail had moved from the entryway. Her hand was on her sword.

"Pinsard," Moder said, a bit louder.

"Oh," Pinsard said, looking up from his book. "Uh, no. At least, I do not think so."

"Put away then," Moder said, and turned to Arsinoe. "Where is giant?"

"Not here," Arsinoe answered. "Close, though. At least I hope he is, or someone else might find us down here, all still and dusty, and wonder at the mystery of it all."

"If they find us at all," Lara said, wiping her hand against her thigh.

"That's the spirit," Arsinoe said.

"Can we not," Pinsard said as he stuffed his book back into his satchel. "I mean, can we, ah, find a way without him?"

"Back at the entrance," Arsinoe said. "Could you have opened those doors?"

Pinsard shook his head.

"Even if we could," Lara said to Pinsard, "We can't leave him. He's her . . . Well, he's her *friend*. I wouldn't abandon you here, even if all the ghouls in the world had dragged you off."

You left Danica, a little voice nagged. *You left Mischief. You let Arlequin and Pierrot get captured just to lure the soldiers away. You sold Surefoot to a chimera. You left them and-*

"You're-" Pinsard lowered his head. "You're right. I am sorry, Arsinoe. We will find him."

Arsinoe smiled her smug smile, and whispered something that sounded cutting . . . But she did so under her breath.

She cares, Lara smiled to herself and walked until she stood before the marble block. It was even larger than it had looked from afar. Above her, the golden demons loomed.

"There are doors here," Pinsard called out. He was standing beneath one of the galleries overlooking the chamber. "But they won't open."

"These ones too," Moder's voice bounced across the chamber, followed by a grunt as she thrust herself against something solid.

Lara stepped onto the dais and walked around the block. Its side was nearly as long as its front, but when she rounded the corner-

"Oh!" she cried. "There's something back here!"

"What is it?" Arsinoe shouted. With the solid stone between them, she sounded very far away.

"A hole," Lara said, "It's like a part of the block is missing. Only- I don't see a way down."

Lara crept to the edge of the pit. It lay within a recess at the rear of the block, as rectangular as the cavity above. There was something on top of the block as well, Lara noticed, just beyond the lip of the stone.

"Could you give me a push?" Lara asked Arsinoe as she came jogging around the other side of the block.

"I could," Arsinoe said, eyeing the hole. "But I don't think the others will be very happy with me afterwards."

"*Lift* me up," Lara clarified. "I want to get on top of this thing."

"That makes more sense," Arsinoe said, and made a cradle of her hands. When Lara stepped into it, she gave her a boost.

Lara caught hold of the lip and pulled herself up. She threw one leg over the other and rolled away from the edge.

When she came to a stop, she found herself face to face with a corpse.

"What is being up there?" Moder called out.

"Just some skeletons," Lara said as she got to her feet, struck by how ordinary the sight of the dead had become to her. "It looks like they were fighting over something."

The bodies were nothing but bone and withered sinew. Whatever garb they had worn had long since shriveled to the merest wisps of cloth. The one at her feet had the back of its skull smashed open. Another pair were still locked together, their clawed fingers intertwined about a black tile of polished stone. It was no bigger than a roof shingle, and a crack ran across its face.

"What is it?" Pinsard asked, his voice drifting from below.

"I don't know," Lara said, taking care not to step on the bones. "It's strange. It almost looks like a pane of glass."

"So, it doesn't look like a key?" Arsinoe asked.

"Not really," Lara replied.

"Is Dramsind up there?"

"*No*," Lara said through gritted teeth.

"What are you still doing up there, then?"

"I just thought there'd be a-" Lara struggled for the right words. "I don't know, a lever. Or a trapdoor. Something like that."

"Is there?" Arsinoe asked. "Any of those things?"

Lara flashed Arsinoe the back of her fingers, and tucked herself into a crouch, readying to slip over the edge of the block.

She hesitated.

It's just a stone, she told herself. *Or a cracked tile. It's nothing. And, even if it isn't, even it is something more, it's still a thing of the demons. Best to leave it alone.*

Lara chewed on her lip and squinted at the cracked black tile caught in the skeletons' grip.

But it must have been important, she reasoned as she began to scoot towards it. *Why else would they have fought over it?*

"What are you doing?" Arsinoe called up to her.

"Just a moment!" Lara replied, doing her best to pry the thing loose.

The tendons of the skeletal fingers crumbled to the touch, freeing the thing. It clattered against the marble before she could catch it.

"Lara?" Moder this time, her voice grown worried.

"Coming," Lara said, her fingers brushing against the tile as she caught it up.

A sour chime filled the air as the thing lit up, blue and pink as the morning sky. Glyphs poured across its face, too fast and too many for Lara to comprehend save one: A blood red lightning bolt, pulsing angrily.

Stormbringer!

A dull rumble filled the chamber, and then the whole room shook. Lara cast the tile away from her, sending it tumbling over the edge of the block . . . But whatever she'd set in motion had clearly begun.

"What did you do?!" Arsinoe shouted.

"I only touched it!" Lara managed as the missing section of the block flew up from below, slamming back into place with a resounding clang. The force of it threw Lara off her feet. Bones scattered as the skeletons flew apart.

"Lara!" Pinsard cried. "Lara, get down from there! The block, it's-"

She missed the rest. She was still pushing herself back to her feet when the entire block began to descend, lurching as it did so. The shift sent her flying forward, the hilt of her sword ramming her so hard in the stomach that the shock made her head swim.

Another rumble shook the chamber. Or was it just the block? Lara retched as she rolled onto her back. As she blinked, she found that Pinsard, Moder, and Arsinoe were now staring *down* at her, their faces receding as the block sank deeper and deeper into the earth. She could see the terror in their eyes.

"No!" Lara shouted, scrambling to her feet.

She jumped towards the nearest face of the shaft. It was no use: She hit the wall and fell back onto the block. Even if she'd had all her strength, she could never leap that high.

Moder did not hesitate. She leapt over the edge and slid down the side of the shaft. A moment later Pinsard had landed next to her with a grunt.

"Come on!" Pinsard called to Arsinoe, who was lingering on the lip of the shaft. "Jump!"

"Ah, Volk!" Arsinoe cursed as she tossed in her spear, tucked in her chin, and leapt over the edge.

She spun a bit as she fell, even managed to land on her side, but the impact still looked like it hurt.

"Bannertail!" Lara cried out, tilting back her head, but all she could see was the rectangular outline of the shaft flying away from them as the block picked up speed.

Then the chimera came sailing over the lip.

Lara crushed one the skeleton's ribcages underfoot as she put herself beneath his fall. He snagged hold of her hair as she caught him and clung to her, shaking as the block plunged into the earth.

"What if it doesn't slow down?!" Pinsard shouted above the thunder of the block's descent. "We'll be crushed!"

"I think not," Moder replied, surprisingly calm. "This is *luft-craet* I am thinking. Like in mine."

Pinsard and Lara blinked at her as the block shook. Arsinoe moaned and rubbed her hip as she sat up.

"Cart," Moder said, flattening her palm. "Goes up and down."

"And what if it isn't?!" Lara asked, staring at the speed with which the walls were flying past them.

Moder considered this.

"Then we are being crushed, like Pinsard is saying."

It was pitch black by then. Lara looked up. The top of the shaft was a pinprick of light, far, far above them. She held Bannertail close and felt his tongue lap against the base of her neck.

The block lurched again, but this time she managed to keep her feet. The roaring in her ears became a groaning squeal as the block quivered beneath her feet.

"You see?" Moder said. *"Luft-craet."*

She was right. They were slowing. The squeal became a low whine until, with one final stomach-turning jolt, they stopped.

"Girl," Arsinoe's voice echoed in the darkness. She did not sound amused. "Where are you?"

"I'm over here," Lara answered, kicking her leg free of the ribcage. "What is it?"

"Ah, never mind-" Cloth rustled and steel scraped against stone as Arsinoe retrieved her spear. "We're still alive. Only . . . What now?"

"You are the guide," Pinsard said, flatly.

"Dramsind was *my* guide," Arsinoe said. "Remember him, boy? Big fellow, a bit quiet?"

"Stop calling me that," Pinsard snapped.

"Shhh," Moder said. "I am hearing something."

Lara heard it too. A sort of low hum, almost musical. Then a bright shaft of light lanced through the darkness.

When her eyes had adjusted, Lara could see that the block had deposited them at the end of a passage connected to a far larger chamber- But the walls and ceiling here were naked rock. Only the floor was as weirdly smooth as the corridors above . . . Though it too was cracked and strewn with loose debris. The metal insects did not prowl here it seemed.

The lamps, or whatever sorcery lit the corridor, were set into the rocks overhead. They were blindingly white, but shed no heat.

"Well," Lara said. "At least we can see where we-"

A piercing shriek echoed through the corridor. It had come from the cavern beyond. Something answered it, something alive, hissing ferally as nail or claw scraped against stone.

"That was no cart," Pinsard said.

"I don't suppose there's a way back up?" Arsinoe said, craning her neck. "Where's that, uh, pane of demon glass you had to go and touch?"

"I threw it away," Lara said.

"Of course you did." Arsinoe squinted at the tunnel.

"What is it?" Pinsard asked. "Ghouls?"

"I have no idea," Arsinoe said, hefting her spear.

Whatever it was, it wasn't alone. The cries grew louder as new throats opened, screeching hatefully as they boiled out of the darkness, a drum-like beat rising behind them.

Moder and Pinsard drew their swords.

"Wait," Lara said, leaning forward, her head turned. "It's not-"

Bannertail twisted out of Lara's grip then, and began to bound down the corridor, stopping only once to see if she was following.

Lara hitched up her breeches and jogged after him.

"Brave little monster," Lara heard Arsinoe say as the others made to follow.

"Do not be speaking about my *dohtor* that way," Moder replied. "Lara! Slow down!"

Bannertail swerved as he shot out into the cavern, his claws digging into the rock as he let out a tremulous bark. Lara slowed too, acutely aware of the sudden drop just beyond the mouth of the corridor.

Before she could begin to guess at its depth, a great twisting column of winged beasts erupted from the depths, squalling and squealing as their leathery wings sent them fluttering past.

"It's alright!" Lara shouted. "It's only bats!"

The others came to a halt behind her, staring as hundreds of the creatures shot past them. Bannertail squalled as they flew up the tunnel, and then they were gone.

"Bats," Arsinoe said. "Then that means-"

"There is way out," Moder finished, and sheathed her sword.

"Yes," Pinsard said. "Look here. There is a stair."

He put his foot on the first rung of a stairway that jutted from the side of the cavern wall. A coppery rail ran directly alongside it, supported by thick beams whose mooring was somewhere far beneath them.

"I wonder how high it goes?" Lara said, leaning back to try and get the scope of it.

A light winked into life high above them, flickering as the column of bats rushed past it. Then another began to glimmer, though it was so high that she could scarcely make it out.

"There's another stair below us," Lara heard Arsinoe say. She turned to see the Telchine peering over the edge of the precipice. "But I doubt we want to go that way. We're deep enough already."

"No," Moder said. "Way out is above."

Another shudder ran through the earth. Dust and loose pebbles showered them from above. Then it was still again.

"Whatever it is you started, girl," Arsinoe said, her eyes trained upwards, "It hasn't stopped."

"We shouldn't stay here," Lara said, wondering just how strong the ancient supports holding up the stairway were.

"Good idea," Arsinoe said. "But why don't I lead us this time, yes?"

Lara nodded, but she glanced back down the corridor, and said: "Dramsind."

"Don't worry about him," Arsinoe said. "I found him down here, remember? Besides, he always-"

The earth shuddered. The stairway groaned. A bright light blossomed in the darkness beneath them, and then a great wave of heat washed up the shaft, hot as an oven.

"We go," Moder said. "Now."

"He'll find a way out," Arsinoe said as she mounted the first couple of steps, practically leaping as she climbed. "You'll see!"

"And what about us?" Pinsard shouted as Lara made to follow.

"We'll manage, boy!" Arsinoe shot back at him. "With a touch of luck . . ."

Arsinoe slowed as something far louder than thunder came roaring up from below, and threw her back against the wall of the cavern. Lara did the same. A tremor made the stairway shiver. Bannertail leapt onto Lara's leg and clung there until it had passed.

"Luck!" Lara spat, slapping her hip until Bannertail climbed onto her shoulder. "We'll need the Watcher's own I think."

"Is there any other kind?" Arsinoe said, tapping at the beetle on her cheek.

* * * * * * *

Lara could feel the fresh, cool air of the outside world brushing against her skin long before they came staggering to the top of the stairs. Only then did they stop to catch their breath, panting at the feet of a far greater gate than the one they had used to enter the mountain.

How they would have opened it, or if they would have lingered there until thirst, the ghouls, or the very earth took them, Lara could not say. Something vast and terrible had broken the gate long ago, crumpling its doors like parchment, though they were as thick as Lara was tall.

"Wulf," Lara whispered.

"Is that what you call Volk, in the north?" Arsinoe asked, her hands on her knees as she heaved for breath. "Wulf?"

"Yes," Pinsard said, "But you should not speak his name so loudly."

"And why is that, boy?" Arsinoe asked.

"It's bad luck," Lara explained.

"Is that all?" Arsinoe said, shooting a sour glance over her shoulder.

The stairway behind them couldn't have stretched more than half a league, but it had felt ten times that length before they had reached its top, the earth trembling as gouts of white-hot fire lanced across the chasm below. The tremors had grown fainter the higher they had climbed, but they never stopped entirely.

For every hundred steps or so there had been a landing from which a corridor stretched. Most were sealed by seamless sheets of metal, but others lay open, their floors white with bat droppings, mold, and chunks of loose stone intermingled with strange objects: Cubes, rods and vases crept over with rust.

As they passed each corridor, Arsinoe had stopped just long enough to cup her hands to her mouth and called out for Dramsind, using the words of the clipped language he spoke. Then she would stop to listen. But if Dramsind could hear her calls, he would not- or could not- answer.

"We could still go back," Lara said. "And, if I'd known what would happen-"

"I told you not to worry, girl," Arsinoe said, turning away from the chasm. "And I don't like repeating myself. So come. The sooner we're out of this place the closer I am to being rid of *you*."

Arsinoe strode towards the nearest rent, her shoulders shimmering as she passed through a shaft of moonlight.

"Ffft," Lara huffed, brushing the fox-squirrel's tail from her face as it turned about. *"Fine."*

Moder took Lara by the arm and squeezed.

"Let her be," she said, "She keeps her word. And sometimes, when there is anger, it is best to be saying nothing."

"Try telling *her* that," Lara said.

"I am not her *moder*," Moder said, letting go of Lara as she fell into step behind the Telchine.

"Well," Lara said to Pinsard as they followed. "I suppose we can both imagine what *she* must have been like."

"Yes," Pinsard said. "No discipline."

"Oh, no," Lara replied. "Just the opposite, I think. Too disciplined. And stiff. Stiff and strict. Easy to annoy."

"Quiet!" Moder shushed.

They followed Arsinoe through the breach, Lara marveling at the way its edges looked like so much melted wax. She was reaching out to touch it when a horrible thought occurred to her: Without Dramsind they could not know if the colorless fire was still burning here.

She squinted at her hands as they walked onto a sweeping shelf of rock, half expecting them to blister and shrivel before her eyes . . . But other than the burn on her wrist, they looked perfectly normal.

For now, she thought. The fire was subtle, Danica used to say. Or was that something she'd read in one of the old woman's crumbling books? Either way, one day she might wake up and find a scaly patch on her skin, like that of a reptile, only the first of many . . .

The sound of Moder's voice drove these thoughts away.

"This is being South?" she was saying. They had come to the edge of the shelf.

"We're higher than I'd prefer," Arsinoe replied, slowing to study the horizon. "But yes."

"We're on the other side then?" Lara asked. "Of the mountains?"

"This is Glycon, girl," Arsinoe said, gesturing at the deep blue expanse that stretched beneath them. "The land of lunatics, dragons, and the fools who worship them."

"Dragons," Lara repeated. "They're real then? Not just stories?"

"Is that so hard to believe?" Arsinoe asked her. "After all the things you've seen?"

Lara shrugged. "I never saw a dragon."

"Well, you're in for a treat then," Arsinoe said, slumping against a boulder. "But first I need to eat, or I'll keel over the side of this cliff."

"Eat," Moder said, looking for a place to settle down. "And I must be shutting my eyes. Just for a while."

"Is it safe to rest here?" Pinsard asked, glancing back at the broken gate.

"We must rest sometime," Moder said, having found a patch of soil. "And I am not so young as you are. So, you will keep watch. Yes?"

Pinsard nodded and stood up a bit straighter.

"Good," Moder said, and laid her head down. Arsinoe was already gnawing on a strip of smoked meat, worrying it between her molars.

Lara knelt and let Bannertail sniff his way across the shelf. Then she walked to its edge, and searched the horizon, not entirely knowing what it was that she was looking for. The only things she knew of Glycon were that dragons dwelt there, and that the Glyconese were known for their cruelty. Their rebellion, ages past, had brought the Kingdom of Aquilia to its knees . . . But the tales of those times she remembered best were those of the wicked Count Faisan, who had betrayed all for the sake of Vasilisa the Beautiful. If there had been songs or poems regarding the geography of Glycon, she'd clearly paid them no mind.

It was cooler on this side of the range, and she found herself missing the warmth of her cloak, lost along with her pack and gloves. But in spite of the chill, the view from where she stood was stirring. The night was cloudless, and the Watcher was quite full. Gazing at it, and the vastness of the glittering sky, she wondered how she ever could have mistaken the cave fishers down below for stars.

Boots scraped against stone as Pinsard came up beside her, his own head tilted to the sky.

"What are they, do you think?" he asked, his voice low so as not to disturb Moder. "The stars."

"They are bits of the Firebird," Lara answered, "You know that."

"I doubt it is true though," Pinsard said. "Heh. When I was little, I used to think there was a blanket hung over the sky with holes in it."

"And," Lara asked, "Behind the holes?"

"A lamp, I guess. Or- I don't know. Another place. Where it was day instead of night."

"That's silly," Lara snickered.

"I said I was little," Pinsard muttered.

"No," Lara said, "I'm sorry. It's kind of nice, actually. A whole other world made out of stars . . . Who knows? Maybe you had it right."

They stood there for a long while, quiet, as the horizon began to turn pink.

"Have you counted them all yet?" Arsinoe drawled as she walked up to the edge and kicked a few rocks from the shelf. "You could do the stones next. Or grains of sand."

"We were just looking," Lara said. She was tired of being baited.

"Stars, stones, sand," Arsinoe gave the shelf another swipe. "None of them will keep you alive, will they? Look for water, girl, if you insist on letting your eyes wander."

"And you," Pinsard said, his voice growing hot. "Do you never stop to look at the sky? Or is that sort of thing beneath you?"

"Speak to me in that tone again, *soluk iblisler*," Arsinoe said, turning ever so slightly to regard him. "And maybe I'll forget my vow to The Ruiner and pluck your eyes from your head. Wear them for a necklace. What a sight the stars would be to you then, eh?"

Pinsard's mouth worked, but no sounds came out.

"Stars!" Arsinoe snorted as she walked away. "Trust me, girl: Look for water. You'll die of thirst in a world made of stars."

XI

Glycon was far prettier than Lara had imagined.

She'd pictured baking wastes and twisting rivers emptying into fetid marshes, where domed temples to The Destroyer loomed and dragons wheeled. But as the Firebird rose and they made the long way down from the rocky escarpments, she found herself gazing upon a green stretch of craggy hills and golden valleys. The hills were thick with unfamiliar wildflowers, their indigo petals coated with fine silvery hairs and, as they pressed through them, dozens of butterflies burst into flight, their wings so like the flowers that it was hard to tell one from the other.

Glycon was hot, yes, and still very dry- Lara soon found herself scanning the valleys for any sign of running water- but there was no denying that it was beautiful.

"How do you like it, girl?" Arsinoe asked as they walked through a low grove of trees with twisted trunks. She looked very natural here, her blueish hair and tinted skin almost making her seem a part of the landscape. "Found a dragon yet? Or are you still counting stones?"

"It's very . . . Green," Lara answered, ignoring the barb. "So there must be rain."

"Yes," Arsinoe said. "But very little during the summer, and when it does there will be lightning. And fires. If we are caught in the open when it does-"

"We *have* storms in the North," Pinsard said, gruffly. He was sweating so badly that his shirt was plastered to his skin.

"Do you?" Arsinoe asked, stopping in her tracks to face him. "I'd always thought that the rain fell upwards there, and people went about with hats on their feet."

"Please," Moder said, tugging at her collar. "Both of you. It is too hot."

"Just don't say I didn't warn you," Arsinoe said, and walked on. Pinsard took a deep breath and trudged after her, his cheeks blazing.

"They're going to kill each other," Lara said to Moder once they'd put some distance between them. "Or something like it, if this keeps up."

"Something like it," Moder said.

"Well?" Lara said. "Shouldn't you stop them?"

"I should," Moder said, giving the front of her coat another tug. "Later."

"Pff," Lara huffed, and quickened her step, acutely aware of Bannertail's weight on her shoulder, and the drip of his tongue as he panted.

As it happened, though, it was the fox-squirrel who led them all to water, his ears pricking as he leapt from Lara's shoulder and tore into the brush. When he didn't return with a bird or mouse clamped between his jaws, Lara pressed through needle-shrub and scaled rocks until she found him lapping water from a gurgling stream.

Lara called for the others before helping herself, cupping mouthful after mouthful to her lips.

"Slowly," she heard Moder urge as Pinsard knelt down beside her. "And wash hands first."

Lara took another gulp and wiped some of the grime from her hands, wondering how dark a tub would turn if she had one to bathe in.

When she looked up, she found herself staring into the black eyes of a tawny-coated rodent, whose head and forelegs were jutting from a burrow on the opposite side of the stream. It was twice as big as Bannertail, and as fat-cheeked as a striped squirrel with a mouth full of nuts.

"Hello there," she started to say, when the head of Arsinoe's lance speared it clean through, pinning the creature to the bank. It let out no cry. The blow had killed it instantly.

"How could you?!" Lara cried as she turned about, Bannertail darting for the relative safety of the nearby brush.

"Practice," Arsinoe said, leaping over the stream, "And good follow through. You want to eat, don't you?"

"What if it was a chimera?" Lara grumbled, though her mouth began to water at the thought of freshly cooked meat.

"It's not," Arsinoe said, giving her spear a shake before lifting the rodent from its hole. "It's just a myrmik."

"A myrmik?" Pinsard said, his hands dripping onto his breeches.

"It means 'ant' in the old tongue," Arsinoe said, laying the thing on its side as she stripped off one of her gloves. "They like to burrow, and collect shiny things like people do, so the first people who came here thought they were giant ants that dug up gold. They aren't, obviously. They're just overgrown rats."

By then she'd taken the myrmik by one of its legs and was skinning it with her bare fingers. Almost the whole of her hand was green rather than gold. If it was a bruise, it was a big one. It ran all the way up to the middle of her wrist.

"The name stuck, anyway," Arsinoe went on, peeling hide from flesh. "They still call this place the land of the myrmekes."

"I have heard word like that before," Moder said, pressing a dampened sleeve to her neck. "A word for warriors who feel no pain."

"Yes, the Myrmidons. Their tribe lived here once, long ago. A strong people the songs say, but the Glyconese enslaved them like all the rest."

"Oh," Lara said, her interest piqued. "Then, you are not Glyconese?"

"Me?" Arsinoe said, looking up from her work. "Do I look like a Gargean zealot to you? Or a daughter of mercy perhaps?"

"A daughter of . . .?" Lara stammered, frightened by Arsinoe's sudden change of tone. She knew that she had a temper, but she'd never seen her so nakedly angry.

"Well, I'm not one, girl, any more than this fat rat is an ant. And you should be glad, for they and their so-called 'goddess' are anything but merciful."

"I'm sorry," Lara said. "It's only- your tattoo. I thought that-"

"My own people gave me this," Arsinoe said, tapping the beetle on her cheek with a green finger. "They gave it to me to remind me of my place."

With that she took hold of a thick fold of the myrmik's hide and yanked, tearing it.

"Your hand is bruised," Pinsard pointed out, flatly. Lara couldn't quite read the look on his face.

"Is it?" Arsinoe said, dipping her hand in the stream and giving it a shake. "Maybe I should give it a rest, boy. Better yet, why don't you make yourself useful and skin this for me while I go and find you all another rat to eat!"

Arsinoe tugged her glove back onto her hand and snatched up her spear before making her way downstream.

"*Her* people," Pinsard said, watching her go. "I wonder who they were."

"Dogs on island," Moder said, crossing the stream and kneeling beside the myrmik. "Very small pack. And now she is alone. She must be very frightened."

"Her?" Lara said. "I doubt it. She hardly broke a sweat fighting the ghouls."

"Is easy to fight monsters," Moder said, her fingers working as she stripped away the myrmik's skin. "Is harder, to change."

* * * * * * *

Arsinoe didn't return with another kill, but her carry-roll bulged with leafy greens and balls of dirt that turned out to be wild onions when she washed them off in the stream. They had gotten a cookfire going by then, and the myrmik was roasting over it on a crude spit.

"I miss my knife," Arsinoe said, pinching one of the myrmik's red thighs and tugging.

Blood dripped and drizzled.

"It's not ready," Lara grimaced.

"I'm not a monster, girl," Arsinoe said, showing her the garlic cloves nestled in her other palm. "Just tired of eating unseasoned meat."

"Tired of *food?*" Moder murmured.

"Here," Pinsard said, offering the Telchine a sharp-edged shard of rock. "You can use this."

"A gift of a blade?" Arsinoe said, raising her eyebrows. "And no coin?"

"It is a rock," Pinsard said, confused.

"Doesn't matter," Arsinoe said, taking it. "But I'll take it, boy, because you clearly don't know what you're doing. Just don't do it again."

"Do what?" Pinsard asked.

"Exactly," Arsinoe said, slicing the myrmik open and pressing the cloves into the cuts.

The spiced myrmik was tough, but like the water from the stream it tasted as good to Lara as any sweetcake she'd ever eaten. She even ate one of the onions, though it made the ones Moder grew seem sweet. Arsinoe gobbled the others down like they were frostberries and gnawed at the leftover joints of the myrmik until there was nothing left but bone. Pinsard stared at this with his mouth agape, until Lara dug her elbow into his side.

As for Bannertail, he eyed the bones piling up near their guide's feet and licked his chops . . . But he didn't get any closer to the woman and her spear.

"How far is it now?" Lara asked Arsinoe as Moder began putting out the fire with her boot. Moder had taken little notice of the Telchine's table manners, having kept her gaze skyward since the first ribbons of smoke had curled from their fire. Lara didn't have to ask what for.

"What? To the sea?" Arsinoe answered, wiping her mouth with the back of her glove. "Six, maybe seven days? We're a bit farther east from my usual route. But I assume you don't want me to just show you the ocean before I turn back around."

"Well," Lara said, trying to remember exactly what their terms had been. "I guess that's what you agreed to, back at the, ah, at the *Carsi*."

"You worry too much, girl," Arsinoe said, getting up. "It makes my head hurt. So, worry not. I'll take you to Zerzura. I'll need to go there anyway for supplies."

"What is that?" Lara asked. "A city?"

"Hardly," Arsinoe said. "But it has a harbor, boats, and sea captains that don't ask too many questions. That is the sort of thing that interests you, yes? Unless you intend to swim from your troubles, whatever they may be."

Lara's nostrils flared, but she shook her head 'no.'

"How far is it to Zerzura?" Pinsard asked.

"If we aren't slowed down by repetitive questions," Arsinoe said, folding up her carry-roll, "I'd say . . . Nine days. Ten at the most."

"Nine days," Lara said. "Do we have enough food?"

"We should find plenty if we follow this," Arsinoe said, kicking a clod of dirt into the stream. "It'll be risky, though. Where there's water there are animals, but also people. And the Glyconese do not like outsiders."

She grinned then, and the beetle's wings flexed.

"Or," she went on, "I suppose they like them well enough, but only when they're working a field or pulling oars inside a galley. Though I'm not certain what they'd make of you lot. I've never seen a Northerner picking maslinki, and 'brother' here is a bit too old to make for a proper Myrmidon."

"And yet you keep calling him 'boy,'" Lara said.

"I do," Arsinoe said, her lips thinning. Pinsard caught Lara's eye and smiled ever so slightly.

"Glyconese," Moder said, taking her eyes off the heavens for a moment. "Are they not where we are going?"

"Zerzura may be a pigsty," Arsinoe said, shouldering her carry-roll and starting down the stream, "But it's a free pigsty. Least it was the last time I saw it. Karks might have taken it since then, but they won't be around for long."

"Karks?" Lara said, scratching at her scalp. She was glad they were moving; the streambed was beginning to get buggy.

"They're another bloody horn-cult," Arsinoe said, "Or was that the Baymins? Ugh. Karks, Jibbiths, Simurgs- I can't tell any of them apart, except to say they're all crazy. Irkalla isn't worth fighting over. Anyone with sense could see that."

"Horn-cult?" Lara said, careful not to trip over Bannertail as he weaved through her legs.

"Why don't we walk more and talk less?" Arsinoe replied, quickening her own step. "I'd prefer we reached Zerzura before winter sets in."

That sentiment frightened Lara more than Arsinoe could have guessed. The terrors of the underworld had made her forget some of her fears, but now . . . They might have the mountains between them and Reynard, but she doubted that his servants had given up their hunt. Where were they, she wondered? Crossing some high pass, a day or two behind them? Was his army still battling the Grand Prince or was it sweeping across Mandross, trampling everything in its path?

She couldn't speak freely, of course. Not in front of Arsinoe. And so, in the end, it was the Telchine who couldn't keep quiet as they traveled downstream, the water's course growing wider and deeper as a dozen smaller streamlets joined it.

Arsinoe talked about food more than anything else, and Lara wasn't surprised; The only thing she seemed to enjoy more than the sound of her own voice was eating. As the soil grew more verdant, the Telchine compared the virtues of the wild greens she plucked: Which were sweet, which were savory, which were better boiled, and which were poisonous. Lara knew of a handful of the plants if not the names Arsinoe used for them. Hemlock were kecksies in her tongue, and horseweed was succory.

Arsinoe also knew the names of the many snakes and lizards that basked along the banks, explaining that they flourished because the Glyconese considered it an offense to harm them- a taboo she blatantly ignored, for she speared and ate as many as she could catch, many of them raw.

Lara couldn't tell a rock agama from a moon-lizard, or a soosan from a jaculus, but she accepted whatever the woman offered. After all, there were no wild chickens to be found here, or eggs for that matter, though there was much small game. Every day, Bannertail caught more songbirds than he could eat and Moder and Pinsard took turns whipping stones at the snout-nosed shrews whose dens lined the banks. Moder was very good, but Pinsard seemed to have been born to it.

"You should keep the hides," Lara said to him, after he'd caught his fifth. "Moder could sew you a new cloak."

"It would not last long," Pinsard said as he cast the pelt into the brush. "Their fur is too delicate."

"I was making a joke," Lara muttered.

"So was I," Pinsard said, sticking out his tongue as he set the shrew over the fire.

Sleep was as difficult as ever, even for their guide, for the richer the soil became the more they found themselves skirting around old mills and mudbrick villages. Soft and inviting as the nearby meadow-groves looked, to take shelter there was far too risky. There'd be no convincing the locals that they were traveling merchants, or refugees fleeing from war and before long every jumble of rocks or thorny bramble looked to Lara like bed . . . But even she counted herself lucky when she noticed how little Arsinoe slept. Without Dramsind to keep watch, she was always the last to fall asleep and the first of them to rise, catching only a few hours in between, lying so still that she hardly looked alive, as if someone had dressed up a golden statue and left it in the wilds for a stranger to discover.

The lack of sleep made Arsinoe even more talkative, if easily distracted. She became almost philosophical as she tried to describe the salty taste of a fruit she called elia, bemoaning that it was out of season. Wine, or something like it she called rakija, was another luxury she longed for, speaking not of how it tasted but of how it reminded her of clouds passing over the moon on an otherwise clear night.

In the mornings, though, she would crave a drink from Hiva called 'kafay.' Moder seemed to know of it and asked Arsinoe if its beans grew in Glycon, to which the Telchine ruefully shook her head, saying that the dragon-worshippers hated the Hivan bean as much as they hated the Hivans themselves.

"More, perhaps," she went on, nibbling on an apparently unsatisfying root. "Getting people to hate each other is easy. But getting them to hate *living*? Well, that's something else."

"Is it that good?" Lara asked her.

"I'd trade a thousand Hivans for a cup of kafay."

"Is good," Moder agreed.

In this way they spent four days, four nights, and the better part of a morning. Then they came to the edge of a low ridge and found themselves gazing upon a river whose shores were lined by dark-barked poplars, each one straight as a column.

"That's the Eridanos," Arsinoe said, planting her spear. "The river of amber, where Phaeteon's chariot crashed into the swell before he died, the pretty fool."

"And who was he?" Lara asked. She could tell by now when Arsinoe was in a mood to show off something that she knew.

"A prince from long ago," Arsinoe said, reaching for her waterskin. "A stupid one, who thought too much of his looks. He wanted to inherit his mother's crown, though he had seven sisters. Even if he'd only had one, he should have known better. No true Telchine would ever have served him."

"Because he was a man?" Pinsard asked. "Is that what you mean?"

"I meant what I said, boy," Arsinoe replied. "Do you think I'd ever listen to you? I am Telchine, or haven't you noticed my skin? On it I wear the mark of the Maiden's glory."

"That must please you," Pinsard said.

"Please me?" She sneered and took a swig from her waterskin. *"Please me?* Tell me, boy, how many summers do you think I have seen?"

"I do not know," Pinsard replied, licking his lips. "Twenty-five?"

"Ha!" Arsinoe chortled. "He is polite, at least. What about you, girl? Or shall I ask Mother?"

"Thirty?" Lara guessed.

"Thirty-two," Moder said, her expression sure.

Arsinoe grinned and began to pluck her glove from her fingers.

"The boy was closer," she said, tugging. "This misery of a year is, in fact, my *twentieth* summer. I'll be lucky to see a fortieth."

"You can't be," Lara said. "I'm only-"

"Look at my hand, girl," she said, freeing her glove. "Look and see how much the Maiden's glory *pleases* me."

Arsinoe held out her hand. It wasn't bruised. It was rusting, turning green like an old copper coin. She flexed her fingers, setting flakes to dance on the breeze. Then she thrust her hand back into her glove.

"Does it hurt?" Lara asked.

"No," Arsinoe said. "Truth be told, it doesn't feel like anything. That's some comfort I suppose."

"I-" Pinsard said, lowering his eyes. "I did not know."

"How could you?" Arsinoe said, sliding down a gravelly slope. "You are only a man, who speaks when he should be listening . . . And I am being too generous! I shall rust and die, boy, before you are ever truly a man."

"Too generous-" Pinsard nearly stumbled as he followed her down the slope, before declaring: "I *am* a man!"

"Are you now?" Arsinoe said, leaping over a rock. "I think not."

Arsinoe leapt from the rock and slid further down the slope before skidding to a halt.

"But you are *pretty*, boy," she said, smirking. "Like Phaeton was, I imagine. Stupid, but pretty. So, when we get to the river, keep yourself off a chariot. I'd hate to see you drown!"

Arsinoe jumped away just as Pinsard tried to match her speed, his long legs ill-suited to the task. When he finally slipped and fell, Arsinoe laughed and barked an insult Lara couldn't make out.

"Do you think she's telling the truth?" Lara asked Moder as they followed, both of them taking far more care as they went. "She can't be twenty. She looks so old."

"She is not looking so old to me," Moder said, watching as Pinsard picked himself up and patted off his breeches. "Not now at least."

* * * * * * *

The hills had been dry and sandy, but the marshy banks of the Eridanos were lush. Reeds and sedges grew in clumps beneath the shade of the lean poplars. Gray cranes stalked the pools, hunting for frogs. Enormous turtles paddled amongst the rushes.

And there were dragons.

Lara did not realize she was looking at one of them when Arsinoe bent down and grabbed Bannertail by the scruff of his neck, ignoring the fox-squirrel's yips and scratches as she kept her gaze trained on the water's edge.

"What is it?" Lara asked, looking for danger amongst the remnants of a dead tree that had fallen into the river. It was nearing midday, and the sunlight on the water was dazzlingly bright.

"Don't move," Arsinoe whispered, Bannertail struggling in her grip.

"I don't-" Lara began to say, when one of the tree's larger 'branches' moved, the bulk of the trunk shifting as it began to rise out of the water.

What she'd taken for a branch was a great clawed forepaw. As it dug into the riverbank, a huge reptilian head emerged from the murk, water spilling from its neck as it turned a single unblinking eye towards them.

It was green and gold and glinted like a polished gem.

"Beautiful," Lara breathed.

"Back. Away." Arsinoe said, starting to do so herself. "Slowly."

As they retreated into the trees, the beast dragged itself onto the bank, its tail making wakes as it lashed through the shallows. Its spiny hide was dark as ivy on a sunless day, but what little of its underbelly Lara could see was quite pale, and stony as a bed of limestone.

The dragon parted its jaws as it resettled atop the riverbank and let out a growling rumble that gave Lara gooseflesh. From snout to tail she guessed that it was easily twenty feet long.

"That's a very big drake," Arsinoe whispered, passing Bannertail to Lara. The fox-squirrel leapt up her arm and tried to hide in the tangle of her hair.

"I thought dragons had wings," Lara whispered back.

"Only the females," Arsinoe replied, gesturing for them to follow her as she pressed into the underbrush. "The males- the drakes- are much smaller."

"*That* is smaller?" Pinsard balked.

Arsinoe didn't reply, but kept moving, climbing up a mossy bank and putting tree after tree between them and the beast basking in the sun.

"This way," she said, pointing to the crest of a grassy ridge just above the tree line. "If he's lazy he won't follow us."

"And if he is not?" Moder asked.

"Then at least we'll have the high ground."

The Telchine's strategy seemed sound enough.

"Do dragons, uh," Lara asked, looking about as they began to climb the slope, "Flock?"

"That was a bull drake," Arsinoe explained as she shoved her way through the underbrush. "An older one too. It probably drove off all of the smaller ones in the area."

"Why didn't it attack us?" Lara asked, still thinking of the thing's chilly glare, and the row of knife-like fangs lining its jaws.

"Maybe it wasn't hungry," Arsinoe said, throwing a branch aside. "Or maybe it was waiting for easier prey. One that old must have felt the bite of a few hunters' spears over the years."

She grinned back at them, twisting the shaft of her weapon for emphasis.

"People *hunt* them?" Lara spat, trying to focus on her footing. Between the brush and the sun in their eyes it was easy to miss the poplar roots twining through the grass.

"They make good boots," Moder said, huffing a bit.

"They do," Arsinoe chuckled. "And it's hard to keep goats with dragons about, so a hunt in these parts isn't as rare as you might think. After all, what young fool doesn't fancy himself a dragon-slayer?"

"Even if I did," Pinsard glowered, "The size of that thing . . ."

"Feh," Arsinoe sniffed. "It's the smaller ones that usually kill people. They lurk in the shallows and strike before you even know they're there. Even children know that."

"There are no dragons in the North," Pinsard growled, speaking through his teeth. "It is too cold."

"And that book of yours," Arsinoe said. "There are no *dragons* in it?"

Lara was certain that, were it not for the swishing of the grass and the creaking of the trees, she would have been able to hear Pinsard's teeth grinding against each other.

"I always wanted to ride a dragon," Lara said as the slope grew steeper. "Not slay one."

"Ride?" Arsinoe repeated, panting. "A dragon? What for?"

"One of the winged ones, I mean," Lara said. "It would be just like flying. Not to mention that I wouldn't have to climb hills all day and night."

"You're a strange one, girl," Arsinoe said, shaking her head. "Even the Glyconese don't ride dragons, and they're mad enough to worship them."

"What about Glyconese?" Moder grunted, her face slick with sweat. "They do not kill hunters?"

"They do," Arsinoe replied. "When they can catch them. But they also need the locals to lead hunts of their own."

"They hunt dragons?" Lara said, "But I thought-"

"Oh, no, not to kill them of course! Heh, that might delay the end. No, their zealots seek out the biggest and strongest ones they can find and capture them alive. But to do it properly takes expertise."

"But what for? Why do it at all?"

"What else? To breed them with *their* dragons," Arsinoe said, catching hold of a nearby branch and pulling herself upwards. "Though who knows? Some say that their priestesses are all naga, so I suppose anything's possible. It must get lonely being a daughter of mercy, surrounded by nothing but eunuchs and Myrmidons."

"I don't understand," Lara said.

"I do," Moder said. "Is bad joke."

"It's a better joke than the nonsense they would have us all believe," Arsinoe snorted. "Some madman chokes down half a gallon of salt-water and manages to babble on for three days before croaking and they call him a prophet? And it was a *him*, of course. That should tell you something right there."

"But what *do* they believe?" Lara asked, gasping a bit as she began to use her hands to climb. "We're from the North, remember?"

"Oh," Arsinoe breathed, "Well, that's easy. They think that dragons will bring about the end."

"The end?" Pinsard said.

"Of everything," Arsinoe said. "First dragons eat us all, or something like that, and then the ocean rises up and drowns whatever's left."

"And they *want* that?" Lara said, stopping to catch her breath. Bannertail traded her right shoulder for her left and yawned hugely.

"I didn't say it made sense," Arsinoe said, taking a moment to breathe herself. "But they *do* believe it. So, they breed dragons. After all, if dragons are going to end the world, it only stands to reason that more of them will speed things up."

"But if Glyconese," Moder said, sucking air as she spoke, "Are hunting dragons- large dragons- and one behind us was being large, then-"

"*Rahatlayin,* Mother," Arsinoe said with a lazy wave of her hand. "To capture a drake that big, *alive*? It would take a whole swarm of zealots just to flush it from the river. I think we would have noticed two score idiots skulking in the bushes, yes?"

Moder nodded half-heartedly.

"Besides," Arsinoe went on, shielding her eyes from the sun as she resumed her climb, "You'd need just as many men to herd it, not to mention the actual hunters to do the hard stuff. Party that size would have cooks, foragers, and horses trained not to spook to pull the cage they'd have to keep it in. Practically a small army."

"A Glyconese one I suppose," Lara murmured, her gut sinking. She'd had more than her fill of running from armies.

"Not really," Arsinoe snorted. "Though knowing the Glyconese, there'd be at least one daughter of mercy waiting to take the credit when the job was done. She would probably have us scourged just for disturbing the hunt. And those scaly-skinned fetches don't go anywhere without bodyguards."

"Myrmidons," Moder said.

"The Ant-Men, yes," Arsinoe nodded, digging the butt of her spear into the hill as they neared the top of the slope. "Though even they won't lift a finger to stop a dragon. I heard that one of the daughters got eaten during a hunt once. A great honor for her, apparently. Heh! I would have paid my own weight in water to see that."

"It sounds awful," Lara said.

"No, it'd be fun," Arsinoe said, turning to shoot Lara a wicked grin as she reached the top of the slope. "And who knows? I've still got some years. Maybe I'll get lucky."

"This one doubts that," a voice said.

Lara put up her hand and found herself staring into the eyes of a woman whose bronze breastplate was draped in layers of delicate green silk. She was sitting atop a strange spotted-blue roan, the horse's reins gripped almost casually in a scaled glove. Her face, impassive and angular, was marked by tattoos that seemed to flow from her eyes like tears. Dark hair hung over her shoulder in a tight coil, and a whip with many barbed heads dangled from her saddle.

Around the woman a dozen warriors stood, close enough to strike Arsinoe with their broad-headed spears. Each wore twin swords on their belts, their faces indistinguishable beneath spiked helms and veils of linked brass.

Myrmidons!

Beyond them, Lara could see dozens of canvas tents being raised by a host of shirtless men hauling ropes and driving stakes into the ground. Others were digging trenches. Yet more were unhitching a team of horses from an enormous wagon bearing an iron-barred cage on its bed.

A cage large enough for a dragon.

"Well," Arsinoe said. "Shit."

"Run!" Lara shouted, turning to do so.

Moder and Pinsard stood frozen to the slope behind her, hands on their hilts as they stared at the score of men who had emerged from behind every large tree they'd passed on the way up the slope. Their bare skin was coated with a clay that matched their drab cloaks and leathers.

It was quite clever, actually. They looked a bit like trees themselves. Though trees didn't usually have eyes. Or bows, for that matter. And they all had those: Recurved bows with arrows nocked and ready.

"There will be no running," the woman said, firmly. "If you do, I will tell the seekers to loose their darts. Believe when I tell you, that end would not be merciful."

Lara slowly turned back about and met the woman's eyes. Her olive skin had a metallic sheen to it, though it was nowhere near as pronounced as Arsinoe's.

"My Lady," Lara said, ignoring Bannertail's claws kneading into her shoulder. "Please, we are only travelers, lost in this country. We meant no offense-"

"This one is a blasphemer!" the woman said, pointing a taloned finger towards Arsinoe, "Who mocks the prophecy of Glyconos and spits at the mercy of The Dragon!"

"You make that sound like an insult," Arsinoe said, planting her foot as she readied her spear.

One of the Myrmidons stirred, and raised his own spear to strike.

"Hold," the woman said, and the man froze at once. Lara could see the look in his eyes now: Glassy and unblinking.

"A quick death would be too kind for this *Akridon*," the woman went on. "Take her alive. And the girl. She may still be redeemable."

"White demons?" one of the Myrmidons rasped. It sounded as though he seldom used his throat.

"An offering," the woman said. "For the chosen, and the glory of her name."

"Her glory," the Myrmidons repeated.

The woman raised her hand. Lara heard bows bend and strings tighten. Arsinoe began to take in a deep breath.

"Stop!" Lara said, lurching forward. One of the Myrmidons turned his spear until its point hovered a hairsbreadth away from her heart.

"You protest, girl?" the woman said, her coiled hair falling from her shoulder as she turned. "What vanity. Perhaps I have misjudged you-"

"Take us if you must," Lara heard herself saying, "But take us to Zerzura. I will see to it that you are richly rewarded if you do!"

"You?" the woman said, her raised arm wavering ever so slightly. "Will reward us? What is this nonsense?"

"Do you seriously look on me," Lara replied, "And see only a girl? Ha!"

The edges of the woman's mouth twitched. Her eyes narrowed.

"Lara," Moder called out, "Lara, wait-"

But Lara could not wait. It was too late for caution.

"I am no mere girl," Lara went on, straightening her shoulders. "I am Larissa, The Queen of Arcasia, and I *demand* that your men lower their weapons at once!"

Bannertail dug his claws into her shoulder as he arched his back and let out a chittering squall.

"The Queen of Arcasia?" the woman said, frowning deeply as she reached for her whip. "Larissa? Hrm. That is a lie, and a lazy one. Larissa is dead. Dead three times over."

"It is no lie!" Lara urged, trying not to think of just how bedraggled she must look. "Look at me. Not at these rags- Look at my face! Surely you have seen one like it on an Arcasian coin? It belonged to my mother, the Queen Persephone, just as my father was once King. Or has news of such things not come to these backwards parts?"

Lara could hear the men on the slope below beginning to murmur as their bow strings slackened. The hunters, at least, had heard of her.

"I *am* the Queen Larissa." she went on, gesturing towards Moder and Pinsard, who looked almost as shocked as the men in gray standing beyond them. "And these 'white demons,' as you call them are the Lady Hirsent and her son, Lord Pinsard, of- of-"

"Of Kloss!" Moder stepped in. "In Carabas, far north from here."

"And this *Akridon* blasphemer?" the woman frowned, gesturing towards Arsinoe with the handle of her whip. "Is she a Lady too?"

Lara turned to Arsinoe. Their guide was giving her a look that was hovering somewhere between shock, hope, and exasperation. It would have been quite funny, under different circumstances.

"She is my bodyguard," Lara lied. "Sworn to defend me to the death."

"Oh, Volk," Arsinoe muttered, but kept her spear level.

"She is very familiar for a servant," the woman said, glaring at the Telchine. "From what this one has heard."

"She is," Lara said, cocking her head. "But it's not surprising. After all, I've known her since I was a girl. Besides, what does it matter? I do not mind her familiarity. She does her duty, do you not, Arsinoe?"

"I *do*," Arsinoe said, swallowing. "Your Majesty."

"You see?" Lara said. "Now, will your men lower their weapons? Or do you intend to go on insulting us?"

Lara tried to take another step forward, but the Myrmidon facing her would not budge. Still, she locked eyes with the woman, and did her best to look as unperturbed by the steel point pressing against her blouse as possible.

"This one has seen your face, girl," the woman said at last. "Or one very much like it. But not on a coin. It may be this one is mistaken, but if not . . . Hmm."

Her grip on the whip's handle loosened, and half a dozen heavy lashes uncoiled from its shaft. Their heads, Lara saw, had steel talons fixed to them.

"Take them!" the woman cried, gesturing with the head of the whip. "Take them and bind them! Or taste of The Redeemer's wroth!"

The Myrmidon standing before Lara exploded into motion, reversing his spear and driving its haft into her gut.

The blow dropped her. Bannertail leapt from her shoulder as she fell. She landed on her side and would have gone tumbling down the hill if Arsinoe was not there to steady her, her own spear lost somewhere in the grass.

"Don't fight them!" Arsinoe whispered, before shouting out, "You *dare* to strike the Queen?!"

Lara had to admit: She sounded fairly convincing.

"Hrhm," one of the other Myrmidons grunted. Two of the others caught hold of Arsinoe, their rough fingers digging into her arms as they dragged her away.

A fist caught hold of a tangle of Lara's hair and yanked. Her neck strained backwards as she rose, catching a glimpse of Moder and Pinsard raising their hands as the hunters advanced on them. Then she was being pushed forward, her right arm wrenched behind her back. Bannertail tried to bite her captor's heel through his boot and then shot into the underbrush before one of the others could spear him.

Run, little one, run! Lara wanted to shout, as one of the Myrmidons took a few stabs at the undergrowth. *This is one thorn bush even I can't save you from.*

The Myrmidon made one final thrust. But when he raised his spear, there was no blood on its tip.

"Good," Lara whispered, and then she was standing before the woman.

"We will 'escort' you, girl," the woman said, gathering up the lengths of her whip. "But not to wretched Zerzura. If you are who you say you are, then you would not be safe there, this one assures you."

"Where will you take us then?" Lara said, wincing as her other arm was forced behind her back.

"To Ladon," the woman said. "There we shall seek the wisdom of The Dragon. She will know if you are a false Larissa or true."

XII

Rocks crunched beneath the wheels as the wagon got rolling again. Lara shuffled to keep up. If she slowed, the shackles would bite into her wrists and the fisher's burn would race up her arm until she blinked tears.

She kept up. The fetters on her ankles were meant to slow her down, but she managed.

Her chains were fixed to the cage resting atop the wagon. Inside the drake lolled, sluggish from the midday heat and the satisfaction of its last meal: The slinger who had managed to lure it into the cage. A few bloody scraps of cloth were all that remained of the man, besides the whistling clay balls he'd used to get the beast's attention. Lara had spent the better part of the morning watching them roll from the front of the cage to the back, and then back to the front again, again and again. Whenever one of the wheels fell into a rut a few of them would jump, but not high enough to clear the side of the bed.

They were as trapped as she was.

She could hear Arsinoe's chains jangling. Their leg irons were joined, and so she was never far behind. The pulse of the Telchine's breath was labored but steady. The daughter of mercy had the Myrmidons take turns beating her last night. One of them had hit her so hard that Lara was certain that he'd broken her jaw but, in the morning, she had managed to chew the stale bread that served as their breakfast.

"So," Arsinoe muttered between breaths, "You're really a Queen, then?"

"I suppose," Lara answered. "Though I hardly ever feel like one."

A whip cracked in the column behind them. Lara hoped it was one of the drovers. Moder and Pinsard were back there somewhere, strung up with the pack animals.

"I know what you mean," Arsinoe said.

"You do?"

"I didn't always have this beetle on my face," Arsinoe grumbled. "When I was younger my people called me *Koriarchis* and carried me around in a litter. They used to think I was The Hollow Maiden reborn. Heh. Can you blame them?"

Chains jingled. Lara could only turn her head so far, but she didn't need to. She could easily picture Arsinoe, her hands splayed beneath her chin and smirking in spite of her black eye and split lip.

"So," Lara said. "What happened?"

Clank went Arsinoe's chains.

"My sister happened. She looked the part just as well as I did. And she wanted it more."

"And she was stronger?"

"Younger," Arsinoe spat. "Quicker. Challenged me when she was only twelve summers. You'd be surprised how hard a twelve-year-old can kick."

"She fought you?"

"Well," Arsinoe answered, "There can't be *two* Hollow Maidens, can there?"

The wagon tilted as one of the wheels fell into a rut. The clay shot pooled into one of the cage's corners. The drake let out a hissing blast of air from its nostrils, its neck craning as it looked about. A moment later the stink of its rancid breath washed over Lara- All musk and rot and yet somehow as sweet as tree sap.

She gagged. Arsinoe began to cough, but not too loud.

"What about-" Lara spat, trying to get the taste out of her mouth, "Your parents?"

"Father was already ten years dead," Arsinoe said, clearing her throat. "Mother watched."

"I'm sorry," Lara said.

"Eh, it was a fair fight," Arsinoe sniffed. "And she let me live. Had to crawl away- like a beetle- and so, I have my reminder . . . But she did let me live."

The wagon sped up as it righted itself, dragging on the chain. Lara quickened her step.

"Anyhow," Arsinoe huffed, chains jangling, "It was nice while it lasted. But what about you, oh Queen? Do *you* have a sister? Or a jealous uncle, something like that?"

"I had a brother," Lara said. "Lionel. I don't really remember him. Or, maybe I do, but I think I must get him confused. With Pinsard, I mean."

"He must have been tall," Arsinoe said.

"He wasn't," Lara said. "He was only a child."

"He's dead then?"

"Yes," Lara said. "He died when I was very young. So did my mother and father."

"Sad," Arsinoe said. "But who killed-"

The sound of hoofbeats shut Arsinoe up. For a moment Lara thought it was the daughter of mercy, come to glare at them, but the priestess was still riding ahead of the wagon. The rider was one of the painted scouts, his lithe horse veering only slightly as it trotted past the cage.

"Kurian *sranja*," Arsinoe snarled when the man was out of earshot.

"What's that?" Lara asked.

"Nothing," Arsinoe said. "Just reminding myself who I need to hunt down when I get out of these chains."

"Don't you mean *if*?" Lara asked.

"No," Arsinoe said.

"You seem very confident."

"I am."

"Why?" Lara said, lowering her voice as she kicked a stone from the road. "Do you . . . Have a plan?"

"I do," Arsinoe said.

"What is it?"

Lara could hear Arsinoe taking in a deep breath, and then:

"DRAMSIND!" Arsinoe shouted. "DRAMSIND! MOTOTO!"

Lara nearly tripped as she spun about, fully expecting the metal giant to come crashing through the poplars, or to rise out of the river itself, his head glowing red and insides humming like an angry swarm . . . But there was nothing. Just the dusty stretch of road, and a pair of startled birds taking flight from the rushes. The drake's eye had opened to stare at them, but it hadn't bothered to stir.

"Eh," Arsinoe sighed. "It was worth a shot."

There were hoofbeats again. This time they slowed. Just to her right, a horse whinnied.

"No talking!" a voice barked, and something whistled through the air. Arsinoe let out a low grunt.

Lara nearly tripped over her own feet as the chains linking them stretched to their limit. In a moment or two the wagon would start dragging her by the wrists- But then the grip on her leg irons loosened, and Arsinoe gave her a little prod.

"Move!" the rider said as he turned his horse about. Lara blinked from all the kicked-up dust.

The rider rode back down the line, and for a long while they walked in silence.

As they trudged, Lara realized that the dark smudge they were making for on the horizon was a town of some sort. A town with a bridge.

"Do you really think he's out there?" Lara asked.

"Dramsind?" Arsinoe said. "Of course. Where else would he be?"

"I mean," Lara said, slowing a touch, "Is he really trying to find you?"

"He better be," Arsinoe said. "I'm the only friend he has."

The wagon hit another rut. The shot rolled across the bed, whistling as they went. The drake raised a paw and took a lazy swipe at them, its claws sinking into the wood when it missed.

"You don't give up on your friends," Arsinoe breathed, her chains jingling. "Didn't anyone ever teach you that, girl?"

* * * * * * *

They marched until dusk, and then they marched some more. What Lara had taken for a town from the road turned out to be either an estate, a temple, or a Glyconese strongpoint. Possibly it was all three. There were certainly enough veiled guards keeping watch on the figures hunched in the fields.

As the wagon rolled by one of the pillared verandas overlooking the bridge, Lara saw a score of dark-haired girls peering out at them. When the drake shifted in its cage some of the girls went to their knees. Others mouthed half-whispered words that blended into a low hissing sigh.

None of them spared Lara or Arsinoe a single glance. She wondered if they'd even noticed them.

When they finally came to a halt, there was food. One of the painted scouts handed them bowls to sup from. The Myrmidons had stripped them of their own, along with their packs, weapons, and belts.

At least the going is lighter.

Supper was some sort of watery yellow paste. It tasted better than it looked but, like the scald Arsinoe enjoyed, it was spiced with something that made Lara wish she had a spring to drink from.

When they were done, the scout took their bowls from them, pausing to stare at Lara before walking back down the line. Then two of the Myrmidons came striding out of the dark. One of them loosened their chain from the back of the wagon and pointed to a patch of ground by the roadside.

"Sleep," he said, planting his spear in the dust.

Lara was too tired to argue. She drifted off quickly, ignoring the Myrmidon's glassy stare.

For all Lara knew, he watched them all night.

When she opened her eyes the next morning, there was a dead mouse lying beside her. It didn't have a head. Something had gnawed it off.

And there were paw marks in the dirt.

She tried to look nonchalant as she rose, blinking at the nearby shrubs. One of them rustled, but it might have only been the wind.

Pain danced up her wrist. The Myrmidon was already yanking on the chain. On the other side of the road the shirtless zealots were hustling to break down the daughter of mercy's house-like tent.

Arsinoe helped Lara up, and then the Myrmidon took up the slack on the chain. The drake was unsettled by the commotion and struck the bars with its tail. They rang.

"Her glory," the Myrmidon hummed, giving the chain a final tug as he went. Lara staggered forward, sucking air through her teeth.

"Water," a voice said. She turned, a curse hovering on the tip of her tongue. It was the scout again. He seemed to be smiling behind his thick beard. In his hands he held a sloshing leather skin.

"Drink," he said.

Lara exhaled and took the skin. As she did so, the scout leaned towards her.

"Tonight," he whispered, his breath hot against her cheek. "When is dark, we set you free. Take you to friends."

For a moment Lara was too stunned to speak. She upended the skin and drank. The water tasted like rawhide.

"Moder, Pinsard-" she started to say, handing the skin to Arsinoe. "The white demons. We won't go without them."

The man frowned at her, his eyes growing small.

"Why?"

"The boy," Arsinoe said. "I have taken his knife."

The scout shot Arsinoe a look.

"We try," he said, and took the skin from her, uttering: "Tonight."

Then he was walking up the line, calling out to one of the outriders.

Before long, whips were cracking and the wagon was rolling again. The road ahead looked just as long and hot as it had the day before . . . But there were still trees, and plenty of brush. Enough for a fox-squirrel to hide in.

Us too, Lara hoped. *And maybe we won't even need to hide? Only the daughter of mercy has a steed. If the scouts-*

"You must have quite the price on your head," Arsinoe said, breaking her concentration.

Lara licked her lips. "What makes you say that?"

"You think Kurians give a shit who sits on some throne a hundred leagues away? And now they've found the sand to spit right in The Dragon's eye to boot? Heh. There must be some great heap of shine somewhere they've been dreaming of these two nights past. Or do I have it wrong?"

Lara sulked for a while.

"What's that?" Arsinoe finally said. "I couldn't hear you."

"What was that you were saying earlier?" Lara said, changing the subject. "About Pinsard and a knife?"

"Oh," Arsinoe said. "That? It's nothing."

"It didn't sound like nothing."

"Just an old custom," Arsinoe said. "Doesn't matter, anyway. Kurians don't have a chance."

"Why not?"

"They might have some sand," Arsinoe said, her manacles clanking together. "But not too much between the ears. I wouldn't lose sleep waiting up for them."

"But," Lara said, turning somewhat, "We should still be ready, right? Just in case?"

"Sure," Arsinoe said. "Wake me if they do."

* * * * * * *

They didn't even have to wait until nightfall.

One of the scouts was riding past the wagon when a Myrmidon stepped out of line and drove the tip of his spear right through the man's breast. The scout's horse reared up as he fell.

Lara heard a startled shout from somewhere behind her, the wild neigh of another horse, and then another one of the painted men shot past her on foot, feet kicking up earth as he ran into a freshly tilled field. An arrow caught him in the back, just beneath his shoulder and he fell, his foot catching one of the furrows sending him spinning head over heels.

The drake hissed, fouling the air as it tested the bars with the flat of its head. The cage shook, and the wagon wobbled on its wheels, but it held.

It took Lara a moment to realize that she was gripping the chain with both hands, as if she might tear the whole thing free from its mooring. She let go, sweating. Somewhere close a man was gasping and grunting for breath. Then there was a wet *crack*, and he stopped.

"See?" Arsinoe said as the wagon lurched to a halt.

The daughter of mercy made a point of guiding her spotted-roan out of the column before having three of Lara's would be rescuers hurled into the dirt before her.

"For silver these ones would deny the will of The Dragon," she said. "And so silver they shall have."

Two of the Myrmidons came forward. One held a pair of iron tongs, the other a box. The scouts didn't so much cry out as whimper as the zealots took hold of them. It reminded Lara of Pasha, whining for his supper.

The zealots kept them in place as the box was opened.

Inside there were bits of silver, round things covered by jagged spines. To Lara they looked like thistle heads.

And then, one by one, the Myrmidons forced them down the scouts' throats.

One of them died quickly, gagging wetly before going limp. The other two weren't as fortunate. They were still alive.

The daughter of mercy merely watched, very still atop her horse. But Lara could tell that she was enjoying herself. She was beginning to share Arsinoe's sentiments regarding the Glyconese.

"Do not let them wander," the daughter finally said, turning her roan without touching its reins. "This lesson has not yet seen its end."

"Her glory," a voice answered. When its owner rode into view Lara was only half surprised to see that it was one of the Kurians, who was not only still alive but tracing a circle over his left breast with the fingers of his right hand.

The zealots slipped ropes about the doomed men's necks. The Myrmidons closed the box and wiped the end of the tongs clean. The last of the Kurians took hold of the ropes and began to walk his horse, his former companions stumbling to keep up with him.

The dead man lay in the dirt, flies already lighting on his face. A whip cracked, and the wagon rolled on.

* * * * * * *

Something's changed, Lara thought when a third rider went skirting past them, the veiled figure slowing as they turned their steed about.

At first, Lara thought they were replacements for the Kurians. The last of them had died sometime during the night, judging by the cries she had done her best to ignore. But these men (if they were men- their robes covered them nearly from head to foot) weren't armed. Their horses didn't even have saddlebags.

That afternoon, they were given an extra ration of water by one of the zealots. The water was cool against Lara's lips.

It's fresh. Someone had to run and get it.

She drank the water down and handed her bowl back to the zealot. But as she tried to read the look on the man's veiled face a shadow passed over her eyes. When she looked up, she saw a trio of birds circling overhead.

No, she told herself, noting the breadth of their wings. *They are too large to be birds.*

That evening, she decided to be bold.

"I want to see the Northerners," she said to the Myrmidon lengthening their chain.

"Hrm," the man grunted, and pointed to an embankment. "Sleep."

"I want to know that they are safe," she said, not budging when he stepped towards her and struck the ground with the butt of his spear. "Tell your mistress that I demand-"

"This one will speak with your voice," one of the zealots said, and jogged past the wagon, bowing and whispering to the drake as he passed.

It was a while before he came back, but when he did six of the Myrmidons were behind him.

"It is permitted," he said, and spoke something low to their watchdog.

The Myrmidon kept his eyes locked on Lara as one of the others freed their chain from the wagon.

"Come," the zealot said, and then they were being led down the line, Arsinoe grunting as she shuffled to keep up. Scores of zealots stared at them as they passed. Or were they only staring at her? It was hard to read their eyes.

At the end of the column, just past the last of the supply wagons, a herd of goats was being kept from wandering by a half dozen zealots sitting about a crackling campfire.

Moder and Pinsard were tied up with the goats. They had been gagged with braided rope meant for the horses. Someone had taken Moder's coat from her. Pinsard had lost his boots.

They did not look pleased.

"You see them," the zealot said, and turned on his heels. The Myrmidon holding their chain gave it a tug.

"I want to speak with them," Lara said, digging her own heels into the dirt. "*Without* gags in their mouths."

The zealot halted, his hazel eyes flicking from Lara to the Northerners. His mouth parted.

"Well?" Lara asked.

"Gags only," the zealot said. "You remove, they speak, and then we go."

Lara nodded. The Myrmidon gave the chain some slack.

"Gags only," the zealot said again, motioning to their escorts.

The Myrmidons fanned out, forming a circle around them. The goats brayed and bleated as they flocked elsewhere. A few of the zealots went jogging after them.

Lara shuffled forward and loosened Moder's gag. Moder spat it out and did her best to wet her lips.

"How are you?" Lara asked, slipping towards Pinsard. Arsinoe jingled as she kept pace.

"Not good," Moder said, swallowing. "And you?"

"About the same," Lara replied, lowering her voice. "I saw shrikes today. They might have been wild, but-"

"I am seeing too," Moder said, her eyes darting towards the guards.

Lara nodded. *Don't say too much.*

She focused on her finger work. Then Pinsard gave his head a shake, and the rope slipped free.

"They took my book," he fumed.

"Is that all you're worried about?" Lara shook her head, incredulous. "We'll get it back."

"They *burned* it, Lara."

"What?" Lara said. "Why?!"

"It was about the Demons," Pinsard said.

"They probably couldn't even read it," Arsinoe muttered. "D*omuz-pislikleri* . . ."

"The Akridon will not *speak*," the zealot warned, unfolding his arms.

Lara could tell their time was almost up.

"Something odd is going on," Lara said, taking Pinsard by the shoulder. "I don't know what, but- Well, we'll get out of this, somehow, I know it. So, don't you give them any excuses."

"I won't," he answered.

She couldn't help but grin.

"You said 'won't.'"

"Enough," the zealot said. "You have spoken. Now you will sleep."

Lara didn't have time to object. The Myrmidon holding their chain spun her about with a yank, and then she and Arsinoe were limping their way back to the wagon.

"That name they keep calling you," Lara risked as they walked. "What does it mean?"

"Locust," Arsinoe answered. "It's what the Irkallans call us."

Lara didn't need to ask why. She'd seen the way that Arsinoe ate.

They returned to the wagon. The drake was restless as usual, rubbing its bulk against the sides of the cage. Lara had long since concluded that Dragons were nocturnal animals. The winged ones probably fed on deer the way that owls ate mice.

"Sleep," the Myrmidon grunted as he refastened their chain to the wagon, stabbing his finger at the ground.

She almost complied without thinking. A week of forced marching had made her head feel fuzzy. But something *had* changed, that much was clear to her. What wasn't clear was how much.

"No," she said.

The Myrmidon did not respond with words. Instead, his arm shot from his side, and the flat of his palm met the middle of her chest. She fell with enough force to take Arsinoe down with her. The ground was very hard, and the pebbles were very sharp.

"Thanks for that," Arsinoe groaned.

Something's changed, Lara thought as she rolled onto her back. *But not that much.*

* * * * * * *

Three days later they came to a crossroad and took the southern fork. The wagon made a wide turn to keep the cage from tipping into the wild brush, which was everywhere. There was no inn to greet weary travelers, no tree to shelter under, not even a marker pointing the way. There was only a pillar of smooth round stones about which animal bones had been scattered.

It's a shrine, Lara realized. *A shrine to Wulf. And why not? Even the Glyconese must worry about insulting the Watcher.*

"*Poznajte-se,*" Arsinoe said as they passed the pillar.

"What's that?" Lara asked.

"Just paying my respects," Arsinoe answered. "What do you say up north? When you want you-know-who to look the other way?"

"Wulf's Fancy," Lara said. "But, uh, you're supposed to be drinking or it's bad luck."

"I'll bear that in mind," Arsinoe breathed, her chains jingling.

The way widened quickly. Fields gave way to orchards that stretched for leagues. Pickers set down their baskets as they passed, bowing until their heads were in the dirt. Carts made way for them. Riders slipped from their horses and traced the tattoos running up their arms as they whispered praises to The Destroyer.

And- every so often- someone's eyes would linger on Lara a little too long and she would wonder: *Do they know?*

The hard-packed dirt beneath their feet became cobblestones. Beyond the fig trees a wide river valley stretched, and a white city of tiled roofs and weathered copper domes sweltered in the midday sun.

Another river, she mused. *Another city.*

This one straddled the river, a dozen arched bridges linking its two halves. Even from a distance Lara could tell it was larger than Irikosa, though it was not until she noticed that the vessels coasting past its docks were no fishing ships or trader's cogs but were in fact galleys- galleys with vast triangular sails and fifty oars to each side- that she began to grasp the true scale of the place. The domed fortress near the city's heart was so large that it could have been a city onto itself.

"Is that," Lara rasped. It had been hours since her last drink of water. "Ladon?"

"Don't know," Arsinoe replied. "Never been this far south before."

"Be silent," one of the zealots keeping pace with them grunted and lifted his arm as though he might give Lara a taste of his switch . . . But he didn't follow through. The gesture had only been a threat.

An empty one, apparently.

Ladon or not, by mid-afternoon they had reached its painted gates. Golden dragons curled across its face, wings splayed as they leered at cities being washed away by vast triangular waves.

They were expected, it seemed. Not only was the way open, but the avenues beyond were lined with people. There were so many of them that all could not stand in the street itself, and so many watched from windows and balconies. These were no Myrmidons or zealots, but plain-looking folk with dark eyes and lined faces. Their clothes were rough-spun wool, their only finery the green sashes they wore about their waists, and the faint golden glimmer of their skin.

The crowd did not cheer as the wagon passed through the gates, or even press forward for a better view of the drake as Lara imagined they would. Rather, they lowered their eyes and began to sway as someone, the daughter of mercy most like, began to chant in what Arsinoe called the old tongue.

Lara had to admit, the woman had a lovely voice.

When she was done, a chime jingled once, twice, three times and then the crowd answered with a chant of their own, a thousand voices speak-singing at once.

The drake, startled, raised its head and rumbled deep in its chest, turning about in the cage as best it could.

Lara reeled back from the reek of its breath, her chains growing tight. The burn on her wrist sang louder than the crowd.

This went on from street to street, and quarter by quarter. Daughters of mercy stood at every corner, inky tears running down their cheeks and arms outstretched. The zealots attending them cradled bronze bowls. Some were brimming with water on which broad-petaled blossoms floated, pink as the dawn. Others were filled with raw cuts of meat, and burning sticks whose heady, pine-like scent buried a dozen mundane city smells beneath it . . . Though the smells were still there. Beneath the bite of cedar, Lara could smell freshly-baked bread, clouds of charcoal smoke, and dung: Horse, human, and otherwise.

Crossing the city took forever. At least, it felt that way. They halted at every intersection. The zealots would hold out the bowls and ceremoniously lay them before the wagon. The chant would be sung, the chimes jingled. The crowd would answer the chant, and so on, street after street, block after block . . . And all the while the drake became more and more agitated.

Eventually it lunged right at the bars, the flat of its head striking them with enough force to splinter their wooden housing. When it lashed its tail one of the bars came loose and went flying into the crowd, striking a pair of men so hard that they both lost their feet.

The crowd quieted for a moment. Then one of the men rose, blood running freely from his forehead. He reached for the drake, who was worrying the bars with its fangs, and clapped his hands together.

"Ti doxa tis!" he shouted, beaming as his own blood blinded him.

The drake split its jaws and roared.

"HER GLORY!" the crowd erupted, a thousand hands clapping in unison. "TI DOXA TIS!"

Lara shrank back, half expecting the crowd to rush the cage, trampling everything in their path. But they didn't. They merely swayed as the daughter of mercy took up the chant, some of them dipping their fingers in the man's blood and wiping their cheeks with it.

The other man was dead. The bar had snapped his neck. Men and women were already lifting his corpse for all to see, their faces awash with bliss.

"These people are crazy," Lara whispered as they put the street behind them.

"I told you," Arsinoe shot back, and then grunted as one of the Myrmidons gave her a shove with the butt of his spear.

"Move," the Myrmidon hissed, giving Arsinoe another unsubtle prod.

Lara picked up her step, trying to ignore the way the drake had turned to eye them through the less-than-perfect bars, its sides heaving with every growl. A few solid hits in the right places and it would be free, and she'd still be chained to the back of the wagon.

But does it know that? she wondered. *Is the look in its eyes cunning, or do they simply look that way, all slitted and sinister?*

Lara couldn't tell, and it was far too late to ask Arsinoe how smart dragons were. If only they could keep moving, get to wherever it was the daughter of mercy was taking them-

But then the wagon was slowing again, and the clay shot was rolling its way back towards her. She looked. Sure enough there was another cross street ahead of them, another crowd of supplicants waiting to display their offerings.

As the zealots held out the bowls, the drake shoved its nose against the bars and snuffled, nostrils flaring.

"Wulf," Lara choked, her eyes watering from the tang.

The zealots bent their knees and laid down the bowls. The daughter of mercy began the chant for what felt like the hundredth time.

The drake backed away from the bars and settled into a broad crouch, its rear legs steadying against the floor of the cage.

LOOK OUT! Lara wanted to scream, but she doubted that the Glyconese would listen, let alone care. She started veering to the right, praying for the bars to hold as the chains connecting her legs to Arsinoe's tightened.

The daughter of mercy finished her chant, and for a moment there was silence.

Then the chimes jingled, and the drake dug its foreclaws into the wood and let out a long, chest-shaking roar, its shoulders hunching like a hill cat about to spring. Lara tensed up, ready to run for her life if the chain came free.

Then another roar split the air.

This one was not only louder, but deeper. It made even the crowd forget to answer the chant. The drake's neck whipped to one side, its head tilting nervously.

A vast shadow passed over the street. Curtains sighed and canopies rustled against stucco. The people lining the avenue went to their knees as their arms reached for the heavens.

Lara looked up.

There was a dragon gliding over the city. It was hard to tell exactly how big it was- it was flying higher than any tower and already banking away from them- but even so she could tell that it was far larger than the drake. It had a crown of horns about its head, and the sun made its sweeping wings gleam like the leaves of early summer. It cried out again, its voice roiling across the city like thunder. Then it passed behind one of the domes of the fortress and she lost sight of it.

The city was silent. The crowd lowered their eyes to the ground and were still. No one dared utter a sound, save for the horses, who stamped and whickered. Even the drake seemed to have shrunk somewhat, its limbs tucked close to its torso and its head flat against the wagon bed.

For a long time, no one moved.

Lara was beginning to wonder if they'd stand there until nightfall, when the peal of what must have been a truly massive bell echoed through the streets. Three times it rang, and then there was silence.

"She wills it!" the daughter of mercy called out. Her voice sounded very small.

"SHE WILLS IT," the crowd murmured, the hush of their voices like a broom on flagstone.

Then the wagon driver clicked his tongue, and they were moving again, the wheels nearly rolling over the zealots who were still crouching in the street.

When they reached the next cross street, they did not stop to receive the offerings of the zealots, jingle the chimes, or sing the chants. The wagon kept rolling and, though it kept at a stately pace, Lara could feel a sense of urgency behind the calm. Even the Myrmidons, who often seemed less human to her than Dramsind, walked with some extra snap in their step.

They turned onto a wide avenue lined with palms- Lara had never seen trees quite like them- and made their way towards a dazzling gate of emerald and ivory.

The bell rang out again: BONG. BOOONG. BOOOONG.

A whip cracked. A score of zealots ran past them, panting. The masses in the street stepped back to give them room.

Someone's getting impatient . . .

The gate swung wide to accept them. Myrmidons parted their ranks. Hairless men swept forward to lead the daughter of mercy's odd horse away, and then they were through.

Beyond the gates a lush garden stretched. Lilies lay in green pools fed by latticed channels. Trees, whose trailing leaves reminded Lara of willows, shaded narrow walkways on which young men and women paced, draped in layers of gauzy silk. Birds with sunset feathers and fanned crests rooted amongst the grasses.

Even if she weren't a prisoner, caked with dirt and chained to the back of a wagon, Lara would have felt very out of place.

There was an island in the middle of this man-made marsh: A tiled plaza ringing a palace so vast that it beggared even Lara's imagination. Here were pillared walkways and looming domes of brass, massive doors of copper and trellised balconies dripping with wisteria. Towers clung to the central bastion as thick as ivy.

Through the bars of the drake's cage, Lara could see the steps that stretched from palace to plaza, where a great host waited to receive them.

Me, she corrected herself, thinking of the veiled riders, the leave she'd been granted to see *moder* and *broder,* the way the zealot's hand had faltered when he'd raised his switch to strike her. *They're not here for the drake. They're here because of me.*

It was The Dragon who waited for her on those steps. The Dragon of Glycon and those who served her.

The approach to the plaza was guarded by more than Myrmidons, who stood at attention in companies five ranks deep. Rows of armed zealots sat cross-legged before the stairs, their heads bowed in supplication. The helmeted, halberd-bearing bronze figures standing sentinel on the landings were actual giants- living and breathing ones, not men of metal like Dramsind or the things collecting dust deep beneath the mountains . . . And there were drakes floating in the pools, their gleaming eyes just visible above the murk. They were clearly of the smaller sort: The ones Arsinoe had told them usually killed people.

"This country you're from," Arsinoe whispered beneath the jangling of their chains. "They on good terms with the Glyconese?"

"Not exactly," Lara answered. "Why?"

"I mean," Arsinoe said, "Just look at all of this. It's impressive, isn't it? In a terrifying sort of way."

"It is," Lara said, keeping her eyes on the drakes.

Others were watching *her*. As they approached the stairs the wagon slowed, turning in a wide, lazy arc as it came to a halt. Imposing Glyconese women glared down at them scornfully, their pauldrons shaped like drake claws, scaled gauntlets resting on swords taller than themselves. One had a bundle of leashes clutched in her grip, at the end of which reptilian chimera with scaly cockrel-heads struggled, like watchdogs drawn to a scent.

The chimera squawked and cackled and beat their flightless wings. The drake answered them by taking a lazy swipe at the bars.

Glancing back, Lara saw they had shed much of the train behind them. Gone were the supply wagons, the scouts and their horses, and most of the zealots. Those who remained were still penning in the goats. A fresh set of Myrmidons were holding Moder and Pinsard at spearpoint.

They were still gagged. Pinsard's feet were covered with scabs and blisters, and the right sleeve of Moder's shirt was brown with speckled blood. But they were still with her. They were alive.

BOOONNNG.

The crash of the bell washed over Lara. It was so loud that it made her feel sick to her stomach. She reached up to cover her ears, but the slack on her manacles was too short to do it properly.

Her ears were still ringing when The Dragon made her entrance.

First the palace doors swung inwards, the carved mural of the multi-headed dragon on its face splitting down the center as a phalanx of young girls in saffron gowns spilled through the gap, chanting in the old tongue as they walked. Behind them came daughters of mercy in deep green robes and breastplates inlaid with turquoise, their glossy hair so long that it practically trailed behind them. They mouthed silent words as they swung smoking censers, parted, and then a great high-backed throne emerged from the palace, held aloft by a dozen men in blindfolds.

It was a tarnished, beaten thing of hammered silver, corroded by salt, sand, and time. It looked to Lara as though it had been fished from the ocean, and yet the figure that sat in it was no naga, snake-skinned or gilled like a fish. Or, at the very least, she did not resemble one. Rather, she seemed an elegant woman of some thirty odd summers, coolly poised despite the ornate tiara she wore upon her brow. Her robes and gown were made up of layers upon layers of emerald silks, on which dragons made of pearl twined.

When they reached the head of the stairs, The Dragon lifted her right hand ever so slightly, extending her first two fingers. The throne bearers came to a halt at once. The girls in saffron ceased their chanting.

The plaza was quiet, save for the hissing of the drakes in the pools, the low jangle of mail, and the frightened bleating of the goats.

The Dragon lowered her hand and gazed down at them. Lara stared back. Queens, she reasoned, did not bow their heads to one another.

At least, not that she'd ever heard tell of.

The Dragon spoke then. Her voice was soft- almost child-like- but it carried very far.

"Who is she," she said, "That dares to seek the mercies of The Dragon?"

"This one," a weak voice answered. "Worthless that she is."

Out of the corner of her eye Lara could see the daughter of mercy inching towards the foot of the stairs. She was bent so low that she was practically crawling, the heads of her whip trailing behind her like a tail.

"And what is this one's third burden?" The Dragon asked when she had reached the first step.

"Krissa," the daughter of mercy answered, placing her brow on the edge of the stair.

"And does this Krissa think to speak with The Dragon's voice? Does this Krissa believe that she is Drakaina, who would offer The Redeemer's mercy with her own lips?"

"This one does not," the daughter of mercy quavered. "This one- This one seeks only to witness the day of The Redeemer's glory. This one-"

"Enough," The Dragon said, and the daughter of mercy quieted. "This Krissa has brought one of the chosen of The Destroyer to Ladon, its way marked with signs. Here then is her mercy: Let Krissa walk the nine paths, and if she still draws breath when she is done, let her go to the sea and weep, for the days of the world are yet long."

"And wicked is the way of men," the daughter of mercy answered.

"Now go," The Dragon said with a wave of her hand. "And seek not for mercy."

The daughter of mercy slunk away from the stairs and retreated back the way they had come, her fingers working at the buckles of her breastplate. When it came free, clanking against the stones of the plaza, she rose, and walked straight past Lara, making for the closest of the walkways that wound past the drake-filled pools of the garden.

On the woman's cheeks, Lara could see real tears staining her artificial ones, but she could not tell if they were of joy or sorrow.

Lara turned away as The Dragon slowly extended her palm.

"Hear now, Ladon," The Dragon said, raising her voice, "The Redeemer's will!"

"WE LISTEN," the crowd answered.

"Before us we see one of the chosen! What are the lives of men, but scattered droplets that fall upon the breadth of the sea and are lost? Yet look here! Look here and rejoice! Do you not see here the coming storm? Do you not see here The Destroyer's Glory?"

"HER GLORY," the crowd shouted. The drake turned its head about and bared its fangs, which prompted an exultant, wordless cry of approval from the crowd.

The drake gave the cage's bars another slap with its tail. Lara glanced about nervously, wondering exactly where the winged dragon had flown off to, and whether or not it would swoop down on them before the ceremony was over.

"Long has been the chosen's road," The Dragon intoned, the golden threads dangling from her tiara swaying as she surveyed the crowd.

"Long and weary. Take him to the long gardens, that he may hunt. May he grow strong, and the daughter of The Redeemer show him favor, so that the end may come. So let it be!"

"SO LET IT BE," the crowd spoke, the wagon lurching as the zealots rushed to comply.

The girls in saffron sang out as the gaudy warriors on the steps clanked forward to replace the Myrmidons as honor guards. One of them made right for Lara, easily twice her size with an over-sized sword and wine-red hair done up in a topknot.

Lara wondered if she had misread the situation and was about to be kicked to the ground before being trampled underfoot when the manacles bit painfully into her wrists. One of the Myrmidons had unhooked them from the wagon and was leading her and Arsinoe towards the stairs.

She spun around as best she could, and saw Moder and Pinsard being similarly led as the goats were herded after the wagon, no doubt to serve as food or sport for the drakes . . . But amongst the hooved legs of the goats she could see something else: A lithe, tailed creature keeping close to the center of the herd, his large ears perked as he ducked his head out to peer at her.

Oh, Bannertail, no, she railed as the fox-squirrel vanished back into the press. *What have you gotten yourself into?*

She wondered if this was how Moder felt sometimes.

The drake and wagon rolled away, followed by the warriors, the cackling chimera, and daughters of mercy young and old alike.

When they were gone, all that stood before the palace gates were the zealots, the bodyguards, and The Dragon herself, sitting on a throne held aloft by slaves.

The Dragon planted an elbow and rested her chin on her hand as she regarded them. An oddly human gesture, Lara thought.

"Bring these ones closer," she said, her voice grown quiet again. "That we may look on them with wisdom."

The Myrmidons took no chances. A pair of each gripped Lara and Arsinoe by the arms before marching them up the stairs. Lara peered at the giants as they passed, wondering at the features lost behind the meshed visors of their helms.

Then the Myrmidons released their grip. Her boots skidded across tile as she steadied herself. From the drag on her leg irons, she presumed that Arsinoe was doing the same. Moder and Pinsard were given far less care. The Myrmidons shoved them to their knees, Pinsard grunting through his gag all the time.

"So," The Dragon said, turning to address Lara. "You are the one who claims to be the Queen of Arcasia?"

"I do not *claim* it," Lara said, rubbing at the burn on her wrist. "I am it."

The Dragon's eyebrows quivered.

"I am Larissa," Lara said, straightening. "And I do not believe that you would have brought us here if you did not think the same."

"Hrm," The Dragon murmured. "In manners, at least, you remind us of the Queen Persephone. She too once thought to insult us . . . A misunderstanding, perhaps, but an insult all the same."

"Is that why you've had us brought here? Had us chained and beaten?" Lara asked, thrilled and terrified all at once. "Because of some insult my mother gave you? Or is this a misunderstanding as well?"

The Dragon stared at her for a long and terrible moment. Then she raised her hand, ever so slightly.

"Undo this insolent one's bonds," she said, "And let her approach."

The Myrmidons stepped back. A lithe figure slipped from the gloom beyond the doors and flitted forward. A woman, Lara thought, though it was hard to tell. Its body was wrapped in leather bands and glossy emerald plate, and its left leg was an artificial thing of brass. Only the skin of its face was exposed . . . but even that resembled a mask to Lara, for it was a sickly shade of blue, and its pale green eyes were overly large and set too far apart.

A naga, Lara realized as the thing swept towards her, its brass heel clicking delicately against the flagstones.

She drew back instinctively, but the naga was very fast. It took hold of the chains binding her wrists with one of its gloved hands, and then its other was dancing over the manacles, something cold and metallic brushing against Lara's skin as it worked.

A key, she supposed.

"Ow," she blurted. The manacles had pinched her skin as they came free.

"My apologies," the naga said liltingly. Lara rubbed at her wrist and was glad of her boots as it bent down to free her legs.

The leg irons came free without any bite. Then the naga stood aside, even going so far as to bow its head.

"This way," it said, gesturing upwards.

"Volk's Fancy, I suppose," Arsinoe said as the Myrmidons began to drag her back down the steps.

"Volk's Fancy," Lara said, and climbed.

The higher Lara climbed, the more aware she became of the figures hovering just beyond the throne. There were more Myrmidon sentinels of course, and a knot of old women- elders, perhaps, amongst the daughters of mercy . . . But there was also a cluster of masked figures whispering close to one another, their belts sagging from the weight of the charms dangling from them. They stared at Lara, hushing as she approached, their lens-like eyes making them resemble a collection of insects.

"That is close enough," The Dragon said, when she was five steps away from the top of the flight. "Cercopes, you may lower our seat."

The men holding up the throne bent down, slowly, moving in unison until the dais on which The Dragon sat was almost level with the floor.

The woman stood, regalia shifting and tinkling as robes slid against robes. Delicate threads of gold spilled over her sweeping pauldrons. Primly, she stepped from the dais and moved to the edge of the steps.

The Dragon looked her over, biting her lower lip ever so slightly. Lara couldn't help but do the same and she was rather struck by how *ordinary* the woman seemed. For, now that they were so close, Lara could see that The Dragon's faintly metallic face was practically unmarked, her only tattoo a dot that sat on her right cheek like a tear-drop. And the longer she looked, even that resembled a birthmark.

"Yes," The Dragon mused, rubbing her forefinger against her thumb. "You do resemble her. And you have your father's eyes, it seems."

"You knew my father?" Lara asked.

"No," The Dragon said. "Only his shadow. But you are no shadow . . . Are you, Larissa?"

Lara did not answer. The Dragon smiled thinly.

"The Princess Larissa will be our guest," she said, raising her voice ever so slightly. "Escort her to my apartments at once and see to her easements."

"Your Wisdom," a muffled, almost metallic voice emanated from one of the masked figures huddled near the door. "Is this not premature? The trials-"

"This is my will," The Dragon intoned, not needing to shout. The masked figures gripped the edges of their gowns and curtsied like a brace of maidens.

A pair of bald men with blindfolds over their eyes scuttled towards her, robes swishing.

"What about Mod-" Lara began, but corrected herself. "The Calvarians, I mean. They are my-"

"We know who they are," The Dragon said, cutting Lara short, though there was no curtness in her voice.

"You do?" Lara said, unable to keep the surprise from her voice.

"Our gaze stretches further than that of any King or Queen," The Dragon said, turning slightly as she stepped back onto the dais. "Rest assured that we have made suitable arrangements for the comfort of the Lady Hirsent. And her son."

"And," Lara said, "Arsinoe?"

"The Akridon?" The Dragon's lips pursed, as though she had bitten into something bitter. "What of her?"

"She was our guide," Lara said. "We would have died in Vulp Vora without her."

"Curious," The Dragon said. "The Kurians spun a different tale. But no matter. A *place* has been made ready for her as well."

"Then you will not harm her?" Lara asked.

"She is our guest," The Dragon said, and settled back onto her tarnished throne. "As you are, Larissa."

The Dragon lifted her fingers, and then the blind men were leading Lara into the cool gloom of the palace.

XIII

Alone. When had she last been alone? Not since the night she had snuck off to see the Crowning festival, and even then Pinsard had come running after her. She remembered how frightened she'd been of the woods, and the snap of branches in the dark. It seemed rather silly to her now, weighed against the things she'd seen since.

She'd seen Tybalt's men dancing with a dead woman. She'd heard a chimera speak with her own voice. She'd run from ghouls beneath the mountains.

But at least she'd not been alone.

The rooms she had been taken to were up somewhere high, with a long balcony that overlooked the river. There was no way down. No easy way, at least. The walls of the palace were very sheer and, even if she could survive the fall, the gardens below were a lair of dragons. The winged female basked there amidst a ruin of fallen trees, its horned head resting on the edge of a deep pond. Lara had taken the dragon for statuary at first, until it had turned to snap at one of the drakes that wandered too close.

Dragon and drake both ate fish from the pond. Perhaps that slaked their hunger, and perhaps it didn't.

She didn't plan on finding out.

The rooms themselves were spacious, but rather bare. Lara supposed that made a certain sort of sense. If one truly believed- hoped even- that the world was coming to an end, doomed to be drowned in an ocean of blood, then there wasn't much point in hanging onto luxuries.

That said, what furniture there was, was very fine. The bed was a proper bed, with a feather mattress. The face of the low table (the Glyconese didn't seem to care for chairs) in the first chamber was a beautiful thing, inlaid with ebony and pearl. There were no cushions to sit on, just mats woven out of braided fiber, but she supposed it might have been pleasant enough to sit there and take a meal as the Firebird sank beneath the horizon.

Were she amongst friends. Were she not a captive.

There was only one other way out of these rooms besides the balcony, and that was through a pair of wrought iron doors. The reinforced iron lattices shielding their colored panes were expertly cast, elegant even, but they were still essentially bars.

Even if she could somehow break the glass, she doubted it would do her much good. For one thing, there were a pair of Myrmidons standing guard just outside. By day she could trace their outlines through the glass, by night they were impossible to make out, but she knew they were there . . . And the doors had no latch or bolt, just a mechanical lock that joined the doors.

It could only be opened from the outside.

The doors had opened only twice since she'd been brought to her "quarters." The first time had been to bring her food and drink, a task performed by the bald, blind men who Lara presumed to be The Dragon's personal servants. She wondered if they really were blind (or even eyeless) behind their sashes, or as mute as their absolute silence implied, but it hardly mattered. They had not answered her questions as they'd glided into the chamber, silk swishing against silk, and ignored her words of appreciation as they slid back out.

Lara hadn't minded much. The men's strangeness was far overshadowed by the sight of the meal they had brought: Sauced meat steaming atop a bed of grains, a glass pitcher of crystal-clear water, and a bowl of purplish, palm sized fruit. She'd bitten into one of the berries and within moments she had wolfed the whole thing down, its honeyed syrup running down her chin as she swallowed. She devoured two more before noticing the delicate knife and fork that had been laid out beside the bowl.

She had sat down before starting on the meat.

That had been yesterday evening. So much rich food, the softness of the bed, and the ordeal of being marched behind the drake had made falling asleep easy. But staying asleep? That was another matter. Where had they taken *moder* and *broder*? Had they and Arsinoe quarters like hers, or were they in some cell deep beneath the palace, under the care of the daughters of mercy? What *did* The Dragon want of them?

Nothing good, she thought as she stared at the bed chamber's bare ceiling. *So, what are you going to do about it?*

In the early morning a great bell sounded from somewhere high above, and the doors opened a second time. This time the blind men were accompanied by a daughter of mercy. This one was far older than the one called Krissa. Her hair was as gray as ram's wool and her inky tears had faded blue.

"The Dragon requests your presence," the woman said as the men gathered up the dishes. "At the fourth bell."

Lara wiped at her eyes.

"Will Lady Hirsent and her son be there?"

"They have not been summoned," the woman answered, frowning at a half-eaten fruit lying near the balcony.

Lara blinked at it too. She hadn't dropped it there, had she?

"You will make yourself presentable," the daughter of mercy said, snapping her fingers at one of the blind men and gesturing at the mess on the floor. "You will bathe, and then dress as befits one The Dragon deigns to honor as a guest."

More blind men brought in a copper tub, its water smelling strongly of mint. Three young women in saffron gowns filed in after them, eyes lowered. They each carried a dress that had been cut from the same cloth as their own. Lara wondered who it was that had been up all night altering them.

"Any of these garments will suffice to replace your rags," the daughter of mercy said, eyeing Lara from head to foot.

"And what if I prefer my rags?" Lara asked.

The creases of the older woman's face deepened noticeably.

"They will have to be *purified*," she said, speaking through her teeth. "The acolyte's fast will have to be extended, but if that is what is required-"

"No," Lara said, gesturing to the dress closest to her. "I was joking. That one will do, thank you."

"As you wish," the woman said, and made a subtle gesture to the girl with the dress before stepping aside. The girl tiptoed past Lara and laid her burden on top of the bed, which the blind men had already tidied.

"Do you require anything else?" the woman said as the others filed out.

"Will you take a message?" Lara asked. "To Lady Hirsent?"

The woman did not answer, but Lara took her silence as a form of unwilling complicity.

"Tell her," Lara said, thinking quickly, "That The Dragon is so very generous to give me such rooms. The river is so much larger than the one you could see from my old balcony, and there are even doors to keep out the dogs. Pasha, our sheepdog, used to lick my face in the morning. This is much better, I think. Though I suppose you don't have dogs, do you? I don't imagine drakes would get along with-"

"The message will be delivered," the woman said, and turned, her hair dragging on the tiled floor as she retreated to the antechamber. The Myrmidons shut the doors behind her.

And, again, Lara was alone.

She doubted her exact words would be repeated, but if they were then Moder would know that she was somewhere high up, with a view of the river, and not in some subterranean dungeon. Her half-truths would provide more details: Her rooms had a balcony, and doors shut tight. Not much, but it would be something to go on . . . Assuming, of course, they somehow managed to escape from their own confinement.

For now, though, there was nothing to do but wait.

"And make myself 'presentable,'" she said, eyeing the bath.

I shouldn't complain, Lara mused as she peeled her shirt from her back. *Moder and Pinsard would probably kill a dozen Myrmidons for the chance of a bath.*

She kicked off her breeches and stepped in.

The bath water was tepid but refreshing. She lay for a while, dozing until the second bell roused her and she set to scrubbing herself. The bar of soap they had left for her was coarse and odorless, but it was just as much of a luxury as the fruit had been.

She was still thinking about the fruit, scrubbing at her shoulders with her palm, when she looked up and saw a fox-squirrel perched on the lip of the tub, staring at her with its head cocked to one side.

"Ah!" she screamed, jumping back in the tub and slipping. A tide of bathwater sloshed onto the floor, and then she managed to catch hold of the lip.

There was a crisp 'snap' as the seal on the doors came loose, and then they flew open. Lara clutched the side of the tub and glared at the Myrmidons who were now peering into the chamber, leaf-shaped swords in hand.

". . . Is hrit?" one of them rasped at her, so quiet that she could hardly make out his words.

Lara turned. Bannertail was nowhere to be seen.

"I, uh," she said, turning back. "I heard something. Down in the garden. It frightened me."

One of the Myrmidons walked in warily, his glazed eyes slowly sweeping the room. Lara did her best to cover herself as he circled about the tub.

The Myrmidon's eyes swept over her as though she were invisible. Then he moved to the balcony, his sword poised to strike.

All of a sudden there was a loud 'crack!' It sounded like a house timber snapping in half, and this time Lara didn't have to lie. She huddled lower in the tub and hugged her knees as the Myrmidon peered over the rim of the balustrade.

"'ree lhrimb sphrit," the Myrmidon whispered, straightening as he sheathed his sword. "'ri dox-lrah 'ris."

The other Myrmidon tried to repeat the phrase, but his voice was so ruined that all Lara could make out was a guttural collection of 'ars' and 'esses.'

"Thank you," she said, waiting for them to re-lock the doors before stepping out of the tub. She resisted the urge to dry herself with the fresh gown that had been laid out for her.

Bannertail had hid himself behind one of the bed cushions. It was a fairly decent disguise, Lara thought, for when curled up he did look a bit like a furry throw pillow.

"How did you get in here?" she asked the fox-squirrel, keeping her voice low.

By way of a reply the chimera chirruped, and rolled about on the bed, begging for scratches.

"Drakes didn't eat you at least," she said, her heart skipping a beat as another 'snap!' echoed against the bare walls.

She walked to the balcony and saw the dragon slowly circling its nest of felled trees, stretching its wings and rolling its head this way and that. Eventually, it put most of its weight on one of the thinner trees. Its trunk splintered from the pressure. 'Snap!'

"Reminds me of Whisper, impatient for his breakfast," she said to Bannertail, who was sniffing at the spilled bathwater. "You're not hungry, though, are you?"

The fox-squirrel lapped experimentally at the puddle, which was gray with soap and grime, and loped over to the table.

"I wish you could understand me," Lara said, softly, tipping the pitcher so that Bannertail could drink. "You could find a way to Moder and come back to show me the way."

The fox-squirrel drank a bit, and then began to clean himself, using his tongue and paws like a cat.

"How *did* you get up here?" she wondered aloud and stepped onto the balcony. She looked down . . . But, no, the walls were very smooth, coated with sun-baked plaster.

He couldn't have climbed.

There was no window above, either. And the only other balcony she could see adjoined the rooms on the other side of the locked doors. The span between them and the one she stood on . . . Well, she supposed the fox-squirrel could have jumped the distance. An ordinary squirrel would have been able to, and he wasn't that much larger than one of them. But *she* surely couldn't. Even if she could, that didn't tell her anything about how he'd gotten there in the first place.

But there was a way. A way to get from the gardens to her chambers, without being noticed by the Myrmidons, zealots, daughters of mercy, and whatever else lurked in the palace, masked or scaled.

There was a way. If only for a fox-squirrel.

She was scratching behind Bannertail's ears when the third bell rang.

"I suppose I should put this on," she said, picking up the dress.

* * * * * * *

"You have no crown," The Dragon said to Lara when the blind men and the Myrmidons had left. The Dragon had dismissed them with the slightest of gestures, and then turned back to the full-length mirror standing before her, turning her head as she slowly ran a finger down her right cheek.

"A simple omission," The Dragon went on. "Easily remedied."

Lara shifted her feet. Besides a crown, she had also not been provided with shoes. And the tiled floor was very cool.

The Dragon's chambers were a few flights beneath her own, split between the balconied space they stood in now and a long, curving gallery below. Both spaces were open to the garden, a series of curling pillars the only thing separating them from the dragons lying amongst grass and pool. It was difficult for Lara not to stare at them, especially the winged one, whose golden eyes always seemed to be staring back.

"One of these might suit you," The Dragon said, waving towards a nearby cabinet. "Choose one, and I will help to affix it."

Lara padded towards the cabinet. Here lay golden tiaras and silver diadems, each adorned with emeralds, peridots, polished malachite.

They were all beautiful, but Lara did not take one.

"What is the matter?" The Dragon said, the jewels dangling from her own headdress swaying as she turned. "You are a Queen, are you not?"

"I never asked to be one," Lara said.

"Nor did I ask to be reborn," The Dragon said. "But people such as us are seldom permitted the luxury of choice."

"People such as us?" Lara scoffed.

The Dragon turned from the mirror and crossed to a nearby table laden with jars, brushes, and a silver basin.

"Queen, Dragon," she said, almost dismissive as she lifted a brush to her cheek and dabbed at it delicately. "To be either is much the same thing."

Lara snorted. "I'm nothing like you."

"Perhaps not," The Dragon said, craning her neck as she wiped at it. "But then, you have yet to know the true burden of being a shepherd to your people."

"I've herded sheep," Lara said.

The Dragon smiled and put down her brush.

"A Queen is a shepherd of a different sort," she said, turning. "Though only in the details. You still must cull the most headstrong rams from the flock . . . And shepherds will always have a need to keep hounds: Hounds to herd by day and hounds to guard by night, when the jackals come."

"In Perun it was hill cats," Lara said, backing up as the woman loomed closer. "Is this what you had me brought here for? To remind me how to herd sheep?"

"Not at all," The Dragon said, reaching to take up one of the diadems. "I am expecting guests. No doubt they too will wish to look on the Princess Larissa."

"What guests?" Lara asked.

"Important ones," The Dragon answered, turning the diadem this way and that. "And if I present you to them as you are now, they may only see one of my acolytes, half-dressed for the deception."

"A crown will change that?"

"How is it that We look to you?" The Dragon asked, her shoulders straightening as her voice grew imperious. "Would you mistake us for a drudge, fresh from the field? Or do you look upon The Dragon, whose truth is that of The Redeemer?"

"I see," Lara said, standing her ground, "A woman. A woman with paint on her face and a fancy gown, trying to keep her neck straight under the weight of the headdress she's wearing."

"That is part of what makes you a Queen," The Dragon said, seeming to shrink somewhat as she held out the tiara. "Try it on, at least."

"What if I refuse?"

"I will not force you," The Dragon said. "Though I might remind Your Majesty that my courtesy, much like my patience, has its limits."

Lara took the tiara. It was a simple thing, two bands that twined at the brow, and there a green gemstone, shaped like a tear. She slipped it into her hair.

The Dragon reached forward and adjusted it, her long fingers working through Lara's curls. With her face this close to her own, Lara could make out the wrinkles beneath the woman's shimmering face paint, the inky flecks lining her eyes.

"Come," The Dragon said, stepping back to examine her. "Have a look for yourself."

The Dragon gestured to the mirror. Lara went to it and stared at the stranger she saw in the glass.

She was taller. Or, rather, she'd never seen herself standing head to foot. Her bare arms were covered in half-healed cuts and scratches, and the skin running up from her left wrist was pale from the fisher's burn. Her face looked lean and fierce to her, at odds with the soft orange dress and finery in her long dark hair.

She hardly recognized herself.

"I had thought we might rosy your cheeks," The Dragon said, inspecting her. "But no. You are perfect as you are."

From the garden below Lara could hear the hissing of the drakes. The winged dragon answered them, her rumbling growl setting Lara's teeth on edge.

"And just in time," The Dragon said, moving to the head of the stairway that joined the balcony to the gallery below.

"Your Wisdom," Lara heard a muffled voice echo against marble. "This one regrets the intrusion, but the so-called 'ambassador' from Therimere-"

"You may admit him," The Dragon said, pausing to adjust her headdress as she made her slow descent.

"Follow me," she said, just loud enough for Lara to hear. "If you would."

Lara took one last look in the mirror, touched her fingers to the tiara, and followed.

The Dragon and Lara were halfway down the stairs when an immense pair of doors swung open to reveal a long corridor lined by Myrmidons. A trio of bearded men emerged from it, their somber, huge-shouldered gowns at odds with the riot of fiery silks and gaudy jewelry they wore beneath them. They looked a bit like what Lara imagined pirates were like. One of them even had an eyepatch.

"Enter," The Dragon said, her voice carrying across the chamber.

At the sound of her voice, the winged dragon in the garden raised its head and growled as its claws dug furrows into the fallen trees.

The men hesitated, unable to hide their discomfort as they minced forward, wide-brimmed hats in hand and heads lowered so as to avert their gaze.

The Dragon made them wait until she finished her descent, and then began to cross towards the garden, her gown trailing silently behind her.

Lara stopped at the foot of the stairs, uncertain of what was expected of her.

"Your Wisdom," one of the men began, straightening ever so slowly. "My master, the Prince of Elegost and Tamarin, Lord of the Argyrian Isles, First Keeper of-"

"A thousand titles will not make your master more than he is," The Dragon said, coming to a halt on the threshold of the garden. "A fat corsair whose raiders sail on ships made of wax seals and lines on paper. Now, come to your point."

"His, ah, Preeminence," the diplomat stammered as the great beast in the garden rose, its wings unfolding, "Would no doubt wish to personally extend his, ah, compliments as to the efficacy of Your Wisdom's, ah, ah, ah-"

The great beast was loping forward now, the drakes quickly making way as it made for the gap between the pillars. The Dragon hardly seemed to notice, all but turning her back as she waited for the man to put his tongue back in order.

"What I mean to say," the man said, starting to worry at his hat, "Your Wisdom, is that I would be more than remiss if I did not, ah . . . Well, given the speculation that we have heard-"

"Princess Larissa," The Dragon said as her namesake entered the gallery, its spear-like claws clacking against stone, "Are you a matter of speculation?"

It took Lara a moment to answer. The dragon was so close now that she doubted running would do any good.

"No," Lara said, waiting for the beast to snap out at her with open jaws before adding, "Your Wisdom."

Under the present circumstances, it seemed prudent to be polite.

"So," The Dragon said, lifting her left hand ever so slightly as the dragon settled behind her, framing her with the enormity of its bulk. "We have permitted you to look on the true Princess Larissa. Is there anything else?"

As the beast came to rest, it laid its head within easy reach of The Dragon, who reached out to stroke its scaly neck.

Lara caught a whiff of the thing's noxious breath and struggled to suppress a cough. The three ambassadors were less successful. They each began to hack and wheeze.

"Yes-" the man finally managed. "Yes, Your Wisdom. You are no doubt already aware of the, ah, the authority given to my office as regards the accounting of revenues and debenture currently, ah, ah, currently outstanding between the sovereignty of Glycon and my master's exchequer. Are you, ah, are you not?"

"I am," The Dragon said, her hand coming to rest behind one of the beast's smaller horns.

"Well," the man said, "If Your Wisdom will forgive us our presumption, might it, ah, might not the, ah-"

Here he gestured towards Larissa, using his half-crumpled hat.

"-the fortuitous position that Glycon now finds itself in behoove us a re-opening, or a rebirth if you will, of discussions pertaining to the, ah, renegotiation of said revenues and debenture?"

"Ambassador," The Dragon said, removing her hand from the beast's neck, "Do you stand before the Court of The Dragon, in the presence of the divine children of The Redeemer, and mean to tell me that you would *dare* sully its sanctity with the petty and vulgar talk of coin?"

As she spoke, the winged dragon lifted its head and snorted at the man, the force of its breath throwing his hat from his hand. Lara could only imagine the smell.

Choking, the ambassador bent to retrieve his hat, casting a frantic look at his attendants. One of them, the one with the patched eye she thought, just managed to nod at him as they retched.

"Well?" The Dragon said.

The ambassador re-straightened, and pressed his hat to his chest with both of his gloved hands, as though he was trying to conceal the gold medallion he wore beneath it. Even from this distance, Lara could see the sweat rolling down his temples.

"Yes," he said, "Your Wisdom."

"Empusa!" The Dragon intoned. The slim naga with the brass leg appeared from behind one of the columns near the doors. "Have the Myrmidons escort these *men* to quarters more befitting the manner of their station. And, as we may eventually deign to speak with them, see to it that they retain the use of their tongues."

The naga nodded, letting out a grating bark as it brought up a flat palm. At once the Myrmidons in the corridor surged into the gallery, ignoring the men's cries of distress and the lash of the dragon's tail as it pushed itself from its haunches.

"Your Wisdom!" the ambassador squealed as the dead-eyed men grabbed him by the gown and began to haul him towards a dark archway set beneath the stair. "Surely, you cannot mean to- The mandates of the treaty, ah, strictly forbid-"

The Myrmidons slowed their step and cuffed the man across the face, stunning him long enough to drag him into the archway without further protest.

"Do spare at least one of their hands," The Dragon went on, addressing the naga. "They might have the need to scrawl their names on parchment before we have finished with them."

"Ti doxa tis," the naga answered and glided after the Myrmidons, her heel clicking with every footfall.

Lara watched her go, trying to remain calm as the dragon turned its head to gaze at her, its nostrils flaring as it sniffed the air between them.

"I do not suppose," The Dragon said, lightly clapping her hands, "That is how your mother would have dealt with such a matter?"

"I do not know," Lara answered, slipping down the stairs and putting some marble between her and the beast eyeing her. "She- When I was young, she- But, those men! Will you really have them cut to pieces?"

"Should I not?" The Dragon answered, making for the stairs that led to the garden. "Their offer was nearly as insulting to us as their master's choice of envoys. Would you have sent such as that whimpering clark to treat with The Dragon?"

The Dragon clapped her hands again, louder this time, and the winged dragon shifted its gaze as it made to follow her.

"I do not think I would send anyone," Lara said, "After what I just saw."

"Your father was less squeamish about such things," The Dragon said as she stepped from the shade, sunlight catching the gleam of her finery. "Though your mother too had her own cadre of 'persuaders.' Not as skilled as my own, I imagine, but talented nonetheless."

"You lie," Lara said, stepping out from behind the stair.

"I can assure you that I do not," The Dragon said, coolly. "The faces of your lineage may have made for handsome coins, Larissa, but the realities of ruling will tarnish even the brightest piece of silver. Your mother's reign was brighter than most. But it was also brief."

"You never knew my mother," Lara spat, the winged dragon letting out a low rumble at the sound.

"Neither did you, it seems," The Dragon said. "Though I fear your education on that matter must needs be postponed. Our second guest shall arrive presently, and we would not wish to appear inhospitable, would we?"

"Inhospitable?" Lara started to say, a list of the indignities she and her family (and Arsinoe, of course) had suffered at the hands of The Dragon's minions racing through her mind, when the air was filled with the hissing and bellowing of the drakes. She could see them craning their necks and was following their gaze when the winged dragon let out an ear-splitting roar, its wings beating at the air as it reared upwards. Lara clutched at her ears and held her breath as a noxious blast of dragon's breath washed over her.

Then Lara saw the cause of the beast's distress: A winged woman- a shrike, it had to be- was gliding over the garden, her taloned feet splaying as she drew closer to the edge of the gallery.

For a moment it looked as though the chimera might collide with The Dragon herself, and Lara tensed to . . . What? Run, hide? Where could she possibly go? But then the winged woman fanned her wings and landed gracefully upon the marble floor of the gallery, giving her feathers a shake as they fell about her like a summer cloak.

A winged monster, Arlequin had called her. *Reynard's personal emissary.*

True to Arlequin's words, the winged woman- or winged maiden rather, for she was very slight and her face was youthful- was far more human than the ones Lara had seen near Gorynych or in Vulp Vora. She was also shockingly nude, unless one counted the amethyst pendant she wore as clothing. Her violet wings served for a hint of modesty, but not much.

"Lady Tisiphone," The Dragon said. "We have been expecting you."

"Then you know why I have come," the shrike replied, her voice surprisingly husky for her frame. She turned her piercing green eyes towards Lara.

She doesn't have hands, Lara noticed, glancing at the clawed digits that served as the shrike's fingers. They hung just above her breastbone, hooked like a clasp.

"We thought," The Dragon said, "That you might care for proof of Her Majesty's welfare."

"I need none," Tisiphone replied, curtly. "Father already knows that she is here."

"And what of 'Father's' master?" The Dragon said. "What honeyed words has The Lord Protector sent for you to sing for us?"

"Only this," the shrike said: "Release the Princess Larissa, now, or suffer the consequences."

"Be careful who you threaten, little bird," The Dragon said. "Or do you forget in whose house you stand?"

The Dragon snapped her fingers together, and the winged beast behind her stirred again, rumbling and hissing as it rose, and befouling the air with its reek until Lara's eyes were weeping.

But, unlike the men from Therimere, the shrike did not so much as stir.

"You can call off your stinking pet," she said, and there was warning in her voice. "I am like my master, and not so easily frightened."

"You *dare* to speak such blasphemy?" The Dragon hissed herself, and now her anger seemed very real. "With a single breath, Lady, I could have one of my empusae put an arrow through your heart. Perhaps I will."

All at once Lara was aware that the gallery was nowhere near as empty as it had appeared. A half dozen figures- all naga with legs of brass- emerged from the room's deeper shadows, curved bows nocked.

"Koschei the Deathless made similar threats when I visited his court at Vassa," Tisiphone said, unshaken. "He is dead now. Father gave his corpse to my brothers and sisters."

The Dragon was silent, her silence lingering as the baubles hanging from her headdress tinkled softly, barely audible over the throaty breaths of the monster at her back. Then she lifted her right hand and flicked her fingers, as if shooing away a fly.

First the naga retreated into the shadows and then, from somewhere far across the city, a bell began to toll, faint but clear. At the sound of it the dragon's head turned upwards, its wings unfolding as it bounded to its feet. Lara danced out of the way of its lashing tail and could not but feel a sense of awe wash over her as it leapt through the columns and took flight, wings beating mightily.

It rose above the walls of the garden, banked slowly about, and was gone. *Off to answer the bell. Like Pasha, going after a sheep.*

"And to *whom*, exactly, do you suggest we release the Princess?" The Dragon asked casually, as though she had merely let out a cat. "Surely, not to you, Lady. She is not that light, nor you that strong."

"No," Lara said, the word slipping from her mouth. Fear had stilled her tongue until now. Fear . . . and the sense that she did not belong here.

But she could not stay silent any longer.

"My master," the shrike went on, seeming to pay Lara's outburst no mind, "Has made the necessary arrangements."

"We do not doubt that he has," The Dragon said.

"Then" Tisiphone said, "You will submit?"

"Listen to me," Lara said, louder now, but neither woman seemed to hear her.

"We must," The Dragon said, shifting ever so slightly, "Consider the-"

"Listen!" Lara shouted, and with a yank, she dragged the tiara from her head and hurled it at the floor. Its jewel came free and skated across the length of the gallery.

"I do not," Lara panted, "Submit."

The shrike blinked her brilliant green eyes and turned to face her. The Dragon did as well, the look on her face enraging Lara all the more, for it was not anger that she saw beneath her golden paint, but pity.

"Your Majesty," the shrike said, feathers splaying as she attempted a curtsy. "Lord Reynard will be relieved to learn that you are unharmed. He-"

"Unharmed?" Lara repeated the word, her words echoing across the gallery. "Unharmed?! You both talk about me as if I were some- Thing! A basket of eggs, or a horse, or a woolpack! Well, I'm not a hen or some purse full of coins to be haggled over! And I am *not* unharmed! Since Crowning I have been living in the wild, running and hiding from your so-called Lord's soldiers, who've shot my horse, hunted me into Vulp Vora, killed my friends- And now you dare to come here and *bow*? Bow, and call me 'Your Majesty,' and try to drag me back to a man who- who-"

Lara wet her mouth. It was so dry.

"To the man who killed my mother- my brother- my father?!"

The shrike straightened and blinked at her again.

"It was not the Lord Reynard who killed your family, Majesty," Tisiphone said. "It was your cousin, Celia Corvino. She, and the Calvarian traitor, Isengrim."

"Isengrim?" Lara repeated, "Pinsard's *faeder*?"

"Lord Isengrim shot your father's horse during a battle," the shrike said, "As he was crossing a high bridge. The fall killed him. No one knew then who had done it, but five years later, after he cut down your brother, and half of-"

"More lies," Lara said, ashamed that she had listened for so long. "Why would he even do such a thing?"

"Ask the woman who calls herself your mother," the shrike replied.

"Shut up," Lara said, her voice hoarse. "Shut up and go away."

"As you wish," the shrike replied. "But first, my master would have me bear a gift to you."

The shrike spread her wings ever so slightly and hooked the amethyst round her neck with one of her black nails. Her right wing extended as she lifted it towards Lara.

"Take it, if you will," Tisiphone said, "As a token of his esteem."

"Get out of here!" Lara snapped, her hand curling into a fist as she advanced. "Get out!"

The shrike leapt backwards before Lara could take a swing, loose feathers cascading in her wake as she released her hold on the pendant and took flight.

"You have until noon tomorrow," the shrike said, hovering above The Dragon, "To make your answer."

With that she dove, spun, and was soaring back over the garden and its pools of hissing drakes. The pendant caught the sunlight as she went.

The Dragon watched the shrike go, her expression impenetrable. When she was no more than a speck, The Dragon raised her hand, and Lara heard the clink of brass against marble.

"Return our guest to her chambers," The Dragon said to the naga who now stood at the top of the stairs. "She must be tired."

The naga nodded and let out a whistling bark.

"What are you going to do with me?" Lara demanded as the Myrmidons trudged into the chamber.

"We have not decided," The Dragon said, "Yet."

The Dragon began to turn from her, but her regalia made her slow. Before the Myrmidons could reach her, Lara grabbed the woman by the arm, and spun her around.

A horrible hissing filled the chamber. The naga archers re-emerged from the shadows, along with others far less human. One had no legs, brass or otherwise. It slithered from an archway, a sinuous tail dragging behind it.

"Where are they?!" Lara snarled at The Dragon, tightening her grip as the woman tried to pull herself free. "Where are you keeping them?!"

"Unhand me!" The Dragon shrieked, the sleeve of her blouse ripping, tearing, and then giving way entirely.

They flew apart, The Dragon tripping over the hem of her own dress. The weight of her ornate crown helped drag her to the ground.

"Where are they?!" Lara shouted and would have kicked the woman in the ribs were it not for the vise-like hands that took hold of her. For a moment she was flying into the air like the shrike, light as nothing. Then gravity took its course and she was dangling between two of the Myrmidons, her wrists and shoulders screaming as they held her aloft between them.

"This one wishes to know where we are keeping her filthy servants?" The Dragon spat as one of the naga helped her regain her feet. "Shall we *share* this wisdom with this ungrateful heretic?"

The Dragon made a gesture, and the Myrmidons gave Lara's arms a jerk before they dropped her. The pain was so intense that she didn't even scream.

"Moder," Lara choked from the floor. "Arsinoe-"

"Who?" The Dragon said, her lips thinning. "Oh. Your Akridon."

She flicked her wrist, and the Myrmidons dragged Lara back to her feet.

"A *Queen* is a valuable thing," The Dragon said. "So are the Calvarians, to an extent. But your pet Akridon? She is nothing. No. Worse than nothing. A blasphemer, still working the evil of the Demons. She is worthy of only one thing."

The Dragon lifted a solitary finger. Something whistled through the air.

Pain, white hot searing pain, worse than a switch, worse than a hot kettle on bare skin, far worse than the fisher's burn on her wrist, lanced across Lara's back, punching the breath from her body.

"Enough," The Dragon said.

The Myrmidons released her. She crumpled to the floor and lay there for a while.

"Where is Pinsard?" Lara finally wheezed though her pain. "Where is my *moder*?!"

"Your mother is dead, Your Majesty," The Dragon replied. "Now, take this one back to her chambers."

* * * * * * *

The first thing Lara did, once the doors to her chambers were shut and the tumblers of the lock clicked home, was look for Bannertail.

He hadn't been anywhere to be seen when they'd carried her in, nor shown a whisker when they'd torn open the back of her gown to dress her wounds. A horrid, masked thing wearing a leather smock and gown had done the work, clicking and hissing with every breath as its long fingers smeared cold ointment over the part of her back where the whip had kissed her. The salve drove the pain away, but it had also slithered over her skin like a thing alive before it settled.

Frankly, she had preferred the lashing.

Now, both the wheezing thing in the mask and the Myrmidons were gone. She didn't bother to change her dress for the new one laid over the bed's coverlet, but began to hunt, overturning pillows, peering over the balcony, and getting down on all fours to check under the table.

She had begun to crawl under the bed when Bannertail leapt onto her legs from behind, his sharp teeth nipping playfully at her bare feet.

"Ow!" she yowled as her head made contact with the underside of the bed frame. "Stop! Stop!"

Bracing her hands against the cool marble floor, she pushed herself out from underneath the bed and stood up, seething. But the fox-squirrel was already gone, sitting atop the table, its head cocked sideways as it licked at one of its paws.

"Come here!" she snapped at him, and then clapped a hand to her mouth.

Bannertail stared at her, willful or oblivious, and continued to groom himself.

"Shoo!" she hushed, waving her hand at the chimera, certain that at any moment the lock would snap, the doors would open, and the Myrmidons would come in with swords drawn . . . But they didn't.

She waited. Bannertail grew bored and trotted past her to settle on the bed. She waited some more. And, after a long while, she was certain.

No one had heard her.

She walked to the center of the chamber, putting herself between Bannertail and the door.

"Help," she called out, faintly, her voice hardly above a whisper.

No one answered.

She turned from the doors and went to the bed, stripping off the ruined gown and slipping the other over her head, shuddering as the cloth rubbed against the slick patch on her back.

She sat down. Bannertail gave her hand a rough lick and crawled into her lap.

"Tonight," she said to him, and gave his neck a scratch.

XIV

They'd both have to come in, or it wouldn't work. Bannertail would need to knock over the bowl, or it wouldn't work. She'd have to be faster than them, quickly figure out the lock, or it wouldn't work . . . And if they saw her, or there were more of them waiting outside, it wouldn't work.

Everything would have to be perfect. And if it wasn't perfect, it wouldn't work. It wouldn't work at all.

The blind men had brought fruit for her supper. That part, at least, had worked. The Dragon hadn't summoned her either. Lara pictured her sitting somewhere, surrounded by slaves and lackeys, her hands worrying the sleeve of her gown, and hoped that it was just so.

Let her worry, she said to herself, and gave the bowl a turn. *She'll have a lot more to worry about when tomorrow comes and we're not here. What will she tell Reynard's shrike then?*

Bannertail stared at her, and at the fruit in the bowl, his honey-colored eyes wide. She clutched the bowl tighter to her chest.

Don't get ahead of yourself, she reminded herself. *You're not gone yet . . . And it has to be perfect. Or it won't work.*

And so, she sat. Sat and waited for dusk and the thirteenth bell, keeping the bowl safe in her hands all the while. And, when the thirteenth bell finally rang, she waited a while longer, and listened to the dragon stirring in the garden below, readying to hunt.

She imagined that the Glyconese kept livestock for it to prey upon . . . Though she wondered. Were she a Glyconese girl, living in the countryside near Ladon, she wouldn't have needed much urging to come inside for supper before it grew dark.

"Lazy girl who shirks her chores," she mouthed as a dark shape flew past the balcony, the spread of its wings momentarily blotting out the Watcher's gleam. "When dragons roar, run indoors . . ."

She took a deep breath, then another, and listened to the beat of dragon wings against the sky.

When she could no longer hear them, she stood up, and went to the window. The Watcher was grinning back at her. And why not? He knew her secret.

It was time.

Bannertail had curled into a ball and fallen asleep hours ago. But when she put the bowl down onto the bed, his head shot up.

"Hungry?" she whispered, and tilted the bowl, letting the fruit spill onto the coverlet.

Bannertail darted for it, a bit unbalanced from his nap. Before he could reach his prize, she flipped the bowl over and trapped the fruit beneath it.

The fox-squirrel stopped short, his claws digging into the bedding, and let out one of his weird bird-like whines, accusing her with his eyes.

"You want it?" she asked, pushing the upended bowl towards the lip of the bed, so that it dangled just so. Then she backed away, keeping her eyes locked on his.

"Well?" she said, taking another step back. "What are you waiting for? Go on! Get it!"

Bannertail pounced on the bowl, nearly knocking it off the bed there and then. One of the palm-sized fruits tumbled through the gap, hitting the floor with a meaty 'plop.'

"HELP!" Lara screamed, already turning, already sprinting towards the table. In her mind's eye she could still see Bannertail looking up at her with alarm, his body tensed to leap after the fallen fruit.

The door shuddered. The dim shapes behind the glass loomed close. The tumblers of the lock clunked one by one.

Lara dove, practically headfirst, at the narrow gap between the tabletop and the tiled floor. Her dress did little to cushion her as she slid under it, scraping both knees and elbows as she dragged herself entirely out of sight.

The doors flew open. Bootheels clicked as the first of the Myrmidons strode in and paused right next to the table. The other stood in the doorway, the silky ribbons of his belt swaying about his knees as he turned this way and that.

Come on, she seethed, breathing as shallowly as she could through her mouth. *Come on!*

The Myrmidon beside her took a few steps, his boots scraping on the tile. Then he stopped again.

"'lacahny," he croaked, heels grinding as he dropped to one knee, his twin scabbards striking the floor as he gripped the edge of the table-

CRASH!

The table jumped as the Myrmidon leapt back up. Shards of the broken bowl clattered as Bannertail let out his high and eerie cry of distress. Lara remembered how much it had sounded like a shrike to her, when she had heard it first. No doubt the Myrmidons thought the same, for the other came running, moving towards the balcony as the first ran for the bedroom, their swords rasping as they slid from their sheaths.

Lara didn't wait any longer, but scurried madly forward, ignoring the scrapes, ignoring her wrist, ignoring even the numbness that washed over her when her back raked against the edge of the table, and then she was up, her arms windmilling for balance as she made for the door.

"Hrrh!" she heard one of the men wheeze, but she was already through. She threw the first door shut, ignoring the sight of both men wheeling about, their dull eyes widening as she grabbed hold of the other and put all her weight behind it.

The door slammed into place. But where was the lock? Where the doors joined there was no latch, no lock and key, just a worked iron boss shaped like a mass of snakes.

No, they're drakes, their heads thrusting out like spokes of a wheel-

She took two of the drakes by the neck and twisted. There was a loud clunk, and then both doors shook as at least one of the Myrmidons ran right into them.

Lara didn't wait for the Myrmidons' second try at the door, but ran to the balcony running along the antechamber, the fingers of her right hand plunging into her mouth as she whistled the way that Moder did at the end of the day.

Come home! the whistle said to all who knew it, *Supper is ready, and I'll be cross if you aren't quick!*

She ran through a gauzy curtain and, sure enough, there was Bannertail, already perched on the railing of the opposite balcony.

She leaned as far forward as she dared, stretched out her arms, and whistled: *Come here, now!*

Bannertail leapt just as one of the Myrmidons came barreling up from behind him, his short sword arcing downwards in a blow meant to split the chimera in half. The blade struck the railing with enough force to chip stone.

Lara caught the fox-squirrel in her arms and danced away from the ledge.

The Myrmidon did not hesitate. He dropped his sword, leapt onto the railing, and launched himself towards her, sailing through the air with clawed gauntlets outstretched.

But he was not a fox-squirrel. He was only a man, a man wearing mail, a tall helm, and a second sword on his weighty belt.

He did not scream as he fell- could not, perhaps- and Lara did not linger to watch, but as she ran back into the antechamber, Bannertail wriggling madly in her arms, she heard a dull 'crack' rise from the gardens below.

It sounded almost identical to the snapping of the tree branches she had heard that morning. A not uncommon sound in this place, she guessed.

The doors shook as the other Myrmidon struck them again, but they were very solid doors, well suited to their purpose. After a third strike the Myrmidon tried to force his sword through the lattice so as to break the glass. When that failed, Lara could hear him faintly, trying to call out the alarm with his ruined voice. If she didn't know what it was, she would have guessed it was the squeak of a rat, scrabbling behind the walls.

No one could hear him, except perhaps the drakes in the garden below. If he was clever, he'd try and find a way to fit the table through the arch and hurl it off the balcony. But then, none of the Myrmidons had struck her as being clever.

It worked. I'm free.

But where now? The most obvious route was through The Dragon's rather bare antechamber and into the palace. But that way was doubtless watched and guarded, and who knew what else stalked or slithered the dark halls at night?

So, no, not that way . . .

There was another room across from the one she'd been kept in, and this one was guarded by nothing sturdier than a stiff gold curtain. She'd only managed to catch a glimpse of it earlier, but she supposed it was where The Dragon slept. Whenever that might be.

WHAM! the doors clanked behind her. The Myrmidon was giving brute force another try.

"Alright," she said, releasing Bannertail from her grip. He shot across the floor and slipped under the curtain. She followed, throwing the drapery aside.

The chamber beyond was very dim, the only light the Watcher's streaming through latticed windows. It hardly looked like a bedchamber. Shelves lined with books loomed beyond a table laden with scrolls, half-spent candles, and strange instruments made of brass. Something that might have been an ornate stool leaned against the far wall . . . And that was it. No doors, no balcony, no exit.

And yet, Bannertail was nowhere to be seen.

Lara searched the shelves, then the windowsills. Nothing. Then she knelt, and peered under the table, but no. The legs were far too narrow even for a fox-squirrel to hide behind, and he wasn't there.

Wham! the doors rang out again, softer now with the curtain between them.

No time to linger.

She was about to whistle when she saw him. Or rather she saw his head, with both ears upturned, poking out from behind one of the bookshelves. There was a gap in the wall, Lara realized. The shelf concealed a secret door.

The fox-squirrel stared at her, and yipped.

"Shhh!" she hushed, crossing the room, her eyes travelling over the ink-scrawled maps and missives on the desk. If she had a packsack or even a pair of breeches she would have snatched up a handful and stuffed them away- after all, who knew what secrets they might contain, or what they might be worth to The Dragon's enemies (and Lara did not doubt that she had many)? As she had naught but her gown, she grabbed a heavy brass candlestick instead, figuring it would make a halfway decent club if someone came upon her in the dark.

The shelf swung open easily. The whole thing was set on a pair of well-oiled hinges and opened onto a narrow stair that led only one way: Down.

There was no light, not even a slit for a window. She could only see the first few steps edged in moonlight, then nothing. If they dropped off, or led to a pit meant for intruders, she would fall before she knew what was happening.

But there was no time.

She slipped through the gap, and pulled the door shut behind her. Something clicked. She was shut in.

Bannertail's claws skittered as he scampered down the steps. When she did not immediately follow, he paused, and let out an impatient bark.

"Quiet, I said," she whispered, her voice dying flat in the deep silence of the passage as she made her way downwards, one hand against the wall in case she needed to steady herself.

Down, down, and down she went, and then there was a gap in the stone. She felt around blindly, tracing its edges. There was a doorway here, and a metal latch, cool to the touch.

Slowly, very slowly, she gave the latch a turn. A bolt or tumbler clicked softly.

She pressed on the door, and moonlight streamed through the crack that appeared. She peered into the room beyond, candlestick ready, and found herself staring down the long gallery where she'd stood that very morning. The marble floor was pale and gleaming. The dark bulk of one of the drakes lay between the pillars.

Not this way, she thought, and closed the door.

She dashed down another flight, her footing surer in spite of the darkness. No one was looking for her, not here. No alarm had been raised, and she doubted The Dragon shared this secret stair with many others, if anyone. And, surely, she would hear one of the brass-legged naga long before she saw one. Or would she? They could be awfully silent when they wished.

Too late to turn back now, she thought, and pressed on, her bare feet flapping against stone in time with the click of Bannertail's claws.

And then she slowed and came to a stop. She could see the steps beneath her feet, and the recessed outline of another latched door. On her right the stairs continued to spiral downwards, into the dark, but on her left there was a featureless passage. A light was washing over its walls, glimmering and trembling like sunlight at the bottom of a well.

Door. Stairs. Or the Hall.

Bannertail crept into the passage and sniffed at the air. He sneezed, a tiny sound, and danced back to the safety of her feet.

Door first, she agreed, and tried the latch . . . But it was no luck. The mechanism was locked shut, perhaps from the other side.

She peered down the stairs and took a few sniffs herself. The air had a sharp, almost fruity scent that still managed to be unpleasant. And it was dark. Pitch black.

Surely, she reasoned, *they wouldn't keep prisoners in the dark?*

Of course they would, her sounder half nagged. *In the dark and worse no doubt. Have you ever heard of a well-lit dungeon?*

It was a fair point. But as anyone who has ever stood at a crossroad might understand, the ominous, unlit way was hardly enticing. Especially when there was a brighter course to follow.

And so, moving very softly, she stepped into the passageway and began to follow it.

"After all," she whispered to Bannertail as he padded along beside her, "We can always retrace our steps."

The hall was long, and at the end of it an intersection, where a dim lamp was set into the wall. The light it cast was very odd, bright as flame and yet somehow murky. It reminded her of the ghost-light that had glowed and flickered beneath the mountains, but when she held her hand close to the glass she could feel its heat.

She was getting on her tiptoes to examine the lamp more closely when the sound of a door slamming sent her scrambling back the way she had come, Bannertail quickly outpacing her.

At twenty paces or so she forced herself to slow. Then she stopped. Her footfalls in this confined space were too loud, and besides, she couldn't hear anything coming after her: No boots. No metal leg clicking against the stone. There was nothing.

But that wasn't entirely true. She could hear *something* echoing down the hallway, as distorted as the lamplight winding across the walls.

She crept back softly, walking mostly on the balls of her feet, and listened.

It was a voice. No, *voices.* One belonged to a woman. The others buzzed and croaked like swamp creatures droning in the night.

She took a left at the intersection and followed the voices down a passage which soon joined another, lined with iron doors. A light gleamed at the end of it, this one as bright as the skull-moon on a cloudless night. And she could hear something else beneath the voices, something almost imperceptible, a low hum . . .

Bannertail leapt onto her back and clawed his way to her shoulder as she crept towards the light.

". . . corruptions are no doubt clouding our verity," one of the crackling voices was saying. "The visions are become unorthodox, Your Wisdom."

"But not yet heretical," a woman's voice answered, smoothly. Lara had no doubt it belonged to The Dragon. "Show us the river again, running towards Delphyne. And be more exacting."

Throats hissed and wheezed as though laboring for breath. Lara shrunk back as the ghostly light of the chamber danced across the mouth of the hallway. Then it dimmed.

She padded forward, candlestick at the ready.

The air grew cold as she went, her skin prickled to gooseflesh. Soon she could see her breath.

Gods it's cold! She rubbed at her arm with her free hand and struggled to keep her teeth from chattering. *Cold as winter.*

Bannertail shivered against her, his head nuzzling into the warmth of her neck.

Just a bit farther. Then we'll turn back.

When they came to the end of the passage Lara stopped and, crouching down so low that she practically crawled, poked her head around the corner . . . And forgot the cold as she found herself staring at a plate from one of Danica's books come to life.

The chamber itself was not much larger than the great room of the farmhouse, though its domed ceiling was much higher. Its curved walls were lined by cracks and apertures from which glistening black ropes snaked across the floor, coiling together until they formed a great heap. Masked figures crawled like beetles amongst the coils, hunched over strange devices that they tapped and pawed at. Clouds of steam gusted through the slits of their masks as they exhaled, hoarfrost glinting across their eyes of glass with every tiny movement.

And above them all, at the apex of the heap, stood a rectangular slab of reflective glass, as tall as a man. Its surface, marred by a single forking crack, was dark as jet- and yet it gleamed as shapes made of light and shadow played across its face.

The Dragon stood before it wrapped in a fur-lined robe, her eyes wan and haunted as they flitted back and forth, searching for something in the dark mirror's depths.

"There," The Dragon said, reaching out her hand so that it hovered just so over the mirror's face. "A ship, moored on the west bank. We would see it."

The masked things sighed, bits of ice tinkling as they shifted, and then the shapes in the mirror flew about wildly, its light flickering over The Dragon until she was bathed in the orange glow of firelight. And- in the mirror- there *was* fire, or what looked like fire, burning amidst gray shapes along a dark and winding ribbon of . . . Water. And in the water, something that looked like a miniature boat, made by some expert toymaker.

No, Lara realized, her eyes widening. *Not a toy. It is a boat. A real one, lying at anchor at the side of some river. And beside it, on the shore, those are campfires, and those shapes-*

One of the tiny shapes moved, leaning closer to the fire, and even from across the chamber Lara could just make out the vague shape of a head wrapped in cloth.

There were men in the mirror. Or a vision of men at least. A vision of the figures on the shore, a vision of the ship, a vision of the river.

A vision.

'And Mehitabel, the sorceress, conjured a vision from out of the black depths of The Mirror of Truth,' the words from *The Downfall of The Demon King* came to her easily. *'And there, beneath the stars, the host of Aquilia beheld the land that was promised. And they were awed.'*

It's real, Lara marveled as she gaped. *A magic mirror- **the** magic mirror. The mirror that dragged Vasilisa beneath the waves- just like in the stories. The naga must have found it at the bottom of the ocean . . . And brought it here, for The Dragon's own sorcerers to call forth visions.*

The Dragon bent closer to the face of the mirror, squinting, and Lara could not help but lean forward herself, until Bannertail scrabbled onto her back, his sharp claws reminding her of where she was.

Pinsard is going to be furious when he finds out he missed this, she thought as she scooted back into the shadows of the doorway.

"We would see this place as it was at sundown," The Dragon said, folding her arms beneath her robe.

"Corruption is imminent," one of the sorcerers croaked through its mask, "Your Wisdom."

"Then do it quickly."

Steam rose in clouds from the masked men as the humming of the room rose to a whine that had Bannertail dancing in circles across Lara's shoulders. Lara hardly felt it. The blacks and blues of the mirror were driven away, replaced by the brilliance of daylight as visions of men flew back and forth within the blink of an eye. And then, for a moment, she could see the ship, as seen from the eyes of a bird. Little figures in blue were hauling the ship closer to the shoreline, while a pair moved about the smudges of the cookfires-

Then, abruptly, the vision faded. The mirror dimmed until it was nothing but a slab of black glass. The chamber grew dark, lit only by the strange lamplight streaming from somewhere below.

"Occlusion," a voice buzzed.

"Fragments to be considered aberrant," another chimed.

"We understand," The Dragon said as she stepped away from the mirror. "The ship, how far? Approximate."

A tall sorcerer near to The Dragon gusted breath as its hands twitched.

"Between eight and nine parasangs," it spoke at last. "Three by the river-measure."

"Possible, then," The Dragon said, making her way down a set of steps partially obscured by the black coils crisscrossing it. "We must see to it at once . . . though first We have our guest to consider."

Time to go, Lara told herself, backing away from the archway, Bannertail shifting to her left shoulder as she scooted. *I've looked too long already.*

"Your Wisdom," the tall sorcerer whined, "Please, understand, even this *attempt* nearly brought us to the breaking point. If we had more time-"

"There is none," The Dragon said. "Now then, Larissa, come out so that We might look on you."

Lara froze and sucked in her breath.

Caught! All her senses screamed at her. She tensed her muscles, expecting at any moment to feel the rough hands of the Myrmidons taking hold of her from behind, or to hear the scrape of scales against stone as one of the naga came slithering from a hidden doorway.

But neither of those things happened. And, somehow, what happened instead was far worse.

On the opposite side of the chamber from where Lara crouched, a diminutive figure stepped from a shadowy alcove, stopping short of the dark, snaking mass of coils that seated the Mirror of Truth.

It was a girl. A girl with curly dark hair in a simple saffron dress practically identical to her own. She could have been one of the dozens of girls Lara had seen singing on the steps of the palace, but for her face.

Lara had seen that face a thousand times before. It was her own . . . *Almost.* The features were too smooth, too perfect, especially about the eyes and nose. And she had no scars, no cuts or scrapes.

Run, she goaded herself. *Run now while they're distracted.*

And yet, she lingered.

"Now then, Larissa," The Dragon said, crossing the room. "When we were speaking earlier, you said that you never wished to be a Queen. Do you remember?"

"Yes," the girl said, her voice sullen.

"I wonder then," The Dragon said, "What it is that you *do* want? What would you wish for yourself, if not a crown?"

"I," the girl said, stopping to consider. "I never thought about it very much, but- I suppose . . . An ordinary life. One where I wouldn't have to live in fear."

"We all live in fear," The Dragon said, "From the highest to the lowest. But, if a mundane life is what you desire, now then . . . That We might be willing to offer you."

"How?" the girl said, pursing her lips.

"There is a girl in my service," The Dragon said, drawing closer to Lara's double. "She resembles you, somewhat. If you so wished it, truly wished it, she might *become* you, Larissa. She would take your place. Then, you might be free."

"Free?" the girl scoffed. "Dead, you mean. There cannot be two of me."

The Dragon froze.

"Do you question my generosity?" The Dragon asked, slipping a hand from out of the folds of her cloak. "Perhaps some correction is necessary?"

"No, Your Wisdom," the girl replied, her bluster gone as she bent low. "I meant no disrespect, it was only-"

The sound of The Dragon's laughter filled the room as the girl cowered. The masked men hissed and clicked, shifting beneath their leathery gowns.

"This one will never do," The Dragon said when her laughter had finally abated. "The real Larissa is far more stubborn."

"Lord Reynard has never met the real Larissa," the tall sorcerer said, his voice whining like an insect's.

"He has several in his keeping who have," The Dragon said, and made a shooing motion towards the girl. "Besides, the face is wrong."

"If we had only been able to cull some of her marrow," Lara heard one of the other masked men croak, and felt her gorge rise in the back of her throat as her double began to *dissolve*, her features running together like melting wax. "We could fashion dozens of Larissas to please the Protector of Arcasia."

The girl's eyes had turned to jelly. Pink slime was pouring from her mouth as she slumped backwards, her spine bending impossibly.

"I should think that would be the last thing he desires," The Dragon sighed, stepping over the widening puddle that had been the girl's legs, "Though the prospect is tempting. Imagine what a headache a dozen 'false' Larissas would cause him. Alas, there is no time for such fantasies."

Whether it was the sight of the patch of slime that had worn her face seeping into the black coils twining about the room, or the sudden realization that several of the masked things were shuffling towards her, the thin wisps of their breath trailing them like pale ghosts, whatever spell hanging over Lara was broken. She backed away at first, not wanting to lose sight of the horrors she had seen in case they gave chase but, as the shadows deepened about her, she turned and ran, the voice of The Dragon and her sorcerers echoing down the hall as she went.

"Nine parasangs," The Dragon was muttering as she reached the turn. "We might turn out the Mormolykeia, if We could ensure they would take prisoners . . ."

"They may prove easier to discipline once the new stock has been introduced," another replied. "It is quite excellent. Natural warriors, well suited to nocturnal combat-"

"Be wary, Darrhon," The Dragon interrupted. "Your sentiments reek of the vanity of men."

"I seek no praise, Your Wisdom."

There was a pause, and when The Dragon spoke again her words were so faint that Lara could only just make them out.

"What puzzles me," The Dragon said, "Is that the emissary did not ask after the mother. She and he were supposed to be close once . . ."

She went on, but her words warbled together until Lara could no longer hear the echoes of them.

Lara threw herself around a bend in the passage and stopped to catch her breath. Bannertail leaned against her cheek, his tail whipping at her hair. Her hand hurt. She realized how tightly she had been clutching the candlestick and loosened her grip.

*They would have killed me. And then handed some **thing**, some puppet-fetch with my face over to Reynard to secretly do their bidding . . . But they would have killed me, either way. And that thing knew it too.*

"There cannot be two of me," she mouthed, reaching up to comfort the fox-squirrel still worrying himself against her neck. "And she wouldn't have you, would she?"

Bannertail rubbed his head against her palm and then leapt from her shoulder, giving his whole body a shake.

Lara took a moment to find her bearings. She thought she had gone back the way she had come, but this place looked unfamiliar. The passage made a sharp turn just a dozen paces from where she stood, and a row of open archways lined either side of the hall.

"Missed a turn somewhere," she muttered, peering back around the corner. The hallway looked much darker than it had just a few moments ago. That made sense, though. The visions in the mirror had brought daylight into this dark place. Now the mirror slept.

The mirror. The thought gave her pause as she slipped back down the hall. *They could use it- they will use it- use it to try and find us when we escape . . . But it couldn't find whatever they were looking for, not without help. It needed guiding from The Dragon and her sorcerers. And it couldn't help them either, to see in the dark. Reynard's shrikes will have a far easier time finding us than them.*

The thought was weirdly reassuring to Lara. A shrike she could shoot down with a bow, providing she could hit it. But the eye of the mirror- if there even was such a thing- was invisible. They would not know if The Dragon could see them huddled close to a fire on a freezing night, or trudging under the full moon . . .

Assuming I can find us a way out of here, Lara admonished herself. *They'll be looking everywhere for me before long, especially if they come calling for some of my marrow.*

She shuddered again. Bannertail cocked his head.

"Need to find the others," she nodded at him. "We'll try that stairway next. If we can find-"

Click. Click. Click.

The sound- footfalls, metallic, made with a single boot- echoed down the hallway, growing louder by the moment.

Click. Click. Click.

It was coming her way.

Lara spun backwards, but there was nothing but hallway behind her. She was too far from the intersection to hide. There was an archway some twenty paces ahead of her, but she couldn't tell where the steps were coming from. If she slipped through the arch, she might find herself face to face with one of the green-eyed naga, or worse.

Click. Click. Click.

Bannertail whined, arching his back.

Lara dashed forward, slapping at her thigh as she ran, and spun around the edge of the archway, ready to use the candlestick as a club as Bannertail darted in after her- But, no, they were alone. This was a chamber of some kind. There was no light, but the dim outlines of what might have been tables loomed in the dark. The place stank of the fruit-like scent she'd caught a whiff of before. The strength of it tickled at her nose, so she held her breath.

Click. Click.

There was silence. Whoever was in the hall was close. Had they heard her footsteps, or the patter of the fox-squirrel's paws?

Click. Click.

Lara drew back from the doorway, breathing shallowly. A moment later a shadow blocked the dim light of the hallway.

Whatever it was, it was right outside the room.

Lara kept still, hugging the wall, her candlestick raised . . . But Bannertail began to sniff at the air, his tail whipping as his ears perked up.

Then Lara heard it too: A scratching sound, like a tiny pair of fingernails working against one of the walls.

There's a mouse in here, Lara realized, her heart racing. *Or a rat. Oh, gods.*

Bannertail gave the air another sniff and let out the smallest of growls.

Click.

The shadow grew larger as a lean figure stepped into the doorway. A pale, bone-handled knife shone in the dark, gripped by a scaly hand.

Lara brought the candlestick up over her head. Two more steps, and she'd strike.

Something skipped and clattered across the far side of the chamber. Bannertail sped after it, quiet now that he was on the hunt.

Click.

The naga stepped into the room and peered about, showing the back of her head as she turned. Lara took a deep breath and raised the candlestick higher, shifting her weight to put more force behind the blow.

Now! Do it now!

She was just beginning her swing when an arm wrapped around her from behind, a hard, gloved hand flying over her mouth as someone- or some*thing*- dragged her backwards, taking hold of the candlestick as she tried to twist away. A moment later a tiny shriek echoed through the room. It sounded too loud for a rat.

"Quiet," a man's voice whispered- ever so softly- into her ear.

She did not ease her hold on the candlestick, but she nodded against his grip.

He relaxed his hold, but only just.

Click went the naga's heel as it planted its left leg just inside the door, reversing the grip on its dagger and letting out a sibilant sigh. Somewhere in the darkness, Lara could hear Bannertail munching on something. At least, she hoped it was Bannertail.

The naga's bluish lips parted slightly. It briefly tasted the air with its dark forked tongue before screwing up its face with obvious disgust.

"Hygienic," it muttered, snorting as its dagger disappeared up one of its sleeves. Then it turned, and hurried back down the hall, the click of its heel quickening as if to make up for lost time.

Lara strained to hear the footfalls over the soft breaths of the man restraining her, wincing at the whiskers of his beard pricking her cheek. When they were alone, she would let go of the candlestick, twist the way that Moder had taught her, and strike him as hard as she could with her palm.

When they were alone.

Bannertail had no such patience. He leapt onto the stranger's arm and sunk both claws and teeth into the hand clamped over her mouth.

The man let go of her . . . But he did not cry out. And when Lara spun about to strike him, she found that he already had Bannertail by the scruff of his neck, oblivious to the scratches it was dealing to his arm.

"Put him down," she snarled, putting up her fists.

The man complied, his fingers spreading wide. Bannertail landed on his feet.

"Don't be afraid, Princess," he said, stepping out of the shadows.

Lara lowered her fists ever so slightly.

It was one of the ambassadors from Therimere. He was missing his gown and fine jewelry. But he still had his boots, both hands, and the patch over his right eye.

"I'm here to rescue you," he said.

XV

"Who are you?" Lara asked.

"A friend," the man answered, tugging at the cuff of his left glove, and frowning at the tears that Bannertail's fangs had made. "A friend from far away. And this is yours, I believe."

He held out the candlestick for her to take.

"What's your name?" she asked, hesitating.

"Procyon," he answered.

"But where did you come from? Who sent you?"

"You can guess, surely?"

"The Prince of Therimere?" she offered.

He shook his head. "Further away than that."

"Frisia," she said. "I have friends in Frisia."

"That you do, Majesty. Your cousin, Roland, for one. He is on Deira. Or at least he was. He has to move often, to stay ahead of the Lord Protector's spies."

He gave the candlestick a gentle shake. She took it.

"Roland," she said, repeating the name. She never knew she had a cousin. "And you'll bring me to him? To Frisia?"

"We'll have to get you out of this place first," he said, glancing down the corridor. "Getting in was tricky. Getting out will be trickier."

"But," she said, "There's a way?"

"There is a way," he said, his left eye winking. "Come, I'll show you."

"I can't," she said.

"Can't?" He frowned.

"My friends," she started, wondering just how much the man knew. "They're still here, somewhere, being held prisoner."

"Your Majesty," the man said, wetting his lips as he chose his next words. "I was sent here to rescue *you*. Do you understand?"

"I won't go without them," she said, as loudly as she dared.

"It will be difficult," the man said, hemming his words. "Very *difficult*. And we haven't much time."

"I don't care."

"Very well," he said, the slightest hint of resignation creeping into his words. "We'll free your friends if we can. But *you* must promise to do as I say. Do you?"

"I promise," she said, wondering if the man expected her to seal it with a kiss.

"I believe you," he said, gently, seeming to have read her thoughts. "Now, follow me."

He moved then, not into the corridor, but deeper into the gloom of the chamber. He was almost entirely silent. She understood how easily he had snuck up on her.

"I can't see," she said.

"Ah," his voice sighed.

Something metallic rasped in the darkness, and then a little flame blossomed in the dark. The man had lit a candle with something he was tucking back under his jack.

"Will this do?"

"Yes," Lara replied, and began to pad towards him.

"Oh," he said, the candlelight reflecting against his good eye, "Your chimera- You might want to pick him up."

"Why?"

"Because he ate one of my sleeping pills."

Lara turned, and saw Bannertail laid out on the floor, his tongue lolling from his mouth as he took shallow breaths.

"Will he be alright?" she asked as she knelt to scoop him up. It was hard to carry him and the candlestick, so she set the latter down.

"I think so," the man said, softly. "He only ate one."

"Oh. I thought-"

"Yes?"

"I thought he had a rat," she said. "I- I heard it scream."

"So did the naga," the man said, and then Lara heard the tiny shriek again, clearer. The man was making it, somehow, though it sounded as if it were coming from the other side of the room.

"A useful trick, isn't it?" he said. "I picked it up long ago."

He moved quickly then, across the room and through another archway. She followed, holding onto Bannertail. Or, rather, she followed the candle. He was hard to make out, a shadow amongst darker shadows.

There were corridors, archways, steps leading downwards. Sometimes she could see things in the candlelight. Glass jars, with flesh inside of them. Dead eyes stared back at her from some, others were nothing but limbs, or organs suspended in fluid.

The man didn't linger. He kept moving, purposeful, as if he knew where he was going. At one point he stopped and handed her the candle as he dealt with the workings of a locked door, fishing a tiny hook and lever from his belt. He fiddled for a moment, and then it opened, as though he'd carried a proper key.

He took the candle back from her, and they went on.

Only once did he douse the light. They were coming around a corner when his hand snuffed it out. She made no sound then, daring hardly to breathe.

A moment later a cold light spilled onto the tiled floor, and a pair of dark, angular shapes glided silently past them, in one doorway and then out another. The light lingered for a while after they had passed, then flickered and died.

They stood in the dark for a long time, silent. She shifted Bannertail's weight from one arm to the other, wondering at how heavy he was.

"Alright," the man whispered at last, and again there was the sound of metal on metal. Sparks flew, white hot, and the candle began to glow again.

"That was close," she said.

"Closer than you think. There are things here that can see in the dark."

Lara shivered, and clutched Bannertail tighter to her chest.

"Do you want to keep going?" the man asked, softly.

"No," she answered. "But we will anyway."

The man muttered something under his breath, very low, but said, "We'll trail for a bit, then. Those three probably know the way better than I do."

"Three?" Lara said. "I only saw two."

"I know," he said, and motioned for her to follow, the candlelight bobbing ever so slightly as he lit the way.

They slipped across the room and pressed into a tight hallway with a gradual slope. More stairs. The air grew moist. It was hot down here. Somewhere she could hear water running. It sounded like it was behind the walls. Every so often they stopped, and eventually Lara could hear what the man was listening for: The musical clink of metal against metal, and the sighing wheeze of exhaled breath.

Before long, they took a sharp turn, and the man ushered her past him before shutting an open door with an iron wheel in its center.

He handed her the candle again so he could turn the wheel. Bolts and tumblers *thunked* into place.

She turned, candle outstretched, and recoiled. The walls of this chamber were lined with instruments: Hooks, chains, barbs and spikes, and other more *creative* devices.

"These are the dungeons," the man said, pausing to flex his left hand before taking the candle back from her. "But we're safe enough. Take a moment and catch your breath."

She hardly wanted rest and was just about to say so when she realized that *he* might need to. He was at least as old as Moder, judging by the silver she could see in his beard.

"Where are the others?" she asked as he leaned against one of the walls.

"Others?"

"The ones who were with you," Lara said. "The other ambassadors."

"Still locked away I'm afraid," he answered. "I should have liked to have freed them, but I couldn't risk raising the alarm when the jailors found they'd gone."

"But what about you?" she asked. "Won't they notice that you're gone?"

"Only if they're paying close attention," he said, and she could just make out the shape of his mouth curling into a half smile. "Just between you and me, Princess, the Glyconese aren't anywhere near as clever as they believe themselves to be."

"And I suppose you *are?*"

"What's that?"

"Clever."

"Oh," he said. "I thought you were going to say 'modest.'"

Lara tried not to smile, failed. She liked this man.

"I found you, didn't I?" the man shrugged. "And you weren't even in your rooms."

"How did you know where they were?" she asked. "Have you been here before?"

"No," he said, "But I've been in lots of places like it. They're a lot more similar than you'd think to look at them from the outside. They're like people that way. Easy to guess the shape of when you've known enough of them."

"But harder to read than books," Lara muttered.

"Oh?" the man said, shooting her a bemused look. "Who told you that?"

"Danica," she said. "A priestess. She taught me how to read."

"She sounds very wise," he said, and rolled his shoulders. "So. Are you ready?"

"Yes," she said.

"Good," he said, and blew the candle out.

She fumbled for a moment in the darkness, but then his hand found hers, and squeezed.

"This way," he said, tugging gently. "And go slow. Slow and quiet."

She let him lead her, padding along as best she could. After twenty or so paces they turned left and squeezed through a narrow archway. The smooth stone underfoot gave way to grated metal. They were in the dungeon proper, now. She couldn't see the cells, but she could smell them. Water dripped. Living things shifted in the dark.

A hundred or so paces later they slowed, and took a sharp right. She had the vague sense that they were walking under an opening of some kind- the air felt fresher, somehow- then they came to a halt.

She couldn't help but wonder if *he* could see in the dark, when she noticed the faint outline of the door directly in front of them. There was light on the other side of it.

"I need my hand," he said, releasing hers.

There was a scraping sound. A latch clicked. Lamplight gleamed as the man cracked open the door.

"Not even locked," he muttered.

Something on the other side of the door whistled, faintly, like steam escaping a kettle. Then, a muffled whimper. Not a scream, but a feeble animal sound, wordless with pain.

"Good," the man whispered. "They're distracted."

"What's- What's in there?" Lara stammered.

"These cells are for the animals," the man answered, beckoning her towards the crack in the door. "Especially the two-legged kind."

Lara peered through the crack. A cell-lined hallway led to a pillared chamber, its floor neatly tiled with a drain near its center. Ropes and pulleys stretched from pillar to ceiling, tied fast to rings of iron.

Bodies dangled at the end of the ropes, two men and a woman, strung up by their heels with arms dangling loose beneath them. They had all been stripped naked, and their skin glittered as they twisted. At first Lara thought it was the gleam of sweat and blood, or the sheen of their golden skin, but then she saw the dozens of needles protruding from their flesh.

Near at hand, a daughter of mercy was leaning over a marble-topped table, her hands sifting through needles yet to be applied. A pair of masked men stood by the ropes, silent. Ready.

The daughter of mercy lifted one of the needles, and flicked it with her finger, making it sing before she moved out of sight. One of the men thrashed at the sound, mewling through the gag in his mouth. In his throes he brushed up against the woman, who let out a deep, ferocious grunt and craned her neck against the anguish of the needles.

What struck Lara was that the woman did not sound at all frightened. Pained certainly. Horribly, even. Lara could not imagine how bad the pain must be . . . But not broken. If anything, she sounded angry.

Terrifically angry.

Arsinoe!

"Seen enough?" the man asked, his hand moving to the latch.

"What are you doing?" she hissed.

"Shutting the door."

"But we have to stop them!"

"*We?*" he said, arching an eyebrow.

"We," she repeated. "I can fight."

"The old woman teach you that too, did she?"

"No," Lara said. "Moder did, and she's better with a sword than you, I bet."

"Perhaps," the man said. "But the thing is, I didn't come here to tussle with The Dragon's goons. I only wanted to see if they were still distracted. And, seeing as they are-"

"But they have her!" she said, a bit too loud.

The man put a finger to his lips, his eyes widening with alarm. They both listened. Somewhere in the dark a prisoner coughed raggedly. Bannertail stirred in his sleep, yawning wide as he squirmed against her palm. From the chamber beyond the doorway there was a muted howl followed shortly by a horrid tinkling.

The man leaned forward, the light streaming through the crack playing over his face as he did so. A deep white scar split the right side of his face from brow to cheek. She was glad that he wore a patch.

"Who?" he practically mouthed. "Who do they have?"

"The woman," she whispered, pointing. "Arsinoe."

"Ah," the man said, scratching at the back of his neck. "The Telchine. Of course."

"You know her?"

"The Dragon made quite a spectacle of marching you through the streets of Ladon," he said, contemplating. "But I did not know that you knew her. Or that you thought of her as a *friend.*"

"She was helping us," Lara said. "She did help us. To escape."

"I see," he said, and let out a deep breath. "Well, if we're going to do this, you're going to need something deadlier than a drugged chimera."

"I had a sword," Lara said, "But they took it."

"I wouldn't count on finding it," he said, taking a knee as he slipped a narrow blade from his boot. "The Glyconese are hardly sentimental about such things. So, here, take this."

"Won't you need it?" she asked.

"No," he said.

She took the dagger from him. It was a simple thing, sturdy but very light. Its blade tapered to a needlepoint.

"Have you killed before?" he asked, simply.

"Yes," she said, surprised by how calm she sounded. "A ghoul. And one of Reynard's soldiers, I think."

"They're supposed to be hard to kill," he said, nodding. "Alright then. Put that down."

He nodded towards Bannertail.

When she hesitated, he added, "We'll come back for him when we're done."

She nodded, tucking him between the wall and the masonry of the doorway. He instinctively curled up into a ball of fur, his long tail serving as a pillow for his head.

"I'll deal with the seamstress," the man said, his fingers working at something hidden beneath his jack. "Can you take one of the guards?"

"Yes," she said.

"Go for the throat," he said. "Or the heart if you can manage it. Anything but a killing blow won't stop a Myrmidon."

"How do you know they're Myrmidons?"

"I don't," he said. "But just in case: The throat, or the heart. Don't hesitate."

"I won't."

"Good," he said, and opened the door.

* * * * * *

One of the masked guards saw them first. He did not cry out- could not perhaps- but stirred from his place near the ropes, his arms unfolding to reveal a pair of taloned gauntlets. That was enough to rouse the daughter of mercy. Her head spun towards them as she reached for the lash coiled at her hip.

The man didn't quicken his step. He was moving down the corridor with speed and purpose, but his pace was far from a run. There was caution in it, and dangerous, weighted intent. It reminded Lara of Moder.

The guard lunged to defend his mistress, his clawed hands raking at the air as he threw himself forward. The man did not dodge. Rather, he let himself be struck . . . Or so it seemed to Lara. There was a quick flash of metal, a gasp, and then the guard went flying, his mask snapping as his head collided with the tiled floor.

What happened next was very quick. There was an almost metallic 'crack' as the daughter of mercy's lash caught the man by the arm. As he stumbled, the other guard made for him, turning his back on Lara as she came racing out of the corridor.

Perhaps the guard hadn't noticed the dagger. Perhaps he didn't consider a girl a threat. It didn't matter. She leapt onto the guard's back and drove the blade into his neck.

She nearly toppled with him as he fell, the horrible *ease* of what she had just done washing over her before both instinct and training kicked in. She landed back on her feet, reversing her grip on the dagger as she steadied herself.

They would have killed you, she told herself, trying not to look at the man crawling on the floor. *They were torturing Arsinoe. You didn't have a choice.*

The sound of a woman gasping drew her attention to the daughter of mercy, who was now staggering against the marble-topped table, partially blinded by the needle protruding from what remained of her left eye. Her whip drooped from her right hand, the end of it still wrapped around the upper half of the man's left arm, which now lay, lifeless, on the ground.

The woman's free hand searched the table, taking hold of a serrated knife just as the man loomed up behind her and shoved her headfirst into the marble.

"There," the man said, coolly. "That wasn't so hard."

"Your," Lara stammered as the daughter of mercy slid from the table, "Your arm-"

"False," he said, jiggling the end of his left sleeve. "I lost the real one years ago."

"What happened?"

The man smiled his lop-sided smile, but he did not answer. Instead, he went to collect the contraption that served as his left limb. The armguard (or, rather, the arm itself) housed a spring-loaded blade. The business end was bloody.

"Did you have to kill her?" she asked, cleaning the dagger against the fabric of her dress.

"You wanted to rescue your friends," the man answered, setting his hand down on the table. "Didn't you?"

"Can *someone*," Arsinoe growled through her teeth, blinking at the sweat running into her eyes. "*Please* cut me down?"

"Don't you want the needles out first?" Lara asked.

"No," Arsinoe spat, and tried to lift her arms, her neck straining at the effort.

Finally, she went limp.

"Fine," she gasped.

Lara looked over the host of needles, unsure where to begin.

"I'll do it," the man said. He'd already managed to do up the topmost straps holding his left arm in place. "Go and fetch your chimera. The harm could be permanent if it's not done properly . . ."

Lara nodded, not asking how the man knew of such things, and padded back down the hall to retrieve Bannertail. She found the fox-squirrel just as she left him, and carefully tucked him against her breast. Then she listened for any sounds of alarm . . . But the noises of the dungeon seemed unchanged. If the prisoners *had* heard the crack of the whip or the cries of their jailors, they had probably taken it for the torture that was likely routine in this place.

She shut the door and hurried back. She could hear the man saying something to Arsinoe in a hushed voice, soft and reassuring. Lara smirked. She doubted the tough Telchine appreciated such niceties.

"I'm back," she said.

"And we're in luck," the man said, gently spinning one of the needles as he removed it from Arsinoe's flesh. "The Calvarians are in the cells just above this one."

He gestured towards a set of steps. They led to another iron-bound door with a wheel at its center.

"How do you know?" Lara asked.

"Daughter was awfully chatty with the man who brought the meals," Arsinoe replied, wincing as the man slid another needle from her shoulder. "If I didn't know any better, you'd think they were lovers."

"Don't scream," the man said to Arsinoe, quickly plucking the last few needles from the woman's belly. She seethed through her teeth, and blinked away tears, but she didn't cry out.

"Let her down now," the man said, "Gently. I need to finish putting my arm to rights before we get on."

"What about them?" Lara asked, pointing at the two men who dangled by Arsinoe's side. She wondered that they had been so silent and still for so long.

"No time," the man said, working. "And besides, they're dead."

"Dead?" Lara gaped. "How?"

"Shock, I expect," the man said. "The daughter must have fumbled with that last needle. Now, will you *please* help her down?"

His voice was still soft, civil even, but there was a heat lurking behind it. Impatience. Lara supposed she couldn't entirely blame him.

Lara set Bannertail down on the table, undid the knot holding Arsinoe in place, and let her down as gently as she could. Once she was on the floor, she applied the edge of the knife to the bonds about her ankles.

Arsinoe stood up, woozily, hissing with pain. Her body was covered by a patchwork of green bruises, cuts, and puncture marks.

"Do you have anything to eat?" she asked, grabbing hold of the table to steady herself before nudging Bannertail with her finger. "Besides your fox-cat, I mean."

"How about some clothes first?" Lara asked, averting her eyes.

"Da, majiko," Arsinoe said, rolling her eyes as she lurched over towards the guard Lara had stabbed. The man was no longer stirring, Lara noticed. A pool of blood had formed on the tiles beneath him.

Arsinoe threw on the dead man's boots, skirt, and tunic, then took one of his gauntlets for good measure. For a belt she practically ripped the one from the daughter of mercy before throwing it over her shoulder.

"Better?" Arsinoe asked, throwing up her arms and quickly regretting the gesture.

"A bit," Lara said, looping the other guard's belt about her waist and stuffing the man's dagger into it.

"You don't have any food," Arsinoe said, blinking at the sight of her dress, "Do you."

"No," Lara said.

"Tch," Arsinoe clucked, sucking at her parched lips.

"Time to go," the man said, his left arm back in place beneath his sleeve. "Grab a blade, Telchine. You might need it yet."

Arsinoe grunted and crossed to an alcove lined with cots. It looked like a cell to Lara, albeit one without any bars. The guards slept there, she supposed.

"Will one of these do?" Arsinoe grunted, tossing aside a curtain to reveal a full rack of polearms of varied make. She selected one of the simpler ones- a short shaft with a wide blade whose reverse was serrated- and gave it a whirl to test its weight.

"It will," the man said, giving the wheel on the door a turn.

"I don't suppose my sword is in there?" Lara asked Arsinoe as she scooped Bannertail up.

"Here's something better," the Telchine said, lifting a linen satchel from a hook at the rear of the alcove and tossing it at her feet.

"What am I supposed to do with this?" Lara asked.

"Put *him* inside of it," Arsinoe said, pointing at Bannertail.

"Oh," Lara said, gently stowing the sleeping chimera at the bottom of the pack before throwing it over her shoulder. There was something else in the pack, rectangular. A book of prayers maybe.

The man called Procyon gave the wheel a final spin and swung open the door. As he peered through the gap he flexed his left hand, as if testing it.

"You first, Telchine," he said, gesturing to the lamplit stairwell beyond.

"It's Arsinoe."

"Arsinoe," he repeated, with an apologetic nod. "Of course. Lead the way if you would be so kind."

Arsinoe's eyes narrowed . . . But she complied, leading with her spear as she crept up the steps.

"Now you," the man said to Lara.

"Me?" Lara said.

"Yes," he said. "Don't worry. I'll be right behind you."

* * * * * * *

The stairwell spat them into a dimly lit arcade ringing a court punctuated by a pale column with drains about its base. The arched ceilings beneath the arcade swallowed the lamplight, but Lara could see at least a dozen cells. Their barred windows provided an easy view of the court and its pillar.

Arsinoe made a sweeping gesture with her hand towards the cells, looking to the man with eyebrows raised.

The man used his good hand to gesture to their right. Arsinoe nodded, and moved towards the closest cell, her focus wavering between the way ahead and the gloom on the far side of the yard.

Lara made to follow, but the man put his hand out to stop her.

"My knife," he whispered, keeping his palm open.

Lara slipped the blade from her belt and pressed it into his hand, shying away as his fingers brushed against her own. Then the man flipped the dagger into the air, caught it, and sent it flying towards one of the deep patches of shadow hanging over Arsinoe.

Something that had been clutching to the underside of the arcade plummeted to the floor, croaking a ragged bark as its limbs twisted vainly to right itself. Arsinoe drove her spear into what Lara took for its head, dancing away from the pink shock of tongue that sprang from its fanged maw.

"Clever bastard," the man said as Arsinoe stabbed it again for good measure. "Must have heard us coming."

"What is it?" Lara asked, trying to figure out if the thing still quivering on the floor was more frog or dog. Its lack of eyes didn't help.

"Your guess is as good as mine," the man said, retrieving his dagger.

"This cell's empty," Arsinoe said, peering through the closest set of bars. "I think. It's pretty dark in there."

"Lara," the man said, using her familiar name. "You call out to them."

"Call out?" she said.

"So they'll know it's you," he explained. "But not too loud."

Lara stepped out from underneath the arcade, gazing for a moment at the darkness looming above them.

"Moder," she said, her voice sounding very tiny to her ears. "Moder, are you there?"

There was silence. Something rustled in the dark, coughed, and then:

"Here," a voice wheezed from somewhere to her left. It wasn't Moder's, but Pinsard's. He tried to speak again, but all that came out was a squeak.

She crossed the court and found him, his pale face pressed against the bars, dark circles beneath his eyes.

"I'm here," Lara said, touching his fingers through the bars. "Is . . . Is Moder-"

"Over there," Pinsard said, pointing to the row of cells opposite the stairwell. "With the-"

Another dry cough racked his body.

"Here, boy," the man said, pressing a waterskin to the bars. "Drink."

Pinsard looked at the man, his face screwing up with confusion.

"It's alright," Lara said. "He's a friend."

Pinsard met Lara's gaze, then bent his neck to take a few swallows.

"Which cell is your mother in?" the man asked when he was finished.

"That one," Pinsard said, pointing again. "Who are-"

"The Lady Hirsent," the man cut him off, turning towards Arsinoe, "She knows you, yes?"

"She does," Arsinoe replied.

"She'll be thirsty too," he said, holding out the waterskin. "Don't give her too much."

Arsinoe hesitated, her tongue working against the inside of her cheek. Then she took the waterskin from the man and crossed towards the cells, giving the column a wide berth.

"What was The Dragon like?" Pinsard asked as the man began to work at the lock.

"A fraud," Lara said. "She's not even a real dragon. Has to wear makeup."

Pinsard smiled. It faded quickly.

"Did they hurt you?" he asked.

"A bit," Lara said.

Snap, went the lock.

"There," the man said. "It's open now."

The man stood aside. Lara threw open the door and took Pinsard into her arms. She couldn't remember the last time she'd done so.

"What about you?" she asked as they parted, glancing at the new bruises beneath his shirt. The shirt was new too, she noticed, and his breeches resembled those that the Myrmidons wore. "Are you alright?"

"They bled us," Pinsard answered, and put his hand against the door frame. "Made us run in wheels. Made us fight."

"Fight?"

"The guards," he said. "Chimera. Other- Other prisoners."

He took a deep breath.

"They wanted us to kill them."

"With your bare hands?" Lara asked.

He shook his head.

"They let us use our swords," he said. "They kept them here, somewhere . . ."

"I have them," the man said, stepping around the nearest pillars with a pair of swords tucked under his arm. Lara hadn't even noticed that he'd been missing.

"Where did you-" Lara started.

"Here," the man said, holding out Pinsard's sword in its black scabbard. "If you're anything like your father, I assume you know how to use this."

Pinsard reached for the sword, eager. Then he froze.

"You knew my father?" he asked.

The man nodded. "I did. He was a great man, your father. We fought together during the war. You have his poise. I am certain you do him honor."

Pinsard did not answer, but he took his sword, loosening the blade to test its edge.

"I thought you were a Frisian," Lara said.

"No, Majesty," the man said, "I too am an Arcasian, far from home. Like you."

The man's left eye winked at her. Or perhaps he merely blinked. In the dark of the dungeon, it was hard to say for certain.

"Moder!"

Pinsard choked out the word and brushed past Lara. She turned. Moder was being led across the court, leaning against Arsinoe like one of the drunks at The Nightingale. The Telchine was struggling under the weight of the larger woman, her spear serving them both as a prop.

Lara ran to help Pinsard steady her between them.

"What is it?" Pinsard asked.

"What's wrong?" Lara added.

"My head," Moder answered, clearly trying to focus her gaze. "Is hard . . . To be keeping eyes open."

Moder swooned then and lost her footing. They struggled for a moment to get her back upright.

"Those fights," Lara started, "Did she- was she hurt?"

"No!" Pinsard blurted. "They hardly touched her."

"They may have drugged her food," the man said, softly. His tone reminded Lara of the need for quiet.

"Why would they do that?" Pinsard whispered.

"To make her more docile," the man answered, "I expect."

"Am fine," Moder muttered. "Cold water. Cold water and air . . ."

"We have to get her out of here," Lara grunted, straining to hold her up.

"We all have to get out of here," Arsinoe rejoined, her gaze returning to the shadows ringing the court.

"Here," the man said, pressing a blade- Moder's- towards Lara. "I'll take her. Don't worry, I'm stronger than I look. But you'll need to take Harrower."

"Harrower?" Lara repeated, taking the sword.

"Everyone west of the Muraille knows the name of the Lady Hirsent's sword," the man said, shaking his head. "Even in Glycon, I imagine. Haven't you heard the songs?"

"No," said Lara.

"No," said Pinsard.

"No," said Arsinoe.

"Ah, well," the man said, and took Lara's place by Hirsent's side.

"*Hwa eart ge?*" Moder slurred, reverting to her own tongue as the man slid her arm over his shoulder.

"Save your strength," the man whispered.

Moder murmured some vague protest, but she leaned against the man, who seemed to have no trouble keeping her upright. He hadn't been exaggerating about his strength, it seemed.

"Now," he said, making for the opposite side of the arcade "It's time to go. Stay close. And keep your ears and eyes open."

* * * * * * *

Lara soon lost count of the rights and lefts they took. The man guided them as best he could, whispering softly which way to turn, but she and Pinsard were soon taking the lead, Arsinoe falling back somewhat to watch their rear.

With every corner they rounded or doorway they slipped past, Lara tensed herself to fight. They were no longer in the darkness of the dungeons, but in well-lit hallways whose stone floors were smooth from use. She had no doubt that there were guards patrolling these places, or perhaps dormitories where the daughters of mercy lay, dreaming of The Destroyer.

A fight here would bring the whole palace down on them, she knew. The thought of what The Dragon would do to them then was terrible . . . But she had to admit, it felt good to have a sword back in her hands.

"Do you know where you are going?" Pinsard asked the man when they had stopped for a moment to catch their breath, taking shelter in an alcove of a wide hall.

The man nodded.

"Most palaces have a back gate," he explained, "For servants, and the like. This one isn't any different."

Pinsard nodded and asked no more, turning his attention instead to Moder, who was making an effort to speak.

"Shhh," Pinsard said, putting his hand on her shoulder. "We are almost there . . . Aren't we?"

"Just a bit further," the man said.

They went on.

Beyond the hall was a corridor whose doors opened onto storerooms lined with barrels, gunny sacks, crates, and- hanging from the ceiling- enormous sets of scales for measuring.

Then the corridor ended, and they stood on the edge of an immense cobbled yard. This was no pleasure garden. It was empty, open to the night air, and there were no trees or shrubs to hide behind. Dozens of windows and balconies looked down upon it. There were lights burning in some of them, and shapes that might be sentries.

"Keep close to the wall," the man whispered, nudging them towards the darker side of the court. The Watcher was west of the river it seemed, but dawn was still a long way off. "But don't run, or they'll know for sure."

Lara went first, fighting the urge to crouch as she hurried along, trying not to look up at the rows of windows staring down at them. She could hear Pinsard's footfalls right behind her, and the scrape of Moder's boots (how fortunate they'd let her keep them!) as they slid against the cobblestones.

"Slow down," she heard the man urge.

Lara forced herself to walk, thinking- hoping- that if they were seen, the Myrmidons would see her dress and Arsinoe's armor and take them for servants of The Dragon, going about Her business.

Halfway across the courtyard, a bell- *the* bell, the one that could be heard across Ladon- began to toll.

Lara forced herself not to run, but came to a halt, and turned about.

"They know," Lara said.

"I think not," the man said, listening.

"But," Pinsard said, raising his sword. "The alarm-"

"It's *an* alarm," the man said, softly. "But not for us."

"Who for then?" Arsinoe asked.

The man did not answer but stood and listened. Lara could hear a woman, or perhaps it was more than one, shouting from somewhere high above. A second bell joined the thunderous peals of the first, and then a third, more urgent.

"Move," the man said then, breaking his silence. "Quick now."

Lara did not need any urging. She broke into a jog, making for an archway on the other side of the courtyard. Somewhere close by she could hear the tramp of boots against stone and, further off but not far enough, the roiling, distressed bellow of the winged dragon, irate perhaps at having been disturbed.

The archway loomed wide before her, and then she was through it, racing along a short, unlit passage. At the end of it she could see moonlight reflecting against the river like silver.

The river!

As she made for the light, she nearly tripped over the dead men lying along its length. There were at least six of them, Myrmidons or zealots she could not tell which. Their necks had been slashed.

"What-" Lara heard Pinsard whisper as he came skidding to a halt beside her. "What happened?"

"I don't know," Lara said, suddenly aware that the stones beneath her feet were sticky with blood. She took a few steps back, but it was everywhere. Even on the walls.

Don't look! Don't look!

She took a deep breath. She was not in the red room. She was with Pinsard and Moder. And Arsinoe. And the man, Procyon, who she realized was right beside her.

He was looking at her strangely, a sad smile on his lips.

"I'm here," he said, his voice echoing down the passage.

"You're late," a coarse voice growled in answer. A shadowy figure stepped between them and the river.

"A delay," the man answered. "There were . . . complications."

"So I see," the voice sneered. The voice was familiar. "Just couldn't help yourself, could you?"

"I suppose not," the man said.

Another pair of men joined the first. One was lean the other lanky. The latter's hair was nearly shock-white, a dark cloak hanging loose over his shoulder.

"The Graycloaks!" Moder spat, struggling against the man as she fought to straighten herself. "Reynard- Reynard is here!"

"Yes," the man said, releasing his grip on her. "He is."

XVI

Moder spun away from the man, nearly toppled, and braced herself against the passage as she clutched for the sword that was no longer on her belt.

"You!" she managed.

"Hirsent," the man said, his head bowing ever so slightly. "It has been far too long."

"Not long enough," Moder said, her head sinking as she tried to keep her balance. She couldn't seem to keep it upright.

"Reynard!" Pinsard spat, leveling his sword. It quivered.

"Reynard? You?!" Lara tightened her grip on Moder's sword. "But he's in Solothurn!"

"I still am," Reynard said. "And I wouldn't do that, if I were you."

For a moment Lara thought the man- Reynard- had been speaking to her, but then Moder launched herself at him, nowhere near as dizzy or unsteady on her feet as she had seemed a moment ago.

Moder's fist shot out, once, twice. Then he caught her wrist in his false hand and twisted until she sank to her knees.

"Let her go!" Lara shouted.

"As you wish," the man said, and released Moder from his grip. This time she did collapse. It seemed to take all her strength to roll onto her stomach.

"I did warn you," Reynard said, the fingers of his false hand flickering.

"Coward," Moder slurred through her pain. "You are drugging me, yes?"

"An old trick," the man said casually, "But necessary. For your eyes deceive you, old friend. These aren't the Graycloaks. Heh. Far from it."

Reynard snapped his fingers. Torchlight filled the passage, licks of flame playing against the faces of men, hard and cruel. Lara put her blade between herself and the dark-eyed man grinning back at her.

"Well," Tybalt drawled. "Caught up with you at last, haven't we?"

"Get back!" Lara said, raising her guard. "Get back, or I'll kill you!"

"Kill?" Tybalt chuckled. "Kill me? And how, exactly, do you intend to accomplish that, Your Highness?"

"Now, now, Tybalt," Reynard admonished. "There's no need to be rude."

"Your pardon, my lord," Tybalt said, sounding oddly humbled as he lowered his eyes. "It has been . . . A long hunt."

"Save your groveling for Carduel," Reynard said. "Are the boats ready?"

"They are, my lord."

"Then see the Lady Hirsent and her son to one of them. As for the Princess-"

Reynard let out a surprised grunt. Moder had taken hold of his ankle. He dragged his leg from her grip and put his other boot down on her shoulder, shoving her to the floor.

"I'm being very patient with you, Hirsent," Reynard warned, "But if you try that again, I'll kill the boy."

"Try it, dog!" Pinsard snarled. "Just you try it!"

"I mean it, Hirsent," Reynard said, turning ever so slightly.

Reynard curled his false hand into a fist.

"Pinsard," Moder rasped, trying to raise herself up. "Do- Do as he says."

"Coward!" Pinsard hissed. "Murderer-"

Those words had hardly passed Pinsard's lips when he let out a short, sharp cry. His blade rang out as it struck the stones beneath his feet.

Pinsard clutched at his hand, blinking at the dagger sticking out of it.

"His hand," Lara said, staring.

"He'll live," Tybalt said, another knife balanced between his fingers. "And he ought to be thanking me."

"Thanking?!" Pinsard hissed as he slid the knife free.

"The view from your hill is pretty, boy," Tybalt said, the dagger seeming to dance as he flipped it head over hilt, "But hard to enjoy when you're dead. I should know. I've made a hill of lofty folk myself. And I don't plan on dying on it."

Tybalt spun the dagger again, his grin fading as he caught it.

"Now kick that sword over here. For your mother's sake, at least."

"I'd do as Tybalt says," Reynard said. "He's rarely so patient, let alone eloquent. Or has it been so long that you've forgotten?"

Pinsard stood a moment, his shoulders shaking.

"I remember," he said at last, and kicked his sword down the passage.

The lanky man (who looked half a Calvarian with his chalky hair and skin) grimaced as he went to retrieve it. His teeth were very yellow, and in the firelight his eyes looked red. He reminded Lara of a white rat that used to live in the barn. Though the rat had been cleaner.

"You too, Princess," Tybalt said. "Your sword."

"No," Lara said.

"No?" Tybalt repeated, shooting his men a look. They chuckled nervously.

"Let us go," Lara said, turning her blade on Reynard. "All of us. Or *he* dies."

Reynard cocked his head and smiled his half smile.

"A bold plan, Majesty," he said. "But I wonder if you've thought it through."

"Not entirely," Lara admitted. "But then, you've forgotten Arsinoe."

The Telchine stepped from the shadows, torchlight gleaming off her skin and the curved blade of her spear. It hovered just short of the small of Reynard's back. A single thrust and he would die, choking on his own blood.

Reynard sighed.

"Not bad," Reynard said. "But you see, I *haven't* forgotten. Have I, Arsinoe?"

"Get in the boat," Arsinoe said to Lara, releveling her spear.

"Arsinoe?" Lara's arm wavered.

Reynard caught the edge of Moder's sword with his false hand and wrenched it from her grip.

"The boat," Arsinoe said as Lara nursed her hand. "Now."

"Yes," Reynard said, motioning for Tybalt and his men to make way. "We've wasted too much time here already, and The Dragon isn't known for her forgiving nature. Come."

Reynard swept past them, tossing Moder's sword to Tybalt as he walked. The dark-eyed man caught it, his lip twitching at something unspoken.

When Lara hesitated, Arsinoe gave her push.

They followed Reynard, the Telchine meeting Pinsard's gaze as they stepped over the dead men.

"Traitor," Pinsard whispered.

For once, the Telchine kept her peace.

"Jacquet, Murgleis," Tybalt rattled the men's names off as they passed, "Get the she-wolf and her brat into the boat."

"Don't touch her!" Pinsard growled as Tybalt's men moved to take them, lifting Moder from the floor himself.

"There's a good boy," Tybalt said. "Now, *move*."

There were two boats waiting for them, tied to a pier that ran alongside the outer wall of the palace. They weren't terribly large, both of them fishing boats judging by the nets and the stink clinging to them. A pair of Tybalt's men sat in each, manning the oars.

There were more boats on the river. Rowboats and narrow ships with triangular sails were jostling against each other as they tried to launch from the quays on the opposite bank, where men and women were all screaming in terror. The bells of the palace were still ringing, louder than ever. Somewhere upriver a great plume of smoke was rising, clouding even the skull-moon as it twisted into the night sky.

"What is that?" Lara asked, staring.

"There's a fire in the city," Reynard said, stepping into a boat. "No one will notice another boat or two trying to flee."

Arsinoe gave her a nudge. Reynard held his good hand out to her, but she did not take it.

"You started it," Lara said, settling down as Arsinoe and another of Tybalt's men clambered in after her. "The fire."

"How could I have?" Reynard said, helping to kick the boat free of the pier. "I was busy rescuing you, remember?"

"But your men did. Didn't they?"

"My soldiers follow orders," Reynard said, nodding to the man at the oars. "Row."

The man swung out the oars and moved them away from the pier. Soon the course of the river was doing most of the work for them.

Lara turned. Pinsard was helping Moder into the second boat as Tybalt and his men piled in alongside them. The boat looked awfully cramped compared to theirs.

"Don't worry," Reynard said. "They won't sink."

Lara glared at the one-eyed man sitting across from her. He returned her gaze a while, and then turned to watch the smoke rising from the city. Lara could see the flames now, a false dawn.

"How did you know?" Lara asked, suddenly.

"I had to guess at first," he answered, still watching the fire. "Your servants wouldn't talk. Not even Pierrot."

He smiled.

"And that old woman you used to live with," he went on, turning to face her. "Now she's a rare one, isn't she?"

"Did you," Lara said, ignoring the lump in her throat, "Torture them?"

"I do not believe in torture," Reynard said, simply. "It is as cruel as it is unreliable. One can make a man confess to anything if only to stop you from hurting him. On that matter, at least, Pinsard's father and I saw eye to eye . . . So to speak."

"Then- They live?"

"Pierrot lives," Reynard said. "But the old woman tried to tear my throat out. I couldn't have that."

"And," Lara said, her cheeks growing hot. "Arlequin?"

"Fever took him," Reynard said. "A mercy, really. Rukenaw was going to have him drawn and quartered."

"But why?!"

"He hurt someone very dear to her, once," Reynard answered. "It was long ago, but still. And why should I refuse her? He was a traitor, after all."

"He was my friend!"

"He was your *servant*," Reynard corrected. "And a servant can never truly be your friend, just as much as a pet could ever be."

His good eye winked. He straightened.

"Or a mercenary," he said, turning again to watch the blaze.

The fire was spreading. The bridge ahead of them was full of people, pressing to escape the flames. People were leaping into the river, thrashing towards anything that could float.

"Faster," Reynard said, and the rower picked up his stroke.

Lara half turned in her seat. Arsinoe was crouched behind her, gaze and spear fixed on the people struggling in the river. Lara had no illusions about what the Telchine would do if they got too close.

"And you," Lara said. "When did you know?"

Arsinoe shrugged.

"It wasn't hard to tell you were running from something," she said. "Pretty girl in the waste with two Calvars? Figured there had to be someone who wanted you back. Someone with more than a gelding and a purse of clean coins. Turns out I was right."

"But how did you-" Lara stammered. "We were in the middle of nowhere!"

"*Carsi* may just be the middle of nowhere," Arsinoe said, "But you get all sorts there. Folk who know folk, even folk in Solyturn, or wherever it is you're from. So, I had some quiet *words* with Prahasta. Heh. You think I paid off my debt to him with a horse that can't breed? Figured I could collect when I got you to the sea."

Somewhere behind them a wail went up as a building collapsed, timbers groaning.

Arsinoe rubbed at the beetle on her cheek. "Didn't count on all these detours, though."

"I," Lara said, taking a breath. "I thought we were friends."

"Dramsind was my friend," Arsinoe said, flatly. "And we left him in the mountains. You? You're not my friend. You're just some stranger I met by the side of the road. One with a bigger price on her head than I expected. Speaking of which-"

"You will be compensated as soon as we reach the delta," Reynard said, growing brusque. "In the payment your master requested."

"He's *not* my master," Arsinoe said.

"No?" Reynard said. Then he settled back in the boat, the fingers of his false hand tapping against the hull as he watched the city burn.

* * * * * * *

The sky grew pink as the river widened, its course diverted by narrow islands and shallow lagoons where reeds clogged the way. White cranes stalked amongst the pools, their heads bobbing and dipping for fish.

The larger ships steered clear of the mire, while the smaller keels and skiffs beached themselves on the eastern shore, driving off a herd of deer-like animals that had been watering in the early dawn. But the boats that held Lara and the others slipped into one of the smaller channels, the rowers picking up their stroke as soon as they were out of sight.

"Drake," one of Tybalt's men called out, his ruddy locks heavy from the damp in the air. He was pointing at what looked like a log.

"Leave it be," Reynard said.

The rowers did their best to give the thing a wide berth.

The channel became so narrow that Lara could have reached out and run her hand through the grasses growing beneath the swell, and then, without warning, the men at both stern and bow leapt over the side and held the boat steady.

"Out," Tybalt barked, no doubt at Pinsard, who was doing his best to lift Moder from her seat. She hardly seemed conscious, more like one lost in a dream. She was trying to speak, but her words were all garbled Calvarian.

Lara wondered what she was trying to say. Then Arsinoe gave her a none too gentle shove with the butt of her spear.

"Don't do that again," Reynard said as he stepped from the boat.

"Sorry," Arsinoe apologized. "Just thought we were in a hurry."

"We are," he said, and offered Lara his hand.

Again, she ignored it, and hiked up her pack as her feet sank into the mud . . . But as she did so Reynard made a sign, and two of Tybalt's men stepped forward to part the reeds for them, doing their best to avert their gaze.

"Be careful as you step, Majesty," Reynard said. "The reeds can be sharp."

"Don't call me that," Lara said.

"As you wish," Reynard said. "Lara."

Lara squirmed but struggled not to show it.

He's just trying to get under my skin . . . And it's working. But he doesn't need to know that.

Tybalt's men half carved, half trampled a path for them through the rushes. Tybalt himself brought up the rear, his two lieutenants 'escorting' Pinsard as he dragged Moder along. Lara managed to cut herself only once, a bit of grass whipping across her leg as one of the men ahead of her let go of a loose clump of reeds.

"Ow!" she cried out. The men about her froze, spinning their heads with worry writ in their eyes.

"Careful, fool!" Tybalt spat at the man. "This is the Princess, not some back-alley slut of yours!"

"Your, uh, pardon, Majesty," the man breathed, rubbing at his crooked nose as he bowed his head. "I didn't-"

"It's fine," Lara said, shoving past him. "It's just a scratch."

"Thank you," the man breathed. "Your-"

"What are you standing there for?" Tybalt snarled. "Keep moving! All of you!"

The men seemed to remember themselves and picked up their pace, though the two clearing the way ahead of her were careful not to let any loose stalks fly.

"I'll give you a scratch, you idiots," she could hear Tybalt grumbling as they pressed on. "I'll give you a few you won't soon forget . . ."

Gradually, the ground grew firmer. The reeds broke, giving way to a wild stretch of grassland punctuated by trees dripping with moss.

Beneath one of the larger trees Lara could make out the dark bulk of a wagon, wreathed by hanging creepers. As they drew closer, she could see horses grazing amongst the brush and men skulking in the shade.

A whistle split the air. Reynard put his good hand to his mouth and whistled back.

Some of the men began rounding up the horses. Others moved to greet them.

"Any trouble?" Tybalt asked one of them, a wiry-haired man with a warg mask dangling from his belt.

"No trouble, chief," the man answered, huskily. Lara recognized his voice: He'd been the one singing back in Vulp Vora. "Nothing here but birds and marsh rats. Not even a drake to keep us company."

The man (and he was not alone) ran his eyes over Lara, his eyes narrowing at the sight of her. Or was it Arsinoe they were sneering at? She couldn't tell. She wondered how many of them had lost someone in Vulp Vora. She supposed that even these men had friends, of a sort.

"Is the wagon ready?" Reynard asked.

"Nearly, my lord," the man answered. "Had to unhitch. Horses were getting skittish."

"Carry on then," Reynard said dryly. "And, as it seems that the Lady Hirsent and her son will also be joining us-"

"Bastard!" Pinsard spat weakly, glaring at Reynard as he fought to keep Moder upright. "Coward!"

The albino cuffed Pinsard across the back of his head, sending both he and Moder tumbling into the grass. When the boy tried to rise, the albino gave him a playful kick to the ribs.

"Enough," Reynard said.

The albino backed off at once, bowing his head.

"The boy's hand needs mending," Reynard went on, meeting Pinsard's gaze as he climbed to his feet. "See to it at once, Corsablis. I wouldn't want either he or his mother hurting themselves more than necessary."

"Yes, my lord," the singer grunted, his men already moving to help 'escort' the Calvarians.

"And what about me?" Arsinoe said, planting her spear. "Or are you the sort to renege on a debt?"

"Ah, yes," Reynard said. "Corsablis? Fetch the box."

"My lord," Corsablis said, swallowing, "We, ah, buried it."

"Then unbury it," Reynard said. "Tybalt-"

"I'm going!" Tybalt snapped, and stormed off, making for the trees.

They applied a quick poultice to Pinsard's hand, tied his wrists together with rawhide, gagged him when he wouldn't stop cursing, and forced him into the back of the wagon.

They tied up Moder too, her legs as well as her hands, though by now she was fast asleep . . . But they didn't touch Lara. The lean man with the long locks- Jacquet- and two more of Tybalt's lackeys stood watch over her, but they kept their distance.

Something shifted against the small of Lara's back. It was Bannertail. The men didn't seem to notice.

"There are fresh clothes if you'd like to change," Reynard said to her. "I can arrange for some privacy."

"I don't want anything of yours," she said. "Ever."

"An easy thing to say," Reynard said, "Before you know what I'm offering."

"I can only imagine," Lara said, rubbing absently at the scar on her wrist.

"Hm," Reynard hummed, and leaned back against the tree to watch Tybalt and his men work.

Both wagon and horses were ready by the time Tybalt's men had dug up the box. They had buried it at a fair distance from their own little camp, and Lara couldn't help but notice how nervous the men seemed as they brought the thing up out of the mud.

Which was odd. It was only a box.

"There," Tybalt panted as he and his men stepped away from the thing. "All yours."

"How do I know it's real?" Arsinoe asked as she walked up to the thing. It was no bigger than a packsack and made entirely of metal.

"Would you like to open it?" Reynard asked, tossing something to her. A key, perhaps. "It wasn't easy to collect."

"No, no," Arsinoe said, palming the object. "Your men's faces speak loud enough. Only-"

"Yes?"

Arsinoe snorted. "Well. I can't carry it all the way to the *Carsi*, can I? I'll need a mule, at least. Or a strong horse."

"Take Tybalt's," Reynard said. "It's bound to be the best. He won't mind, will you Tybalt?"

"No, my lord," Tybalt said, minding.

Two of the men reluctantly helped Arsinoe secure the box to the back of a surprisingly pretty dapple with a blond mane. When they were done, they rejoined the others, sweating.

"What's in there?" Lara asked.

"Freedom," Arsinoe answered, taking the dapple by her reins.

"Yours, maybe," Lara said.

Arsinoe turned and wiped the hair from her eyes.

"I don't know, girl," she said. "You're a lot tougher than you look. Most folk don't make it out of the waste. Or the mountains. Or Ladon."

The beetle flexed its wings.

"For what it's worth," Arsinoe said, "I think you'll be just fine. Even your idiot brother."

"Is that supposed to be an apology?" Lara asked.

"No," Arsinoe said, and clicked her tongue.

The horse made her objections, tossing her head and whickering, but soon the two were crossing the grass-flats, making north.

"Mount up," Reynard said. "Every fanatic The Dragon can spare will be hunting for us by now."

Reynard stood silent as Tybalt's men hustled to comply. The singer and the albino climbed onto the wagon. A few others slung themselves into their saddles, but the bulk of them merely shouldered their gear. Not all the men had mounts, it seemed.

"And me, my lord?" Tybalt said, pointedly. "Or am I supposed to *run* all the way to the sea?"

"Only for a while," Reynard said, taking the reins of his own horse, a rather unremarkable brown courser. "But once the Telchine has put some distance between us, send a few of the men after her. To see her safely on her way."

"Kill her, you mean," Tybalt said.

"Yes," Reynard said. "And have them make certain that anyone who finds her body also finds the key to the box."

"Ah," Tybalt said, sucking at his lips. "I see."

"And now, Majesty," Reynard said to Lara, gesturing to the wagon, "If you would care to join your friends . . . Blanc, help her up, would you?"

The albino threw his black coat over his shoulder, gripped the side of the wagon, and extended his right hand. It was like Reynard's left, a prothesis, but it was far less lifelike, a thing of metal rods and wheels with three claw-like fingers.

"C'mon, girl," the man said, flashing his yellow teeth. "It won't bite."

"She did what you asked," Lara said, turning to Reynard. "Didn't she?"

"She did," Reynard said. "And she was paid what she was due."

"Then why?"

"I have need of another false trail for The Dragon to follow," he said, smoothing his beard. "And you might be surprised by how many whores and mercenaries have secret hearts of gold."

He paused for a moment, tapping his index finger against his lips.

"Not literally, of course," he said. "Or they might pay for themselves. Although, with this one . . ."

His men chuckled. Even Tybalt.

"Don't kill her," Lara said. "Please."

Reynard stared at her. So did Pinsard, she noticed, though he could not speak.

"You beg?" Reynard asked, unamused. "For her?"

Lara looked at Pinsard, and saw only confusion in his face, an unspoken question mixed with his naked rage.

"I do," she said.

"Even though she betrayed you?"

"Yes," Lara said.

One of the white cranes rose silently out of the marsh, gliding over the reeds.

"How like your mother you are," Reynard mused. "And your father too, I think. So. *Lara*. Shall we bargain?"

Pinsard shouted something into his gag, his head shaking back and forth. Reynard shot Blanc a look. The man nodded, and began to turn about, the claw he had for a right hand clacking.

"No, don't hurt him!" Lara said, all in rush. "I'll do it! I'll bargain."

"Very well," Reynard said, calling off Blanc with a gesture. "Let us say that I *did* spare her. What would you give to me in return?"

Lara's mind raced. What could she offer him that he did not already have? He had already stolen her kingdom, and now he had stolen her as well . . . What else could he possibly want? To hear her plead and beg? To steal her dignity from her? But, no, he'd already taken that. At least a shred of it. And once he had her in Carduel he could pick at her at his leisure, like The Dragon had.

That was it. She was certain of it. It wasn't her body that he wanted. It was her. Herself. Her heart and spirit, to break and reshape. And he was already doing it. Even now he was worming his way into her mind with this game. What would she surrender? How much?

"Well?" he said.

When would it end? How much could she endure in the haunted city? And how much of her would be left when he was done? The fate she would have suffered at The Dragon's hands was far more merciful. To die and be replaced by a fetch was one thing. But to one day stare into a mirror and not recognize oneself . . .

And then, all at once, the answer came to her. It was so simple. And she had almost forgotten.

"I know something," she said.

"Oh?" he said, unfazed. "And what could you tell me, Lara, that I do not already know?"

"I saw something in The Dragon's palace," she said. "A secret. And if I don't share it with you, The Dragon will find me. Find you. And she'll kill us both."

Now it was Reynard who was silent. Out of the corner of her eyes, Lara could see his men shooting each other nervous glances.

"Go on then," Reynard finally said.

"First," Lara said, "You will swear to me that you'll let Arsinoe live."

Reynard hesitated, the fingers of his false hand flickering.

"Swear it," Lara said, straightening up. "Or we both die in Glycon."

"Very well," Reynard said. "The mercenary lives. On that you have my word of honor."

"Hah," Lara spat.

"Shall I swear by my mother's name?" Reynard asked, his voice flat and cold. "Or would you have me seal my promise with a kiss?"

"No," Lara said. "Your word will do."

"Then we have a bargain," Reynard said. "Now, this secret of The Dragon's that you keep. What is it?"

"She has the mirror," Lara answered. "The Mirror of Truth, that Vasilisa the Beautiful carried into the sea."

There was silence. Then the men began to laugh.

But not Reynard.

He put up his hand, and the laughter died.

"You saw it?" he asked, looming close.

"I saw the river in it," Lara said, taking a step backwards. "And a ship, and men, and the night turn back to day. She was using it to hunt for you. But you were already in the palace. She didn't know where to look."

"My lord," Tybalt said, stepping forward. "This is horseshit! The girl's bluffing-"

Reynard turned his head, ever so slightly, and Tybalt stilled his tongue.

"Where?" Reynard asked.

"In the palace," Lara answered.

"Where in the palace?"

"I don't remember," Lara lied.

Reynard smiled at her thinly.

"Jacquet," he said. "Take my horse. It seems you will have to be me for a while."

"Palleon would do it better," the man said, before adding, "My lord."

"Palleon is not here. Is he?"

"No, my lord."

Reynard handed him the courser's reins and proceeded to rummage amongst the horse's saddlebags.

"Just to make certain that I completely understand the situation," Tybalt said, "You're going back to The Dragon's palace, for . . . What? A magic mirror? One you didn't even know existed until a few moments ago?"

"That's correct."

"What are you going to do, break it?"

"No," Reynard said. "I'm going to steal it."

"Of course," Tybalt said.

"Do you question my logic, Tybalt?" Reynard asked. "Or is it my skill that you suddenly find lacking?"

The question had sounded casual, but Tybalt seemed to shrink beneath Reynard's gaze.

"No, my lord," he said. "I am, and I shall remain, your humble servant."

"But for how long, I wonder?" Reynard mused. "How about it, Tybalt? You have the girl, a decent head start, and at least a thousand mercenaries that I know about who trust your coin. Who knows? I might even die here. You could make a decent go of it, don't you think?"

Tybalt licked his lips.

"What if you do die?" he asked. "What then?"

"If I were you," Reynard answered, "I would run. Before Rukenaw or Tiecelin decide that you had a hand in it."

The muscles in Tybalt's neck worked as he swallowed his next retort.

"Get them to the coast, Tybalt" Reynard said, slinging both pack and sword over his shoulder. There was a polished ruby set into the sword's hilt. It reminded Lara of something, but she couldn't remember what. "And get them there in one piece, or I'll know the reason why."

"The cart, Highness," Tybalt said, turning to Lara. "Get in. Don't make me ask twice."

Once again, the albino offered her his mechanical arm. This time Lara took it, choking at the scent of the man's breath as he pulled her into the wagon. He was clearly no stranger to onions and garlic.

She met Pinsard's gaze as she settled across from him. The anger in his eyes was all but gone, and he couldn't seem to meet her gaze for long before turning away.

He was ashamed, she realized.

She gave his boot a kick.

We'll be alright, she mouthed. *Just don't do anything stupid.*

He nodded and scratched absently at the poultice.

Then Tybalt climbed in after her, slamming shut the tailboard and pounding it a few times for good measure.

"Git!" Corsablis grunted, giving the reins a shake.

The team began to move.

"It's a pity we must part so soon," Reynard said. "It's a long voyage to Carduel, and we still have so much to discuss."

"Don't you have somewhere to piss off to?" she asked, flashing him the fingers.

"And here I thought you'd have a hard time making conversation with Blanc," he sighed. "Perhaps he'll tell you how he lost his arm."

The albino chuckled darkly. Then the wagon shuddered as the team began to pick up speed.

"Farewell, Lara," Reynard called after them. "'Til we meet again."

She watched as he straightened, glanced at the sky, and began to walk back the way they'd come. Perhaps he meant to take one of the boats. Perhaps not. He slipped down an embankment and then he was gone, lost amongst the grass.

* * * * * * *

When it was clear that Reynard was truly gone, Tybalt stood up in the back of the cart and beckoned to the men riding behind them.

"Murgleis," he said when the lead rider was within earshot. "Take two more men and go after her."

"Go after who?" the man asked, spitting something foul into the grass.

"My horse," Tybalt said. "Who else?"

"And the sellsword?"

"Kill her. And leave the box for the lizard-lovers to find, just like the Lord Protector wanted."

"No!" Lara choked. "He gave me his word-"

"One more peep from you," Tybalt said, "And I'll have Blanc here start breaking the wolf pup's fingers, starting with the thumbs. Got it?"

Lara nodded, biting back her rage.

"Good. Now, what are you waiting for?" Tybalt asked Murgleis. "Kill the bitch. Or do I have to tell you again?"

"But, he- I mean, Lord Reynard said-"

"Do I look like Lord Reynard to you?" Tybalt asked, leaning over the side of the cart. "Or do I look like the man who's going to put a knife right through both of your eyes if you don't get his horse back?"

"I, uh-" Murgleis' mouth flapped a bit. "Chief, I don't-"

"I want my bloody horse back, Murgleis. Now get going, or I'll find someone else who will!"

"Right," Murgleis grunted, turning his horse. "Vaurien, you and Cafard follow me!"

The three riders broke from the column and galloped back the way they came.

"Were that wise, chief?" Blanc asked. He'd thrown the black coat over his head, and he was sweating in the heat.

"Why?" Tybalt asked, slumping into the back of the wagon. "You going to blab?"

"Naw," Blanc said. "But she might."

He shot a glance at Lara.

"Oh yeah?" Tybalt said. "You going to rat me out, girl? Or would you prefer I call you Larissa?"

Lara thought of Pinsard's thumbs, and kept her mouth shut.

"You're a quick learner," Tybalt said, and stretched out his legs so that his heels rested on the sack lying beside her. "That's good. You'll need to be quick if you're going to be the Queen of Arcasia."

He yawned, hugely.

"You can speak now, if you like."

"You call them back," Lara hissed through her teeth. "Do it, now, or when we get to Carduel I'll have Reynard grind you into mincemeat."

"Go ahead and try it," Tybalt chuckled. "He loved your mother, girl, and he killed her. You think he'll care about some mercenary, face down in a swamp?"

He settled back and began to clean his fingernails with a sharp-looking knife.

"Besides," he said, seemingly unconcerned by the sway of the cart, "He needs me, girl. Maybe more than he needs you. So, try it. You may be his puppet Queen, but me? I'm the Prince of Cats. And I always land on my feet."

He stopped to examine his thumbnail and yawned.

"Blanc," he said, putting away his knife, "Wake me if there's trouble."

* * * * * * *

"So," Blanc said. "You want to hear how I lost my arm?"

"No," Lara said.

She stole a look at one of the knives that Tybalt had sheathed in his bandolier. He was sleeping so close that she could reach out, snatch it, and drive it into his heart before-

Tybalt's hand reached up to pat at the blade.

"Something I can help you with, Your Highness?" he asked, cracking her a sideways glance.

"No," she said.

"That's good," he said, and went back to his nap.

She raised a hand against the glare and pretended to watch the horizon, waiting for . . . What? Tybalt to fall asleep? Moder to wake up, and break out of her bonds? The Dragon's soldiers to catch up to them? Of these, only the last seemed even remotely likely, and it was far from preferable.

After a while she stopped pretending and let her gaze wander over the shimmer.

Not that there was much to see. The drylands beyond the delta were hot, dusty, and- of course- dry. Even 'trail' was far too generous a word for the meandering stretch of packed dirt they were following, its course dotted here and there with needle grass. Still, there was life: Long-eared hares hid in the grass, and snakes too, diamond-backs with rattles at the end of their tails. Tybalt's men made a sport of shooting at them.

Corsablis seemed to be the best shot. A short, recurved bow lay across his lap, and when he saw a hare running through the brush he'd set down the reins, pluck an arrow from a quiver tucked into the catchall, and let it fly. Some managed to zig or zag out of harm's way, often cheating the Watcher by less than a hair's breadth, but most of them ended up tumbling into the dust with an arrow through their middle.

He had one of the men jogging behind them fetch him a particularly fat specimen, and sang as he skinned it:

"Petals will not do for I

How will I snare my lover's sigh?

Not with rags or maiden's-dew

And cinders on my cheek

But silks and lace about my waist

And jewels like stars to light my face

How else should I win his sweet embrace?"

When the last of its fur came free, he tossed the hare's bloody corpse into the dust.

Lara tugged her packsack closer to her side. The swell of the fox-squirrel's breaths against her hip managed to be both reassuring and nerve-racking.

Don't wake up, she urged, silent.

"Come on," Blanc said, planting the palm of his false hand on the barrel next to him. "My arm. Ain't you the least bit curious?"

"I said I wasn't," Lara said.

"Not asking *you*, m'lady," the albino said, tossing her a rough nod. She guessed it to be the extent of the man's courtesy. "I'm talking to the whelp here."

He gave Pinsard a shove with his boot.

Pinsard didn't react. He kept very still, his gaze locked on the bed of the wagon.

"How about it, whelp?" Blanc leered. "It's not a long story, but it's a good one. Won't bore you, I'll bet."

"Why don't you leave him alone?" Lara asked.

Blanc's grin soured. His jaw worked, but he kept his mouth shut.

"Now, now," Tybalt said, brushing a tiny insect away from his face. "We still have a way to go, Highness, and you aren't exactly Queen yet. Or did I somehow manage to sleep through your coronation?"

Lara didn't dignify the question with a reply.

"Right," Tybalt said. "So, by all means, Blanc. Regale them with your wit."

Blanc's lips parted as he smiled his yellow smile.

"Some years back," he said, "There were a Calvo. Right hero he used to be: Tall. Strong. *Proud.* Weren't he proud, Corbie?"

"As a peacock," Corsablis answered.

"And that were the trouble, weren't it? Calvo got so puffed up he forgot 'is place. Forgot who 'e was. Where 'e came from. Got so as he bit the hand that fed him. Same hand as took him and his bitch in, same hand what kept 'em safe though his brothers and sisters were burning up all the countryside, putting babes in the ground 'wif their own mums."

"Leave off, Blanc," Corsablis said, giving the reins a shake. "You never had a mum."

"Ah, piss off," Blanc shot back. "Everybody's got a mum. Ain't that right, whelp?"

Blanc gave Moder a vile look. She was still out cold, her head resting against Pinsard's left shoulder.

"Think a man would be content," Blanc said, clawed thumb grinding against metal palm as his eyes wandered. "Satisfied, right? A pair a legs like hers? And that sweet Calvo hair. Phew! Fancy must be awfully fancy, eh?"

Pinsard jerked his head towards the man, the rawhide binding his wrists together straining as he turned.

"There it is!" Blanc chuckled. "There's that look, alright. That Calvo pride. Just like 'is old man, yeah?"

"Yeah," Corsablis said. "Only smaller."

"He's tall enough," Blanc said bitterly, and he turned to Lara, his grin widening. "And getting bigger by the day, I bet. Bigger the dog the worse the bite, ain't that right? And when this one is big enough, well . . . I'd watch my hands, m'lady. I'd watch my hands. Watch 'em while I still had the two to scratch my ass with."

He reached forward and snapped his claws at her, less than a handsbreadth away from her face.

"Is that supposed to scare me?" Lara asked, blandly. "You do know we've been to Vulp Vora, right?"

Blanc's grin vanished again. His clawed hand clacked shut as he seemed to search for a retort.

"I'm thirsty," she said before he could find one. "Is there any water?"

"There's water," Corsablis answered, not turning his eyes from the trail as he passed a bottle gourd over his shoulder.

Blanc took a swig from the gourd, and held it out to Lara, water dripping down his chin.

"Them first," Lara said, nodding to Pinsard and Moder. "They've been in the sun all morning."

"What? You giving me orders now?" Blanc asked, blinking.

"Do what she says," Tybalt said, using the sideboard for leverage as he got to his feet. "We don't want Reynard to, how did she put it? Mince us?"

"Grinding you, chief," Corsablis said. "Into mincemeat."

"That was it," Tybalt said, stretching. "My, what a kind and merciful Queen you'll make, Your Highness. Even so, why don't I do the honors? I have a steadier pair of hands than Blanc does, at any rate."

Tybalt took the gourd from Blanc, his attention drawn to something up ahead. Absently, he began to wet a bit of cloth.

"Better slow up a bit, Corbie," Tybalt said. "And tell the boys to keep their eyes peeled."

Corsablis put his fingers to his lips and whistled. The men riding on their flanks shifted in their saddles, perking up.

Lara lifted herself into a low squat and followed Tybalt's gaze. The land was green a half a league or so ahead of them, low trees and shrub growing on either side of a deep, rocky cut. Beyond it she could see nothing but a deep blue expanse.

"River?" Lara asked.

"The sea," Tybalt corrected, sucking at his teeth. "Can't you smell it?"

She took in a deep breath. He was right, she could smell it: A strange salt tang, almost foul, but earthy, like soil after a storm.

"There's a boat waiting just below those cliffs," Tybalt went on. "But that ravine's a perfect place for an ambush. And Murgleis' running late."

"Maybe he cut ahead?" Corsablis offered.

"You give him too much credit," Tybalt drawled. "Tch. Knew I should have sent Jacquet with 'em."

"You want us to wait?"

Tybalt shook his head.

"Maiden's a good filly. But not that good. Just take 'er easy, Corbie. I wouldn't want to spill."

Tybalt's face screwed up with concentration as he knelt beside Moder, putting the damp cloth to her lips and dabbing at them until her lips puckered.

"There's a thirsty girl," he said, squeezing a bit of water into her gasping mouth. "Alright. You're next, boy."

He shot Pinsard a sour grin and sidled over. Lara's eyes flicked towards the short sword dangling from his belt.

"Blanc," Tybalt said, "Keep an eye on Her Highness while my back is turned. She's been sneaking glances at my knives all morning."

"Yeah, yeah," Blanc grumbled. "Only I weren't finished. 'Wif me story."

"The Pincher's dear dead papa cut your arm off," Tybalt said, loosening Pinsard's gag. "But wouldn't you know it? You lived to tell the tale. Happy?"

"My father was a great-" Pinsard began to say, but Tybalt forced the gourd into his mouth.

"Yeah, yeah," he said, tilting the bottle. "Drink up, you little snot."

Pinsard choked a bit, but he managed a few mouthfuls. When he was done, Tybalt shoved the damp cloth into his mouth.

"Suck on that a while," he said, turning about. "Now how about it, Majesty? Still thirsty?"

He tossed the gourd. She caught it.

"You used to frighten me, you know," she said, freeing the stopper.

"Used to?" Tybalt shot her a bemused look. "I don't frighten you now?"

She took a quick draw, ignoring the taste of garlic clinging to the gourd's mouth.

"I had nightmares," she went on. "Monsters outside the door. A room red with blood. I was more afraid of you than I was of demons, or ghosts, or dragons."

She snorted.

"'The Prince of Cats?' Why, you're nothing but a pack of mangy dogs that Reynard's trained to fetch and carry."

She tossed him the gourd. He caught it.

"And what does that make you then?" Tybalt asked. "Not a lioness, surely-"

"Whoa!" Corsablis cried out.

The horses neighed, stopping up short. The wagon skidded to a halt, bouncing as one of the wheels rolled over a rut. For a brief moment Tybalt lost his footing, staggering until he was able to catch hold of the sideboard.

"Wulf!" Tybalt spat, dousing her with his spittle. "I said take 'er easy! Not stop!"

"Sorry, chief," Corsablis replied, "But something's up."

Tybalt straightened, turning his attention back to the rocky cut between the cliffs. They were close now. Lara too found herself scanning the grasses along the ridge. But there was nothing to see, no archers or zealots . . . Just a cloud of dust, rising from the mouth of the cut.

"There," Corsablis said, pointing.

"I see him," Tybalt said, leaning forward.

Lara could see him too. It was Jacquet, all in red atop Reynard's brown courser, his horse kicking up a cloud of dust as they tore out of the ravine.

"Wha-" Lara started to say, when something pinched against her thigh. It felt like a horsefly bite. She stifled a yelp and swatted at her leg.

Jacquet's steed swerved, making a hard right. Then both horse and rider were galloping along the edge of the cliff.

"Where's that bloody twist going?" Tybalt snarled.

"Dunno," Corsablis said, scratching the back of his head. "But he's slowing down."

The horse's pace slackened to a canter. Then Jacquet slipped from his saddle and fell into the underbrush.

"Cushion up!" Tybalt spat. "Now!"

Corsablis whistled. The men on foot began to hustle towards the wagon, unshouldering their crossbows. The pair of outriders on their flanks began to circle back . . .

Again, something stung Lara's leg.

She tore her gaze away from the ridge and raised her hand to strike at . . . Nothing. There was nothing. Just the dusty pair of prints where she'd smacked her leg. And something that looked like a scratch.

She put her hand to the red lines.

Then Bannertail's paw shot out of a fresh tear in her pack and worried the back of her palm.

"Ow!" she cried through gritted teeth, and then, without thinking, she picked up the pack and put it in her lap.

"Here," Blanc growled, squinting at Lara. "What's that?"

"What's what?" Tybalt spat, drawing one of his knives. "Where?!"

"Her bag," Blanc said. "It moved. Least I thought it did."

Tybalt turned slowly and shot the man a look that would have curdled milk.

"Her bag?" Tybalt breathed.

"You told me to watch 'er!"

"I told you-"

"Chief," Corsablis said, nervous.

"-to watch her. Not her bag. Not her pretty tits-"

"Chief," Corsablis repeated, louder.

"Watch *her*. So she don't stab me in the-"

"Chief!"

"WHAT?!" Tybalt barked.

"It's Maiden, Chief."

Tybalt turned. Lara turned. They all turned.

The ocean wind had picked up, coarse and cool. Swirling clouds of grit danced and spun across the mouth of the rocky belt between them and the sea. Out of the dust a figure rode: A rider atop a fine gray dapple.

It was a woman, her piecemeal armor wrapped in swathes of Glyconese green. She was carrying a broad-headed spear in her gauntleted right hand.

Arsinoe.

"I'll deal with you later!" Tybalt said to Blanc and vaulted over the side of the wagon.

Arsinoe trotted towards them, bringing the dapple to a halt at about a hundred yards.

The men raised their crossbows. Corsablis plucked an arrow from the catchall.

"Hold your fire!" Tybalt called out.

He's worried they'll hurt his horse.

"Don't suppose you've come to return Maiden to me?" Tybalt said as he walked past his men.

"No," Arsinoe said.

"Why then?" he asked.

"I like to keep my promises."

She dismounted. He stretched out his arms and rubbed his fingers against his thumbs.

"My men," he said. "Dead?"

She nodded.

"Which one squealed?"

"One of them," she replied.

"Murgleis was one of my best," Tybalt said. "You must be pretty good with that spear."

"I am," Arsinoe said, advancing. "But I had some help."

"Help?" Tybalt sneered. "From who?"

"A friend."

She began to jog.

Tybalt's arms crossed and uncrossed. Something flashed in the sun. Arsinoe weaved with her spear. Metal clashed against metal, and a pair of blades went spinning into the dirt.

"Not bad," Tybalt drawled, and drew his sword.

Arsinoe waded forward, the spearhead lashing out like the head of a snake. Tybalt seemed almost to dance around the strikes, and then lunged forward to drive his blade straight into her gut . . . But she was already leaping backwards, her body bending like a reed as she sent the spear windmilling towards his head.

He seemed to collide with her before the blow could land. For a moment he had hold of her spear, and steel rang as his blade flashed and cut. Then he hooked her right leg under his left, and they struggled against each other until they flew apart, his arm hooking and thrusting until the flick of her spear forced him back.

"You can dance too," Tybalt panted as he gained some ground. "But for how long?"

"*Siktir!*" Arsinoe spat at him, her spearhead skating across the sand as she went for his legs.

"Yeah, yeah," Tybalt grunted, sidestepping the strike as he freed another dagger from his bandolier.

Bannertail squirmed under Lara's palms, his claws pricking her legs. She loosened her grip on him and began to rise.

We can't just sit here and watch!

And, sure enough, all of Tybalt's men were doing just that. All but Blanc. He had drawn a blade- Moder's- and had balanced the tip of it against Pinsard's chest.

"Don't even *think* about it," he said, shaking his head.

Lara shot Pinsard a glance, her eyes flicking towards the bag. His brows narrowed with confusion, but he nodded all the same.

"What's that, now?"

"Nothing," Lara answered, her voice little more than a whisper as her fingers moved with deliberate care towards the straps of the packsack.

"Give that 'ere!" Blanc snapped, his clawed hand shooting out to snatch the pack away from her.

Blanc stared at the pack and gave it a shake.

"What's this then? Some weapon? I know it ain't the gem of Zosia, cause that's in-"

Blanc couldn't feel the sting of Bannertail's fangs as he shot out of the hole he'd been gnawing and latched onto his metal wrist, but the shock of it was enough to distract him. He was still gaping when Lara barreled straight into the albino, knocking him backwards as she took hold of his left wrist and began to twist.

"Ahhh-ahh!" Blanc shrieked, his grip on Moder's sword loosening. He let go of the pack and tried to swing his false arm around, the claws snapping at her hair.

"Blanc!" Corsablis shouted, turning about. But before he could trade his bow for blade, Pinsard was on him, the rawhide that bound his wrists together digging into the man's neck.

"Bitch!" Blanc was shouting at her. "You bitch!"

They stumbled and twisted. He was at least twice her size. She applied more pressure, bending his wrist back, back, back . . .

The albino let go of the sword, growling and spitting as he finally caught her hair in his claws. He yanked, once, so hard that she felt her scalp giving, but then Bannertail was on his face, the chimera's sharp teeth sinking into the man's cheek as its claws dug at his eyes.

Blanc released her and grabbed at Bannertail, catching him in his metal claws and tearing him from his bloodied face.

"Got you, you little- hrhk!"

Blanc stared at the blade in his breast. The blade had punched right through his black padded jack.

Lara gave him a kick as she slid Harrower free. Bannertail leapt onto her shoulder.

She whirled about. There were half a dozen crossbows aimed in her direction. Pinsard still had Corsablis by the neck, but both he and the wiry-haired man were frozen in mid-struggle.

"Let 'im go!" one of outriders- the one with the crooked nose-growled at Pinsard. "Now!"

Lara spared a moment to glance at the fight raging amidst the dust. Arsinoe was pushing Tybalt back, forcing him towards the ridge, but only just. There was blood running down her left arm, while Tybalt looked barely winded. Even his parries looked effortless, almost casual.

Then he lunged straight into one of Arsinoe's thrusts, driving his sword straight towards her breast. She managed a block, and rowed the shaft of her spear as she gave ground. When Tybalt drove at her again, she put her back to the cliffs and let him do the pushing. He didn't need much encouragement.

She's not stalling. She's leading him away from us! But, why?
Because she's not alone? Because she has-

"A friend," Lara said.

"Do it!" the crooked-nosed man urged again. "Or by Wulf, we'll shoot you both!"

Corsablis did his best to object, but all he could manage was a gasping choke as Pinsard tightened his grip.

"Let him go, Pinsard!" Lara ordered.

Pinsard shot her a look. *Why?* it said, and *No!*

"Let him go!" she commanded.

Reluctantly, Pinsard loosened his grip. Tybalt's men didn't lower their bows.

"My voice," Corsablis rasped, throwing Pinsard off him as he leapt from the cart. "My bloody voice!"

"Shut it, Corbie," the crooked-nosed man said. "I'm second now that Blanc's-"

He gave Blanc's black and white form a nod.

"Now, why don't Her Majesty drop that sword?" the man went on. "Least until the chief is done dancing with Princess Elissa."

"I don't think so," Lara said, fully aware of the men creeping up on the wagon behind her back.

"Oh?" Corsablis wheezed, ignoring the glare of the crooked-nosed man as he rubbed at his throat. "And why not?"

"Because I know something you don't."

"And that is?"

"DRAMSIND!" Lara shouted, as loudly as she was able. *"MOTOTO! MOTOTO!!!"*

Tybalt's men all looked at her like she'd lost her wits. She supposed it would look that way if it turned out that she was wrong.

"What's that?" Corsablis coughed. "Calvo for-"

To Tybalt's men, it must have looked as though one of the ridges was starting to collapse, rocky soil exploding from the right side of the ravine until there was so much dust in the air that Dramsind himself resembled a great metal horse. And indeed, he was galloping towards them on all fours, the wail of his rage bouncing off the gully walls like the cry of some terrible chimera.

"What is it?" one of Tybalt's men quailed.

"I don't care!" the crooked-nosed man shouted back. "Shoot it!"

Lara cut Pinsard's bonds as they opened fire, their quarrels spinning and splintering as they glanced off Dramsind's metal hide.

He came on, gaining speed.

The outriders' steeds panicked, one rearing as it threw the crooked-nosed man into the dust. Lara saw Corsablis running after the other rider, his warg mask bouncing off his thigh as he screamed for him to slow down and wait, wait, wait.

The rider did not slow. But Dramsind did, smacking one of the men out of his way as he rumbled forward. The man didn't even scream as he went flying headfirst into the dust with an audible *snap*.

"The joints!" the crooked-nosed man was shouting, trying to gain his feet. "Go for 'is joints!"

Pinsard tore the wet cloth from his mouth and searched for his sword amongst the blades stowed behind the driver's seat.

Dramsind slammed another of Tybalt's men into the hard-packed dirt. A particularly brave or stupid fellow drove a short-handled spear straight through the tendons of Dramsind's right knee.

The giant staggered for a moment, but his sinews were made of the same stuff as his body, and when he straightened both blade and shaft shattered.

The man backpeddled, turned, and started to run. But it was far too late. Dramsind's fist struck his head like a boulder falling from a great height.

The wagon shook as the team snorted and stamped.

"Get out!" Lara shouted to Pinsard, kicking open the back gate. "Before they all bolt!"

"Take it!" he shouted, shoving his sword into her off hand as he bent to pick up Moder.

She was stowing the sword under her arm when a rough hand grabbed at the hem of her dress and tugged. She whirled around, already swinging at a man who had half-climbed onto the wagon. Harrower glanced off his mail, but the strike threw him from the cart.

The wagon team bolted.

She jumped.

She landed on her feet and staggered forward. Bannertail leapt from her back, disappearing amongst the dust.

There was dust everywhere now, so thick she could barely see through it. Somewhere close a man was shrieking in terror. The pounding of Dramsind's limbs against the earth sounded like the priest in Perun, beating on his drum.

She couldn't see Pinsard. She couldn't see Moder.

"The joints!" the crooked-nosed man cried out one last time, and then there was a terrible 'crunch,' and he was silent.

She choked on the dust. She could hear the wagon, rattling and rumbling, and the steady tread of Dramsind. His dark bulk loomed out of the dust, vapor steaming from his joints as he stared down at her balefully, his red gaze piercing even the thickness of the dust as it played across her face.

She dropped her sword.

"Dramsind," she said, calm but firm. *"Kutuju."*

His arm extended as it wound back, the fist curling.

"Dramsind!" she said, louder. *"Kutuju!* Do you hear me? *Kutuju!"*

He froze. The swarm inside of him beginning to dull.

"Motaju? Tifeke?" he asked, his voice suddenly seeming to be two voices. They were clearly at odds with each other. *"Motaju?"*

"Kutuju," she said, again, as clearly as she was able. *"Motaju Kutuju."*

"Kutuju," he said, his voice one again.

The red glare dimmed as he lowered his arm. The swarm in his breast grew silent. He was absolutely filthy, dust-coated and mud-speckled, with bits of foliage stuck under his breastplate. It would take some time to free the worst of it, she thought.

But there was no time for that now.

"Pinsard!" she called out, choking on the kicked-up dust as she bent to retrieve their swords. "Pinsard!"

"Lara?" Pinsard's voice replied. "Where are you?"

"I'm here!" she shouted.

The wind picked up and, and then she saw him, kneeling in the dust beside Moder.

"Is she-"

"Still asleep," Pinsard said, panting. "I can't- I cannot carry her any farther. She's too heavy!"

"We'll do it together," she said, thrusting his sword at him. "Later! How's your hand?"

"Hurts," he said, wincing. "But I can use it."

"Good," she said, breaking into a sprint. "Now, come on!"

"Where are we going?"

"To save Arsinoe!" she answered, "And kill Tybalt!"

* * * * * * *

The Telchine was good.

He couldn't deny that. And she was quick. As quick as he'd been when he was younger. Quicker even. Quick and brutal. A single misstep and it would all be over.

It was a pity she was tiring. He hadn't had so much fun in years.

"Pity," he breathed, aiming a cut at her head.

She weaved to the left, glid under the cut, and drove the point of her spear up towards his throat. The block was far too easy, a simple shove with his dagger against the haft. Then she presented him an easy target: Her pretty, gleaming neck, glistening with sweat.

A trap.

He took the bait anyway, slashing at her collarbone. Sure enough, she brought the spear up in time. His sword bit into the haft with a crack.

She sprung the trap. Her feet slid on the looser soil of the ridge as she drove the butt of her spear straight towards his crotch.

Good choice! But too slow.

First, an easy parry. Then a quick cut across her leg with the reverse. It was just a scratch, really, but she wasn't expecting it. She beat the blade away and gained some ground as he spun around her flank for a kidney strike.

She grabbed his wrist before he sank home the knife- so quick!- and tried to throw him. But her footing betrayed her. Part of the dune they stood on collapsed and she stumbled backwards, releasing him.

Now!

He came at her, hard and fast, favoring the sword, trying to force her back, towards the edge of the cliff. She rowed her spear as she backpeddled, slipping and stumbling as the ground grew rockier.

Finally, she tripped, the butt end of her spear catching on the ground as her heels gave out beneath her.

"Hah!" he cried, lunging.

He saw her feet find purchase as she coiled. The spearhead flew towards his face. All her floundering had been nothing but a ruse.

Too late, he leaned away from the strike.

It wasn't enough. The curved edge of her spear carved open his cheek as it shot past his head. There was no pain, not yet, but he had felt the shock of it against his skull.

The cut had been deep, right down to the bone. An inch or two to the left, and the blow would have killed him.

Would have. If she hadn't missed.

He let his dagger fall from his hand as he caught hold of the haft. He brought his sword crashing down on it. All his strength was behind the swing.

The spear splintered in two. He tossed away the business end, beat aside the remains of the haft, and kicked her in the thigh, just below the new cut.

When she fell this time, it was for real. She tried to roll with the fall, but the rocks made it difficult. She panted, her body coated with sweat, dust, and blood.

"I used to think that Telchines bled green," he said, spitting his own blood from his lips as he knelt to retrieve his dagger. "Turns out that's just a children's story."

She crawled a bit further, towards the edge of the cliff. He padded after her casually, vaguely aware that *something* had gone amiss behind him. The Princess and the Pup had tried to escape, no doubt. But they were just children, against a dozen of his best.

Nothing he couldn't sort out.

"No escape that way," he said, kicking a bit of dirt at her. The pain of his cheek was coming on. He wished Murgleis hadn't taken Cafard with him. He could knit up a wound almost as good as a priestess. "Come on, I'll make it quick."

She spun onto her back as her arm shot out. The rock struck him just above the bridge of his nose. It wasn't enough to break it.

But it hurt.

"Slow then," he said, wiping the blood from his mouth with the back of his hand. "No rush. We have all the time in the-"

His ears were ringing, his head pounded, but he heard the scrape of boot on stone, the skip of rock. He turned just as the Pup came at him, gripping his sword with both hands.

The boy swung for his head, almost as fast as his father had been. Tybalt only just managed to deflect the blow, and when he riposted, the boy leaned away from the strike, nimble for all his size.

"Wulf!" Tybalt swore, finding himself giving ground as the boy pressed forward, his long blade slashing and whirling as he switched his grip.

Fancy moves. Proper. The kind his mother must have taught him. And with both hands, even the one he'd put one of his knives through.

Well, this time he'd maim him. Maim him for good.

Reynard could hardly complain about that.

Tybalt caught the boy's blade with his dagger, began to glissade his own sword down its length-

A shadow on his right, the flash of steel. The girl! He shoved the boy's blade away and nearly spun into her thrust. He slammed it aside, slicing his knuckles on the edge of her blade.

"Ah!" he cried, thrusting with the hilt of his dagger, aiming for the girl's head.

The blow fell short. A killing blow would have landed, of course, would have punched right into the nape of her neck-

Something flashed on his left. The boy again! He brought his sword up just in time. The girl tried to bull straight into him, but he rolled around her, driving his elbow into her as he danced away.

Should have killed her. Easy blow to the kidney.

But orders were orders. Reynard wanted her alive.

"So," he panted, "You two really think you can take me?"

"We three," the Telchine said, shakily. She had the pointy end of her spear back in her hands.

"We three," Lara repeated. "Together."

"Right," the boy said, already moving to flank him.

"Left," the Telchine said, sidestepping one of the larger rocks.

"Now!" the girl shouted.

They came on.

The Telchine was exhausted. The girl was only half-trained. The boy couldn't use his right hand properly. But Tybalt only had two hands. And they were young. They didn't have forty summers dragging them down.

He couldn't fight them all. Not without killing them.

He parried. He riposted. He fought dirty, kicking dust up into the boy's eyes, aiming blow after blow at the Telchine's bad leg.

It wasn't enough.

They pushed him to the edge of the cliff, the boy's sword slashing open his sword arm just above the elbow. He needed ground, but there was none. There was nothing behind him but the cliff and the sea. The waves pounded against the rocks. He had nowhere left to go.

Nowhere but down.

There was blood in his mouth. The left side of his face felt like it was on fire.

To the Watcher with Reynard.

He hucked his knife at the boy, smashed the Telchine's spearhead aside, and lunged at the girl, snarling.

He could see the fear in her eyes. She hadn't expected it. Thought she was safe, thought he wouldn't dare. She thrusted at him- an easy parry. He reversed his grip. A quick slash to her throat and it would all be over.

He took her blade in the gut, just below his breastplate. Her first thrust had only been a feint.

Mother had trained her well, the bitch.

He took a step backwards as he dropped his sword. He could hear it clattering against the cliffside as she slid her own blade free.

She leveled her sword at the base of his neck.

"I just wanted my horse back," he said.

"And you killed my brother," she said.

"I did," he said. "Brave lad, him. Didn't suffer. 'Less you count the fear."

He looked down the length of the blade and glanced at the sea.

"But then," he shrugged, "Who isn't afraid to die?"

She had the grace to let him jump.

* * * * * * *

"Do you think he landed on his feet?" Lara asked as she peered at the rocks below. It was such a long fall that she couldn't see his body amongst the waves.

"I doubt it," Arsinoe said.

When Pinsard offered her his shoulder, she took it without complaint.

"Why did you come back?" he asked as they made their way back down the ridge. "Revenge?"

"Revenge is a fool's errand, boy," Arsinoe said. "But I told you I'd guide you to the sea."

She gestured with her off hand.

"I swore it by The Ruiner. Remember?"

She forgot her leg for a moment, sucking in her breath as she took a bad step.

"Here," Lara said, taking her other shoulder.

They walked. The dust whirled about them.

"The one-eyed bastard got away, by the way," Arsinoe said. "I managed to wing him, but he rode off before I could finish the job."

"That wasn't him," Lara said. "Just one of his men wearing his clothes."

"Really?" Arsinoe said. The beetle quivered on her cheek. "Volk, it looked just like him."

Lara looked about. The horse that Jacquet had ridden was gone. So were Tybalt's men. At least, the ones who weren't lying dead in the dirt. Dramsind was little more than a statue now, not even swaying with the wind. She doubted he would move until Arsinoe told him otherwise . . . But Tybalt's men didn't know that.

The wagon hadn't gotten far. The horses were pawing at the dust not far from the mouth of the ravine. Tybalt's filly, Maiden, was grazing on the ridge nearby.

"I need to sit," Arsinoe said.

They helped her to the wagon. She practically lay down on the tailboard. Her leg was red right down to the ankle.

"That needs mending," Pinsard grimaced.

"So does that hand," Arsinoe replied. "Where's mother?"

"We'll fetch her," Lara said, "Just lie still."

"You got it," Arsinoe said.

Moder was still dozing in Dramsind's shadow, propped against a rock. Her blond locks made her easy to spot.

They had nearly reached her when they came upon the body of Blanc. He was lying face down in the sand, Bannertail perched on his shoulder. The fox-squirrel's ears were perked, his tail erect.

"I think he's dead," Lara said.

The fox-squirrel lashed his tail and began to lap the blood from his paws.

"This is a Calvarian coat," Pinsard said, kneeling by the body. "My father wore one just like it. Ugh, but it stinks."

"Take it anyway," Lara said. "Your skin is red enough as it is."

Pinsard lifted the coat from the dead man and threw it over his shoulders.

Lara had to admit: It looked right on him, somehow.

"You should not be wearing that," a groggy voice said.

Moder was awake and on her feet.

"It is looking well on you," she said, rubbing at her eyes. "But I am still being your Moder."

EPILOGUE

More than half the men on the boat were from Tyris, not Frisia, so when they saw a woman on horseback and a giant at the mouth of the bay, many thought that one of The Dragon's slave catchers had finally come for them.

A few of them ran for the cliffside, taking their chances against the jagged rocks. Skelmis, who had escaped from a vamvaki field five summers past, dove straight into the sea, fearing to be returned to the lash more than he did the adder-fish lurking in the shallows.

But Daimonax, who was the ship's lookout in spite of his gray hair, could soon tell that these strangers were not Glyconese, and he called for the others to come back.

Eventually, they listened and did as he said. But they did so slowly, for even though the strangers were not the servants of The Dragon, nor were they the men who the one-eyed man had told them to expect.

And they were a strange lot.

The woman on the horse certainly had the look of Tyris: Golden-skinned, with hair as wine-dark as the sea. She was even marked on the face like a slave, but she wore the scaled armor and green robes of a Gargean zealot. If she was a daughter of mercy, she was an odd one.

The giant was clad from head to toe in antique plate, thin-limbed despite his bulk. He had no weapons, no robe or pack, only the dull metal box that he gripped as one might a gunny. But he was still a giant.

Two were pale-skinned, fair-haired Vanir warriors from the North. The woman was hard, tall and lean. The boy was young, but dangerous-looking in his long black coat. They had osprey eyes: Blue and pitiless.

There was a girl with them too, a Luxian by her looks. She was no more than twenty summers old, with tall boots on her feet and a sword tucked into her belt. A creature like an alopex sat on her shoulder, shading itself with its own tail. She hardly looked like a warrior, but she was pretty.

A face like a coin, as they said in Arcasia.

As they neared, Hylas stepped forward to parley. Which was proper; He was their captain.

"Who are you?" he asked the Telchine.

Like the others, he assumed that she was the leader. But it was the girl who answered.

"Travelers," she said, simply, her accent strange.

"What do you want?"

"Your boat," the girl said. "Take us to Frisia."

The men laughed.

"And why should we listen to you?" Hylas asked.

"If you don't," the Telchine said, pointing at them with one half of a broken spear, "I'll have Dramsind here punch through your hull before we send you all to Domdaniel."

The giant stirred at her gesture, his head swiveling towards them oddly as he laid the box in the sand.

The men reached for knife and cutlass. But the girl whispered something to the Telchine, harsh and pointed. The woman rolled her eyes but lowered her arm.

"Please, forgive my friend," the girl said, "She makes a poor jest. We will pay for our passage. If you will take us."

"The one who hired us is paying us to wait for him in this cove."

"You'll be waiting a long time," the girl said. "Besides, we'll double whatever he's paying."

"Double?" the captain scoffed. "How? Even if there's gold in that chest, it won't be enough."

He pointed at the box lying in the sand. Strange how the others seemed to shy away from it.

"Roland of Arcasia," the girl said. "He'll see that you are paid."

"And how is it that you know of Count Roland?"

"He's my cousin," the girl said.

* * * * * * *

By dusk, the sky had turned royal. Pink ribbons played across the dark waters, and the clouds above were streaked with gold. They had long since lost sight of the coast. There was nothing behind them. Nothing ahead. Only the sea.

"What's wrong?" Lara asked Arsinoe. She looked . . . Well, not green, exactly. But pale. Sick. "Is it your leg?"

"No," Arsinoe said, her grip on the ship's side tightening. "But I-I've never been on the ocean before. It scares me."

"Can't you swim?"

"I *can*," Arsinoe said. "But all this water . . ."

Suddenly, she leaned over the gunwale and vomited her supper into the sea. Some of the crew cheered. Others swore. Coins changed hands. They'd been having a wager, it seemed.

"What a waste," Arsinoe said at last, wiping at her mouth.

"You did not have to come," Pinsard said.

"You say the sweetest things," Arsinoe said, spitting into the swell for good measure. "But what else was I going to do? Retire on the coast, start raising drakes for the Drakaina?"

"What about Prahasta?" Lara asked. "Don't you have to pay your debt to him?"

She nodded at Dramsind, who was reclining against the door to the aft cabin, an uneaten bowl of beans lying by his feet. The crew was already in the habit of stepping around him, leaving both him and the box alone.

"Eh, let him wait," Arsinoe shrugged. "I can afford a few enemies. That box is worth a thousand *Carsis*. Maybe more. If I hadn't come back for you, I could have been the Lady of the Singing Sands. For what that's worth."

"It certainly sounds," Lara said, "Romantic?"

"It's not," Arsinoe said. "But don't think I had second thoughts about coming back for you."

"Well," Pinsard said. "Thank you."

"What for?"

"For changing your mind."

"I didn't have to change my mind," Arsinoe said. "I mean, we *are* married."

"Married," Pinsard said, blinking. "Wait, what?"

"You gave me a blade," Arsinoe said. "A stone blade, but a *blade* nonetheless. Where I come from, that's as good as a marriage proposal. And I took it. So, man and wife. Congratulations. Should we break the news to mother?"

She turned to wave at Moder, who was still discussing the merits of Northern knots with one of the ship's mates.

Pinsard grabbed her by the arm, and let go just as quickly, as if he'd touched a hot stove.

"Sorry. But, I-" Pinsard sputtered. "And then, then that-"

"Please, don't have a fit," Arsinoe said. "You didn't know, did you? And besides, I tossed it into the brush. You're not exactly my taste, Pinsard. Got it?"

Pinsard nodded and let out a long sigh.

"What?" Arsinoe snorted. "Don't tell me you're disappointed?"

"No. It's not that."

"What then?"

"You called me by my name," he said, smiling ever so slightly.

"You earned it," she said, and there was no bite to her words. "Rushing in to save me, fierce as Orthus. Pfft. Who knows? Maybe they'll be singing tales about you someday."

"Well," Pinsard said, brushing his hair from his eyes, "I suppose that I *do* have a sort of rugged heroism."

They both stared at him. He sniffed and leaned against the gunwale.

"So, what now?" Arsinoe said. "Was all that nonsense about your cousin for real?"

"It wasn't a lie," Lara said. "I have friends in Frisia. Arlequin said so. So did Reynard."

She took a deep breath.

"I don't think he was lying about that."

"Who's Arlequin?" Arsinoe asked.

"He was my groom."

"Your groom."

"My groom," Lara said. "He was a good man."

"Let's see now," Arsinoe said, counting her fingers one by one. "Married. Rich. Friends with a Queen . . . If only little sister could see me now."

"Do you," Lara asked, "Still think about her?"

"All the time," she answered. "And now, if you'll excuse me, I'm going to steal Dramsind's supper."

* * * * * * *

Lara was tired but she could not sleep.

The night was cloudless, the skull-moon hanging just above the horizon. The waters were black, and the way the moonlight played against them reminded her of The Dragon's mirror. Was she looking down on them, even now? Or had Reynard already stolen it . . .

She sat up, ignoring the stare she received from the fox-squirrel dozing in her lap, and rubbed at her eyes.

"We are not sleeping either," Moder said.

She was leaning against the prow, clutching at the rigging for support. Pinsard was with her, his sword laid across his lap.

Lara joined them. Bannertail leapt onto the forward spar and danced along its length.

"What if he falls in?" Pinsard asked.

"He won't," Lara said. "He's too clever."

The ship creaked as the sea lapped against its hull.

"You don't think The Dragon will catch him," Lara asked Moder. "Do you?"

Moder studied her hands. Then she shook her head.

"And he won't stop," Lara said. "Not unless we kill him."

Moder did not answer. She did not have to.

"Alright," Lara said, her voice soft. "Alright."

"Are you afraid?" Moder asked.

"I am," Lara admitted.

"Good. Only fools are having no fear."

"Then," Lara said, "He's afraid too. Isn't he?"

"Yes," Moder said, and they were quiet for a time.

The fox-squirrel tired of his game. He jumped from the rigging and slipped into the hold, hunting for rats.

"He stole it," Pinsard said. "He stole my faeder's sword."

Moder blinked. But she did not look surprised.

"You knew?" Pinsard asked.

"No," she said. "But I am knowing *him*."

She shut her eyes. When she opened them, Lara could see her tears.

- 374 -

"Forgive me," she said, wiping at her cheek. "When I am thinking of him- when I saw him- It was many years ago, but . . . It is breaking me all over."

"He was your friend," Lara said. "Wasn't he?"

"He saved my life," Moder said. "And he destroyed it."

Her face hardened.

"But I am being destroyed before," she said. "A hundred times. A thousand. And still, I go on breathing. And so do you. So do you."

They held her then. Held her close.

* * * * * * *

Lara woke once more, before the night was through.

Arsinoe was sitting atop the forward spar, trying to balance one of Tybalt's knives on her palm. Lara watched for a while, listening to the jib groan as it slowly swung to starboard. The helmsman let out a low whistle. They were tacking south again.

"How do they know where they're going?" Lara said, squinting. "I can't see anything out there but waves."

Arsinoe gave up on the knife and pointed upwards.

Lara craned back her head. The Watcher was but one light amidst a sea of stars, their vastness split by the silvery road that marked the fall of Hydra from the heavens. All the jewels of the earth could not match their splendor.

"So," Lara said. "Do you still think the stars are useless?"

"I do," Arsinoe sighed. "But they are beautiful."

Acknowledgements

This novel took me on a far longer, stranger journey than I would have imagined when I set out to write it. To all those who helped me weather the seas, I thank you. Special mention must be made (of course!) to my dedicated editor, Marguerite Hickernell, fight choreographer Alec Barbour, who laid the groundwork for the finale, and the patient support of Kirsten Foster, who has to deal with me whenever I think everything I'm writing is garbage. Your own mileage, of course, may vary.

www.ingramcontent.com/pod-product-compliance
Lightning Source LLC
Chambersburg PA
CBHW030354030726
47497CB00002B/341